D1607615

Just Ella

Annette K. Larsen

Y
LARSEN

12/19
14.24

For All My Sisters
Both actual and honorary
And most especially for Jana
Because you know I couldn't have done it without you.

Chapter One

I'LL ADMIT THAT my decision was impetuous. Only the crates and barrels crammed into the wagon would hide me from view as it pulled away from the kitchens, but it was my best chance. The supply wagon had just been sitting there, and upon overhearing the men talking about their plans to visit the caravan of traders in the village, the possibility of a taste of freedom made me reckless.

So here I sat, bumping along, hoping I could make it through the gates without being caught.

I dared to peek around a barrel to check on my progress and saw that we were rounding the edge of the castle. We had only to make it through the gardens and we would be at the gate.

Crouching down once more, I sent a plea to heaven that my ramshackle plan might succeed, but only a moment later, a guard called the wagon to a halt.

Cursing my luck, I scooted back and ducked even lower, anticipating a good amount of disappointment and humiliation. I heard a ripping sound as I moved and knew that a hole had been torn in my dress. I ignored it and held my breath, hoping the wagon would be allowed to move on without an inspection.

"Princess."

I scrunched my face in irritation and looked up at the guard gazing down at me. I stood, knowing my adventure was over. The guards surrounding the wagon were no surprise; however, the swords pointed threateningly at the drivers were.

"What are you doing?" I demanded.

"Are you well, Princess?" asked one of the guards.

"Of course I'm well." I tripped over crates and scrambled out of the wagon bed, ignoring the hands that offered assistance. "And these men had no idea that I was in their wagon until you made them stop. Put your weapons down at once."

"You got in on your own?" The guard's confusion was understandable, but I still found it irritating.

"Yes, now let these men be on their way."

As they reluctantly lowered their swords, I noticed several servants watching the spectacle, and started to worry about the potential ramifications of my actions. I had only a moment to hope that my mother would not be told before I heard her voice ring out across the courtyard.

"Ariella."

My stomach dropped and I looked up, then immediately back down as I encountered the eyes of the queen, so similar to mine, as she stood rigid on the palace steps.

"Coming, mother." Gathering my poise, I hurried past the baffled guards and confused servants, my head held high as I joined my mother.

The fact that she had witnessed my failed adventure only added to my humiliation. I followed her into the castle and up the stairs to the sitting room attached to my parents' chambers.

The door shut with a snap. "Explain yourself."

I sighed, resigned to simply tell the truth. "The caravan of traders have come and I wanted to see them."

"So you decided to go in the back of a supply wagon?"

"It's not as though there's any other way I would be able to go."

"There is nothing amid the trinkets of traders that would interest you, and travelers are notorious swindlers. But that is not really the point, is it? Why would it even enter your head to attempt to ride out of the palace in the back of a wagon? Why, Ella?"

I didn't know how to answer.

"It's dangerous. Do you not know that? Do you know what it looks like when you so openly defy me?"

I kept silent.

"Your defiance, your complete lack of decorum and your sneaking around the servants does not look right and it *must stop*."

I stared at the ground and clenched my teeth, trying to keep the hurt at bay. My mother was embarrassed by me. "I don't *sneak* around them. I'm just interested in the things they do."

Her tone softened a fraction. "I know that you are curious; you always have been. But if you insist on indulging your curiosity, then you will not do so in *public*." I could feel her gaze boring into the top of my head, but I refused to look up and it wasn't long before I heard the retreat of her footsteps and the sound of the door as it snapped shut.

I stared out the window onto a spectacular view of Dalthia. The palace lawn sloped down past the gardens to meet the wall surrounding the extensive grounds. Beyond that barrier, the common village sprawled out until it met the river, which wove through the dense trees like a silk ribbon through a braid. On the other side of the river were the houses belonging to the nobility, and far beyond what I could see, nestled between rolling hills, rested many outlying villages and estates.

But I was too caught up in my own thoughts, my own hurt and disappointment, to appreciate any of it.

"Fine," I muttered defiantly. If my mother wanted me to hide where no one would see me, then I would go back to the maze.

I hurried down the grand staircase and out the door without acknowledging the guards in my usual friendly manner.

Making my way through the public portion of the gardens, I held my head high, knowing that several noblemen might be following my movements with their curious eyes. The palace served not only as my home, but as the central meeting place for all government. The landlords who oversaw the outlying villages had regular meetings with my father, as did the magistrates and peace officers. I expected the scrutiny of noblemen, but still hated it.

A smile tugged at the corners of my mouth as I reached the hedge walls of the maze and entered. I inhaled the intoxicating fragrance, remembering the hours my sisters and I had spent running through this house of nature.

The maze had been my playground as a child, but at twelve years old I was pronounced too old for such frivolity. So I had stayed away. Because I *wanted* to do as I was told—to be everything they expected me to be. But clearly, my ability to act properly had not been helped by avoiding the maze. So it was with a fair amount of spite that I returned here now.

Walking into the rooms of nature-grown walls, I saw a great deal of change since I used to play here—or perhaps I just saw it differently. Compared to the rest of the gardens, the maze was much less tidy. Some plants and bushes grew into the paths I followed; others had climbed the hedges and hung overhead, their blossoms dripping from the sky.

The maze was arranged with narrow pathways mingling with wide open rooms. A few of the rooms were almost entirely enclosed, but most tended to run into each other in a rambling, nonsensical way.

The scent of lilac and roses filled my lungs, easing the tension in my shoulders. I wished I could take down my light hair so the breeze could blow through it, but I knew that I wouldn't be able to tame it into submission myself. I loved my hair, but its thick, loose curls made it unruly.

It was difficult to remember the layout of the maze, but I found a round room with every color of rose bush sweeping the perimeter, surrounding a large tree in the center. I remembered the tree and was happy to discover that my height, combined with the height of a bench now situated beneath it, would allow me to climb it.

I chewed my bottom lip and cast my eyes around to see if I dared attempt such a thing now. I hiked my skirts and stepped onto the bench, then grabbed a limb and used the back of the bench to lift me higher before pulling myself into the branches of the tree. Fifteen years old. A princess. And still I did it.

Fifteen years old, but in just a few weeks I would be sixteen, and I dreaded the day. Somehow I knew that Prince Jeshua would start to pursue me in earnest once I was all of sixteen. Avoiding him had become a talent of mine over the years and was one of the reasons I was so good at being places where I didn't belong. He could have chosen any one of my sisters, but he had fixated on me. I pushed the unpleasant thought aside and climbed higher.

Pleased with my own daring, I looked at the leaves surrounding me and realized I was largely obscured from the view of anyone not standing directly below the tree. I stepped carefully from branch to branch, hoping I might watch people unobserved from this height.

Once I could see above the hedge, I found a gap in the leaves and gazed around, proud of my success as I watched a visiting nobleman and woman as they strolled arm in arm. I looked farther and caught sight of a gardener I'd never seen before. He was quite young, not much older than myself, and rather rough looking. He dressed in earth tones—a loose fitting shirt and brown breeches. He was tall and lean with dark, tousled hair. A satchel hung across his body, some sort of foliage sticking out of it. When my eyes returned to his face, I realized that he had stopped his work to watch me, his eyebrows raised.

Then he smiled—not as though he were being polite or tactful, but just because he was amused. Because of me.

My eyes widened and I crouched down. Apparently I wasn't as well hidden as I had thought. What was I thinking? If my mother heard of my antics, she would put an immediate end to any and all excursions.

I started to make my way down. If I could get out of this tree without anyone else seeing me, then perhaps I could find another tree in a more secluded corner of the maze, or one with thicker leaves.

I was just about to step onto one of the lowest branches when the gardener appeared just a few paces from the tree.

"Stay aloft a bit longer. There is someone coming." He

disappeared before his words had fully registered. When they did, I found myself hugging the large trunk and hoping that whoever ventured near would soon be gone.

I heard their approach and tried to take even breaths. Through the gaps in the leaves, I caught glimpses of the couple as they strolled, unconcerned, along the path and out the other side.

As their voices faded, I breathed easier until a noise startled me.

The gardener had jumped onto the bench below. "All clear, Miss." The lightness in his face and voice left me stunned until he reached a hand toward me. "Do you need a hand?"

I lowered myself, hoping to look dignified—or at least as dignified as one can look when climbing a tree—but didn't know how to get out of the tree once I ran out of branches.

"Sit down here." He slapped the lowest branch and I did as he bade, my legs dangling as I prepared to lower myself.

"Hands on my shoulders now."

My eyes widened, but I did as he asked. He grabbed hold of my waist and lowered me to the bench. My hands dropped from his shoulders and I tried not to stare.

"You're all right then?" he asked.

"I don't usually climb trees."

He quirked a corner of his mouth. "That I had already guessed." He jumped from the bench then handed me down. "I've not seen you wandering the maze before."

My mind was a jumble. I wasn't used to people speaking so freely with me. My silence seemed to remind him of our difference in station and his face lost its laughter. He stepped back.

"A good day to you, My Lady."

He turned but I stopped him. "I thank you," I blurted. "For your —assistance."

He inclined his head, pinching the brim of his hat. "A pleasure."

"I'm Ella," I said on impulse. It was an almost unconscious decision, introducing myself as Ella. Only my family knew me as Ella.

Perhaps I would have felt too high and mighty introducing myself to this down-to-earth, rough character, as Ariella—Her Royal Highness, the princess—Ariella.

Instead of lightly grasping the tips of my fingers and bowing low over my hand, as I was accustomed to, he took hold of my hand with both of his and gently inclined his head while smiling at me with his eyes. "Glad to meet you, Ella." I gave a small, inaudible gasp. No one outside of my family addressed me without my title. No one. I wondered for a moment if he were being purposefully disrespectful, but he seemed entirely unaware of the gaffe. "My name is Gavin."

I gave a fleeting curtsy and replied, "A pleasure," out of habit. I knew I must have had the appearance of a startled deer—eyes wide and wary, rooted to the spot.

"What brings you to this portion of the gardens? I'm not used to seeing people strolling all by themselves."

"Oh, well," I stumbled, knowing very well that he hadn't seen me *strolling* at all.

"Hiding away?" He seemed genuinely curious about this point.

"I suppose."

"Hm." He seemed a bit puzzled. "I have never seen a noble who wished to hide away."

"I'm not nobility." It was an automatic response because it was the truth.

"Oh, you're not?" he seemed amused by this. "Then perhaps a lowly servant who has stolen her mistress' clothing? Or maybe the daughter of a dressmaker, taking liberties with her parents' goods?"

That's when I realized he hadn't recognized me. He must have never had the opportunity of seeing me up close. I suddenly appreciated my impulsive decision to introduce myself as Ella. Perhaps if he could get to know me—even a little bit—before he found out who I was, then…I don't know…we could be friends? Was that even possible?

"So, you assume if I'm not nobility, I must be a thief?" I tried to sound affronted, but felt a bit giddy about the whole situation, and ended up sounding more amused than anything.

His grin broadened. "And what would you have me believe, miss? I'm no expert on dresses, but I know it takes a lot of coin to look as good as you do right now."

My mouth dropped open a bit. "I believe that is the most backhanded compliment I've ever received, sir."

"Sir?" he let out a laugh. "The lady in the fine dress calls me 'sir,' and I'm to believe you are not noble?"

"And what exactly do you have against nobility?"

"Nothing, really. I'm simply used to working for what I want and need. Nobility already have that and so they seem a bit...." He trailed off.

"What?" I asked in horror. If he had such a low opinion of nobility, I couldn't imagine what he would think of me.

"Well, lazy, if you must know."

I let out a breath of unbelief and searched my mind for an argument.

"You know," he continued, "for a person who claims *not* to be nobility, you've certainly got your feathers ruffled."

"You think that because I am given less responsibility than others that I have less value in society?"

Compassion crossed his face, as though sorry to see my distress over the matter. "No. You are simply a different sort of society—one I don't understand."

"But we are all part of the same society."

He laughed, but stopped himself quickly. "That, miss, is entirely untrue. I am surrounded by nobility constantly, but I do *not* interact with them. I'm completely separate—they don't see me." The fact that he did not recognize me made it difficult to argue the point.

An inexplicable sadness settled over me. I was speaking with one of my subjects who believed he was unimportant and invisible. And I could do nothing about it.

"That's really what you believe?" I asked, hoping, perhaps, he was exaggerating or joking.

He gave me a sad smile and shrugged. "I apologize if my bluntness offends you. I figured you would leave if you were upset by me."

"That would be very rude of me."

"It's what I'd expect."

"Why? Because that's what a noble would do?"

"Well." The confusion was back, forcing him to make a slight concession. "Any other noble." It was somewhat gratifying that he no longer felt compelled to lump me with the nobles he despised. However, the fact remained—I wasn't a noble. And I knew he would think even less of me when he knew what I was.

I wouldn't lie. "I told you, I'm not—"

"Come now, Ella. Your tree climbing hasn't got me fooled." He used an almost paternal tone, his eyes laughing. "You are nobility, aren't you?"

I buried my hurt. "No, I'm something worse."

"Oh, come now, I don't think that badly of people. The only thing that might be worse is royalty." How charming he was, even when insulting me.

I stood silent for a moment, wondering if he would catch on. When he continued to gaze at me, I simply said, "Exactly."

A look of horror crossed his face and I gave him a sad smile before turning to leave.

"Oh," I heard him stuttering behind me, sounding utterly mortified. "No, I...my apologies, miss—Your Highness," he corrected himself sharply. "Princess, I'm so very sorry, I..."

I shook my head as I turned to face him again. He looked so different: the confidence, the grin, the amusement were all gone, replaced with a look akin to physical pain. "It's all right," I said quietly. "You're not wrong." I should have inclined my head, waiting for him to bow before I left. Instead I lifted my hand in farewell.

Unwilling to return to the palace, I walked deeper into the maze. My conversation with Gavin had not ended well, but that was no reason to give up my explorations. Coming here had been *my* choice, and I would not leave until I *wanted* to leave. Admittedly, I was disappointed. Speaking with Gavin had been enjoyable; he had been open and had a charming, teasing manner. It was a shame our first encounter would be our last. Even if he didn't despise me for my station, he would no longer be comfortable conversing with me. I was a royal—a lazy, entitled royal.

I was mortified anyone would perceive me that way. And the worst part was that he was right. None of my talents or endeavors were really useful, and I also despised royalty some of the time. Royal suitors were frequent guests in a castle that housed seven princesses. And though some were pleasant enough, I had met my fair share of princes who were supreme examples of arrogant, entitled royalty. Prince Jeshua was one of the worst. Perhaps that's why it bothered me so much. I found being put on the same level as those I scorned appalling.

I entered one of the open rooms and sat down amidst the lush greenery and fragrant blooms, trying to decipher my feelings. I was sad and angry and insulted, yes. But Gavin had sparked another feeling. I felt invigorated—more invigorated than I ever had while defying my parents and evading royal guests, and I was anxious for this excitement to last.

Chapter Two

THE NEXT AFTERNOON I sat in deep contemplation, a pencil in my limp hand and blank paper in front of me. I had received a very small glimpse of a friendship I longed for but which was unlikely to be. Still, I couldn't shake the possibility from my mind.

My father would arrive soon. Over the past several years, I had spent a great deal of time in the library, getting lost in the worlds created in books while avoiding the world I lived in.

I was fourteen when my father discovered my tendency to linger here. One day I had walked in expecting to find myself alone, as usual, but when I pulled out a book and turned, my father was sitting in a chair, a book open on his lap but his eyes on me. I jumped in surprise then laughed at myself in relief.

"Good day, Father."

He gave me a serene smile, the kind he only showed when there were no servants or nobles around. Dark hair brushed his shoulders and a trim beard framed his mouth. Even sitting in a chair, his broad build and considerable height made him an imposing figure. "Good day, Ariella. And what are you doing in here?"

"Just…looking for a book."

"Are you here often?"

"Oh," I began, not wanting to admit I could be found there every day, for several hours. "Fairly often. And you?"

He smiled at my question. "A little every day if I can manage it. I find that a break from my responsibilities helps me to focus."

I noticed the weariness about his eyes. My father's responsibilities were so much a part of him that I had never before considered how he might struggle with them.

"Come here, let me show you something." He leaned forward, setting his book on the low table in front of him. I approached, somewhat hesitant. I wasn't used to spending time with just my father; he didn't have time for it. But that day, he took the time to show me the document he had been reading, which included the names of all the lords that had jurisdiction over different parcels of land, with notations about how many tenants worked on the property, as well as the goods produced. I found it fascinating. Not so much the subject, but the fact that my father shared his own insights with me.

It became a habit. If he had the time, he was usually in the library around the same time each day. Whenever I joined him he spent his time teaching me about our country. Sometimes we spoke of its history; other times it was his plans for the future, a problem with an outlying village, or the methods he employed when dealing with foreign governments. It was all so interesting and I had to wonder why I spent time learning dancing and etiquette along with my sisters when I could be learning things of importance.

So when my father entered for our lesson the day after my encounter with the gardener, I put away my drawings and tried to focus on him, but eventually interrupted with a question. "Father—" He looked up, surprised. "You don't interact with commoners much." His eyebrows shot up at my abrupt change of topic. "I was just wondering, why is that?"

He sat back and studied me for a moment before taking a deep breath and answering seriously. "I suppose you might consider it self preservation." My brow furrowed and he continued, "I make decisions every day that will affect countless people. It is vital that I remain rational and logical. If I get caught up in the feelings of individuals, it becomes almost impossible for me to make sound decisions."

I stayed silent, letting his words sink in and hoping he would expound, but he moved on to other things and our time was soon up. His words stayed with me, though. As I walked out to the gardens, I wondered if this reasoning was the same my mother used for keeping me away from the servants. It was a battle I had been fighting for several years even though I could never quite understand why I felt so drawn to them. As a child I had loved everyone—as I suppose most children do— but I had the misfortune of having not only a watchful mother, but three older sisters who thought it prudent to steer me away from such feelings.

When I was six years old, Mia and Jensa had seen me kiss the cheek of my nursemaid in thanks and had chastised me severely for it. I held the title of princess and needed to act like one.

I tried to be detached and distant and think of myself as better. I tried, desperately wanting to please my family, but never comfortable playing that role.

And so it was a great relief to have taken this step—to have reclaimed the maze and given myself permission to be a little more of myself. My father's reasons for keeping himself distant helped me to understand him, but it also made me realize that I did not feel the same. I wanted—and perhaps even needed—to know our subjects as individuals.

I entered the maze and felt satisfied in my decision to be there. I went a different direction than I had the day before and ended up winding my way close to the outer wall. The path opened up rather suddenly onto a large area of blossoming trees mingled with statues. Several archways led away into other paths and areas. I recognized the juncture and remembered that a couple of rooms were easily missed.

Crossing the open space, I found a gap in the hedge hidden behind one of the largest trees. I slipped through into an enclosed space very much like a room.

Vague memories were all I had of this room; my childhood had been spent running through the more open areas of the maze. It was nearly a perfect circle, with a round pond in the middle. Flat rocks had been laid to make a stone floor surrounding what must have been a spring. More rocks stacked on top of each other formed a low wall surrounding the water, only about as high as my hand. The water flowed out of a small opening in the outer wall, escaping under the hedge. The perimeter of the room was lined with stone columns, trellises and benches, all intermixed with plants and flowers. A lone tree shaded the far end of the pool, sending the petals from its white blossoms to drift lazily on the water's surface before rushing away. It was enchanting.

This room had been very carefully planned and created with a subtle feeling of...vibrancy. Something extra had been put into this room, as though it meant more to the caretaker than the others.

My attention was directed at the tree, considering whether or not it would be a good one for climbing, when I sensed a presence behind me. I turned to find Gavin standing barely inside the room, and stared at him for a moment, trying to decipher the emotion running across his face. He certainly looked embarrassed, but there was something else. It wasn't anger, or even irritation, as I might have expected. Concerned wasn't quite right, but it was closer.

He looked away from me, taking in the serenity of the room surrounding us, and when his eyes returned to me, I saw it. Vulnerability. It had taken me so long to pinpoint the emotion because I had not expected it.

Why would he feel vulnerable? I took in my surroundings once more and realized that he must be the one who cared so well for this room.

And I was intruding.

"My apologies—I'll leave." I walked toward the doorway where he stood.

"No, Princess. Please, I will not interrupt." He gave an awkward bow and stepped back.

"Wait," I called, before he could leave. "Please don't let me keep you from your work."

He seemed to consider for a moment, never meeting my eyes. "If you're certain it won't be a bother."

"Why would it be a bother?"

"Part of my job is staying out of the way. Especially after insulting a member of the royal family."

I sighed. "Though I may be royalty, I'm still the one you found climbing a tree yesterday. I don't consider your presence a bother."

He bowed his head, the corners of his mouth turning up just a little. "Very well."

As he worked, I sat down, only to realize the tension rippling through me, my hands gripping the edge of the bench. He was busy clearing out twigs and wilted petals stuck to the rocks that surrounded the pond. I couldn't still my feet or relax my hands and finally gave up on the idea of sitting. I stood, walking along the stone laid path, admiring the vines and flowers that climbed the trellis and hung above the bench where I had been sitting. Knowing that this young gardener had woven himself into every detail of this room made me want to know more about him. The colors of the different flowers blended in harmony with one another and seemed brighter, fuller than the others in the gardens. I couldn't resist running my hand over many of their leaves and budding blossoms. I reveled in the feeling for a moment until I felt a twinge in my finger. "Ouch!" slipped from my lips and I pulled my hand away from the offending branch. It wasn't really painful, but the surprise of it had sent the exclamation out of my mouth before I realized it.

"Careful of those roses," Gavin said as he came up behind me. I turned to look at him in embarrassment. "They bite back," he said with a smile. Maybe there was still a chance that I could get to know him.

I shook my hand at my side to relieve the stinging. "Yes, I noticed."

He came closer, pulled off his gloves and put them under his arm, then held out his hands. "Here, let me see." I let my hand rest in his and he bent over it, inspecting my fingers. "You said your name was Ella."

"Yes," I answered, wondering at the question in his tone.

15

"I do not remember any princess by that name."

"Short for Ariella."

"Ah." He looked up. "That name I might've recognized." He let go of my hand. "You should put some salve on that."

"Thank you. Though you needn't feel obligated to assist me."

"Nonsense. As one of your concerned subjects, it is my duty to help you any way I can."

I stepped back. "As I said, no obligatory concern necessary." I turned and walked back to the bench.

I caught a glimpse of Gavin's confused face before he asked, "Have I offended you, Princess?"

"No, of course not." It wasn't really a lie. I was certainly *trying* not to be offended.

He walked toward me. "I can tell I did something wrong, but I don't know what."

I sighed. "It's really not your fault. It shouldn't have bothered me."

"But it did," he stated. "And I'd like to know why." His voice was gentle, earnest.

I wanted to have a friendship with this young man, and in order to do so, I knew I had to be honest. "Because of who I am, it's often difficult to judge a person's sincerity." He didn't say anything, so I went on. "I've heard countless flattering words in my life, about anything and everything I do. I never know who to believe." I tried to look at him, but couldn't. "It makes friendships difficult; friendship requires sincerity, not flattery." I glanced up and saw that his expression appeared a bit bewildered, like he had seen something for the first time—something confusing.

"I can understand that," was his eventual response.

I let out a breath I hadn't realized I'd been holding. I never shared confidences with anyone.

He walked closer, which surprised me in and of itself, and sat down next to me. I was speechless, and relieved when he started a conversation.

"So," he said, turning toward me, "tell me the most absurd thing someone has said to you in order to flatter their way into your good graces."

A smile broke over my face as comments began flying through my head, from the most blundering to the most eloquent compliments. "Oh," I sighed in amusement, "I don't know that I could pick just one."

"So, tell me more than one."

That was the beginning for us. It was tentative and shaky, but I came back the next day and the day after. We continued to talk and I continued to explore. I loved being in the maze and I found myself ever more drawn to the ponds throughout—their soothing sound and reflective surfaces. I had never played in them as a child, knowing it was strictly forbidden; but one day, with Gavin by my side, I stopped resisting and acted on impulse.

"Might I ask what you are doing?" Gavin questioned as I stooped to remove my silk slippers.

"Have you ever waded through water?"

His brow furrowed deeply. "Many times, but only out of necessity."

"You never thought it might be fun?"

"No. And I stand by that." He seemed as if he desperately wished to stop me from doing what I was about to do, but I knew he wouldn't.

"I've never waded in water just for the fun of it," I told him while I gathered the many layers of dress into my hands in preparation. "I think it will be rather enjoyable." I stepped over the low stone wall and into the shallow pool. The water barely reached my ankles, but it still felt wonderful. I took several steps, letting my toes skim the bottom as my feet glided through the water. I turned to Gavin, who watched me in a bemused sort of way. "It really is quite a lovely feeling."

"Is that so?"

"Yes, it is so. You should try it," I answered as I let my feet slip gently through the water, careful not to let my skirts skim the surface.

He studied me, a curious expression on his face, and asked, "If you have such an affinity for these gardens, why have I never seen you here before?"

I thought about his question for a moment, mulling over my attempts to be proper, which had lead to so much of my discontent.

He came closer and I was roused from my musings.

"I actually used to spend a good deal of time here. But it's been several years. So...," I changed the subject. "Are you going to wade with me or not?"

He chewed his lip. "I'd rather not, Princess."

I stopped. "Don't call me that."

"Why?"

"Just—" I couldn't explain it. "Don't call me that."

"Then, what am I supposed to call you?" He asked, genuinely confused.

"By my name, of course."

"You expect me to just call you Ariella?"

"I would prefer simply Ella, but I'll take what I can get."

His eyes were slightly panicked. "I don't know if I can do that."

"Why ever not?"

"Because you're royalty." He said it as though I might have forgotten.

"Then pretend I'm not."

"You say that as though it's the easiest thing in the world."

"Isn't it?"

He looked exasperated. "No, Princess, it's not." My brow furrowed at hearing the seriousness in his voice. "You look like royalty, you act like royalty—"

"The first time we met, you had no idea that I was royalty."

"I've learned from that mistake."

"What do I do that is so royal?"

"It's not so much what you do, but how you do it. You carry yourself like a royal."

My eyebrows rose at this. "Even when I'm climbing a tree? Or tramping through water barefoot?" I walked to the edge of the pool, splashing as I went.

The corner of his mouth twitched. "Though I will admit, the sight of you wading through water is undoubtedly a refreshing one,"—his eyes roamed over my face and down to my wet feet—"you look like a princess, and you cannot avoid that."

I rolled my eyes and climbed out of the water onto the stone barrier. "It's just a dress." I stepped off the little wall, landing lightly in front of him. "It's just ribbons and silk; none of it means anything." I turned and started away from him.

"I wasn't talking about your wardrobe, *Ella*."

I smiled at his using my name, then turned back. "But if you weren't referring to my clothes, then how exactly do I look like a royal?"

"I meant that the way you act shows just how much better than me you are."

My mouth opened in horrified shock. How could he think—?

"Not," he said, seeing my reaction, "not in an arrogant way. Not the way other royals act. Not as though you *think* you're better. Just that —" he struggled for words, "—just that you *are*." His shoulders sagged at this admission and my eyebrows knit together in confusion. "You're better, you're...more beautiful than anyone I've ever met."

I just stared.

"You are what royalty *should* be."

"But I don't want to be royalty." The words were out of my mouth before I realized I was thinking them.

He smiled softly. "I know."

I looked away, shaking my head in confusion.

"I meant it as a compliment, not an insult."

I took a breath in, forcing myself to trust that what he said was true. "In that case, thank you?"

I laughed a bit at the way my thanks had come out as a question. I wasn't sure if I should be thanking him or not and my uncertainty broke the tension.

"You're welcome?" He laughed along with me, then became serious. "Might I ask you something?"

"Of course." I found it curious that he would ask. I thought we had moved beyond that.

He hesitated for just a breath before asking, "What would happen if someone found us here together?"

My shoulders tensed, but I willed myself to maintain my composure. "What do you mean?"

He narrowed his eyes. "You know what I mean. How much trouble would I be in?"

My gaze fell to my fidgeting hands. "You wouldn't."

"I wouldn't?"

"My mother would know it was my idea. I wouldn't let the blame fall to you." He seemed puzzled by my response. "I'm the one intruding," I clarified. "You're only doing your job."

"You're not intruding."

I smiled. "I have to go." I stooped to pick up my slippers and walked away from him. "Meet me here tomorrow morning."

"Is that an order?" he asked lightly.

"No," I said over my shoulder before lifting the hem of my skirts and hurrying gingerly along the winding stone path. Just before I slipped out of sight, I glanced back to see him looking mystified.

Before I left the maze, I stopped to put on my slippers. I wasn't quite brave enough to allow anyone to see me barefoot. When my feet were appropriately covered I made my way out of the maze and up to the palace drawing room where my sisters and I had lessons. As I went, my hands automatically straightened and smoothed my hair and dress so as to avoid any unwanted questions.

When I arrived, my sisters were seated and our language instructor stood at the front of the room, waiting for me. I slipped into my seat, not meeting anyone's eye. As our instruction began, I heard a whisper in my ear.

"Barely on time once again, Ariella?" I glanced up to see Lorraina smirking.

"Why do you care?" I asked, trying to pay attention.

"Oh, I don't. I was just making an observation. You don't seem to put much stock in punctuality lately. It's a very unattractive habit."

I decided not to respond. Out of all my sisters, Lorraina was the most difficult to get along with. Though nearly two years younger, she considered herself far superior to me. She prided herself on being the picture of princessly perfection. And perhaps she was; it was merely her personality I found lacking.

When our lessons ended, I wandered slowly back to my room, in no hurry to arrive there or anywhere else. I could think of nothing in the palace to excite me.

In my room, I found my maid, Gretchen, in my wardrobe, her dark blue uniform pristine as always, her sandy hair tied back and covered with a matching kerchief. She was running her hands gently over the fabric of my dresses.

I had many times wondered if Gretchen would flee if I were to extend a hand of friendship to her. During the year I was twelve, my nursemaid was dismissed and Gretchen, as her daughter, took over as my lady's maid. We were close to the same age, but in my efforts to please my family, I had never tried to befriend her.

In the beginning, she chattered out of nervousness while she worked, and I loved her stories of growing up in the village. But as she learned her role, her nervous chattering stopped and I missed the friendship that felt so close, yet seemed so impossible.

I hoped that now I could change things, perhaps have a friend in her.

She stood now with a smile on her lips, as she put the fabric of my dresses over her arm or up to her body, no doubt imagining what it would be like to wear one. I had often wondered if those who served me envied or pitied my wardrobe. It was stiff and uncomfortable, but undeniably exquisite.

My moment of observation ended as she caught sight of me and flew into a panic. She dropped the fabric she had clutched so lovingly in her hands and stepped back, her head bowed, her hands stiff at her sides.

"My apologies, Highness. I'll put your things to rights straight away."

"Oh, I don't mind."

She continued to stare at the floor, her voice shaking. "I shouldn't have been dawdling." She went down on both knees and gathered a few ribbons.

I knelt beside her. "It really is all right." But she continued to move about frantically. I caught both her hands in mine. "Gretchen." She ventured a quick glance at me. "I don't mind." I tried to keep her attention. "Do you believe me?"

Her eyes showed even more alarm. "Yes, of course, Highness. I would never doubt you."

"I'm not upset or cross with you. Alright?"

She held my eyes for a moment, then nodded her head in the affirmative and went about straightening the very slight mess. I took a deep breath, as much to encourage her to relax as to draw courage for myself. "Gretchen, I have an idea…"

Her hands stilled and she gave me her full attention. "Yes, Highness?"

"I wonder if you would like to try on one of these dresses, just to see how it might look."

She seemed shocked, almost scandalized. "Oh no, Highness. That would be—I'm sure I could not."

"You could if you'd like. I think it would be fun." I held my breath, hoping she might let down her guard and take pity on me. I had the most adamant wish that she not be frightened of me.

She still seemed uncertain, so I decided to approach it from a different angle. I stood up and looked through my gowns. "Which one do you like best? Do you have a favorite?"

She took a hesitant step toward me, her hands fidgeting continually. "Yes, Highness. I do."

"Which one?"

She stepped forward tentatively and pulled out a gown of sage green. The fabric was heavy with a beautiful luster that made the shade of green deepen when it was in shadow.

"I wore that for Jensa's eighteenth birthday."

She nodded, no doubt remembering.

"Would you like to put it on?"

She appeared sorely tempted, but seemed to come to her senses. "No, Highness. I should get back to work."

She started away from me, but I found myself blurting out, "Gretchen, please."

She stopped and turned, looking thoroughly stunned at my pathetic, pleading tone. "Begging your pardon, Princess?"

It was unbefitting for a princess to whine, and I certainly didn't want to seem ungrateful. I had a comfortable life—more than comfortable—and I knew that Gretchen and every maiden like her envied me. And I truly did wish her to stay.

"I just—I would very much appreciate your company."

Confusion still blanketed her features.

"My sisters and I don't have much in common. I find myself a bit lonely sometimes."

"I will stay, of course, Highness, if you wish."

"I do wish, but I don't want you to stay because I asked you to, or at least not because a princess asked you. I'd like you to stay because you would enjoy yourself. So, I leave it up to you. I am inviting you to stay, but you are free to go if you'd prefer."

Gretchen's lips pursed in thought, then a smile started to pull at the corner of her mouth before she said, "I have wondered what it might be like to dress up as a lady."

"Shall we find out?"

She paused for only a moment then fairly skipped over to me.

We ended up switching clothing since I was curious what it would be like to wear regular, plain clothing. I discovered that above all else, it

23

was easier. Not so much to worry about or keep in place.

Apparently Gretchen agreed with me. "This is ridiculous!" she exclaimed in exasperation as she tried to move about in the green dress. "How can you get anywhere without falling on your face?" She blushed after her outburst, but I just laughed.

"With great difficulty," I replied. "Plus, you're shorter than I am, so the hem is more underfoot. And keep in mind this is a ball gown, so it's even less practical than my usual attire."

She quirked her mouth to one side and shook her head in disbelief. "I can't believe you actually *dance* in this."

I shrugged. "You get used to it."

She looked skeptical. "I suppose."

"So, how do you feel?"

She pulled her shoulders back and lifted her chin. "Quite regal," she answered, and I laughed. "And how about you?" she asked. "How does it feel to be dressed as a commoner?"

I spun around effortlessly. "It feels easier."

She stifled a giggle, then looked about as if realizing something. "Oh, Highness. We must get you dressed for dinner or you'll be late." She was quite right, and we both went about helping each other out of our costumes and into our own clothes. I worried she might go back to being aloof, but as we changed and she settled behind me to do my hair, I managed to keep a light conversation going. It almost seemed too easy, but then I realized there was a good chance she found herself as lonely as I did.

✳ ✳ ✳

Each morning over the next week, I went out to find Gavin wherever he was working in the maze. I would stay there for an hour or so while he continued to work. Sometimes I brought a book and read out loud to him. He continued to call me "Princess," and I continued to correct him. From there, our friendship grew into the most precious thing I'd ever had the pleasure of owning.

I enjoyed sitting on the ground—usually in the middle of a

pathway. Anyone else would have been scandalized by such a display, but Gavin seemed to find it as amusing as I did. I caught him smiling several times as I tried to tame my skirts—watching them billow up around me.

If he was working near one of the many ponds throughout the maze, I would wade for a moment or two, or at least put my feet in as I sat at the edge. After a couple weeks I felt more and more in the way as Gavin worked and I did nothing.

I could speak three languages and play two instruments; I was aware of the five acceptable reasons to go to war; and knew the protocol for greeting any guest that might enter the place. But when it came to everyday, practical situations, I was useless. So I started insisting that Gavin teach me to perform some of his everyday tasks so I could feel useful.

"So, I take a hold of it here…" At present he was teaching me about weeds, and though he had vehemently tried to dissuade me from dealing with the weeds myself, I was more insistent than he was prepared for. Thus, I was down on hands and knees beside Gavin, my hands covered in dirt and my hair slipping from its proper place.

"You'll want to get a hold of it as close to the ground as possible," he advised me.

While I knew this task was minimal and unimportant in the grand scheme of things, I found a real sense of satisfaction in learning to do something useful. I pressed my fingers into the dirt and grasped the little fiend once more. "Like this?"

"Yes." He drew out the word as though amused that I sought guidance about something so simple. "Now just pull steadily." I did so, and to my surprise it came loose—roots and all. "And that," he said, turning to me, "is how you get rid of a weed."

"Fascinating." I couldn't help staring at the bit of green in my hand, then at the spot where it had previously resided.

I looked over to see Gavin trying desperately to keep a straight face. "What?" I asked, sensing he was somehow laughing at me.

"Nothing," he claimed, and then quickly dove into his work so he could turn his head away and laugh to himself.

I reached out and touched his arm to get his attention. "Tell me what's so funny. Did I do it wrong?"

He turned toward me, keeping his mouth from turning up, but I could see the amusement in his eyes. "No, you did it just right."

"But?"

"In all my years of working with plants, I've never considered that weeds could be fascinating."

"Oh." My brow furrowed as I realized I had made a fool of myself. "Yes, you're right of course. It's not fascinating, I was just…" I saw another weed and decided to try it again, if only to give myself something to do. I was embarrassed at having shown my naivety.

"What are you doing?" he asked quietly.

"Getting rid of another weed." And I did just that.

"I can do it." His tone was careful, not wanting to hurt my feelings.

"I can do it too. You've taught me very well." I kept my eyes on my chosen task as I wrapped my fingers around yet another noxious offender.

"You're getting your dress dirty." He sounded as though this would end the matter, thinking I might abhor the idea.

"So?" I finally looked him in the eye, daring him to say something of my station or my upbringing.

His gaze flitted about, as if searching for an appropriate response, and eventually settled on a simple, "Alright." Apparently, he still didn't know quite what to make of me.

Chapter Three

THE NEXT MORNING I walked into the garden room to find Gavin tending to some ground creepers that wound themselves around the other plants. He faced away from me as I entered, and I heard him singing to himself—a lilting folk song in a deep, resonant voice.

> *My lass is a beauty,*
> *A sight to behold,*
> *And when she does kiss me,*
> *I cannot feel cold.*
> *Our love is the purest,*
> *Our love is so sweet,*
> *For she's my fair lady—*

"You should perform for Father."

He whirled, halting his song. "Princess—Ella," he corrected. "You startled me. I'm not used to being snuck up on."

I settled on the ground next to him. "It was not my intent to sneak; you simply didn't hear me."

"It's those blasted silk slippers, they don't make a sound." He turned his attention back to his work. "I should make you wear some proper, clomping shoes."

"You have a handsome voice."

He shook his head as though I were being overly kind. "I'm sure it's nothing compared to what you're used to hearing."

"You'd be surprised."

He stopped his work to look at me. "Would I?"

"Musicians at the palace are rarely concerned with showcasing their musical talents. None of the words hold any meaning beyond wanting to be in good favor with royalty. It seems like a sad way to use one's talent."

"Or the smart way."

"What do you mean?"

"I'm sure those musicians gain far more by being in favor with the royal family than by using their talent to express themselves and earn nothing."

My brow furrowed. "I hadn't considered that."

"That's because you don't think about money."

I was insulted, but I knew he hadn't meant any offense. "My parents aren't fools, Gavin. We all know those songs are meant for flattery."

"Then why do you keep inviting them back?"

"It is not for our benefit that they play."

"Then whose?"

"The court's, visiting royalty or nobility—anyone besides us."

"I don't understand."

"It's important we maintain the image of being reverenced by our people. I know it sounds shallow—and sometimes it is—but if those who dine with us don't witness the respect given us through those songs, then there is a chance they will think us weak. If we do not appear to be in full favor with our own people, our enemies may believe they can exploit that."

"Hm." This noise was short and abrupt. I really didn't know what it meant.

"It's a tricky thing," I confided, "because while it is important to appear in power to those on the outside, I fear it makes us appear shallow and vain to our own subjects. Like you. And thus we lose the respect of our own people."

"I never said you were shallow and vain." He wasn't defensive, but spoke softly, as though reassuring me.

"And the rest of my family?"

He dropped his eyes—I wasn't surprised that he thought of my family as shallow and vain. And I certainly didn't blame him for it; as I had said, our conduct had various effects on different people.

I opted to change the subject. "When you are not tending to these gardens, what do you do?"

"I have many responsibilities at home."

"Where do you live?" I asked, realizing I didn't know.

"Just outside the palace walls. There is an area designated for palace servants to live if they so choose. My family has been tending these grounds for generations."

"Really?"

"Yes. I started working with my father when I was twelve years old."

"Does your father still work here?"

He looked away. "Not anymore."

"Why not?" I asked quietly, worried that perhaps his father no longer lived.

"His leg. It's pained him for many years, but about a year and a half ago, it became impossible for him to stand all day, bending his knee constantly."

"So you took over his responsibilities?"

He nodded.

"Was your father glad to be done, or was it difficult for him to give up his work?"

"He hated it. Being unable to work is not easy on a man's pride."

"How did he manage?"

"Learned a new trade." He smiled as he answered. "Swallowed his pride and turned himself into an apprentice for a wood carver. He's made some rather impressive pieces of furniture."

The pride he felt for his father shone in his eyes.

"He's found satisfaction in a new skill and left me in charge of the maze."

"You work only in the maze?"

"I assist in the main gardens from time to time."

"Is that lonely? Aren't you by yourself most of the day?" If so, I could certainly sympathize.

He shook his head and smiled. "It suits me. Besides," he paused, his eyes scanning my face. "It's less lonely now."

I looked down as heat filled my face. "And you enjoy it?" It wasn't really a question. I could clearly see he enjoyed his work.

He nodded. "I find a great deal of satisfaction in what I do, assisting the earth in its growing."

"Taming the wildlife?"

He let out a small, breathy laugh. "Not taming, more...sculpting." His pride was obvious, almost profound, especially as I watched him work.

"I wish I were able to do some sort of useful work," I mused aloud.

He stopped what he was doing, his expression curious. "What do you do with your time?"

I dropped my eyes, not wanting to admit to the pathetic endeavors of my day. "Nothing of consequence."

"You're not going to tell me about anything about your life?"

I supposed there were a few things I didn't mind admitting. "I have tutors, I read, I draw, and I have lessons with my father several times a week."

"Lessons with your father?" he asked, surprised.

"Yes," I confirmed with some pride.

"Teaching you what?"

"Teaching me the reason that flattering musicians play at banquet." He smiled as he went about his work. "Teaching me the history of the relationships we share with neighboring kingdoms. Really, he tells me anything he thinks I might need to know and answers any questions I have."

"Have your other sisters received the same instruction?"

I shook my head. "Not to my knowledge. Then again, I don't think he's found any of my other sisters lurking in the library."

He grinned. "So you lurk, but you don't sneak?"

I stifled a laugh. "Apparently."

Taking off my shoes, I walked to the pool. My gown today had an inconvenient train that I had to drape over one arm before stepping into the water. There was a statue in the middle of the pool, which I had admired many times. In fact, it was the only statue I had found that I actually liked. Statues were in abundance everywhere in the garden and I ignored them for the most part. All the others depicted proper courtship– a gentleman and a lady sitting on a bench, turned toward each other but not touching; a gentlemen down on one knee holding the hand of a lady who looked shyly away. They were all so civil.

But this statue—this was different. I walked through the water and circled it, studying it from every angle. It appeared fluid and soft, and the scene depicted was not one of civility, but of laughter and gaiety. The gentleman and lady were dancing together, but not a stately dance like I was used to. They were standing with their right shoulders pressed together, facing in opposite directions and smiling at each other. Each of their right arms went in front of the other's torso, resting on their partner's hip. Both balanced on one foot as if in mid-step, with their left arms thrown outward as they laughed.

"Princess?"

"What?" I was startled out of my reverie by Gavin's voice. He walked to the wall closest to me and stepped onto it.

"You looked distracted." He appeared amused by my antics.

I had often thought to ask Gavin about this statue, but had never found the nerve. I admired it so much that I didn't want anything to ruin it for me, but my curiosity finally won out. "This is different from every other statue I've seen in the gardens." I ran my hand over the smooth stone, appreciating the energy it portrayed.

"There are others like it."

"Where?"

"There are four statues like this one throughout the maze. Each is in a room much like this one—closed off and easily passed over." He admired the statue from his perch on the wall.

"That's curious. Why would the most lovely and moving statues be set aside?"

He shrugged but his eyes swept over me. "You'd better come out of the water before you drop your skirts, Ella."

"Very well." I turned from him under the pretense of looking at the statue once more, but in truth, I wanted to hide my smile from him. He had requested something of me without any titles, without any formality at all. I composed my face and headed toward Gavin, who offered his hand to assist me. I took it, noticing its rough quality and the firmness with which he grasped my hand. Men of my class never grasped a lady's hand. I greatly preferred the security I felt in Gavin's grasp.

This was only the second time he had moved to touch me and I felt a little thrill at the thought. When I was firmly on the ground, I allowed my hand to stay in his, wondering how long he would retain it if I didn't pull away. He gazed at our entwined hands as if wondering how they had ended up that way. Without looking up at me, he drew his hand away from mine, allowing his fingers to slowly graze my palm. A tingle crept up my arm and into my neck. I shuddered ever so slightly, but it was enough to rouse Gavin. He stepped back and went stiff.

"Till tomorrow, Princess." He inclined his head slightly, then turned away.

"Ella," I quietly corrected him.

"Till tomorrow, Ella," he said over his shoulder and walked away.

"Good bye, Gavin." I replied, though I'm not entirely sure he heard me. I said it much more quietly than I had intended.

It took me a moment to gather my thoughts. What had just happened? He had simply withdrawn his hand, and yet my pulse was quicker than it had been a moment before. I did my best to shake it off as I resolutely gathered my slippers and headed out through the maze.

✳ ✳ ✳

Gavin broke up our usual routine a few days later. When I found him he was striding toward me with a conspiratorial grin and the look of someone bursting to share a secret.

"What?" I asked.

"Have you ever explored the forest before?" he asked, referring to the forest just beyond the rear palace wall.

I blinked in surprise. "No, of course not."

His grin broadened. "Oh, Ella, how much you have missed." And with that he sat me down on the nearest bench and proceeded to remove my slippers. I bit my tongue, determined not to ask what he was doing for fear he would think I disapproved. My patience paid off as he pulled some sturdy shoes from a satchel slung across his body and put them on my feet. "It's a good thing your dress isn't too fancy today. We're going to walk a little ways."

"Where?"

He just grinned.

"We're not actually going into the forest are we?"

"Yes."

"How?"

He seemed positively exhilarated. "You'll just have to trust me. Do you?"

My answer was immediate. "Of course."

"Then, come along, Miss Ella." He grabbed my hand and I trotted along behind him as he strode through the maze, into a room that came right up to the back wall.

"Do you plan on hoisting us over?" I felt honestly confused. Short of actually climbing the wall, I didn't see how we would get into the forest beyond. "There isn't even a tree we could climb," I pointed out as he pulled me through the room.

He stopped at the back wall, covered in years and years of ivy growth, and turned to me. "I'm about to share a very great secret with you. Are you ready?"

I was thoroughly delighted and absolutely intrigued. I'd never seen Gavin so enthusiastic. "More than ready, sir."

He turned to the wall, took hold of the ivy, and with some effort, pulled it aside to reveal the wall beneath. Only there was more than a wall there. There stood a narrow wooden door set into the rocks. I froze, astonished.

"I—" I had no words. How was it possible that there was a door— an unguarded, unprotected door—in the middle of the wall?

"Few people know about it," he explained as I continued to stare, wide-eyed. "Your parents, the captain of the guard—"

"How do *you* know about it?"

"I'm the one that uses it regularly."

"But how—"

"My family was given charge of the grounds, and the maze specifically, several generations ago. We often need to collect good soil, plants, or even rocks from the forest and this was the simplest way to get there. We were entrusted with the knowledge because we had proven our loyalty."

"Isn't that dangerous?" Agitation tinged my voice.

"Isn't what dangerous?"

"Having a door blatantly set into the middle of what is supposed to be an impenetrable wall?"

He held his hand toward me. "Let me show you."

Forcing myself to grab hold of my composure, I took his hand. He heaved the door open enough for us to slip through, then reached beyond the opening to push away more vines. Gavin pushed me through and then followed. He closed the door with some effort, and I saw that the same rock that made up the wall had been attached to the back of the door. When it closed, it blended into the wall seamlessly. Gavin dropped the vines into place and watched me as I scrutinized the place we had just come through.

"That's…incredible." It was perfectly hidden. If you looked closely enough to see through the ivy, you only saw rock. "How do you open it from this side?"

He stepped forward and showed me a certain rock that he reached under to release the latch.

As the shock of such an odd discovery wore off, I let my gaze sweep around and felt a thrill run through me. I was outside the palace walls, unescorted, with Gavin. The possibilities had me grinning in sheer joy while I breathed in the scent of freedom.

Nearly all of the trees were very old, and therefore very large. Vines crawled across the forest floor and up many of the trees, giving them the look of having trunks made entirely of leaves.

I finally turned back at Gavin, my body tense with excitement. "You mentioned exploring."

A satisfied grin split his face. "I did." He took my hand. "You don't mind walking a bit?"

"Walking sounds infinitely better than sneaking out in a wagon," I assured him. "Lead on. I'll be right behind you with my proper clomping shoes."

Gavin led me away from the wall, weaving his way expertly through the trees.

"Are we going to be able to find our way back?" I asked, looking over my shoulder as the wall disappeared from view.

Gavin laughed lightly. "You may not be able to, but I will."

I walked on, enjoying the sound of his laughter and the feel of his hand pulling on mine. "Whose shoes am I wearing?"

"My sister's. I stole them away without her knowing."

"So, you're a thief, are you?"

He stopped, his face comically aghast. "Of course not, Ella. I am merely a borrower of things that I need."

Without the sound of our footfalls, I heard something. "Is that water?"

He dropped my hand and started walking backwards. "Yes, Princess, it is."

"Princess?"

He didn't respond, only raised his eyebrows in anticipation of whatever it was we were going to find before he turned and walked on.

We started up a slight incline, and I was about to pose another question when I saw a waterfall through the trees. I gathered my skirts and dashed ahead, too eager to walk. It wasn't all that large or magnificent. It only dropped about ten feet in a solid wall of water that was perhaps six feet wide. But it was lovely, and I found myself oddly soothed by the sight and sound of it.

"What do you think?" Gavin's voice roused me from my pondering. My feet had stopped of their own accord at the end of the trees.

"I love it," I breathed out.

"I thought you might, what with your obsessive tramping through puddles in the garden."

"How long have you been keeping this a secret?"

He shrugged. "It's a good spot to pull plants from." I let my gaze wander away from the wall of water and focused on the wildflowers and grasses growing along the stream's bank. It was quite spectacular. I drew closer to get a better look at the waterfall and the pool it created before rushing on down the stream. The waterfall appeared to have nothing but air behind it.

"What's behind it?" I asked.

"Behind what?"

"The water. It isn't hitting any rocks or anything; it's a solid sheet of water. Is there space behind it?"

When Gavin didn't respond, I tore my eyes away from the water and looked at him. He simply shrugged, a bemused expression on his face.

"You don't know?" I was shocked that he might have never bothered to find out.

"Unlike you, I am not so inclined to go jumping into water for recreational purposes."

"Well," I started, as a wicked little idea began to percolate. "We'll have to remedy that, won't we?" And with that, I grabbed his hand and proceeded to pull him toward the water.

"Ella?" He used a wary, warning tone.

"You said we were going to explore and so we shall." I was only a couple of feet from the edge of the water when Gavin broke my grip and wound his arm around my waist to halt my progress. He stood behind me with one arm locked around my waist and the other holding onto my arm.

"Now, wait just a minute. You can't just plunge into a pool of water."

"Why not?" I should have said something cleverer, but I felt a bit scatterbrained, all thoughts having fled when Gavin's arm went around me.

He made a noise of exasperation. "Why not, she asks. Because, *Princess*, what's going to happen when you show up for your lessons completely drenched? Or, what happens when we both show up on the palace grounds completely drenched? I don't know about you, but I don't want to have to explain that to anybody."

Unfortunately, he had a point. "Don't call me Princess." He had been so relaxed today, so willing to be himself and let me be myself. I hated that he felt the need to remind me of my rank. I was tempted to be angry and walk away, but I also wanted to see how long he would keep his arms around me. Simply out of curiosity, of course.

"I was just trying to make a point." Some of the force seemed to have left his voice, and I realized that when he spoke I could feel his breath on my neck.

I swallowed. "Point taken."

He seemed to take that as a sign that I was no longer going to do something rash, so he let me go and stepped away in one quick movement. I could tell he still watched me though, and decided not to turn around just yet. My confused emotions were likely written clearly across my face. His stepping away was too abrupt, but I wouldn't let myself think that he wanted to stay there. I couldn't think that because even if he felt something for me, or if I felt something for him...

We could be friends, but my station would not allow for anything more, no matter my feelings.

"Do you have many friends in the village?" I asked to distract myself.

"I suppose," he answered as he stepped up beside me.

"What do they think about the time you spend with me?"

"I haven't told anyone. I didn't think it prudent, for either of us."

"You think it would cause trouble."

"Yes."

"Then why do you do it?" It was a question I had wondered over many times.

I felt his gaze on me and reluctantly turned to face him. His dark eyes searched my face before answering. "Probably for many of the same reasons you spend your time with the likes of me. Because I want to. And I trust that you know the importance of keeping our friendship to ourselves."

I turned back to watch the waterfall, pleased with his answer, but trying not to show it. "Am I keeping you from your work?" It was a genuine worry of mine.

Gavin just smiled. "I always get my work done. You don't need to worry about that."

I relaxed, breathing in the misty air and watching the water falling for several minutes...until I heard raindrops hitting the foliage around us.

It was only a sprinkle, but it broke my concentration, and after letting several drops fall on my upturned face, I turned to Gavin, who tried to hide his smile.

"Now I have an excuse to be drenched," I teased.

"Oh, no you don't." He grabbed my hand and headed resolutely away from the water. "We have to get back now, or else people will wonder why in the world you were lingering in the rain. Come on." He started to jog along, trying to pull me with him, but my skirts wouldn't allow it. I let go of his hand so that I could use both to hitch up my skirts and go faster, focusing on not tripping as I ran in unfamiliar shoes over unfamiliar ground.

We reached the wall and I couldn't see how he would manage to find the door, but he didn't hesitate, just pulled the ivy aside and there it stood. The clouds continued to drizzle as I stepped through the curtain of ivy, back into my world. I paused to catch my breath as Gavin pulled the door shut.

"Are you all right, Princess?"

I rolled my eyes. "*Don't* call me that," I insisted, then turned to leave.

"Wait." Gavin stopped me and backed me up to sit on the nearest bench. "Your shoes," he explained as he pulled out my slippers and made quick work of switching his sister's sturdy shoes for my silken ones. "All right." He pulled me to my feet. "You'd better hurry. It's getting worse."

And indeed it was. I was getting soaked. "I'll see you tomorrow." I waved hastily and wound my way out of the maze and up to the castle.

Chapter Four

I ASKED GAVIN to take me back to the waterfall a couple of days later. He agreed readily, and we snuck off into the forest. This time I was armed with a satchel that held my art supplies. After making sure I was comfortably settled in the grass, he went about his work searching for large smooth rocks to line a garden path, and I went about sketching. We both worked silently for several minutes until he spoke abruptly.

"I've been wondering something."

I looked up to see him kneeling at the edge of the stream, peering over his shoulder at me. "What's that?" I asked. He was very selective about the things he asked me.

"Do you remember the first time you realized you were royalty?"

I replied without giving it much thought. "I suppose I've always known."

"There was never a moment when it hit you that you were meant for greater things than most people?"

His question was humbling and made me a little sad. Truthfully, I had never seen myself that way. Being royalty had become tedious and I often resented it, which was precisely why I was sitting out in the forest with him. "No, I never had a moment like that." Strictly speaking, it was a truthful answer. I had never felt I was meant for greater things.

"You just always knew what you would become?"

I looked out at the forest. I wanted to answer his question, but found my answer difficult to put into words. I supposed it would be simplest to say I dreaded what I would become.

"Ella?"

I focused on Gavin and tried to answer. "I suppose I have an idea of what I am expected to become, but," I smiled to myself as I admitted, "I think I'll end up disappointing everyone."

"I very much doubt that." He went back to work and I decided I needed a distraction.

I set my drawings aside and climbed to my feet. As I walked past Gavin I said, "You know, I still think we should find out what is behind that waterfall." My feet were already bare and I managed to get one foot in the water before Gavin hauled me away from it. I squealed at him to let me down.

He did, keeping himself between the water and me, and muttered, "I swear, you're bent on destruction."

On the verge of laughing, I gave him an innocent look and asked, "Aren't you the least bit curious?"

"I'm not letting you drench yourself."

I sighed in feigned resignation. "Fine."

He stood, guarding the way to the waterfall until I was sufficiently ensconced in my drawing once more. He tried to appear serious and stern, but I could tell he was fighting hard against a smile. I loved that look. I tried to sketch his face, but didn't have enough time to do it justice before he turned back to his work.

"Tell me about your family."

"What do you want to know?" he asked without looking up.

"How many brothers and sisters do you have?"

He turned to me, his hair in his eyes, and my pencil captured a couple more lines of his face.

"I have two sisters and one brother." He returned to his task, but I continued to ask about his family and learned, bit by bit, that his sister, Janie was only a year older. They tended to get along half the time and then bicker endlessly the other half. Fynn was twelve, but thought he was

41

older, which gave his mother fits. Kinley was nine and the baby of the family. Gavin admitted to spoiling her and having a tendency to laugh whenever she sassed their mother.

"I can't help it. It's like watching a miniature reflection of my mother. She sticks her fists on her hips and purses her lips just the right way. Even her tone of voice is spot on." I smiled as he stood demonstrating the stance. "My mother is furious whenever she catches me laughing, but I can't stop myself. I've taken to leaving the house when I can't keep it in."

I was trying to hold in my laughter, reminding myself that I should finish capturing his smiling face on paper. When we lapsed back into silence, I was able to sketch a rudimentary likeness of him, hiding it among my other papers when he came back to sit with me.

Later that evening, I sat in my room, filling in the details of his face, knowing that at some point I would have to let go of our friendship and this drawing may end up being my only link to him. It was a miserable thought.

✳✳✳

The next week, I gathered my courage and went back to the waterfall on my own.

Gavin had taken me enough times that I felt sure of finding my way without difficulty. I would have enjoyed Gavin's company, but he was determined to keep me out of the water, and I was determined to get in. Each time we had returned, I had continued to threaten to find out what hid behind the water. I think he knew I wouldn't really do it, but he still wouldn't let me get too close to the water without him there to prevent me doing something reckless. In truth, I enjoyed the little game. When he focused on not allowing me to drench myself, he had less time to think about maintaining an appropriate distance..

As much as I enjoyed the game, though, I couldn't abandon my curiosity. So I headed into the forest on my own, armed with my least cumbersome dress and an extra set of under things packed into my satchel.

42

"Ella, where are you going in such a hurry?" Mia asked as I tried to slip by. She stood regal and confident as always. As the oldest, she would likely be the next queen and carried herself as such.

"Just out to the gardens," I said as I moved my satchel behind my back.

"Drawing again?" Jensa asked. Her tone was somewhat condescending.

"Yes, I am." I refused to agree with her that drawing was frivolous. She was much too serious in general. Where Mia was confident, Jensa tended to be uptight and critical.

"Really, Ella. Must you always—"

"Leave her be," Mia encouraged, putting a hand on Jensa's arm. "She's not hurting anything." Turning back to me, she said, "Enjoy the gardens, Ella," before turning away and taking Jensa with her.

I scurried away without a farewell.

I used all my strength to open and close the hidden door, and found the stream and waterfall easily enough. Perhaps being in the forest by myself should have made me uneasy, but the bright sunlight filtering through the leaves and the sound of the birds singing put me completely at ease.

I approached the water. It appeared to be only waist deep, so my inability to swim would not be a problem. I took one last look around to ensure I was alone, then stepped out of my dress. In truth my under things weren't any less covering than my dress had been; they were simply a bodice and skirt of plain white muslin. I removed my shoes and set them aside, along with my dress and extra set of under things.

The water was colder than I had expected, but not unpleasantly so. I crouched down, submerging myself up to my neck and taking a moment or two to enjoy the feeling of being entirely surrounded by fresh, cool water. My feet were braced against the bottom of the stream to avoid being knocked off balance by the current.

I smiled to myself, imagining how my family members might react if they saw me.

Once acclimatized, I stood up and pushed myself through the waist-high water, reaching out with one hand and pushing it through the waterfall. I took a deep breath and walked through the cascade, gasping as water rushed over my face. I blinked and wiped the water from my eyes, pleasantly surprised at what I found. The rock face behind the falls was smooth and set back about five paces from where the water poured down. The water churned around me and as I approached the rock face, I discovered that the ground rose and I stepped up out of the water. By the time I touched the back wall, the water only reached my ankles.

No sound but the water reached my ears. I couldn't hear the bird's song or the wind in the trees or the rustle of leaves. I was entirely separated from the world and that fact left me strangely...exhilarated. The water from the falls slid down the underside of the rock and created a sort of constant rain.

It was only a simple cave, but I felt possessive of it and proud of my discovery. Sitting in the shallow water, I stared at the water pounding down in front of me and thought back to Gavin's question, when he had asked what being royalty meant to me.

I knew it meant slightly different things to all of my family members. My parents were aloof, as though a tangible barrier sat between them and all their subjects. Perhaps the weight of an entire kingdom did that to them, but all I could think was that it wasn't what I wanted.

I could see what being royal did to my sisters. Some of them displayed an arrogance that worried me. Lorraina was only a year and a half younger than I and worried me the most. She was vain, self centered, and even malicious at times.

As for me, I saw it as unfair, for many different reasons. I shook my head, forcing myself to enjoy this solitary place, breathing in and out, feeling the mist on my skin. Perhaps I would tell Gavin about my excursion. Perhaps. But for now, I would just be glad for the ability to come here if I ever had a need to be entirely alone.

With that encouraging thought, I walked back into the water, through the falls and out into the sunlight again. The sounds of the forest seemed out of place after hearing only the roaring of the waterfall, but I welcomed their liveliness. Heading toward shore, my foot slipped and I found my head submerged in the water. I struggled to regain my balance and came up sputtering and panicked, clinging to the shore. Forcing myself to calm down, I wondered if I should consider myself lucky and get back home as soon as possible. But just as I had claimed the maze, I wanted to claim this place for my own, and I didn't want to fear it.

Taking a deep breath, I slipped carefully back into the water. I practiced maintaining my balance while battling the current. If I pushed against the water with my arms, I could compensate, at least to a degree. I tired quickly, however, and determined that I would have to practice again.

The sun's scorching rays were a welcome relief as I climbed into the open air. My kingdom held undeniable beauty. The great mountain that sheltered our castle and served as a natural border rose majestically, greenish blue and immovable, to meet a pristine sky so blue I had difficulty believing it was real.

I changed behind a couple of close-growing trees at the base of the hill, then squeezed the water from my hair and tried to restore it to some semblance of order. I wrung out my clothes before wrapping them in a shawl and putting them in my bag. I decided against putting on my shoes, instead walking barefoot back to the maze, enjoying the feel of the earth under my feet. A lightness filled me; whether from knowing the secret of the waterfall or from abandoning propriety and tromping around barefoot, it didn't really matter. New life had been breathed into me. The looks thrown my way while entering the palace with bare feet and disheveled hair made me smile. I couldn't find it in myself to be ashamed.

I bounded up the stairs to my room with no poise at all, and had to suppress a grin when I hurried past Lorraina, who stopped suddenly upon seeing me and didn't recover before I passed her by. I slipped into my room and shut the door firmly, unable to keep a broad smile from my face as I considered my excursion. It was liberating.

I turned around, startled by the sight of Gretchen tidying my room. She gave a shy smile and dropped a quick curtsy. "Afternoon, Highness."

"Good afternoon, Gretchen." I tried to smother my grin but I was too happy in that moment and had to smile.

Gretchen looked back to the bedding she was straightening. "Might I ask where you've been, Princess?"

Her question surprised me. "I..." I paused, searching for an appropriate way to phrase it. "I was...exploring." I could barely keep a straight face; I was much too pleased with myself.

✳ ✳ ✳

The very next day, Gavin asked me if I'd like to visit the waterfall again. I was more than happy to comply and enjoyed the fact that I had a sumptuous secret to share. Keeping quiet seemed silly now that I had a confidante.

We passed through the wall and I lead the way, confidently following the invisible path to the waterfall. We sat a ways downstream so Gavin could hear as I read aloud. It was different seeing Gavin lying back, doing nothing. His work was so constant that seeing him at his leisure felt odd, though I enjoyed it.

My voice halted mid-sentence when he blurted out, "Aren't you going to try today?"

"Try what?" I turned to see him propped up on one elbow.

"You know very well what. I keep expecting you to scamper into the water and throw yourself beneath the waterfall, but you've sat here the whole time as if the thought never even crossed your mind."

"That's because I'm no longer curious."

"Really?" He looked as though he didn't believe me.

I looked down at my book. "I already know what's behind it."

"How's that?"

"I came here yesterday and looked for myself."

"You did what?"

I jerked my head around to look at him, worried by how angry he sounded. "What?"

"Do you have any idea how dangerous that was?"

I gave a bemused smile. "It wasn't dangerous at all."

"Ella, you can't just go off and—"

"Of course I can," I said calmly. "I can and I did, and I likely will again."

He groaned and slumped back. "I should never have shown you that door," he muttered.

It surprised me how much those words hurt me. "What is so terribly wrong with me satiating my curiosity?"

"That's not what worries me." I furrowed my brow in confusion. "Ella, you went outside the palace walls, unescorted. What if someone else had seen you? What if someone with less than noble intentions had come upon you?"

"When have we ever seen anyone else out here?"

"Just because we haven't doesn't mean we couldn't."

"Well, I'm sorry you regret confiding in me, but I'm not going to stop coming here."

"I don't want you to stop coming here. I love that you come here. But you have to let me come with you."

"Because you can protect me from the wicked world?" My voice was mocking, mean.

His eyes narrowed. "I can hold my own," he said in absolute seriousness.

For the first time, I considered his build in relation to something other than his striking looks. The years of hard physical work had resulted in toned muscle and rough, strong hands. He would be good in a fight. The thought made me swallow.

"Can you say the same for yourself?" he challenged.

I looked down at the book I'd been reading, rubbing one hand over the cover in agitation while my face burned. The guilt I felt at his reprimand surprised me. "All right," I conceded. "You can come from now on."

He moved close to me, then brushed a curl behind my ear. "I'm sorry," he said softly.

I had to keep myself from closing my eyes as the warmth of his touch rippled down my spine. "I'm fine."

"I'm still sorry."

I rested my chin on my knees, staring at the water for a minute. "How old are you?" My quiet question broke the silence.

"Eighteen," he answered, close to my ear. "How old are you?"

I turned to glare at him but was momentarily distracted to find him leaning toward me, smiling. I had the oddest urge to kiss the smirk off his face.

Forcing myself to look at his eyes, I resumed my glaring. He knew my age. Everyone knew, because everyone prepared for the festivities. "I'll be sixteen in five days," I said caustically.

He just kept smiling. "Happy birthday."

Chapter Five

MY EYES OPENED when there was only a hint of pink to indicate the dawn. I sat in the alcove by my window, watching the sky lighten. Today was my birthday—my sixteenth birthday—and I knew it would be horrid. We always had beautiful birthday celebrations, but the sixteenth was an all-day affair, and royalty from surrounding kingdoms were invited to come join in the festivities.

While a large party on my behalf was certainly enough to make me dread the day, the more horrifying aspect was that a certain prince was in attendance whom I had no wish whatsoever to see. Prince Jeshua of Tride had been one of the first to assure us of his presence at the celebrations.

I heard my door open and turned to see Gretchen coming in. It took her a moment to realize I was no longer in bed, but sitting at the window.

Her smile was less tentative and completely genuine. "Highness." She dropped a curtsy out of habit. "I didn't expect you up yet."

"When I woke up and remembered it was my birthday, I couldn't go back to sleep."

"Too excited for the day's festivities?" she asked as she knelt to light the fire.

"No. Terrified is more like it. I'm rather dreading the whole day."

She stopped and stared at me for a moment. "Why ever would you be dreading your own birthday celebrations, Highness?"

"Let's just say that there are some guests I would not have invited if I'd been given the choice."

Her eyes widened. "Indeed, Princess?" She opened her mouth to say more, closed it as if thinking better of it, then ended up asking anyway. "May I ask who?"

I smiled at her curiosity, and even more so at her questioning me. Though tentative, our friendship seemed to be slowly limping forward with my prodding. I went to sit beside her on the rug spread before my fireplace. "Do you know who Prince Jeshua is?"

"He's the crown prince of Tride, I think."

I nodded, but said nothing else. She furrowed her brow, then raised it in surprise as her mouth dropped open slightly. "Prince Jeshua is the one you wish wasn't coming?"

I nodded.

"Why not?"

I pulled my knees up and wrapped my arms around them. She went back to lighting the fire as I explained. "Jeshua has...taken an interest in me."

"What kind of interest?"

"A romantic interest...I fear. He always pays me special attention whenever we're together—even though I practically ignore him while my sisters fawn over him."

"Is that a bad thing?"

"Jeshua is...not kind." I was trying not to be harsh in my description of him, but found it difficult to find nice words for his behavior. "He's very self-centered and usually quite arrogant."

"Aren't most princes that way?" she asked, then blushed at her own boldness. The question was so blunt and innocent that I laughed out loud.

"Perhaps they are. Maybe it's not just Jeshua I don't like, but all princes." This thought depressed me a little and I sobered quickly. It was true that I was not close to any royal of my acquaintance, but I had assumed that eventually I would find someone who understood me and sympathized with my views. But perhaps Gretchen was right. Maybe with the way I had come to view royalty, it would be impossible to find a suitable husband who didn't put my teeth on edge.

"With so many guests today, it shouldn't be too difficult to avoid him," she suggested.

I thought about that. It would be a very large affair. Perhaps, if I was careful, I could avoid Jeshua for the most part. "Well, I can certainly try. Maybe I'll attach myself to some other royal for the day." I snuck my toes out from under my nightdress and pushed them toward the fire. I wished I could simply sit here with Gretchen for the day, but we both knew there was a schedule to keep. I forced myself to sit at my vanity and allow Gretchen to work her magic.

It would be a day of celebration in all the cities of Dalthia. Most would have a simple celebration in the evening, but here in the capital the celebrations took up the entire day. There were four different events: first, a breakfast with my family, then a picnic for lunch to which everyone was invited, and I do mean everyone—royals, nobles and commoners. Then for dinner, a large banquet would be held for nobility and visiting royalty. The evening would end with one of the most extravagant balls anyone was likely to experience.

I dressed more plainly for breakfast than usual, with my hair braided loosely and hanging over one shoulder. One of our traditions was to make the family breakfast a very relaxed affair. We had it in a private dining room with no servants present and no interruptions allowed. The table was set beforehand with all the food and drink we might require, then we were left to serve ourselves. I suspected this would be my favorite part of the day. My interactions with my family of late had been very limited, so it felt good to be reminded that when we were left to ourselves we tended to get along—and even have fun.

Before we served ourselves, we turned to my father expectantly, knowing what was coming.

Father stood, glass in hand, and we all reached for our own glasses.

"Today, our dear Ariella is sixteen years old," he started into his usual birthday speech. "There will be much celebration today, and there will be many people who will wish you the best. So let me be the first: may you find in this new phase of life a purpose that brings you joy and satisfaction."

"And a husband!" Marilee called out, bouncing a bit in her seat.

I rolled my eyes but my father responded seriously. "While marriage is certainly something to be considered, there is no need to be hasty."

I raised my glass. "Agreed, Father."

He smiled and we all raised our glasses. "To Ariella's contentment," he said.

"To Ariella's matrimony!" Marilee chimed in.

"To anyone's matrimony but my own," I said over the laughter that followed, in an attempt to ward off any further talk of marriage. I would let my older sisters concern themselves with matrimony. At this moment, I wanted no part of it.

"To Ariella." My mother's voice concluded the matter and each of my sisters repeated, "To Ariella." We all drank and then broke into buzzing conversation as we served our own plates.

I was grinning and found myself wishing this dynamic with my family were the norm instead of the exception. We took ourselves far too seriously.

My good mood lasted throughout breakfast, but was quickly squelched as I crossed the grand hall, still laughing with my sisters, and found Jeshua waiting there for us. Both my laughter and my feet stopped of their own accord. It had been almost a year since I had seen Jeshua. He was now twenty-one and everyone agreed he would soon be looking for a bride in earnest. I just prayed that all my instincts were wrong and that he wouldn't look to me.

"Prince Jeshua!" my father boomed in greeting. "We didn't expect you here so early. Are your parents here?" He reached out to shake Jeshua's hand.

"No, I decided to ride ahead. I was quite disappointed when I arrived and was told you could not be disturbed." He sounded as though being barred from seeing anyone he wished to see was unthinkable.

"Quite right," my father confirmed. "It is tradition to have a very private family breakfast on birthday mornings."

I tried to shrink back behind Kalina and Jensa. I did not want his attention at this moment—or ever, for that matter. I ended up next to Marilee and she tugged me closer so she could whisper in my ear, "Perhaps we won't have to look far for a husband for you," and then settle into a fit of giggles. I started to shush her, but found it unnecessary as my three older sisters stepped forward to greet His Highness.

I escaped shortly afterwards to prepare for the picnic.

I shut the door to my chamber and leaned against it, sighing. Gretchen regarded me quizzically and I answered her unspoken question. "Jeshua is already here."

She smiled and shrugged a bit. "Might as well enjoy his admiring looks."

"That's the thing. He doesn't give me admiring looks. He...*leers* at me. It makes my skin crawl." I turned my back to her so she could help me out of my casual morning dress. Though the picnic was outside, it was not a casual affair. With so many nobles and quite a few royals in attendance, we had to be at our best. I sat and talked with Gretchen for the better part of an hour before I was expected to make my appearance.

She redid my hair in a loose chignon just before it was time for me to go. I turned to her, trying to draw courage from her friendship. "You'll come down soon, won't you?"

"Yes, Highness, I'll only be a few minutes behind you. Don't worry, I'll be there even if you don't see me."

"I'd better see you. You may be one of the only sympathetic faces I encounter." I wondered if I might see Gavin at the picnic as well, and the thought made my stomach quiver.

Gretchen put her hands on my shoulders and took a deep breath, encouraging me to do the same. "Now, do *try* to have a good time,

Highness." She tried to give me a stern look, but it was lost in her teasing eyes. "It is your birthday, after all."

I groaned. "It really is ridiculous that I dread my own birthday above all other days. Although," I realized, "breakfast really was a very nice affair. I actually got along with my sisters."

"Well, see then?" Gretchen exclaimed, grabbing onto this bit of good fortune. "If that's not a birthday miracle, I don't know what is. Now, go down and wait for the rest of your miracles. They're bound to come."

I closed my room, ready to head down the hallway with a smile until Jeshua pushed himself away from the wall beside my door.

I sucked in a horrified breath and tried not to frown too deeply as he bowed. I curtsied and tried to take control of the situation. "Prince Jeshua, are you lost?"

He gave me an arrogant smile while his eyes raked over every inch of my person. "No, I believe I've found what I was looking for."

"Oh. Well, good day then." I dropped a very quick and dismissive curtsy and turned away from him.

He caught up easily. "I thought I might escort you out to the picnic."

My lips pressed together, not knowing what to say. He hadn't asked permission; he just assumed he could. I hated that about him.

I refused to take his arm, but it made little difference. He ended up putting his hand to the small of my back as we moved through the palace and insisted on helping me into one of the carriages that waited, ready to transport us from the palace to the picnic spot on the side of the hill. We rode with my two youngest sisters, Marilee and Lylin, who effectively squelched all conversation by giggling and talking to each other behind their hands almost the entire way. Marilee was spoilt and silly but she had so much joy and so many smiles that it was easy to overlook her silliness. Lylin was much more shy but tended to come out of her shell when prompted by Marilee's over-exuberance.

We reached the hill and my sisters hurried off before I could prevent it, leaving me once more with Jeshua, whose hand went immediately to the small of my back as he walked along, too close for my liking. I tried to ignore the uncomfortable feeling this possessive contact gave me. Walking along in the sun, my feet quickened in anticipation. Perhaps I might be able to enjoy this outing—if only I could get rid of Jeshua. Making our way up the side of the hill, we encountered more people and I was obliged to stop and greet those who came up to me, wishing me well. Thankfully, this forced Jeshua to step back.

I enjoyed the chance to interact with others, but also wished I could greet the commoners. They kept a respectful distance and only the children were bold enough to approach. I received many hugs around my waist from little girls in pinafores, and many shy handshakes from boys who blushed from head to toe when I bent to kiss their cheek. I wished there were some way to get to know them better.

Through it all, Jeshua stayed close at hand, resting his hand on my arm or back at any opportunity. When we had almost reached the top, I spotted one of my sisters.

"Kalina!" I called, hurrying over to her and out of Jeshua's grasp. I grabbed onto her outstretched hands as though they were a lifeline. Out of all my sisters, I felt closest to Kalina, perhaps because she was just older than me.

"So, the guest of honor has arrived. And you're even on time." She sounded surprised.

"Of course I am. What possible reason could I have to be late?"

Her eyes cut over to Jeshua for a split second. "I could think of some."

I was sure she would like nothing more than to have a gentleman be as attentive to her as Jeshua was to me, but her insinuation made my jaw clench. "I have no designs where Jeshua is concerned," I murmured.

She laughed. "It's nothing to be ashamed of, Ella."

"But, I'm really not—"

"I'll go let Father know you're here." She moved to extract her hands from mine, but I held on tighter.

"No," I insisted. She may not believe me, but I wouldn't let her leave me alone with him. "I want you to stay with me and it's my birthday, so you must give me what I want."

It was the sort of thing I would never say, but which everyone expected. While I cringed inside that I had resorted to being the spoiled princess, Kalina just smiled and entwined her arm with mine. We set off together, though she cast more than a few longing glances back at Jeshua as I continued my greetings and we eventually sat down with our family.

I sat down under the awning that had been erected for my family, drawing close to my sisters. Our conversation turned lighthearted, but any laughter was shushed by my father. We were in view of the entire Kingdom, and he wanted us to act with dignity.

I enjoyed watching the vast amount of people spread across the hill. I caught sight of Gretchen about halfway through the meal and entertained myself by watching her interact with those around her. I kept hoping to see Gavin's face in the crowd, but couldn't find him.

Convincing Marilee to walk about with me was easy enough, and she chattered amiably while I only half listened, searching the crowd for Gavin. When I did see him, his eyes were already on me, a smile threatening to spread across his face, though he kept it barely concealed. His eyes were teasing as he inclined his head in greeting then pulled his shoulders back and gestured toward his clothing. I held my lips in check, though I could feel my entire face smiling. His usual earth tones were gone, as was the dirt. His shirt was a deep blue, a color I had never seen on him before, though the sleeves were still rolled up out of his way. His trousers were cream colored, completely useless where his profession was concerned, but the effect was stunning.

I smiled despite my best efforts, then looked with curiosity to the people surrounding him. A girl sat nestled into his side, both arms wrapped around his upper arm as she rested her head of dark ringlets on his shoulder—this must be nine-year-old Kinley. A middle-aged couple sat behind him. The man had Gavin's dark hair with gray starting to run through it. The woman had plump cheeks and was keeping a sharp eye on the boy, who I guessed was Fynn. His gangly body hung just on the edge of falling into maturity. He was staring at Gavin, his face screwed up in concentration as he turned my way to see what had caught Gavin's attention. I turned my face away.

"Ariella?" Marilee's voice broke my concentration and I turned to her.

"Yes?"

"I asked you why we've stopped." She looked in Gavin's direction. "And what were you staring at?"

"Nothing." I pulled her along, but couldn't help one more glance in his direction. He was still staring at me, and I couldn't help the blush that heated my cheeks.

I wanted to sit down with my family, but saw that Jeshua was there, in earnest conversation with my father, so we continued to wander until it was time to leave.

Walking down the hill, I decided to take a precautionary measure as I drew level with my father. "Will you be starting the ball with me, Father?"

Surprise lit his face. "You can start it with whomever you wish, Ariella."

"Well, I wish to start it with you. Is that all right?"

He gave a ready smile. "I would be honored, my dear." He bowed his head as though humbled by the idea. I slipped my arm into the crook of his elbow, and we shared a carriage for the ride back.

Once inside the palace, I excused myself and raced up to my room to avoid being waylaid by Jeshua. I breathed a sigh of relief as I shut the door behind me.

I went to sit by the fire, smiling as I thought of my brief glimpse of Gavin, then frowning as I anticipated the ball and the inevitability of Jeshua asking for a dance. As I sorted through every possible way to avoid him, Gretchen came tumbling into the room, dropping a quick curtsy with a "Princess."

"Gretchen." I smiled at her ruffled appearance.

"I declare, that man follows you about like a stalking predator."

I was gratified that at least one other person had noticed. "He's much worse today than he usually is," I admitted, though I didn't tell her how worried that made me or how I had been expecting it.

"At first, I couldn't figure why you wouldn't want the attention of so handsome a man, but the way he looks at you, it's as if..." she struggled for a moment to find the words, "as if he owns you."

My brows furrowed of their own accord. It was precisely what I had been thinking. "Why can you see that but no one else can?"

She perched on the chair next to mine. "I was on the lookout for it. I might not have seen it if you hadn't mentioned your worries this morning."

"I suppose people see what they want to see. Everyone loves the idea of a fairy tale wedding. For some reason, people suppose that princes and princesses have more romantic lives than other people. And perhaps that's true in some regards. Maybe our lives are more romantic, but that doesn't mean there is any more romance in our lives."

"I'm not sure I know what you mean." Gretchen sounded confused and I laughed at myself. I had been thinking aloud and didn't really know if what I had said made sense even to me. But something about it was true...

After lounging around with Gretchen for a few minutes, we got to work transforming me into the guest of honor for the dinner and ball. I was actually excited to step into my dress. This was the first time I had refused all the suggestions of the dressmakers and had a gown made that was entirely my choice. It was cream colored with scrolling embroidery trailing down the center of my skirt and fanning out to cover the bottom edge.

Gretchen pulled my hair up, but I had her leave several curls out to drape over one shoulder. It was not in keeping with today's trends, but I did not much care.

My time ran out and I left the haven of my room. I had the foresight to stop at Lylin's room so we could walk down together and kept up a steady stream of animated conversation with her, pretending not to notice Jeshua as he lingered at the end of the corridor. Seating at dinner wasn't a difficulty, since the royal family sat at the high table. Thus I enjoyed dinner without looking over my shoulder every minute. There were several toasts in my honor—some sincere, many that were flowery nonsense, and all of which embarrassed me.

When dinner wound down I was almost relaxed as I drifted away from the table with Kalina and Marilee. Our conversation paused for a moment and Prince Jeshua took the opportunity to pounce.

He took me by surprise, and I was unable to keep my sisters from leaving as he seized my hand and forced it into the crook of his elbow.

"Ariella, I do believe you get more beautiful each time I see you."

I swallowed in distaste, wishing he would stop his infernal habit of touching me whenever he was close enough. "Thank you," I forced myself to respond.

"So beautiful, in fact, that I'm afraid I will have to impose and demand I be allowed the first dance with the guest of honor."

My nostrils flared in fury, but otherwise I managed to keep my face calm.

"I've already asked my father to share the first dance with me, Prince Jeshua."

"I'm sure your father would let me escort you onto the dance floor in his stead," he suggested magnanimously before pressing his lips to my hand.

I pulled my hand away. "I'm starting the ball with my father."

I turned my back on him, determined to find my father before Jeshua could try to bend me to his will. Fortunately, he was already striding toward me, his face lit with anticipation. My father and I had become quite close; in fact, I rather adored him—especially at this moment. He looked every bit the part of the noble king, dressed in all his finery, stepping forward to grasp my hands with so much poise and confidence that no one could doubt his authority.

"Ariella, dear." He kissed my hand and tucked it around his arm.

"I wanted to escort you down myself so I can see your reaction."

"My reaction to what?" I wondered.

"Your reaction to the location of your birthday ball."

Now I was confused. Were we not having the ball in the *ball*room? I allowed him to lead me through the castle, knowing that he wanted it to be a surprise. And it was a surprise when we ended up in the courtyard. Lit with torches and star light, it was a breathtaking sight.

"Whose idea was it to hold the ball here?" I asked as we made our way into the party.

"Your mother's. She's noticed your affinity for spending time out of doors and thought you would enjoy this."

I loved it. And I was glad we were here instead of closer to the maze. The maze wasn't something I wanted to share.

It took me a moment to realize we had stopped and my father was waiting for my reaction.

"It's divine." I kissed his cheek. "Thank you, Father."

"You are most welcome. And now," he said, taking my other hand into his, preparing to dance, "we shall commence this party in grand fashion."

The musicians, taking their cue from my father, started to play, and I was swept away into the revelry of my sixteenth birthday ball in very grand fashion indeed. There could be nothing so grand as being led about a dance floor on the arm of my father, the king.

"You are a lovely dancer, Ariella."

I smiled. "Why do you sound surprised? We have all been taught the art of dance."

"Yes, but you don't just dance. You breathe it. You're a natural."

I blinked in surprise. "Thank you."

When the dance ended, he stepped back, bowing gallantly. "I suppose I'll have to share you now. There seem to be quite a few gentlemen waiting for their turn." He escorted me off the dance floor, leaving me with my sisters before extending his hand to my mother.

"Princess Ariella?"

I turned and saw an unfamiliar gentleman. I could tell by the decorations on his clothing that he was a prince, but I could not remember ever learning his name. I dipped into a curtsy.

"Prince Terius, Highness," he introduced himself. "Might I have the pleasure?" He extended one hand toward me and the other to the dance floor.

"Of course." I slipped my hand into his and let him lead me into the dance. On closer inspection, I realized he was very young, possibly my own age.

"It's a lovely evening," he commented without looking at me.

"Yes, the weather has been perfect."

"How are you enjoying yourself?" Still, no eye contact.

"Well enough. And you, sir?" I asked in hopes of getting him to look at me.

"I can't find any fault with the celebration."

What an odd response. "Did you expect to?"

"My standards are drastically higher than the average person."

I wondered if he included everyone in the realm of 'average.'

"But you approve?" I was trying to get a firmer grasp on our conversation and finding it increasingly difficult.

He shrugged, scrutinizing the courtyard. "I'm not sure I'd go so far as to say that I approve."

I was starting to dislike this gentleman, but cast about for another subject. Dancing in awkward silence seemed like a worse alternative. "Have you met any of my sisters?"

"Not as yet. I suppose I'll end up taking a turn with at least one of them. They're pretty enough that I wouldn't mind."

There were no words.

"And do you think you'll catch anyone's eye this evening?" he asked, his chin raised practically to the sky.

"I beg your pardon?" I asked, trying not to sound as affronted as I felt.

"I assume you're doing your best to make a match this evening. It's

61

why my father encouraged me to ask for a dance."

I was glad he could not see my glare. "You think the point of the evening is for me to choose a husband?"

He finally looked at me. "Of course," he answered, his voice dripping with arrogance.

"But I hardly know anyone here. Don't you think I should get to know a person beforehand?"

He shrugged, his eyes wandering away again. "In my experience, knowing someone before you marry them makes little difference." In his experience? What experience could this runt of a man possibly lay claim to?

"Well, I can assure you that at the very least, I plan on knowing whether or not I like a person before I marry them."

"That's one way to approach it, I suppose."

I decided a change of subject was needed before I told this young man exactly what I thought of him. "And from whence do you hail, Sire?"

Surprise crossed his face, as though I should already know. I hoped I had offended him. "From Saldine."

"So, you traveled quite a ways?"

"Yes."

"I hope your return home goes very smoothly."

"Thank you," he said without any conviction.

I allowed the awkward silence to fill the space between us, and when the dance ended, we said only what was required for a polite parting. As soon as he stepped out of earshot, Marilee latched onto my arm, inquiring, "That was the Prince of Saldine, wasn't it?"

"Yes." I sighed, still annoyed at him. "Prince Terius. He's rather horrid, to tell the truth."

Marilee looked disappointed. "I had heard he was a bit conceited, but I hoped it wasn't true. He is quite handsome."

"Yet painful to listen to."

"Oh, here comes another," she whispered. I turned to see that, indeed, another prince was heading toward me. The night was sure to be taxing.

Fortunately Prince Terius was the worst of the lot, and several of the gentlemen I danced with were quite pleasant, and very polite.

The most interesting moment of the evening was dancing with Prince Goran.

"What can you tell me about your sister Mia?"

The question took me off guard. "Why do you ask?"

"Your father made a point of introducing us."

My eyebrows shot up. "Really?"

"She seemed embarrassed by it, and I wondered if you might know why."

"Yes. Well, to my knowledge, my father doesn't usually try to foist us onto unsuspecting gentlemen."

He blinked in surprise. "That's not what I meant," he assured me.

"I know, but that may be what she thinks."

"I wondered why she seemed nervous during our dance." His sincerity and forthrightness were encouraging. He seemed very decent. I just hoped Mia hadn't felt humiliated by my father's actions. She had reached marriageable age a couple years ago, and I knew she was anxious to fulfill her duty and be wed. Still, none of us wanted to be manipulated into marrying. I hoped my father would allow us the time to choose on our own, but since none of us had married as of yet, he may have been getting anxious.

I focused on my dance partner once again. "I'm sure she's fine. She was probably just taken off guard."

He smiled at the reassurance and we ended our dance with a curtsy and a bow before he led me off the floor. He had certainly given me something to think about, but I found myself quickly distracted as Jeshua seized the moment and claimed the next dance.

"I'm not used to having to fight for a lady's attention," he breathed in my ear, and I tried to pull back. I could think of no response polite enough to say aloud, so I pressed my lips together and focused on each colorful swirl of skirts as couples twirled around us.

"I had anticipated that we would have a good deal of time together today, but have found myself gravely disappointed."

"I have many guests, Jeshua. I must attend to as many as possible."

"I am wounded, Princess," he whined. "To think that you consider me just another guest."

Before I could retort, he continued. "But don't you worry. I understand that you must appear impartial at an event such as this. I will simply have to make the most of our time together."

My stomach twisted as he pulled me closer, and I clenched my teeth, trying to gain some control over my emotions so I would not flee the room altogether. He did not say anything further, instead taking every opportunity to breathe in the scent of my hair, brush his chin against my cheek, and draw languid circles on my back with his thumb. I survived his attentions, but extracting myself from his presence took a concerted effort on my part.

By the time my last partner took me in hand, I could feel my limbs starting to wilt. So much attention had pushed me beyond my limits. As I stood clapping along with everyone else at the dance's end, I congratulated myself on holding my poise throughout and then rallied all my energies to continue smiling as I bade our guests farewell.

Gretchen had fallen asleep waiting for me. She apologized profusely and freed me from my dress, allowing me to fall into bed, wondering when I might see Gavin on the morrow.

Chapter Six

THE NEXT AFTERNOON, I found Gavin hard at work and settled on a nearby bench to read. I was lying on my back with my book held over my head, trying to concentrate on the words, but after fifteen minutes of going over the same two pages, I gave up.

"Will you take me to the waterfall?"

He leaned out from behind the bush he was pruning. "You know you don't have to ask."

I rolled my eyes, annoyed that he would refer to my ability to command. "And you know that I *do* have to ask." I sat up. "Do you have time or would it put you behind?"

He took off his gloves and ran his fingers through his hair. "I always have time."

I grabbed my bag from under the bench and stuffed my book into it, glancing around to be sure nothing had dropped out. I threw the strap over my head and looked up to find Gavin standing a few feet in front of me, holding a single rose. I froze in surprise.

"Happy birthday," he said with a grin.

I smiled and took the flower. "Thank you. Now what ever will I get you for your birthday?"

He turned and started walking. "In order for you to get me anything, you would need to know my birthday."

"You're not going to tell me?" I asked, sticking the rose in my hair.

"It really doesn't matter," he said dismissively. I disagreed, but let it go. He was taking me to the waterfall, so I really shouldn't be arguing with him just for fun.

As he closed the door and let the ivy fall in place, he narrowed his eyes at me. "You aren't going to jump in the water, are you?"

I turned away, grinning at his concerns. "I can't promise anything," I called over my shoulder.

He groaned, trudging behind me. "If you end up drenched, you'll never get back into the castle without someone asking questions."

"Perhaps I brought a change of clothes." I kept walking, resolute, thoroughly enjoying our sparring match.

"And you're just going to change out in the middle of the forest?"

"What do you think I did last time?"

His footsteps ceased and I looked over my shoulders, but didn't stop. "Your brow is going to end up permanently creased if you keep frowning like that."

I hurried along, then blushed as I realized our conversation was not at all appropriate. Still, he seemed more concerned than shocked, so I tried to shake off my embarrassment. When I stopped at the edge of the trees a few paces from the stream he finally passed me by, shaking his head. I loved that I could exasperate someone so thoroughly.

He turned back to me, his expression serious. "Ella—"

"I'm not going to jump into the stream," I finally admitted. It was fun teasing him, but I wanted him to relax. "That was not my plan for today." I sank down to the grass, trying for a look of innocence. He just studied me. "You don't trust me?"

He hung his head and muttered something unintelligible, then looked up and sighed. "I'm going to gather some herbs for my mother." He pointed across the stream. "They're just over that rise, so it will only take me a minute. You're going to stay here?"

"I won't even get the hem of my dress wet."

"All right." His reluctance made my lips twitch upward. He removed his shoes, rolled up his trouser legs, stepped across the stream and continued up the slight rise. As soon as he was out of sight, I pulled my own shoes off. In accordance with my promise, I gathered my dress up around my knees, far out of the water's reach, and slipped my feet in. I went carefully, being sure not to slip. I really didn't want to get wet just then, so I watched each step and tried to make it across the stream using rocks as stepping stones. Halfway across, I stopped to contemplate my next move. The next rock sat a little farther and I wasn't sure I should risk the jump. Before I could decide, I heard Gavin whisper, "What are you doing?" and looked up to see him scrambling down the rise.

"My feet are wet; my dress is not," I defended myself.

"Shh," he hissed, splashing into the water and scooping me up.

"Gavin," I objected.

"Quiet," he insisted. Dropping me on dry land, he pulled me behind him as he hastily grabbed up my satchel and our shoes. "Someone is coming."

My heart tightened and I ran with him behind two large trees growing close together next to the small cliff over which the water fell. I crouched down with him, my heart racing. If we were seen—if I was seen outside the palace walls—if Gavin and I were seen together—I did not want to imagine the consequences.

We were each on hands and knees, crouched as low as possible. We watched as a group of men came over the rise. They were scattered, walking at a leisurely pace and talking. It appeared to be a hunting party on their way home from an afternoon of sport. My pulse quickened as I saw my father striding down to the stream, with Jeshua close behind on his left, and Jeshua's father, the King of Tride, to my father's right.

They all crossed the stream easily, most sloshing through without a thought. It appeared that my father had arranged this expedition for some of the more important royals and nobility that were visiting for my birthday. I closed my eyes, praying they would amble right past us without pausing. But, of course, they took advantage of the stream. They dropped their gear and crouched to drink or splash water on their faces.

My father came within a few paces of us and gazed out over the forest, appreciation in his eyes. Jeshua soon joined him, hands behind his back.

"Your Majesty," he greeted with less arrogance than I had come to expect from him.

"Jeshua, how have you fared this afternoon?"

"You know how much I enjoy a good hunting excursion."

"Don't we all?" my father agreed.

"Yes," Jeshua answered. "However, I have to admit that I have some ulterior motives."

"When does he not?" I muttered and heard Gavin stifle a laugh.

My father just chuckled. "I had a feeling. You haven't quite been yourself."

"Yes, well." I couldn't recall ever seeing Jeshua flustered before. "I would like to discuss the possibility of a marriage contract."

The blood drained from my face.

"Ah." Father seemed unsurprised.

"Please no, please no, please no," I whispered under my breath.

"And which of my lovely daughters has your favor?"

"Princess Ariella."

No! I clamped both my hands over my mouth to keep from shouting out loud and shook my head furiously.

"Ariella?" This *did* surprise my father, and I hoped he would say no. "She's barely sixteen, Jeshua. She is too young." There was a hard edge to his voice, a warning.

"Of course she is. I would not think of approaching her with this subject now. But I am also confident that my feelings will not change over the years to come. I would trust you to decide when the time is right."

"And if I were to ask her opinion of you, what do you suppose she would say?" I was grateful for the skepticism in my father's voice and hoped that Jeshua's charm would not win him over.

"I think she would likely be embarrassed by such questions." *What?* "She needs time to allow our relationship to grow, to gain confidence in her own feelings. That's why I would not dream of bringing the idea to her now."

I stopped breathing in horror. He sounded so sincere, so horribly genuine.

"I know that she is young, but I also know that I want her by my side when the time is right."

His speech made my stomach burn. How could he believe such a thing? How could he be convinced that I had any interest in a relationship?

A new voice spoke up. "You know our realms have had a solid relationship for several generations. Think how much stronger this would make us." My heart pounded faster. It was the king of Tride. His support would lend even more weight to the suggestion. How could this be happening?

"Is my suit acceptable, Your Majesty?" Jeshua asked.

I wanted to see their faces but was afraid to move. I desperately wished for my father to say no. Even a tentative no, anything but –

"Yes, Jeshua. I believe I will accept your offer. "

I was being crushed, suffocating under the weight of those words.

"But you will trust me to know when the time is right."

"Of course, Sire. I would have it no other way." Jeshua's voice was all deference and respect.

I thought of the farce my life would be if I were to become a princess of Tride, or a queen. I forced myself to swallow a sob as I huddled, listening to the ruination of my life.

"Jeshua—" Concern was threaded through my father's voice. "She does care for you?"

"I assure you, Sire, we are well matched." He hadn't even answered the question.

"They are well suited, I have no doubt," Jeshua's father spoke up. "I've noticed the way they watch one another." Why did he have to interfere?

"Well then, I look forward to the union." My father's voice had a ringing finality to it. I could imagine the handshake. It was done, just like that. It took no time at all. I heard them walk away, heard the murmur of voices as they continued to talk about the planned union. I hated that I could not follow and hear the rest, but I was frozen, unable even to take a breath.

Silence enveloped me until the sound of their retreat was long gone. I pushed myself to my knees, gasped a painful breath of air, and finally released my sobs. The anger and hurt were so deep.

My anger was for Jeshua—for having the arrogance and gall to convince my father that I cared for him, that I respected him. I had never felt as though I hated anyone up to this point in my life, and I certainly didn't want to start now, but I couldn't think of any other word to describe my feelings toward him.

The hurt I felt was because of my father. He had given me over to Jeshua so easily, with only the ridiculous claims of Jeshua himself as an assurance of my feelings. As I thought more on that betrayal, the hurt won over and I pressed the heels of my hands into my forehead.

"Ella?" I had almost forgotten Gavin was there. He brushed my hair back off my forehead, touched my shoulder, my knee, then finally pulled me into his arms. I draped myself over his shoulders as his arms drew me closer and I continued to sob. My emotion was out of control, and I held him tighter in an attempt to keep myself together.

After a few minutes, I forced myself to calm down and finally settled enough that Gavin's grip loosened and I made myself pull back. I met his eyes and then quickly looked away as the compassion written on his face made me want to return to his arms. I fumbled for my satchel, pulling out my shawl so I could dry my face. Turning to lean against the tree, I tried to look Gavin in the eye but couldn't.

I sniffed and tried to laugh, but it didn't work. So I just whispered, "I'm sorry," and closed my eyes.

I heard him sit back. "You're apologizing?" His voice was bewildered but I just nodded my head, sweeping the tears from my cheeks. "Why?"

"I should not have let my feelings get the better of me." Diplomacy was my position of retreat.

"You think I expect you to hear something like that and not react?"

I stared down at my hands. "I shouldn't be surprised."

"Of course you should," he insisted, sounding almost angry.

His validation made my voice thick with unshed tears as I admitted, "I hate him—so much. And my father gave me over to him without so much as blinking." I shut my eyes again as more tears fell. "I can't do it."

"You can't do what?" I felt his hand on my knee once more as he tried to keep me focused.

"I can't be courted by Jeshua. I can't marry him. But I don't know how to avoid it." I sat still for a moment, and when he made no response I looked up at him.

"You say no," he said bluntly.

"No one says no. That's not how my world works, Gavin." My voice had risen, but I didn't bother lowering it. "You do what is expected of you because it's the right thing to do."

He leaned toward me. "How can it be the right thing to do," he asked, wiping a tear from my cheek, "if it makes you feel like this?"

I pushed past him, climbing to my feet. "My feelings will not be the issue." The bitterness gave my voice a hard edge.

"So that's how your world works?"

I picked up my satchel. "I'll be late for dinner. We have to go back." I stumbled as I tried to put my shoes on while standing.

"Talk to me, Ella." Gavin shoved his feet into his own shoes as I looked at him, trying not to cry again.

"No." I hurried away and he chased after me.

"Ella?"

I whirled on him. "What do you want me to say?"

He rocked back a bit. "Say anything."

I turned from him and stalked away. "I don't want to say anything.

I don't want to think about it. I don't want to acknowledge it in any way. I want to scrub my ears out and pretend it was never said. I don't want anything to do with it!"

Gavin caught hold of my flailing arm and forced me to stop my stomping retreat. "All right." He pulled me to him and I couldn't stop myself from crying into his chest.

"How could he do that?" I cried.

The silence stretched out for a moment and then Gavin gently asked, "Would he have agreed if he knew how you felt?"

I blinked as I considered and had to admit, "I don't know." I let him hold me for a moment more before I broke away. "I really do need to go back."

He nodded and fell into step beside me, a reassuring hand on the small of my back. I did need to go back, not because I would be late for dinner—I had plenty of time for that—but because I felt much too vulnerable out here. A storm was gathering inside me and I wanted to be alone when it broke.

We didn't talk as we trudged back. I was so deep in thought that if not for his hand to guide me, I would have wandered aimlessly.

Safely back in the maze, I sat down. Suddenly the prospect of being alone with my thoughts—of truly having to think about what had just happened—scared me senseless.

"So, what do you think of my world now?" My eyes were dry.

Gavin sat beside me, resting his elbows on his knees. "I think it's more complicated than I thought."

I cast about for something to focus on and my eyes landed on the far corner of this closed-in room. There sat another of the statues I so admired. Another dancing couple, happy and carefree, sat partially hidden behind the foliage. "Wouldn't it be lovely to be a part of their world? Just for a moment."

He followed my gaze and considered the statues. "You could, you know."

I let out the tiniest laugh, finding his assertion to be very funny.

Gavin's face, however, remained earnest. "That is a common couple, in a common dance. That's my world."

My face felt slack as I stared at him and then turned to consider the statue once more. I got up to take a closer look and examine the details. Their clothes were plain, utilitarian and practical; a kerchief covered her head and a cap stuck out of his pocket.

"How did they end up here? And why are they hidden away?"

"Your mother commissioned them." I turned to him, shocked by this revelation. "Your father chose to hide them away after she refused to get rid of them."

"How long ago was this?"

"I believe it was just after they were married."

"And how do you even know of it?"

He smiled. "My family has been here a long time."

I continued to focus on the statue, unwilling to think of other things.

"Do you dance?" I asked Gavin.

"Why, yes, of course. Dances are a common pastime."

"How common?"

"There is a gathering tonight, in the square."

As he told me this, an idea stole into my head and took root. I knew it was a ridiculous notion, but I wouldn't let it go without trying.

"Take me with you," I pleaded.

Gavin's brow furrowed and then his eyes widened as he comprehended my meaning. "Ella, you cannot."

"But why?" I could hear the whining tone in my voice and hated it, but I was desperate.

"You think you could just walk into the village without the entire kingdom being in an uproar? Your family would never allow it. The people would not know how to react to such an action."

"I could dress like a commoner, no ribbons, no silk. I could tie up my hair in a kerchief. I could—"

"Ella," he interrupted. "I have told you before, it is not just your

73

clothes that make you look like a princess. I—"

"Please, Gavin." I had only been this rash once before, and my wagon ride had ended almost sooner than it began. But the prospect of doing something so completely outside of myself, with Gavin, was so glorious that I could not let the idea go. "You said I could be part of that world."

"I didn't mean—"

"At least help me consider it."

He looked torn. "Ella, I cannot deny you anything you ask for and you know it."

"This is not a royal command, Gavin." I walked over to him. "This is just me asking you. You can say no if you like, but I am asking as a friend. I have to get away from all this just for a while." I met his eyes, knowing only he could help me do this.

He gazed back at me, seeming distracted, and asked, "Get away from what?"

I stared at him, incredulous. "You would condemn me to sit in my room and think of my future life as a shackled companion to Jeshua of Tride?" I took both his hands into mine. "Please, Gavin."

He closed his eyes at my mention of Jeshua, then looked down at his hands in mine. He finally blew out his breath and said, "All right."

"Thank you." I squeezed his hands in gratitude.

"But only," he added, "if you promise that if we cannot find a safe way to do this, we will not go."

I smiled and promised.

Chapter Seven

WE ENDED UP enlisting the help of Gretchen. She was reluctant, but once I told her my reasons, her indignation on my behalf compensated for any nerves. She lent me one of her dresses, some shoes, and a kerchief. She helped capture my curls into a simple bun and made me walk around the room. "You can't walk so perfectly, Princess."

"You realize you'll have to call me Ella when we are out of the palace?"

"Yes," she said dismissively. "Now try to walk as though you have a purpose, as though you are simply trying to get there. Don't think about how you look."

"I don't think about how I look, this is just how I walk."

"It's too pretty, Highness."

I made a concerted effort to walk with less grace. Gretchen laughed at me and quickly covered her mouth. I threw up my hands after a while.

"How do you expect to get outside the wall, anyway?" Gretchen asked.

I didn't want to risk telling her the truth about the hidden door. "I'm leaving that up to Gavin. He said he has a way."

She shook her head. "And when exactly did you become friends with Gavin?"

I dropped my gaze. Gretchen was the first person to know anything about my friendship with Gavin. "We've been friends for..." I had to think about it. It felt like several months to me, but in reality had been far less. "About a month now."

When it was time to go, I left the castle with Gretchen, and we went through the kitchens to avoid the guards. Once outside the castle she went to leave the palace grounds through the servants' gate and I went to meet Gavin in the maze. He raised his eyebrows when he saw my covered hair and common clothing, but didn't comment as I left a bundle of clothing hidden in the room with the door. He was nervous about our expedition and encouraged me to walk swiftly and stealthily around the outside of the palace wall. We met up with Gretchen before entering the village, and Gavin walked a little way from us. They each told me that young ladies and young men rarely arrived together unless they were engaged, but once the dance started, everyone mingled freely.

As I walked alongside Gretchen, I couldn't help beaming. Several times we caught each other's eye and broke out laughing. At one point Gretchen leaned toward me and whispered, "I cannot believe you talked me into this."

"You don't think this is fun?"

"It is fun, but I still can't believe I'm doing it." She looked me up and down as we walked. "You're still walking too perfectly."

I shrugged, but attempted to adjust my step.

Despite my too-perfect walk, we traversed the distance to the dance without any mishaps. We were greeted by the sound of fiddles, drums, and flutes being tuned and tested. I looked around in amazement, taking in the humble surroundings and cheerful faces. Like the buildings, the faces were creased and worn, but there remained a light in their eyes. The time for arduous daily tasks had passed and the evening beckoned, enticing them to cast their cares aside and enjoy the company of others.

As the musicians started their first song, the dynamic of the group shifted. All the women and girls had been talking and mingling on one side of the square while the men and boys had been doing the same on the other side, but as that first chord struck, everybody moved into a flurry. Gretchen dragged me into the middle of the square along with all the other women, where everyone joined together. Some found partners immediately and set off dancing, while others formed groups, circling together with joined hands, then splitting off again.

I tried my best to follow Gretchen as she, like everyone else, danced her way through the crowd. We joined with several groups, one after the other, and I felt I was just getting a hang of the rhythm when a gentleman whisked Gretchen away. She looked back at me as he pulled her away, no doubt worried that I might feel lost without her. But I gave her a smile and went to join in another group circle when I felt a gentleman's hand on my waist as his other hand took mine. He lead me away in the same fashion Gretchen had been, then spun me around to face him and off we went. I admit I was shocked and more than a little embarrassed–dancing with a group was one thing; dancing with a partner was another. Looking into his face, I realized that I had been hoping to see Gavin, but the man was a stranger to me.

My step was clumsy at best, but my partner didn't seem to notice; he just led on, dancing me to and from every corner of the square. By the time the music started to wind down, I had relaxed and was starting to enjoy myself as I became more familiar with the dance. The last note sounded and my partner spun me. I cheered along with everyone else, elated to be a part of this wonderful custom.

As the applause died away, my partner leaned close so I could hear him. "You are a lovely dancer, miss."

"And you are far too kind," I responded.

"Nonsense," he argued with a broad grin. "I could tell you weren't completely familiar with the dance at first, but you caught on and followed very well."

"Thank you," I replied, settling on the simplest reply I could come up with. I knew an overabundance of manners might make me seem suspicious.

My partner had opened his mouth to speak again when Gretchen appeared at my elbow.

"I'm sorry," she said breathlessly. "I tried to stay with you, but—"

"It's all right," I assured her, but I linked my arm through hers nonetheless. I didn't want to lose her again. I still felt out of my element.

My dance partner startled me when he spoke. "Gretchen, aren't you going to introduce me?"

I turned to Gretchen in surprise. "You know him?"

"Since the day I was born." Gretchen said. "This is my brother, Eli." I wasn't sure what to do at this point. I knew how to greet royalty and nobility, but I didn't know what the commoner custom was. I tried to follow Eli's lead as he extended his hand. I put out mine and he grasped my fingers more firmly than I was used to and without any bow said, "It's a pleasure."

"This is Ella." Gretchen finished the introduction. No one but Gavin, Gretchen and occasionally one of my sisters called me Ella, so it wasn't a risk to use it here.

Eli released my hand. "I saw the two of you sticking together, so when Benjamin stole Gretchen from you, I thought it appropriate that I step in. I hope you don't mind."

"Not at all."

"And how do you know my sister?" he inquired.

I tried to remember the story that we had come up with, but was saved by the fortuitous arrival of Gavin as he ran up to our group, relief apparent in his eyes. "Good, I found you." He put his hand on my elbow and looked me over as though making sure I was all in one piece.

"Yes, Gretchen has been taking excellent care of me, showing me around."

"You're not from here?" Eli asked.

Gretchen, Gavin and I exchanged looks, waiting to see who would be the first to take up the lie. Gretchen was the quickest. "She's here to visit a sick aunt. We met at market early this morning and I agreed to show her around."

"And how long will you be staying?" Eli's smile broadened, and though I appreciated his friendly nature, pretending to be someone else was more difficult than I had anticipated.

"I'm not sure—it depends on how long my aunt has need of me." Before Eli could ask any more questions, the musicians started another song and Gavin was quick to pull me into the fray. I was elated to be dancing with Gavin. He was relaxed and confident here. He didn't hesitate in touching me when the dance required, and his hold was firm. I was secure in his arms.

The next time we stopped to rest, I asked, "Why are some of the women holding scarves?" Quite of few of the women danced with a scarf in one hand. It added to the general beauty of the dance, but I thought there might be a more meaningful reason, and I was right.

"It means they're married or engaged. This way, the married folk can enjoy the gatherings, and none of us single fellows will try to dance with them."

The simple logic of this custom struck me. Instead of married folk being forced to either stay at home or simply watch, they could join in and not have to worry about being viewed as inappropriate. It seemed to cut out some of the courtship games.

The rest of the evening was a blur—a wonderful, exhilarating blur. I spent much of the night in Gavin's capable hands as he lead me through each dance. My favorite was when a new song started and Gavin leaned in.

"Ready?" he asked, eyes dancing.

"For what?"

"This is the dance shown by the statue you love so much. During the chorus we'll take hold of each other and spin as fast as we can. Ready?"

"More than ready."

We started in a circle of four, hands on our hips as we did a little footwork then shuffled round the circle before repeating the footwork and shuffling the opposite direction. Then the chorus began and we separated from the group, wrapped our right arm around the other's waist and used out weight to propel us in a circle.

I was flying and exhilarated. Spinning during each chorus left me dizzy and I had to hold onto Gavin while I laughed and regained my balance, my insides fluttering as he pulled me close. I always hated to leave him when I had to dance with anyone else, but it was necessary.

I danced two more dances with Eli and two dances with partners whom I never formally met. It was exhausting, and yet I never wanted it to end.

As the last notes of the last song faded into the night and the applause died away, Gavin put his mouth to my ear and a warmth trickled down my neck. "Gretchen will walk back with you, but I'll be right behind." I nodded and left through the crowd with Gretchen. Near the castle, the servants had dispersed. Gavin joined me once more and we waved Gretchen on her way as she headed to her own home. Once Gavin and I reached the hidden door, he held it open for me. "This is where I'll leave you."

I turned to look at him, his face inches from my own. "Thank you, Gavin. This was amazing." It sounded trite, but I couldn't think of any other way to express myself.

He smiled, and my stomach flipped over as his eyes flitting to my mouth and back. "I'm glad you enjoyed it. Goodbye, Ella."

"Good night."

He closed the door, and I let a grin steal over my face before retrieving the clothing I had hidden in the room. I changed quickly, keeping my ears perked for any passersby. I heard nothing and encountered no one going back. The guard at the front entrance gave me an odd look before making his face blank once more, but I just hurried past and back to my room. I slipped into my nightdress and fell into bed with the beautiful sounds of common music playing in my head.

Chapter Eight

I WOKE THE next morning to find the sun higher than it usually was when I awoke. I smiled in spite of myself, recalling the glorious evening I had experienced. The dancing, the people, the music, and the joy—it was all so ridiculously lovely, I could hardly keep from laughing.

Then I remembered. I remembered the reason I had insisted on escaping the palace in the first place and I pulled my covers up over my head.

Jeshua. Slimy, slithering, repulsive Jeshua had asked my father for permission to marry me. And the worst part was that my father had actually agreed. That was it: the end of my life wrapped up in a neat, two-minute conversation that hadn't included me. My stomach twisted. Everything inside me squirmed at the idea of being wed to a man I had avoided since the moment I met him. I couldn't do it. And yet how could I not? A promise had been made; an agreement had been reached between one royal family and another. How could a contract like that be broken?

I wanted to hide forever. Last night I had begged my way out of dinner, but it wouldn't work twice. Today I would have to face Jeshua— at breakfast, at lunch and at dinner. I would have to be polite and pretend not to know.

The door opened and closed quietly.

"Your Highness?" It was Gretchen.

"Yes?" I mumbled from beneath my blankets.

Her footsteps came closer. "Are you alright, Highness?"

I pulled the covers away from my face. "Yes, Gretchen, I'm fine. I was just… thinking."

"Indeed, Highness. About what?"

I waved it off. "It's not important."

"Whatever you say, Princess," she replied with a mock curtsy and a coy smile.

"I suppose it has to be 'Princess' now that we're back in the castle," I said in amusement. I threw back my covers and slid out of bed, slipping my feet into fur bed slippers and scurrying across the floor to my wardrobe.

"So, which lovely dress will you wear today?" asked Gretchen. Her fascination with my gowns gave me an idea.

"I don't want to wear something lovely today." The idea grew rapidly. "And I don't want you to do anything fancy with my hair either."

"But Highness—"

"I want to look as plain as possible, understand?"

"But why?"

"I can't get out of this betrothal, especially since I'm not even supposed to know about it, but maybe I can make *him* change his mind."

Gretchen gave me a pitying smile. "I will make you as plain as possible, Princess, but I doubt it will make any difference."

I shrugged. "I at least have to try."

But trying didn't do me any good. I only made it five paces outside my bedroom when my mother walked by and stopped me. "My darling, you must go change. We have guests for breakfast and I'm sure you want to look your best."

Annoyance crossed my face, but she ignored it. "Go on. And be quick about it."

I considered taking as much time as possible, but figured it probably wasn't worth the upset it would cause. Besides, if I were to walk in late, it would draw more attention to me, and that was the last thing I wanted.

Gretchen didn't seem all that surprised when I returned with the news. I changed quickly, then Gretchen pulled a few of my curls free of the bun she had arranged so they framed my face. I stopped her before she could add her favorite pearl hairpins.

When I left my room for the second time, I met Marilee.

"Do you know who is still here?" Marilee asked, fairly bouncing out of her shoes.

"Who?" I asked, knowing she would want to share the news instead of hearing that I already knew.

"Jeshua! His parents have gone but he is staying an extra day." She squeezed my arm in excitement. "What do you make of *that*?"

I offered a strained smile. It was difficult not to smile when Marilee was like this. "I'm sure I have no idea."

During breakfast I said little, frowned constantly, clanked my utensils together in what I hoped was an annoying fashion, and purposefully spilled my drink in the direction of Jeshua's plate. He either didn't notice, didn't care, or thought it was somehow endearing, because he gave me his most gracious and self-aggrandizing grin and patted my hand a time or two. By the end of breakfast I was so annoyed that I no longer had to act clumsy on purpose; it came along with my frustration.

To my complete delight, Jeshua didn't stay the entire day, but left immediately after breakfast along with several other guests. All of my sisters and I bade him goodbye at the doors of the great hall. And though he directed most of his attentions toward me, Jensa and Kalina gave him five times the farewell that I did. My farewell was restricted to formalities and politeness, while my sisters practically hung on him. When he finally extricated himself from their attentions and was able to leave, I was left amid my sisters' sighs and giggles as they discussed his visit, their meaningless comments fluttering about.

"Surely his visit was more than just a visit."

"Of course it was; he *is* of the marrying age, after all."

"So which of us do you suppose he's chosen?"

"Perhaps he hasn't chosen at all."

"You think he came to browse?"

"I think it's entirely possible."

"I think he's chosen Ella." I continued to gaze out the door, refusing to acknowledge Marilee's comment.

"Why do you say that?" Lorraina's voice made it clear that she thought Marilee dimwitted.

"Have you seen how he looks at her?" Now it was Marilee's turn to make it clear that she thought Lorraina was dimwitted.

"That doesn't mean he's chosen," Lorraina snapped. I wondered if she had secretly taken a liking to Jeshua. "In fact, I think Kalina is right. I don't think he's chosen at all."

No one responded. Lorraina had a way of taking the fun out of any conversation that wasn't going her way.

I felt someone at my arm and looked down to see eleven-year-old Lylin resting her head against my arm. "I don't want anyone to get married," she whispered. I squeezed her hand, but kept silent.

"Mia." My father's voice broke the silence, ringing through the empty space of the entrance hall. "I'd like to speak with you."

At hearing my father's request, Mia's eyes became very wide and I knew she and all of my other sisters were thinking the same thing: Jeshua had chosen Mia.

I wished they were right, but knew my sisters' curiosity where Jeshua was concerned would not be satisfied for several years. I watched Mia fidget and had the impression that it was not excitement, but more apprehension that caused her to wring her hands.

Sitting through my lessons was difficult, but I escaped to the maze as soon as possible. I passed Gavin, working on some shrubbery in the main garden and caught his eye, hoping he would be able to join me soon. It was cooler today than it had been lately, so I had my cloak on. But when I entered the garden room, I took it off and laid it on the ground so I could sit and draw. It wasn't as chilly in the maze and I enjoyed the feel of the breeze on my skin.

In a few minutes Gavin came through the hedges, dusting dirt from his gloves and knees. "Will you teach me some dances?" I asked before he even looked up. He removed his gloves, glanced up and stared.

"What?" I asked, wondering if there was something amiss.

He shook his head slightly. "Uh, nothing. You just look...different than you did last night."

I rolled my eyes slightly, moved my skirts aside and got to my feet. "Mother wanted me to look especially well this morning because Jeshua stayed for breakfast. I had a difficult time not gagging on my food the entire meal." I stepped toward him, not wanting to speak of Jeshua. "Now, will you teach me better how to dance? I was quite lost about half the time last night."

"You didn't look in the least bit lost."

"So say you," I teased, but I was serious as well; Gavin would never speak unkindly.

"But not just me. So says Eli as well."

"Eli?" Gretchen's brother? What did he have to do with anything?

"Yes, he was quite taken with the mysterious stranger from who knows where. He was wondering how I know you." He seemed to be watching my reaction closely, and a tingle ran across my skin.

"Just tell him who I really am and he'll go running for the hills. Now teach me how to dance."

He sighed. "You already dance very well." But he came toward me nonetheless.

As he began teaching me, he continued our conversation. "And what exactly makes you think Eli would go running for the hills if he knew who you were?"

"What?" I asked, having already forgotten our conversation. My focus had shifted to our dancing, to the ease with which Gavin put his arms around me, to my own nervousness. Dancing with Gavin proved very distracting when there was no one else near to dilute my awareness of him.

"You said Eli would go running for the hills if he knew who you were."

"Oh," I responded. "Well, it's true." Gavin moved to spin me under his arm but I had lost my focus and my dress was not meant for dancing. I tripped over my own feet and ended up tangling myself in my skirts. I went down and in his attempts to catch me, Gavin fell with me. I landed on my backside and he landed on his knees. For a moment neither of us spoke, but then we saw each other's faces and started laughing.

He moved to sit down beside me. "Are you all right?"

"Yes," I sighed, embarrassed. My backside hurt a bit, but I wasn't about to tell him that. Instead I reached down and untangled my foot from my petticoats. "I should have changed before I came out here."

"It is a bit dangerous, isn't it?" he asked as he grabbed a handful of fabric at the bottom of my skirt and examined the layers. My eyebrows rose of their own accord but I kept my mouth shut and tried not to smile. Any noble or royal who might have seen such a display would have had him flogged. "Imagine if you had fallen into the pool." He got to his feet and offered both his hands to me. I took them and allowed him to haul me to my feet.

"Well, I feel graceful," I said. He hadn't released my hands and the thought distracted me.

A smirk slipped across his mouth. "You are graceful, even when you fall."

He was making fun of me. "Oh, certainly."

"No, really. Everything you do is graceful, and I haven't figured out how you do it." He positioned me in a more formal stance and started moving through the steps of a different dance.

I sighed. "I suppose those lessons were useful after all."

He stepped us into a fast twirl, propelled by each other's weight. The feeling of these quick carefree movements was intoxicating. I closed my eyes, enjoying the feeling of moving with Gavin. When I opened them, the world spun around me and Gavin had to pull me closer to keep me from falling—again. I was starting to feel clumsy. I found my face very close to his and forgot my clumsiness. His mouth had me distracted. "So much for grace," I breathed before finally looking to his eyes.

I found him staring at my own mouth and felt it go dry as his hand trailed down my back before pulling away. He finally met my eyes and lifted a corner of his mouth before twirling me outward and inclining his head, ending our dance.

✳ ✳ ✳

My father announced Mia's engagement the next week. Not to Jeshua, as my sisters had suspected, and not even to a prince, but to a noble who had been quietly doting on her for years. That's why my father's introducing her to Prince Goran had been upsetting to her. She had fallen in love, which surprised me. I had always thought that Mia's lack of prospects were due to her practical nature. She had never been one to romanticize situations and seemed content to wait for the appropriate man. We had all expected her to marry a prince who would be able to rule alongside her when the time came. My father had always made it clear that the crown would be passed to one of us as the next queen.

So when we heard of her engagement, we were all anxious to know how the situation had come about. Lord Havington was twelve years her senior with a naturally reticent disposition and had been hesitant to pursue her when she came of age. So he had bided his time, slowly getting to know her. It was my father that finally prompted him to act.

"After Lord Havington saw the way that Father was pushing me toward Prince Goran, he came up to me, looking very determined, and told me that I should not marry the Prince. When I asked him why, he said, 'Because I would like you to marry me.'"

We all smiled and I even heard Marilee sigh.

"Of course, I have cared for him for quite some time, but he never gave any indication that he truly had an interest in me. It was such a relief to have him finally speak his feelings. We had talked much and even flirted a little, but I was worried about what people might think. He is much older."

"That hardly matters," Jensa encouraged. "Especially now that you are a little older. I think it will be a great match for you."

"So when will the celebration be held?" Naturally, this question came from Marilee, always looking forward to the next social event.

The seven of us were gathered in the study. We had come here for lessons, but our tutors had given up when they realized we would not allow our discussion to be interrupted by anything as menial as lessons.

I joined in the conversation, truly happy for Mia. She had found someone she loved and it gave me hope for several reasons. First, at least my ideas of romance were not completely unattainable. Second, there seemed to be no disappointment over his not being royalty. And third, she had done it without the rest of us knowing. Perhaps I could keep my secrets as well. However the more I thought about it, the more unhappy I became. Despite the gift of love that Mia had been given, I remembered that such a chance could not be mine. My future had been determined already. As my melancholy settled over me, I quietly extricated myself from the room.

Hurrying up the stairs, I pulled pins from the thick chignon holding my heavy hair captive before shutting myself in my chamber. I lay my forehead against the door and let out a sigh of relief. Crossing to the vanity, I dropped the pins on the tabletop and vigorously shook my hair out with both hands before throwing it all over my shoulder. The confines of fashion and etiquette dictated the way I had to wear my hair in public, but I preferred it this way; gold waves in wild disarray—it suited me. I finally looked in the mirror and gave a startled scream when I saw Gavin's reflection staring back at me, frozen where he stood by the fireplace, holding a vase of flowers. I spun so quickly I nearly toppled over and had to brace myself. His eyes were wide and held no hint of amusement, only a sort of panic.

"I—" The words escaped him. He cleared his throat and tried again. "I was told that one of the princesses wanted an arrangement of flowers, so I took the liberty of arranging one and when I brought it to the house mistress, she showed me to this room and told me that all the highnesses were doing their studies and I should just place them where I thought best, so I…." He trailed off, no doubt assuming I could finish the thought.

My hair fell into my wide eyes and I pushed at the pale strands without thinking. "Oh…" was all I could manage to say.

"I would have been gone before now, but I couldn't decide where they looked best and I had no idea of anyone returning any time soon. I certainly didn't know it had been you who requested them, though I suppose I should have guessed." He stopped himself from rambling any more. We each continued to stare at the other and I imagined that the panic I saw in his eyes was most likely mirrored in my own. "I should go," he declared in a would-be casual voice, and started walking to the door.

"Gavin," I managed to speak. He stopped and turned stiffly toward me, his eyes running over my hair and then away. "The vase," I said, motioning toward the flower arrangement he still held in his hand. He looked down, realizing he still held it. "On that table would be fine."

He tripped a little as he moved back to the table and dropped the vase in its center. He didn't quite meet my eyes and inclined his head vaguely before reaching the door.

"Thank you," I managed before it shut.

I tried to still the mad pounding of my pulse, realizing that being indoors with Gavin was an entirely different experience than being outdoors with him. Here, in my chambers, there was no open air to diffuse his presence, no breeze to cool my blush. I turned to look in the mirror, wondering about the way Gavin's eyes had seemed drawn to my hair, and how he had acted almost guilty about it. I felt more like myself with my hair down, and wondered for a moment if he saw me differently when I wasn't conforming to the rules of society.

I decided to make a little test out of my suspicions. The next time I went to a village dance—and I would go again—I would wear my hair down, with only a kerchief to subdue it, and see if it had any effect on Gavin.

After forming this simple plan, I was brought up short, wondering why I felt the need to test Gavin's reactions. Was it because of his reaction just now? Seeing how far I could push our relationship? Was I trying to manipulate him? No, that wasn't it. I just wanted to know...what?

I closed my eyes and let out a sigh. I wanted to know if he saw me as more than a friend, because I now found it impossible to ignore the fact that I thought of him as much more than a friend—and that frightened me. Because if I embraced those feelings and let them grow...then what? I didn't know, but at the moment, I chose not to care.

I didn't want to let Gavin go.

Chapter Nine

MY STOMACH WAS in nervous knots as I approached the maze the next morning. I hadn't been nervous about seeing Gavin since our first meeting. The encounter in my room kept running through my head and I welcomed it, relishing the memory of those feelings. They had been potent, real. I wondered if those feelings would return when I saw him again, or if it had just been his unexpected appearance in my personal space that had caused the chaos in my soul. My back was tight and rigid as my hands rested against my stomach, attempting to calm my anticipation. I shook my hands out at my sides, trying to relax, trying to breathe normally and reacquire the casual manner I had managed to achieve around Gavin.

I was so distracted by my nerves that I jumped when he appeared at my side. He raised his eyebrows, alarmed.

"I'm sorry," I apologized for my overreaction. "I wasn't paying attention and you startled me." He simply cocked an eyebrow and then turned his eyes to the ground as he rotated a small tool in his hands.

"Would you like to help me with something?" he asked, keeping his eyes on his hands. That was odd for Gavin. He always looked me in the eye, so much so that it oftentimes made me uncomfortable. Having him ask me a direct question without so much as a glance in my direction was peculiar.

"Of course," I managed to answer.

His project was in one of the open rooms. It had a large tree in the middle surrounded by a circular bench. The tree had several branches hanging too low and they needed to be trimmed. He explained the process and then handed me a knife. I stared at it, holding it gingerly. I had certainly never held this kind of knife before, and if felt awkward in my hands.

"Come on up here." Gavin stood on the bench, pulling a branch down, the muscles in his arms becoming more defined as they worked.

"I'm going to cut off my hand, or yours," I warned.

He smiled, a glint of mischief in his eyes. "I trust you. Come on."

The undercurrent of flirtation in his manner roused my curiosity, so I carefully hoisted my skirts with the unfamiliar knife in my grasp, climbed up onto the bench, and stood close to him.

Gavin took a moment to grin at me before directing his attention to the branch in his hands. He told me where to cut off the thin shoots, and I gave it a try.

He shouldn't have trusted me. He had to dodge out of the way when the knife went through the first branch and sliced toward his right shoulder. I dropped the knife and covered my face with my hands, horrified that I had come so close to hurting him. "I'm sorry, I'm so sorry," I mumbled through my hands.

"Shh," he said, wrapping one arm around my shoulders. "I'm fine." He actually sounded *amused*.

I pulled my hands from my face and hit him squarely in his chest. "I *told* you I would hurt you!"

"You didn't hurt me." He still sounded like he found the situation funny. "I anticipated that happening. I was ready for it."

"You anticipated that happening?" My voice hardened with each word. "Then why did you let me try?"

He shrugged a shoulder. "I wanted to see what would happen."

His hands were lightly gripping behind my elbows. I pulled my arms free and stepped off the bench. "You're a rogue!" I called over my shoulder.

He jumped down and followed. "What?"

I turned on him. "You find it amusing to scare me out of my wits?"

Having heard the tremor in my voice, the mischief left his eyes and he studied my face. He approached me and once again pulled me to him with one arm. "I didn't mean to frighten you. I'm sorry. I was just curious."

My forehead rested against his chest; his chin grazing my hair. "What were you curious about?" It was difficult asking a coherent question. I was distracted by the fact that he embraced me. It was only with one arm, but it was much more contact than he usually initiated. The only other time we had been this close was just after I'd overheard my betrothal. I wanted to wrap my arms around him, but couldn't summon the courage. Instead I clutched the fabric of his shirt at his sides.

"I wanted to see you in a new situation."

I frowned, confused. "Why?" I mumbled into his shirt.

"I've only ever seen you in this maze, with only me. Then last week—seeing you at the dance was—different. And yesterday in your room..." I was suddenly very glad he couldn't see my face. It burned.

"So you decided to risk my stabbing you out of curiosity?"

He chuckled and drew back slightly. I looked up at him and he raised a shoulder. "Stabbing me wasn't actually part of the plan."

I shook my head, trying not to smile and relinquished my hold on his shirt. He dropped his arm, but didn't move away. "Do you still need help?" I asked after a moment of charged silence.

His face lit up at my willingness. "How about you hold the branch and I'll use the knife?"

"Will I be safe?" I asked facetiously.

"Perfectly," he answered as he walked backwards away from me.

Back up on the bench, he pulled a branch down and had me take a hold of it before cutting off several offshoots. After letting it go, he pulled down another for me to hold, but I folded my arms, regarding him with suspicion.

"What?" he asked.

"You could do this just as well on your own. It might even be easier."

The mischief came back in his eyes as he ignored my question and pulled my hand up, placing it on the branch, though his eyes never left mine. "I like it when you help me."

We worked silently for several minutes, going around the tree. The silence was...tense. He just watched me much of the time and I couldn't help staring back. I think we were both trying to work out what was happening between us. Though in my estimation, it was not so much what was happening with *us*, but with *him*. He was different—more bold, more comfortable.

When the tension started to make me feel anxious, I decided to start the conversation again.

"I want to go to another dance."

A broad smile stretched across his face. "Just tell me when."

"You're the one who knows when they are," I pointed out. "So you'll have to tell me."

He finished the last branch and moved so close that I could feel his body heat. His head dipped slightly toward mine, hovering for just a moment before he pulled himself back. "I will," he promised, then jumped down and offered a hand to me. For the first time since we started our task, he didn't meet my eyes. It was not the same as earlier when he had looked at the ground. This time he seemed more ashamed or...guilty. My thoughts went to the moment when his face had dipped toward me; I thought perhaps he might kiss me. Was that why? It had happened so quickly, I couldn't be sure. The entire afternoon, the air around us had been thick with so many unspoken sentiments that it was impossible to make sense of it all.

It was time for me to return for my lessons, so I started away. "I'll see you tomorrow?" I meant to say it as a statement, but it came out as a question.

He smiled at my question. Not the roguish grin from the past half hour, but a soft smile, a familiar smile. "Of course, Ella."

His straightforward response put me more at ease. I had enjoyed the roguish grin, the boldness, but it felt good to leave with a morsel of normalcy.

As I walked back to the palace, I thought of the prospect of going to another dance and realized it would be a good idea for me to obtain some common clothing. I didn't want to deprive Gretchen of hers, not when I was perfectly capable of buying some myself. Well, not exactly myself. I spoke with Gretchen about it that evening, came up with something to trade, and had her do the actual shopping. She came back the next morning with a full-length white chemise and a blue apron dress to go over it. She also got me shoes, a shawl and two kerchiefs. I would fit in nicely.

***

The next time I went back to the maze, I armed myself with a book. I found the tension between us interesting—exciting—but I wasn't ready to be roped into another project where I had to stand only a step away from Gavin and feel the pull between us once more.

I found him beneath a bush, elbow-deep in soil, trying to dig it out. It was the kind of project he would never ask me to help with. Perhaps he wasn't ready for another heady encounter either. I sat five paces from him, tucked as much fabric from my dress beneath me as I could, and opened my book, reading silently to myself so I wouldn't distract him.

A moment later, he pulled himself out of the hole he was burrowing and said with mock offense, "You're not going to read to me?"

I smiled easily, enjoying his disheveled hair and dirt-streaked face. "I didn't think you'd be able to hear me under there." I turned the page back and started reading out loud. He ducked beneath the bush and returned to work.

Forty-five minutes later he let out a groan as he fell back, arms splayed out at his sides, drenched in sweat and breathing hard. "I don't know if I'm going to win this fight."

I stood and surveyed the hole. "Certainly not today."

"What happened in the book?" he asked, his eyes closed against the sun.

"I told you you wouldn't be able to hear."

"I can't hear every word, but I like listening to your voice."

I sank down next to him, ignoring my billowing skirts, and opened the book, preparing to summarize what I had read.

"The next dance is tomorrow," he said before I could begin.

My head shot up. "Really?" The excitement in my voice was obvious. "You should show me another dance."

He turned his head toward me and cracked one eye open to look at me as though I were crazy. "Now?"

"Oh." Of course he couldn't show me now. "No."

He smiled, hearing all too clearly the disappointment in my voice. "How about this afternoon?"

I tried to suppress my grin of triumph. "All right."

He put his forearm over his eyes to block out the sun more fully. "I don't think I'll ever understand your fascination with common dances."

"Have you ever seen a formal ball?"

"Of course not."

"If you had, you would understand."

He didn't respond, but the lower half of his face showed his amusement.

I wanted to keep our conversation going, so I searched my mind for a safe topic.

"Tell me more about Janie," I requested, wanting to know more of his family.

"What would you like me to tell?"

"Does she have a special gentleman in her life?"

He lifted his arm away from his eyes. "A special gentleman?"

"You know what I mean." I looked down, refusing to blush at my choice of topic.

"She does," he finally answered. "In fact, I think she'll be engaged soon."

"Really? And how does that work?"

"How does what work?"

"Proposals, betrothals, engagements, marriages. How does it work among common people?"

"It depends. There are those who find themselves attached to someone and simply propose. If their families do not object, they are married a few months later. Then there are those who only want a reliable companion or someone to take care of them. Their parents will talk with other parents and try to find a match. If a match is found, they become engaged, usually for a year. They spend time together, get to know each other, and if they find themselves still happy with the situation after a year, they are married. If, at some point during the year, one or the other realizes that they simply can't accept the other as a spouse, then the engagement is broken."

"What if they end up falling in love during the year?"

He smiled at my question. "They can choose to marry sooner if they wish."

"And what about betrothals? Do parents ever agree to a marriage when their children are young?"

"Once in a while, but the only times I've heard of it, it was because the families were very great friends."

"Hm." I found this all very interesting, especially the idea that even if an engagement had been agreed upon, they could choose to break it if they ended up not liking each other.

I watched my fidgeting hands as I asked, "Have you ever thought about who you might end up with?"

"Not lately," was his only reply, and I couldn't bring myself to inquire further.

The silence settled around us before he spoke again. "You're really not going to say no to your betrothal?"

I looked up, surprised by his abrupt question and serious tone. "I'm not even supposed to know about it. How do you propose I go about rejecting a proposal I should never have overheard?"

"You could at least make your dislike known." He usually said such things in a teasing manner. He was not teasing now.

"Believe me, I'm trying," I said, glancing down. When I looked back at him, he looked like he was going to say something else. Instead he threw his arm over his eyes once more and I wondered if he was angry. I sat frowning for several minutes until he sat up and sighed. My eyes remained fixed on my lap as he pushed himself to his knees and came to sit beside me. He ducked his head, trying to see my face better.

"I would say no if they gave me the chance," I whispered into my lap.

He sighed once more before putting an arm around my neck and resting his chin on top of my head. "I know."

✳ ✳ ✳

The next evening, Gavin and I snuck out of the castle grounds. Gretchen had done my hair in a low bun, helped me rub dirt into my new common dress, and tied my shawl around my waist in an attempt to help me blend in. After Gavin and I left through the wall, we met up with Gretchen again, and though we were all nervous, they seemed to find sneaking around as fun as I did.

Gavin left us to walk on his own and as I strode alongside Gretchen, I pulled all the pins from my hair and shook it out, letting it settle in its natural waves down my back before retying my kerchief over it. I would have preferred to go without the kerchief, but knew it would make me too conspicuous.

Gavin rejoined us just at the edge of the square and I watched his reaction as he approached. He seemed a bit stunned, staring at the waves of blonde now loose from their confines. He stepped up beside me, his hand grazing down my hair then settling at the small of my back for a moment before dropping away. His fingers squeezed mine for just a moment before going to join the men, while Gretchen and I moved into the group of women. I fanned my face, feeling suddenly overheated.

The buzz of energy around me soon distracted me. I gripped my hands together, trying to contain my excitement, but ended up bouncing up on my toes instead. Knowing what to expect made the anticipation all the more wonderful. Instead of everything being a fantastic, confusing blur, I could take in the experience more fully, enjoy it even more. When the crowds of men and women flowed together, I felt immediately swept up in the atmosphere and the feeling of this gathering. It was so different from my day-to-day life. These people—these hardworking, wonderful people—held so much joy, so much *life*. And I got to be a part of it.

As I twirled through the crowd, Gavin caught me in his arms and spun me to join a group of couples dancing in a circle. The women would clap while the men did high-stepping footwork. Then the men would clap while we women danced from one foot to the other, swishing our skirts from side to side. I had seen a group doing this at the last dance and so had some idea of what to do. I breathed deep, trying to take in the revelry.

Throughout the night, I found myself closing my eyes when I danced with Gavin, trying to experience more fully the feeling of being held by someone I cared for—to hold onto those moments of utter abandon and elation. When he played with my hair, I would close my eyes, inhaling the scent of soil and fresh air that came off his skin as a tingle started at my scalp and ran down my neck. It only happened twice, but I wanted to engrave upon my mind what if felt like, especially since he stopped as soon as he realized what he was doing. But those few moments made me feel...adored.

It struck me as odd that it took the simple gesture of a common gardener to make me feel that way, when I was "adored" constantly by all my subjects.

Each time he touched me I felt a thrill rush through me. Even when he wasn't touching me, I could feel something in the air between us —a pulse of energy trying to pull us together. But I made myself remember that we were in the middle of a large gathering of people, even though it felt like we were the only two people in existence.

As the dance wore on I felt my envy growing each time I caught sight of the swirl of color created by the scarves used by married or engaged couples. I wished for one of my own, wanting to be spoken for, but wanting to choose the person on the other end of my own lovely scarf.

Chapter Ten

WHEN THE LAST song came to an end, Gavin wrapped his arms around me from behind as we cheered with the crowd. As he tightened his arms around me, he bent his head and casually kissed my cheek, right by my mouth. It all happened so naturally, so innocently, that for a moment I thought perhaps he hadn't realized what he had done.

But as he loosened his grip and pulled his lips away, he became very still. I had no idea what to do or how to act, but when I felt him start to slowly remove his arms from around me, I knew I didn't want *that*. So I trapped his hands with my own where they rested on my stomach and turned my head slowly to look at him.

His face was still close and his eyes were on my mouth. He moved closer just a fraction, then stopped himself, looking into my eyes. I held his eyes for a moment and then glanced at his mouth, hoping he would recognize the invitation.

He did. In the midst of a crowd of cheering people, Gavin slowly brushed his lips against mine. The little air left in my lungs rushed out just before he kissed me fully.

It did not last long, but it was exquisite. And it might have gone on longer, but the cheers were dying down and the crowd was beginning to disperse. He gave me a suppressed smile and then took my hand and headed away from the square. As he pulled me along, I put my fingers to my mouth, wondering at the sensation his lips had left on mine.

As we walked farther from the square, our hands entwined, we found ourselves alone. Gavin looked around and then pulled me off the main path and into a small space between two buildings. He turned to face me as I stood with my back almost touching one of the walls. He seemed nervous.

"What is it?" I asked, concerned that something had upset him or perhaps he was regretting kissing me.

He took a deep breath then said, "I just didn't get to—" And he was kissing me again, more deeply this time, and I allowed my arms to wind around his neck. He wrapped one arm around my waist and leaned the other on the wall behind me as he kissed me, over and over. When he stopped, I was grateful to have the wall supporting my back as I regained my breath and my bearings. We looked at each other for a tense moment, then he leaned in and kissed my lips lightly. His proximity made me dizzy. "I'm sorry," he murmured against my mouth, then pulled back. "I just didn't know when I would get a chance to do that."

I stifled a giggle, embarrassed at how giddy I felt. "Gavin, we're alone constantly. I think you might have found an opportunity."

He kissed me once more, then took my hand and led me back out into the street. "Yes, but I don't think I would dare to kiss you inside the palace grounds."

I furrowed my brow. "Why ever not?"

"I'm not that brave," he answered matter-of-factly.

I was silent, wondering what in the world bravery had to do with it. But as we reached the road that led up to the palace, I had the misfortune of having my question answered by the appearance of about a dozen armed guards on horseback. They were just coming out of the palace gate, beginning to fan out as if preparing to search. They had only gone a short way when one of them noticed me. My common clothes may have fooled the folks in the village who never really saw me, but every guard knew my face and the faces of each member of my family. A signal was given and they immediately turned to converge on my position.

"Oh, no." The exclamation was involuntary and suffused with dread. I had never been particularly fond of my father's soldiers, but with Gavin at my side, I was terrified. What would happen to him?

As Gavin saw the guard approaching, he instinctively pulled me behind him in a protective gesture. But this only made the situation worse. The guards' attitude toward Gavin became infinitely more aggressive, as they now viewed him as an aggressor toward me. Half of them swung down from their horses to approach on foot.

"Step away. Now," one of them demanded in a tone that indicated he would not ask twice. Gavin hesitated.

"It's all right," I whispered frantically. "Just do what they say." I was desperate for Gavin to not get himself into any more trouble. But the sight of a dozen crossbows pointed at him, and inadvertently at *me*, made him stand his ground. I saw that the guards were about to act and so decided to do something myself. I stepped away from him, relieved when he did not try to stop me.

The captain of the guard, keeping his eyes on Gavin, addressed me. "Please step behind me, Your Highness."

I would have, but I was too afraid that with me out of the way, they would hurt Gavin, so I tried to explain. "He hasn't done anything wrong; it was my choice to go with him."

The guard's eyes flickered to me for a moment, then he gestured to his men and they relaxed their position somewhat. He gestured again and I flinched as two men stepped toward Gavin and deftly brought him to the ground. His wrists were shackled before I knew what was happening.

A guard took me by the arm to escort me up to the palace, but I yanked it away. "I am perfectly capable of walking by myself," I snapped at the guard. "And there is no need to handle him so roughly; he has done nothing wrong."

He bowed slightly. "Of course, Highness."

I stole a short glance at Gavin as they hauled him to his feet, before starting on my own up to the palace. As we made our way, I heard Gavin being manhandled despite what I had said, and hoped I would be able to fix this mess. How could I have let this happen? I had become too comfortable, too confident in our success. I had done this, and Gavin would pay the price.

I walked into the glaring lamplight of the great hall prepared to meet my father's stare. But my father hardly even glanced at me. His eyes were riveted on Gavin, who was thrown down in the middle of the floor. He didn't look as though he had been hurt. He came to his knees and stared at my father, terrified.

As I was deposited at my father's side, he kept his eyes on Gavin but he addressed me. "Are you alright, Ariella?" It was difficult for me to determine whether concern or anger was most dominant.

"Yes, Father. I am perfectly well." I hurried to reassure him, hoping my obvious well-being, as well as my calm response, would convey that I had not been in danger.

His voice filled with venom when he addressed Gavin. "You are fortunate indeed that the princess is unharmed; otherwise your fate would be far worse."

I paled at his implication. "Father—"

But he bowled over me, his eyes searing through Gavin. "You took a member of my family away from the palace, yes?"

"Yes, Sire." What else could he say?

"And how much time in prison do you think your crime warrants?"

I couldn't breathe. "But, Father—"

"I do not know what your intent was in kidnapping my daughter. I do not know if you were working alone, but I assure you my questions will be answered." He fairly roared now.

"Sire—" Gavin pleaded.

My father stood in his rage. "Do not speak. I have not given you permission to speak, therefore you would do well to hold your tongue and consider your crime."

"But he has done no wrong!"

"Quiet, Ariella!" It was the first time my father had raised his voice to me. "He took you away from this palace; that *is* something wrong."

He used his fingers to signal the head guard, who immediately stepped toward Gavin who was kneeling on the stone floor with his head bowed. The guard yanked his head up by his hair and I stopped breathing. They meant to begin his punishment right now, and it was going to be painful.

"No!" I shrieked, stepping toward Gavin but stopping myself. The guard hesitated and I looked back at my father, reaching a hand toward him, pleading. "Father, please! He's a friend! He didn't take me away; he only did what I asked. Please stop this," I begged. I could hear the horror in my own voice, the disbelief and the desperation I felt. It was as though I were being torn in two, as though my arms—one outstretched to halt my father, the other itching to pull Gavin from harm's way—were pulling me in opposite directions, and if I moved at all, I would be torn to pieces.

My father only gave me a fleeting glance, continuing to direct his rage at Gavin, who knelt below him, still held by his hair. "Friend, you say? And how did you come to know this 'friend'?"

"He's a gardener, he tends the grounds. I befriended him. I pestered him endlessly." My only thoughts were of taking the guilt on myself. Any punishment my father could inflict on me would be nothing compared to what he would do to Gavin.

"And then he took you away from the palace." My father shot me a glance that chilled me to my core. "Am I to excuse that?"

"I made him," I blurted out. "I wanted to know what a commoner dance would be like. I ordered him to take me with him." This was, of course, a lie. "I told him that if he didn't he would be disobeying a royal command. I gave him no choice."

"That doesn't matter!" His voice echoed through the corridor.

"Yes, it does!" My voice rang shrilly through the air, stronger than I would have thought it could be. "This was not his idea. It wasn't a plot. It wasn't a kidnapping. It was my choice, Father. He does not deserve this and it would be unjust to punish him in this way. The fault is mine and mine alone."

My father paused. He had always prided himself on being a just and benevolent ruler. I could see his mind working. To throw Gavin in prison or impose any physical punishment would be unjust and extreme, but my father had to do something. Taking a princess away from the palace was unacceptable, and there had to be some consequence.

"*Please*, Father." It was strange to hear myself beg.

He turned to me. I had never asked anything of him before. He came to me and said in a low voice, "Your concern for his welfare is much more than it should be." He said this in an accusatory fashion, staring at my face as if searching for something he didn't want to find. "And it makes me wonder if you care for him much more than is prudent, Ariella. Perhaps you should consider, just for a moment, how your actions have affected not only this *friend* of yours, but your family as well." I saw it then: the devastation, the undiluted fear in his eyes, and I closed my own in shame. "I am not unfeeling, but this situation is inexcusable. I cannot make this allowance and you know it."

I felt him move away from me and opened my eyes as he turned his attention back to Gavin. "Young man," he addressed Gavin, his voice carefully controlled. "Were you, in fact, ordered by the Princess to accompany her to this common frivolity?"

Gavin's body wilted in defeat. He didn't want to lie, but he knew the truth, however innocent, would appear traitorous and likely cause his imprisonment. "Yes, Sire," was his hoarse reply.

I breathed a silent sigh of relief, but still feared the consequences as Father began to pace. He was weighing every possible option and every consequence. I prayed he would see it my way but knew very well that his analysis of the situation would be much farther-reaching and more complex than my own. So I waited.

Finally, he raised his voice to give the order. "Understanding that my daughter put this young man in a compromising position, with an impossible decision, there will be lenience. However, it must be understood that such behavior is unacceptable. The young man may retain his freedom, for I can say he has broken no law. However, he will not be allowed to enter the walls of the palace grounds. And under no circumstances is he to be allowed to come anywhere near Princess Ariella."

"Father—"

"Guards, you will escort the princess back to her quarters. The young man is to be escorted outside the palace walls." With that, he turned and stalked away. I looked back to Gavin, but only had a fleeting glimpse of his marred expression before I was seized by the arm and dragged to my room. Once there, I just stood, numb, as I wondered what on earth I should do next. My mind finally cleared enough to convince me to go to the window and see if perhaps I could get a glimpse of Gavin. It was too dark and too far. I could see nothing, and I wept.

Chapter Eleven

MY FATHER'S PUNISHMENT for me was simple. He acted as though I did not exist. He was angry with me, that much was obvious, but he never told me his reasons. I'm sure it had something to do with etiquette or family honor or simple disobedience. Regardless, I couldn't summon the energy to care. I secluded myself for several days, ignoring both the maze and my lessons, going nowhere but to the library and back, except for mealtimes. The only time I avoided the library was when I knew my father was likely to be there. I didn't spend any time with my sisters. Even when I returned to my lessons, I would listen in silence and then escape to be alone. All I could think was that I somehow had to escape my life, so I threw myself into the lives of the characters in the novels that had been so much a part of my life before I met Gavin.

Gretchen was my only companion at this time. We talked for hours. She at least understood the entire story; she knew Gavin didn't deserve the treatment he had received and she didn't look down on him. She knew how crushed I was to be separated from one of the few people I had ever called a friend.

But it wasn't just that I was separated from a friend. I had come to realize my father was right. I cared for Gavin too much. I cared for him as much more than a friend. I began to think I even loved him.

It sounded silly even in my head, but it felt true. Because the moment I admitted it to myself, the pain in my chest tripled and my sobs had me doubled over, helpless. If it were only my life I was dealing with I would have sought him out immediately, but I wasn't ignorant. I had to think of him. If he were to be seen anywhere near me, the consequences for him would be unthinkable. I had already ruined his life. I would not ruin it further.

Only two weeks after Gavin was pulled from my life, my family went on holiday. I almost laughed out loud when Gretchen told me she had been instructed to pack my things for a holiday at the sea shore. We never went on holiday; I didn't realize my father knew the meaning of the word. The reason for the outing was to show off our happy family— to demonstrate that my father had everything under control after the incident with the gardener and his wayward daughter. It was a show, and I was likely to be center stage.

Whenever we were in view of the public, I made an effort to pull myself from my brooding and at least appear alert. As heartbroken as I was, I didn't want to seem sullen and depressed, for that would help nothing.

Once we were settled on the beach, with no one but my family and our servants close enough to see my face, I gave up the act and became caught up in my own contemplations. I sat a little apart from my family, staring out at the crashing waves, allowing the sound to rinse through my mind.

"Ella?" I turned at the sound of Kalina's voice. She sat next to me, studying me as though I were a puzzle. "Are you all right?"

I turned away. "I'm fine."

"You know," she started tentatively, "Mother and Father haven't told the rest of us anything. We know something happened. All the servants are talking about it, but we don't know what it was." She paused, but I just stared ahead. "Won't you tell me? I know there was someone named Gavin—"

"Please don't." I shook my head, trying to get the sound of his name out of my head. "I'm sorry, Kalina, but I can't tell you what happened." I climbed to my feet and walked through the sand up a small rise and sat down on top of it. I was still in view of my family, but I turned my back, hoping to discourage anyone from approaching. I couldn't talk about him. I couldn't try to explain to my sisters who he was and what he had been to me. So I stared at the water and let the wind blow in my face until my eyes stung.

Lylin and Marilee ran into my line of vision, holding their shawls out to let the wind catch them, making them flutter. I smiled, happy that they were still able to enjoy being young. They hitched their skirts up so they could run more freely and were quickly reprimanded by my mother. They each curtsied in acquiescence, then stifled smiles as they ran off once more.

Lylin fell at one point, but it wasn't until we left that my mother discovered the cut on her hand. Lylin only shrugged, but my parents took her directly to a healer anyway.

My sisters and I walked down the main street of the little seaside town, looking in shop windows as our guards walked on every side. My sisters' chatting was not quite as enthusiastic as it should have been after a day by the sea. They kept casting worried looks in my direction, knowing this holiday wasn't quite what it appeared to be. My discontent dampened the mood, for which I was sorry, but not sorry enough to explain myself.

When we rejoined our parents, Lylin was smiling and rolling her eyes at their hovering. We climbed back into the carriages and returned home amid the same strained conversation as when we left.

The next day I headed straight to the library, returning to my voluntary exile.

❋ ❋ ❋

I was sitting in one of the cushy chairs by the huge fireplace in the library when I heard the door open. I sat up, worried it was my father. Instead, my mother came into the room and sat in the chair opposite me.

"Ariella."

"Mother."

She sat stiff and formal for several moments, then let out a breath, allowing her posture and brow to relax as well. "Will you tell me about it?"

This question so surprised me that I just stared. I expected a reprimand, a demand for an explanation, a lecture about decorum, propriety and behaving while in public. Instead she asked me that.

"About what?" I finally replied, wanting to be sure before I lay my heart on the table.

"I want to hear anything you want to tell me, Ella. I know I have no right to expect you to bear your heart and soul to me. I've never been a confidante for you." She looked at me with regret. "But if you need a listening ear, I'm volunteering."

My lip started to quiver as I realized how much my mother missed because of her title. I'd never seen life any other way, so I had never begrudged her absence, but in that moment I realized she might just be lonely as well. I bent toward her, lay my forehead on her knee and found myself gasping for breath.

For the first time in years, I cried into my mother's lap. I sobbed on her shoulder. I told her how I cared for Gavin and how foolish I had been to think my actions would not affect him. "And now he's gone."

She rocked me in her arms and asked softly, "He was one of the groundskeepers?"

I pulled away, brushing the tears from my cheeks. "Yes, he took care of the maze."

She smiled. "That's one of my favorite places, you know."

"Because of the statues?"

Her eyebrows shot up. "How do you know about the statues?"

"He told me."

She smiled. "Yes, the statues are one of the many reasons I love the maze."

"Will you tell me about them?" I asked her, in much the same fashion she had asked me.

It took a moment for her eyes to focus on me, then she said in a quiet voice, "Not tonight, but soon." She paused, then sat up straight and looked me full in the face. "Was he good for you? Did you learn something about yourself?"

I regarded her with curiosity, wondering what had prompted this turn of subject, then answered honestly. "Yes." My eyes filled with silent tears as I thought, *He made me see myself.*

"Then I cannot reprimand you," she said, that same look of remembrance in her eyes.

"It wasn't just that," I said, more to myself than my mother. "He taught me about myself, but he also taught me so much more. He taught me about the world outside. That maze was my haven, and now the thought of entering it—" I broke off, unable to finish.

"Have you been out at all since he left?"

"I can't go without him. It doesn't feel right."

She gave me a quizzical stare and then asked, "Have you thought about riding?"

"Riding?" I asked in astonishment. She knew how I felt about horses.

My mother's mouth pulled up at one corner. "Yes, riding. I think it's high time you learned to handle a horse."

✳ ✳ ✳

I hoped this inclination of my mother's would soon pass, but such was not my luck. The very next day when I went to my lesson, I was informed that I would spend one hour after lessons in the stables. When the time came, I walked very slowly to the stables. A myriad of scenarios ran through my head, all of which involved me being thrown and trampled by a horse and meeting my doom.

I arrived at the stables and was met by a courteous manservant who gave me a slight bow.

"Good morning, Highness. My name is Weston. I've been expecting you."

"Well then, I suppose it's a good thing I showed up," I replied, trying to figure out what to do with my hands as I stood awkwardly in the stable doorway.

"You have some reservations?" he asked with a kind smile.

"Several."

"I assure you, Princess, you have nothing to worry about. And I'm afraid it is Her Majesty's express wish that you learn to ride, so you really don't have much of a choice." He said this in jest, with a smile in his eyes that set me at ease—at least somewhat.

"Well then, I suppose we should get to it."

"Of course, Princess, if you would allow me one moment."

"Yes, of course."

As Weston bowed away, I began taking in my surroundings. The stables were quite magnificent in their own right, and though the horses terrified me, I could also see their beauty.

When Weston returned, we had a quick disagreement about which saddle I would use. He had brought a ladies' saddle, which looked so precarious and awkward that I insisted he put me in a normal saddle, one where I might have a fighting chance at staying upright. He eventually acquiesced, and we continued with my first lesson.

My hand shook as I reached out to stroke the mare I was doomed to ride. I jumped when she made a sudden movement and heard Weston cough behind me, no doubt trying to squelch his laughter. When he finally persuaded me into the saddle, I sat tense, breathing methodically through my nose as I tried to be calm. The horse shifted and my chest seized up as I clutched the reins. The size and strength of the horse beneath me was overwhelming. While one part of me hated that feeling, another part enjoyed that I was feeling something other than that black hollowness. I forced myself to keep breathing, determined to keep trying, and made it to the end of the hour. By that time I was able to relax at least a little.

I stepped away from the horse as my lesson ended and turned to Weston.

"Will I be seeing you back here tomorrow, Princess?"

I knew my mother wanted this for me, but my decision to continue had little to do with her wishes. I needed something in my life other than books and sadness. "Yes," I replied simply and dipped into a quick curtsy as he bowed me out of the stables.

The next day I returned to the stables willingly, almost eagerly. The tension and apprehension were still there, but I had to find a way to fill the hole inside of me, and this seemed as good an idea as any.

***

Four months later found me on a horse whenever I could manage it. It was the best remedy I had—the best way of working through my heartache. Once I had gotten over my initial fear, riding came naturally to me. I believe my instructors started wishing I had retained a bit of hesitance. When Weston realized just how much time my training would require, he turned me over to another groom named Emmett. I felt perfectly comfortable on a horse, and this made any instructor uncomfortable. Regardless of my competence, I was still escorted by Emmett whenever I went riding because they did not think me quite capable enough to be on my own, and because they saw me as reckless. And I was, but I was also very good on a horse.

There was one afternoon I had a particular need to be alone. I tried to convince Emmett that I was competent enough to ride on my own.

"I'm sorry, Highness, but I cannot let you ride off by yourself. You are still quite new at this. I have to stay with you." I had a feeling this had more to do with my father than anything.

I sucked in my anger. "Fine, but I'm not waiting," I replied before kicking my horse into a mad gallop.

Emmett's frustration grew to new levels over the next weeks. I found great satisfaction in trying to outride him. I never quite managed it, but it was fun to try, and it made him crazy.

After a month of that, I pulled myself into the saddle one morning and saw no one else preparing another mount. Emmett just looked at me, clearly uneasy while Weston answered my look of surprise. "Her Majesty has asked that you be allowed to ride out on your own for no more than an hour."

I grinned in triumph and trotted off.

Chapter Twelve

THIS DAY MARKED six months. Six months ago, Gavin had kissed me and then been dragged from my life. I had not seen him or heard anything about him since.

I could have. If I had asked Gretchen, I'm sure she could have told me something about him. But I didn't ask and she didn't offer. The temptation to ask for some scrap of information, for some clue as to what kind of life he led, was constant, but I knew that if I asked once, I wouldn't be able to keep myself from asking over and over again. And I knew that it would hurt, and keep hurting.

I'm not proud of it, but enduring my life was all I could do. I went through the motions and avoided every question my sisters put to me about the gardener. I took satisfaction in music, drawing, books, and my newly acquired horse, Fancy. I also continued to talk with my mother and feel invisible in the presence of my father.

But today, I skipped my lessons. For the first time since his departure, I fought past my trepidation and went into Gavin's garden room at dawn, leaning against the flowering tree as I watched the sky lighten above me. I had noticed a difference in the maze as soon as I walked in. It was still well kept, but not in the same way. Gavin had spent every day working in the maze, so his absence was obvious.

In truth, I didn't want to be here. I didn't want to feel this feeling and be this person. I didn't want to give in to my hurt and my missing him. I wanted to be strong. But I didn't feel strong. I wondered how losing him had stripped me of my courage. After all, I had had plenty before I met him. I had stepped outside myself; I had ignored the rules and made a friend out of a common gardener. Where was my courage now? Where was the curiosity and determination I had used to pull him into my life?

I missed those parts of myself. And it frightened me that I couldn't seem to find them. It was as though in falling for Gavin, I had given those parts of myself to him, and he had taken them with him.

But I needed them. I needed those parts of myself that made me Ella. I wanted to feel strong—to be strong.

But on this day, I just sat there, hoping that tomorrow I'd be able to find myself.

***

The next week I decided to do something—anything—to reclaim myself. Gavin had been my link to a people I had been curious about throughout my entire adolescence. He had made me feel a part of them, even if I did not know them. And now I had only Gretchen. So it was through her that I started learning the names of the servants in my household. It was the only little rebellion I dared indulge in. I studied their faces and remembered their names, not wanting to see them as "the servants," but as individuals. It was all I could do.

As another month passed, I started to notice the slackening of the hold my father had on me, so I decided to take it a step further. I started using the names of the servants as much as possible when addressing them. I looked them in the eye when asking for something and thanked them for it later. At first their response was hesitant, but eventually, instead of greeting me in an obligatory monotone, their voices held real feeling, and a smile lit their eyes. It was a small thing, but even that bit of connection was a comfort. It reminded me of the world outside these walls, and helped to ease the loneliness I felt at being separated from those who had made me feel so alive.

I found satisfaction in my success, but that small happiness was invariably interrupted by Jeshua. He came every six months without fail, and trying to convince him of my indifference while keeping up the pretense of ignorance was exhausting.

The celebration for my seventeenth birthday was a much smaller affair than the year before, but there was still a ball, so I was once again forced into Jeshua's arms.

I managed to avoid him for the entire first half of the evening, but he inevitably snuck up behind me, his hand on my waist, breathing on my neck as he bent to speak in my ear.

"Happy Birthday, Ariella."

I flinched as the tip of his nose grazed my ear. "Thank you, *Prince* Jeshua."

"I've been trying to win a dance with you all night, but you've moved from partner to partner too swiftly."

The only reason I wasn't dancing now was because the musicians were not playing.

"Perhaps you could make it up to me by giving me the next three dances."

My stomach turned. "Actually, all that dancing has left me parched. I was just going in search of some refreshment."

"An excellent idea." He tucked my hand into the crook of his arm and set off toward the tables lining one wall.

Walking with him was better than dancing, but drinking only took so long, and he pulled me onto the dance floor. I distracted myself by thinking of the village dances while trying to maintain a comfortable distance from him.

By the end of the third dance, there was barely any space between us and my arms hurt from trying to keep him away.

I remained vigilant throughout the rest of the night and avoided any further dancing with him, falling into bed completely exhausted.

The next morning, I was sitting in the breakfast room, my sisters having already finished, when Jeshua joined me, taking the seat to my left. I swallowed as nervous dread filled my stomach.

"Good morning, Ariella."

"Good morning, Prince Jeshua," I answered while dodging the hand that reached toward my hair. He pulled his hand back but leaned toward me, resting his arm on the back of my chair. "Are you enjoying your stay?" It took all of my self control not to run from the room.

He just smiled. "I always enjoy my time in your home."

I nodded, trying to ignore his fingers as they pushed a lock of hair behind my ear. My father walked in at that moment and I was able to slip away as soon as he caught Jeshua's attention. I needed to find one of my sisters so that I would not be caught by myself again.

✳ ✳ ✳

It had been one year, and I started to reclaim myself. Perhaps not all of myself, but I stopped simply enduring life and again participated in it. I became more familiar with the servants. I even tried to mend my relationship with my sisters. I continued to ride—recklessly much of the time, especially when I was by myself. I convinced my mother to join me on some of my outings, and during those rides, I learned her story. Until Gavin had told me about the statues, I had never had reason to suspect that my mother's life had been anything out of the ordinary. When we developed the habit of riding together, I found the nerve to ask her about it.

"I wasn't like you," she told me as we walked our horses side by side. "I didn't try to be anything but what was expected of me...until after I was married." Her eyes cut over to me. "And you can imagine how well that went over. Your father and I knew each other fairly well, at least on the surface. But when I was brought to this place to start my life with him as a queen, I realized I had expectations that were not going to be met. I thought being a queen would give me freedom and authority. I thought I would be given responsibilities. I was a queen, for heaven's sake; surely that meant something." I could hear the old frustration in her tone but I could also see that at present, she was content. Something had changed over the years.

"So it wasn't what you expected?" I asked.

"No. I had freedom, but not in the way I wanted. I could have anything I desired, but I could not give advice or input on anything but clothing and decor—and even those things were left mostly to the experts. So instead of stretching the boundaries when I was young and still at home, like you are, I started pushing and shoving soon after I got married."

"What did you do? Were you rebellious?" I asked conspiratorially.

Mother laughed. "Not in the way you're thinking. I put on an excellent show. I was a new queen after all, and it was important for me to earn the respect of the people. So my little rebellions were always within the parameters of my position. I just tended to think more outside the norm than they would have preferred."

"Like the statues?"

She inclined her head. "Exactly. I was encouraged to choose statues for the garden. I could have any that I wanted. To everyone else, this meant I should speak with the usual artists and commission some statues very similar to all the rest in the gardens. But I couldn't stand those statues. They were meaningless; they had no feeling. It seemed as though the subjects themselves had been statues instead of real people. I never even met the usual artist. I went looking for a very different kind of statue, found an artist willing to make them, and commissioned four statues. But when they were brought to the gardens, your father was mortified. He couldn't believe I would bring common statues onto palace grounds. We had quite a rousing fight about it." I could see her suppressing a grin and wondered what my parents had been like when they were newly married. "Eventually we struck a compromise, though I still think it was weighted in your father's favor. I could keep the statues but they would be put out of the way, so that only those with an adventurous spirit would be able to find them."

"I'm glad."

Mother glanced over at me and tried to hide a smile, then asked, "Why?"

"Because most people wouldn't understand. And those out of the way rooms...one of them became mine—" I sighed, trying to push Gavin from my mind.

I directed my thoughts back to my mother and father—to their relationship and to my relationship with them. "Mother?"

"Yes?"

"Why won't Father speak to me anymore?"

"He speaks to you, Ella."

"No," I stated. "He gives me information or orders. But he no longer speaks to me, and certainly not with me." I shook my head, realizing how much this had started to bother me. "What did I do wrong?"

"Ella," she said as though it were a silly question.

"It's not a ridiculous question. I know you all think it's obvious, that my conduct was somehow a horrid breach in protocol, but I just don't see it." There was sympathy in her eyes, but I knew she didn't understand. "He was a friend," I said, pleading for understanding, "a very dear friend—and I don't have many of those. I don't have any at all."

The horses plodded along, accompanying our silence until my mother answered. "He's afraid for you."

"Afraid of what? That I might discover there is no difference between me and anyone else? That we are no better?"

"He's afraid you'll lose focus."

"Lose focus of what? I'm not focused on anything!"

"Your father wants to see you all well settled. Mia will be married next week, and we expect Jensa will settle within the year. But neither of them will be able to take the crown. One of you will be the next queen. Surely that is something to focus on. We must think practically."

I gave an incredulous sigh, then turned to meet her gaze. "Father wants to see us all well settled?" I confirmed and she nodded. "Happily settled?" I clarified and she nodded again. "Mother, Father would be more than happy to promise any one of us to any royal who came along claiming an interest."

Her eyes were sad. "Oh, darling, you know that's not true."

"Jensa is marrying to make Father happy, you know. She doesn't love Prince Goran. But it makes good sense and Father encourages it." She made a noise of disbelief, but I continued. "Think about it, Mother. Think about the way they look at each other."

She sighed as though tired of this thread of conversation and looked at the horizon for a moment before turning back to me with serious eyes. "Ariella, there are worse things than marrying for practical reasons."

I was taken aback by the defensiveness in her voice. "Did you marry for practical reasons?"

She met my eyes, almost defiant. "Yes, and now I love your father and we have a good life." That may have been true, but I still reeled at the idea that my parents had not loved each other when they married.

I tried to regain my argument. "So, he never decided to ignore you like he has me?"

"Your father is not ignoring you," she said gently, trying to convince me.

"Yes, he is." Some of the hurt leaked into my voice. "He doesn't act like my father anymore. He acts as though I'm just another subject."

Her patience had run out. "You were sneaking around behind our backs and putting yourself in danger. Do not act as though you are an innocent in this. You did do something wrong."

"No one even knew it was me, Mother. That's how separate we've kept ourselves from our people." Her eyebrows raised, surprised at this new line of attack. "There was no danger. It's been almost a year, and I'm an adult now. It's time for him to let it go." I was being disrespectful, but it had to be said somehow.

She had regained her composure. "He was afraid for you."

"Yes, afraid I would lose my heart to someone who deserved it, instead of letting him *give me* to someone who deserved my title."

My mother just continued to gaze at me, my speech having had no effect on her. She looked disappointed—disappointed in me, and I had to look away. She nudged her horse into a trot and made her way toward the stables. I continued to walk Fancy for a bit, then nudged her along, wanting to reach the stables before my mother had gone.

My mother was just walking out of the stables when I pulled to a halt. She stopped and watched me dismount, then walked over to me after I had handed Fancy's reins to Charlie, one of the stable hands.

She faced me, then told me, with more conviction than I had ever heard her use, "Ariella, your father would never *give you* to anyone."

I didn't know what to say. She looked at me for a moment more, then strode off toward the palace. I stood there, wanting to believe her, but recollecting all too well the conversation between my father and Jeshua. As of yet, my father had said nothing to me of Jeshua. During his infrequent visits, Jeshua continued to slather me with attention, my indifference barely keeping him at arms length—most of the time.

The temptation to tell him just how unwanted his attentions were was almost overwhelming, but the crushing inevitability of my situation left me feeling helpless and weak. Without Gavin in my life, I had far less reason to fight Jeshua's advances.

I shook myself from my thoughts and took a moment to put my pain away before I went back to the palace. I would normally have sought one of my sisters for company, but I found myself craving solitude instead. I retreated to the library—an occurrence usually reserved for Jeshua's visits—and climbed the small set of stairs along one wall that led to a balcony, stretching the entire length of the library. I didn't plan on spending much time here. I was simply in a wandering mood. Finding nothing of interest, I was headed back toward the stairs when I heard the library doors swing open.

I still wasn't in the mood for conversation, so I retreated out of sight in the hopes that whoever had entered would find what they sought and leave quickly.

Then I realized what time it was and chastised myself for not remembering it beforehand. My father came here nearly every day at this time.

I should have just walked down the stairs and faced him, but I was too much of a coward. Or I was too tired, or too...fragile. I didn't think I could hold myself together if I had to face his disappointment, or worse, his indifference.

I sat down to wait, knowing he wouldn't be able to take much time out of his day. The door opened again and I got up to see if he had left. Instead I saw my mother come in, already changed and refreshed from our ride.

"Hello, darling." My father sounded surprised but pleased to see her. I moved over a bit so I could see both of them.

My mother sat in a chair facing my father. "Forrester, I'm concerned."

He closed the book he had been perusing. "Concerned about what?"

"Your treatment of Ariella." I pulled back in surprise, and so did my father.

"I do not wish to discuss Ariella." He opened his book rather pointedly and my mother removed it from his hands.

"I'm afraid you're going to have to."

He sighed. "What is there to discuss?"

"You are alienating her. This punishment has gotten out of hand. You are treating her unfairly."

"I am doing no such thing. Her behavior was unacceptable and I will not reward it."

"It's been a year." Her voice rose, and I was shocked to observe this private conversation. "It's time for you to stop and consider what you are doing." My mother held his gaze without flinching. "She is the most responsible, the most sensible of our daughters. You should be preparing her to be a queen, not shunning her for her curiosity."

"She needs to learn, Lorilai. She must learn from her mistakes."

"And what do you suppose she's learning from your treatment of her? She's learning that her father and her king is cruel and without compassion. Do you have any idea how bright she is? How aware she is of the world around her? How many truths she has gleaned from the time she spent with that boy?"

"That boy was a misfit and a disgrace," he declared and stood up.

"That boy taught her more about herself and about her kingdom than anyone else." My father scoffed. "Do you have any idea what she thinks of you?"

"What are you talking about?"

"Forrester, she's losing her respect for you." She paused to let this sink in. "And frankly I don't blame her. You certainly haven't done anything to earn her respect lately."

"I don't have to earn anyone's respect." His voice was vicious, which was almost more shocking than the way my mother had spoken.

My mother sat for a moment, unaffected by his outburst, then said calmly. "You know that's not true. Please don't act as though the world has suddenly changed just because Ariella defied you. We all must earn every *bit* of respect. That's the only way—"

My father held up a hand to silence her. "I know." He blew out a breath, then sat back down in his chair, looking tired. "If a king does not have the respect of his people, then the only thing he rules is fear." It sounded like a recitation—something he had been taught long ago.

"And fear holds no loyalty," my mother added.

"Perhaps that's the problem." My mother's brow furrowed, confused, so he went on. "I've known many fears in my life, having faced many threats. But none compared to what I felt when we found her missing. The thought that she could simply disappear without anyone noticing horrified me. It still does." He ran a weary hand over his face. "Well, Lorilai, what do you suggest I do?"

My mother smiled, "Let go of your anger and start talking to her again—at the very least."

He nodded his head, then got to his feet and crossed to my mother's chair. She lifted her face as he leaned in to kiss her.

I stepped back, needing to look away. My eyes stung and my chest ached. It hurt to see people who were truly in love; it always made me wonder if it could have been me. If Gavin hadn't been forced away, could we have loved each other that way?

✳✳✳

The next day, I went back to the maze and sat in his room, wondering why I had abandoned this place of solace. True, there was a sadness that came with being here, but I still loved it. This place brought back so many memories of genuine happiness. And despite Gavin's absence, I found comfort here. So I continued my visits. Instead of retreating to the library or escaping on horseback, I took my books to the garden room.

I was headed there the day before Mia's wedding, book in hand, when I heard someone call my name. I turned to see Jeshua walking toward me and tried not to let my face scrunch in distaste. He bowed when he reached me. "My dear Princess, how good to see you."

I curtsied. "Prince Jeshua. Have you come for the wedding?"

"Yes. It's certainly reason to celebrate."

"We are very happy about the union." I started walking—away from the maze—knowing he would fall into step beside me. It was bad enough that Mia's wedding had prompted an additional visit from him; I certainly would not allow him to taint the maze. I wrapped both my arms around my book, holding it to my chest.

"It is a shame that she could not have made a better alliance."

I breathed deep before responding. "I don't think it's a shame at all. While alliances are important, we are hardly in the position of needing to seek them out. There was no reason to manipulate Mia's life when our peace is not being threatened."

I glanced at him to see shock and even a bit of disapproval in his features. "Your father has said that?"

"*I* have said that. I am only telling you what I think."

"That is a relief."

I wanted to ask why but kept my mouth shut and shared another opinion instead. "I hope never to be manipulated in such a manner. It would be torturous to marry someone not of my choosing."

"I'm sure your father would never align you with anyone

126

unworthy."

His response was not a comfort.

We entered the castle and I had the good fortune and running into Lorraina and Marilee.

"Prince Jeshua, you have come!" Marilee rushed up and swept into an enthusiastic but perfectly respectable curtsy, forcing Jeshua to bow and greet her with a kiss on her hand.

I edged away at a sedate pace, knowing that she would chatter for a bit before allowing him to greet Lorraina who stood behind her, back rigid, nose aloft.

I didn't see him again until dinner, where the celebratory spirit was lively enough that he focused more on his wine than on me.

The next morning was filled with enough last minute preparations that I avoided Jeshua altogether and was able to attend and enjoy the wedding in peace.

The ceremony left me almost breathless. The radiant light in Mia's eyes throughout the entire day was a testament to her happiness—a happiness afforded her by her choice. The stream of envy running through my heart was continuous, but so was the joy I felt for Mia. So I focused only on the joy until late that night, when I allowed myself to cry into my pillow.

Chapter Thirteen

It had been seventeen months since Gavin left. I tried not to keep track of the time but had failed completely.

I was sitting on the edge of the pool in the middle of the Gavin's garden room, my feet immersed and my skirts pulled up scandalously high, out of the water's reach. In all my visits to this room over the years, the only person who had ever been here was Gavin. Besides, even if someone had seen me, I wouldn't have cared.

I spent most of my mornings in this fashion, and could usually be found riding in the afternoon. I now knew the land surrounding the palace as well as anyone. I had spent months simply exploring and re-exploring the forest, foothills, and shoreline, usually trailed by Emmett, who had given up on trying to curtail my explorations. I felt completely at ease when I rode, but I still favored the garden room. For though the adventure of riding and exploring gave me distraction, it was the water round my feet and the books propped on my knees that gave me solace.

Today my book was a sad one, a story of lost love and one of my favorites. As I read, I allowed myself to say the characters' lines quietly to myself, as if they were my own. It wasn't until I saw the blotches on the page that I realized I was shedding silent tears. I shook myself and brushed the tears from my cheeks. I had been so lost in my story that I had lost track of time as well as my surroundings. As I became conscious once again of my garden room, I realized there was a shadow to my right that should not have been there. I stood quickly, clutching my book to my chest to keep it from falling in the water and whirled around. I could only hope it was not Jeshua, appearing for another unanticipated visit and come to destroy yet another piece of my life.

But it wasn't Jeshua.

"Gavin," I breathed out, then had to remind myself to breathe in again. There before me stood a taller, broader, and more handsome Gavin.

"Hello, Princess." I was too surprised to take note of the formality. He stood several paces from me, his feet planted wide, his hands clasped behind his back, slowly taking in my appearance.

"You're here." I felt stunned but elated.

"Yes, I'm here." There was sadness behind his words.

"I—" Words escaped me. I didn't understand. I cast around for some idea to hold on to, then realized I still stood in the pool.

"They allowed me to come back to work under the supervision of the head groundskeeper."

"How?" I asked as I stepped from the pool onto the dry stone pathway.

"They no longer see me as a threat to you."

I stuttered for a moment, then said the only thing that came to mind. "I don't understand." Then I realized it didn't matter if I understood. Gavin was back; he was back in my life. I was just about to take a step toward him to let him hold me in his arms when he spoke.

"I am engaged."

My hands dropped to my sides and my tiny book slipped from my fingers and fell softly into the water dripping at my feet. All the air in my lungs escaped in one tortured breath as his words registered, and I became rooted to the spot. I felt my entire body sink, my chest collapsing in on itself, crushing my lungs. Here he was, standing before me—back in my life, within my reach—and I was losing him all over again. As dozens of emotions filled my body, I tried to form a response. I took in a deep, stuttering breath, and instead of letting it out in a sob as I wanted to, I forced a painful smile, barely holding back the tears as I said, "I'm happy for you." I took in one more steadying breath and excused myself before walking past him and slowly away, trying to remain upright.

I do not remember making my way, barefoot, back to my room. I do not remember crawling into my bed fully clothed. I only remember that the emptiness, which had filled my chest for years, had now been replaced by a terrible, throbbing ache. It was a pain so deep I almost couldn't feel it, and yet I couldn't breathe. The time for me to be at my lessons came and went without my noticing.

I tried to put a name to what I felt. And the only word that came to mind was…broken. I felt broken, and it was Gavin who had broken me. Never would I have anticipated that. Never would I have thought that Gavin, of all people, would be the one to break me. Never would I have imagined that loving someone could be so utterly painful.

The afternoon and evening slipped away. I got out of dinner by pleading ill and permitted only Gretchen to enter my room. She insisted on helping me out of my gown and into my nightdress so I could lie down comfortably. She didn't ask any questions, seeming to know by the emptiness in my eyes that I would not yield to interrogation. It was her understanding that prompted me to say, as she turned to leave, "Gavin is back." I heard her stop as I stared, unseeing, at the ceiling. "He is going to be married."

I will forever be grateful to Gretchen for what she did next. She broke every rule as she lay down beside me and draped her arm around me.

I cried myself to sleep.

Waking in utter darkness, I tried to decipher the noise that had brought me out of my miserable sleep. Gretchen was no longer beside me, and I wondered if her leaving had awoken me. Then I heard it. Someone was walking away from my door, and I realized the noise that had woken me was a low knock. I tried to summon the energy to go to the door and peer outside but instead decided I would wait till morning. So I lay my head back on my pillow and closed my eyes.

But sleep did not come. I lay there for I don't know how long and tried not to think of him. When a dim glow appeared at my window, I gave up the idea of sleep and decided to sate my curiosity. Slipping off my bed, I pulled my covers with me, draping them around myself as I walked slowly to my door, the excess fabric dragging behind me.

I opened the door and peered out, expecting to see nothing. Instead I found a book lying on my threshold. Even before I picked it up, I knew it was my book—the book I had been reading when Gavin found me. It felt damp against my fingers as I picked it up, and I vaguely remembered letting it drop from my hand just after Gavin told me he was marrying someone else. He must have plucked it from the puddle of water. He must have found my door in the middle of the night in order to return it to me.

It was an act of kindness. Yet, as I allowed the book to fall open in my hands, I despised him for it. I hated him for doing something so simple, yet so thoughtful, so obviously prone to make me want him so soon after he had denied me that option. I turned back into my room, shut my door and went back to my bed. I lay upon it with my covers still clutched around me, holding the book to my chest and staring into nothingness as day took hold of my room.

When Gretchen came back I asked her to make excuses for me—to tell my parents or sisters or whoever might ask that I was sick or exhausted or anything to keep them away from me. I lay in bed, with the book clutched over my heart for hours. I had no appetite. I just kept thinking of those words he had spoken to me, and the book he had returned to me, and the sadness on his face when he told me he was engaged. I couldn't make it fit together. My first thought was that he did not love this girl who would become his wife, but that thought—that Gavin would marry someone without loving them—was incomprehensible to me. Surely he would not do that to himself, or to this girl. Of course, many people did marry without love. On a list of priorities for marriage, love barely made the top five for many.

But this wasn't most people. This was Gavin—my Gavin. Gavin

who laughed at the world if it became too serious, Gavin who didn't see me as a princess the first time we met, Gavin who had become the very best friend in the world, Gavin whom I had fallen in love with. It felt cruel, and yet Gavin could never be cruel.

It was with these thoughts that morning turned to afternoon, and it was still several hours before I got up.

When I finally summoned the energy to pull myself out of bed, I could think of only one thing to do. And so I fairly stalked out of the palace and into the grounds, an extra set of under things bundled in a shawl and clutched to my chest. I didn't know where else to go, so I decided to go back to the waterfall. I had not been since Gavin had left. My time outdoors had been occupied by riding alone, until recently, when I had allowed myself to return to the garden room.

At this moment though, I felt an intense need to be apart from the world. Walking through the gardens, I kept my eyes straight ahead, then made my way through the maze, to the room with the hidden door. Pulling the ivy aside, I froze, remembering the warning Gavin had issued so long ago about never going by myself. I didn't care. He had lost the right to sway my decision when he had chosen someone else. I pushed the door open, using all my strength because of its lack of use. Once in the quiet of the trees, some of my guard fell and I became aware of the wetness on my face, but I ignored it, unwilling to acknowledge my pain here in the open.

Two minutes later found me crouched in the shallow water at the rear of the cave behind the falls, my hands and forehead pressed against the back wall as I gave free reign to my emotions. With the constant dripping from the ceiling and my initial trip through the cascade of water, my tears mingled freely with the tears of this lonely space. It felt as though the roaring silence wept with me as my sobs were drowned out by the constant howl.

I admitted there, in that tiny part of the world belonging to me alone, that my time spent away from Gavin had in no way lessened my attachment to him. I had always thought of him as *my* Gavin, the one that would always be a part of me. Now it seemed that even that small measure of comfort had been stripped from me, leaving me torn and in more pain than I thought possible.

When my tears finally stopped, I sat leaning against that rock wall and tried to let my mind drift into nothingness, to hear only the rushing water and nothing else. I tried not to hear Gavin's voice or see his face. I tried not to remember that when I had first seen him the day before, my first impulse had been to kiss him. And I tried not to wish I had done exactly that.

I also tried—desperately tried, and failed—not to think of the time he *had* kissed me. The first time so very long ago in the middle of the village square, and then later that same night, on the side of a street. I tried not to remember how right it had felt to have his arms around me, how safe and loved I had felt.

Darkness was falling, but still I remained half submerged in water with my back against the rough rocks. Yesterday, Gavin had been lost to me physically; tonight I knew he was lost to me in every way except the physical. He was here, and yet he was farther away than he had ever been before.

The light was starting to fade when I finally picked up my exhausted, shivering body and climbed back onto dry land. I picked my way through the woods in a daze, dragging my feet and my shawl as I went.

✳✳✳

One week after Gavin's return, I saw her—the woman that would be his bride, though she seemed to be more girl than woman. I saw her come from the outer building that housed the laundry. She must have been a laundress, one of many who served me without my knowing. Truth be told, I had been hiding behind a hedge, watching Gavin work. Yes, I was spying. Though I knew the futility of it, I couldn't squelch my need to be near him somehow. And so I found myself skulking behind a hedge when it happened.

I noticed her approach before Gavin did. She separated herself from several other women and fairly skipped toward the place where Gavin worked. She was radiant. No wonder he had chosen her. He was likely her first love, her only love. She would make him her entire world. When she reached Gavin, he sweetly took her hand and kissed her cheek in greeting. She in turn smiled, blushed, and glanced away. I retreated, unwilling to torment myself any longer, especially after I realized that though his gestures were genuinely sweet, they were not passionate. He liked her and may have even adored her, and though I wondered more than once if I were kidding myself, I couldn't help but draw the conclusion that he was not in love with her.

Whether or not that was true didn't matter. He had chosen to marry her, and therefore he could not be mine.

I would have thought before now that any contact with him would have been better than wondering what had become of him. How horribly wrong I was. The last year and a half had been awful, but I had at least had the ability to go numb. The ache of being without him had smoldered into something manageable, something residing on the fuzzy outskirts of my consciousness. I had continued living my life, finding peace in the memories of being with him. At least before, while I was missing him, I could assume he was missing me.

But now—now he was here, every day. I knew he was close enough at any given moment that if I wanted to seek him out, I could. And yet I did not. I could not. I would not. Because now—now she was here.

The day I first saw *her* was also the day Jeshua came for another visit. I had been walking the corridors, the sound of my feet hitting the stones making me feel alone. Passing through a corridor overlooking the great hall, I saw Jeshua arrive and suddenly felt far less brave.

If only Jeshua actually cared for me. If his face broke into a genuine smile of pleasure when he saw me, his courting me might have been bearable, even pleasant. Instead he would greet me with a faint and very smug smile, his eyes roaming over me as though he were very satisfied.

Everyone else who saw this satisfaction called it admiration, or appreciation of my beauty, or even doting affection. *Doting affection—* nothing could have been further from the truth. You cannot have affection for someone you know nothing about.

Perhaps he did appreciate my beauty. I was often told that I was a rare beauty, but it never really meant much to me. I looked much like the rest of my sisters.

And so, subjected to Jeshua's company once again, I forced myself to smile politely and act as though his every glance did not disgust me. It was interesting to watch my parents during these times. My father would glance my way once in a while with satisfaction and give Jeshua a nod of encouragement. My mother tended to go out of her way not to look in my direction and wore a continual expression of composed indifference. While I didn't appreciate either sentiment, at least my mother had the sense not to openly approve and especially encourage this ritual of... whatever this was.

After dinner I was forced to endure a walk with Jeshua. We walked south, away from the lowly village houses and toward the rolling foothills instead. We walked as he rambled and I let my mind wander.

"Ariella?" I was pulled abruptly from my thoughts when Jeshua halted our stroll and said my name. Apparently he had caught me not paying attention.

"Yes, I'm sorry. What were you saying?" I tried to focus.

He turned to face me and took my hands in his. I resisted the urge to yank them away. "You are quite distracted tonight. Whatever could be on your mind?"

I was taken aback. Jeshua never asked me questions about myself. I wondered whether or not I should answer truthfully. Perhaps a partial truth would be best. "I was just thinking about an old friend."

"Well, aren't you sweet. Worrying over someone until you're driven to distraction." He reached up and brushed my cheek with the back of his fingers. I tried not to flinch away from his cold touch. Bad enough that he held my hands captive, but did he have to touch my face? He had never been this bold, and it worried me. Had the time come?

Was he going to propose soon? Was he here to speak with my father about making it official? The thought made me shudder.

"Are you chilled?" Jeshua asked, running his hand over my arm. I tried to step back, but he held me in place.

"A little," I lied, my voice tight. I hoped he would take my cue and return me to the palace. I had only a delicate shawl with me, having left my cloak behind in the hopes of keeping the evening stroll as short as possible.

"Well then, perhaps we should find a way to warm you up and help you forget your worries at the same time." He said this in what I supposed was meant to be an alluring voice as he moved deliberately closer to me.

Oh, no.

We were standing next to a low stone wall on the perimeter of a pasture. I tried to step back, away from Jeshua, but my foot met with the wall and I lost my footing. I exaggerated my stumble, saying, "Oh!" as I pulled my hands free, trying to create some distance between us. The idea backfired.

Jeshua's arms encircled me in an embrace far closer than circumstances required. "Don't worry, I have you." He smiled to himself, and I didn't bother to hide my horror. This could not be happening. "Don't look so frightened, Angel," he reassured me, no doubt misinterpreting my horror as nervousness or even anticipation. He bent his head toward me and I turned my face away. His lips brushed my ear as he whispered, "You're in very capable hands."

There was barely a moment to be disgusted by his implication before I felt his lips just below my ear and suddenly felt dirty. "Now," he whispered, placing a dry, rough kiss on my cheek, "shall we endeavor to chase all your worries away?"

I'd never been so revolted in my life. It wasn't just that I loathed him in the first place. It was the way he pulled my body into his, the way he turned the moment into something very intimate without stopping to consider the way I reacted.

In fact, I didn't know *how* to react. He had moved so quickly that I froze, my muscles locked up against his advances, until I felt his disgusting kisses moving closer to my mouth.

I pushed against his chest, leaning away. "Jeshua, don't.... This is…" But before I could get any further protests past my lips, he sealed them off with his own.

I pushed him away as quickly as I could. "This is not proper, sir," I told him as I wrenched myself away, stumbling out of his hold. "I have to return home." I continued up the lane, unable to restrain myself to a simple walk—I ran flat out, my shawl flailing in the breeze. I didn't care what he thought; my repulsion drove my feet forward until I was shut safely in my room. I went to my wash basin and scrubbed at my lips and my neck, determined to rid myself of the creeping, crawling sensation plaguing my skin. I needed to somehow shake loose the feeling of his hands on mine. I had to do something, to act.

Chapter Fourteen

I WENT TO my closet and yanked out the common dress and shoes I had purchased from the village so long ago. I threw my cloak around my shoulders, stuffing my common garb into its folds and out of sight, then made my way out onto the grounds and into the room with the hidden door. I changed from my gown to the homespun dress. I took the jeweled ribbons from my hair, tying it into a disheveled knot before covering my head with a kerchief. I left my cloak in the room with my dress and tied a knit shawl around my waist in case it became chillier. I had discovered this was the reason common women so often looked as though they had double-layered skirts. Lastly I replaced my slippers with what Gavin had once referred to as "proper clomping shoes" and heaved the door open.

So it was with only the aid of the dimming light and a kerchief covering my head that I snuck away from my home. I could have easily recruited Gretchen to come with me, but she didn't know about the door and I didn't want to involve her, especially when I was so thoroughly defying my father.

I just wanted to be by myself, to be away from the palace. I planned to simply walk the cobbled street, to clear my head of thoughts of Jeshua and fill it instead with sights of simplicity and camaraderie.

But as I walked down alleys and lanes, I discovered that for the most part they were deserted. Or if there were people left in them, they were headed for the square. It didn't take me long to deduce that a dance was taking place. I hesitated. Going to a dance would likely throw me into Gavin's path. I considered giving up my plan and returning home, but just the thought of being inside those stone walls made my chest constrict.

I wouldn't participate in the festivities, only watch. And if I did see Gavin? Well, it was an occurrence I would need to get used to.

Approaching the square, I was overwhelmed once again by the sense of *life* here. The festivities were already well underway. The dance being performed as I entered the square had all the women circled around the outside, doing steps and twirls, using their skirts to add to their movements. The men were in the middle doing rhythmic stomping punctuated by clapping. I could have easily slipped in with the circle of women, but I stopped in the shadow of a building instead. There were many older villagers sitting around the edges of the square, talking with one another and watching the dancers. Couples walked hand in hand and women chattered together.

I smiled, reveling in the noise and chaos, enjoying the commotion. As the song ended, some people came away from the dance while others joined in. Just ahead of me, a gentleman not much older than myself sat on a bench. He caught my eye, smiling politely, and I did the same. But then he did a double take. "Ella?" he asked, sitting up straighter.

More than a little surprised to hear him call me by my nickname, I looked closer and realized I recognized him. "Eli?" It was Gretchen's brother who had danced with me the very first time I had come to one of these gatherings.

He stood up, a grin splitting his face. "How are you, Miss Ella? We haven't seen you in ages; I thought you had gone for good. Are you here with your aunt again? I hope she is well."

"Yes," I blundered, relieved he had reminded me of the story of a sick aunt that I had told to explain my haphazard appearances at these events. "Yes, my aunt is very well. I am simply visiting this time."

"Well then, I must tell my sister you are here; I know she became quite fond of you when you were here last."

"I was very fond of her as well," was the best thing I could think to say. Truth be told, I was not prepared for someone to recognize me. It had been a year and a half, for heaven's sake! But I suppose if anyone would recognize me, it would be Eli. Being Gretchen's brother, he had been a part of our little group. My mind sought frantically for something to say that wouldn't make me sound guilty. "And how are you, Eli? Are you well? Is Gretchen well?"

"We are both doing very well, thank you. Remind me where you hail from?"

"I..." Fortunately I was spared the need for a response by the appearance of a young lady with a scarf in her hand.

"Eli, you must come dance with me," she said as she latched onto his arm.

He kissed her forehead in greeting. "I will, darling, but first you must meet Ella," he said, gesturing to me.

She extended her hand. "How do you do?"

"Quite well, thank you."

"Ella is an old friend of Gretchen's who has come back to visit. And Ella, this is my wife, Layla." He made the introduction and slipped an arm around Layla's waist.

"You're married. How wonderful. Congratulations."

"Thank you very much," he said then his eyes widened as if he had just remembered something. "You know who else is getting married?"

I widened my eyes in interest and he went on. "You knew Gavin, didn't you?"

My chest went tight and my eyes widened even farther.

"In fact," continued Eli, "I'm sure he would like to say hello; I know he is here somewhere."

We both started scanning the crowd and Eli pointed into the sea of swirling bodies as he said, "Right there."

I followed his pointing finger and spotted not Gavin, but his betrothed. She circled with a group of women, but then broke away as a gentlemen's hand took hold of the scarf she held. My eyes went from the scarf, to the hand, then the arm, shoulder, and finally rested on his face —Gavin's face. He had looped the scarf over his wrist as she held both ends of it, and used it to guide her into a twirl. I stood mesmerized. I had seen many times how these scarves were used, but watching Gavin, it was much clearer just how personal the dance became with that scarf. It made its way around necks, over arms, through fingers…connecting them so physically. It made me ill—seeing them together in that way.

"That's his fiancée he's dancing with now."

I nodded mutely at Eli's words, trying to keep my face neutral.

"We were happy to see those two make a match. Gavin has had a rough time this past year."

I cleared the emotion out of my throat. "He has?"

"Never did figure out why he was let go from his position at the palace. But he hasn't been the same since."

I swallowed. Neither of us had been the same. "When did they meet?"

Layla answered this time. "Oh, they've known each other for years. I'm surprised it took this long for his parents to arrange it." She turned to Eli, pulling on his hand. "Come on, the next dance will start soon."

Eli smiled, allowing himself to be pulled away. "It was good seeing you again. I'll send Gavin over to say hello."

They joined the throng of dancing and I stood frozen for several seconds before forcing myself to move. I could not stay there, waiting for Eli to deliver his message to Gavin. Suddenly the open square and noisy chaos were oppressive and overwhelming. I fought my way through the crowd, gaining access to the open street and the shadows of night before looking behind me.

Gavin was standing in the spot I had occupied only a moment before, turning left and right, looking panicked. I don't know why I didn't go right then, but something held me still. I trusted the shadows to veil my presence and saw the moment that Gavin peered toward me, toward the street that took the most direct route to the palace and started walking toward it.

The shadows would not hide me once he entered the street and so I hurried away until I reached the road to the palace.

I kept glancing over my shoulder, expecting Gavin to catch up with me at any moment, but he wasn't there. I allowed myself the time to untie the shawl from over my skirt and wrap it around my shoulders. Though the breeze was not strong, nor very cold, I felt the prick of it against my skin as if it were shards of ice. I walked—resolute and numb —toward my home, my head bowed in grief, my heart anxious that Gavin might still catch up with me.

Looking behind me again, I bumped into a man coming the opposite way. An apology was on my lips, but he grabbed my arm roughly.

"Have a little respect, wench."

The stale stench of wine wafted over me and air became lodged in my throat.

"Nothing to say?" he demanded, pulling me closer to his sneering face.

"I'm sorr—"

"You know." His blurry eyes cleared a little as they raked over me. "Walking alone can be a dangerous undertaking, miss."

He clamped his hand over my mouth, spinning my back to him and wrapping his other arm around me, pinning my arms to my sides.

How had this happened? How could I have been so foolish?

The man was easily three times my size and had his hand so firmly over my mouth that my attempt at screams could not possibly have been heard by anyone. He heaved me off my feet and carried me easily toward the dark wood. I kicked and I flailed, hoping I was close enough to the palace walls to be seen, but it was useless. No one knew where I was. No one would notice me missing until morning.

All at once, my attacker stopped walking and his grip slackened as my mind registered the sound of heavy breathing. Crumpling to the ground as he released his grip on me, I turned to see him trying to loosen the arms circling his neck. I pulled in a deep breath and screamed when I realized a second man was slowly but surely cutting off my attacker's air supply. The brute swung his arms over his head, trying to hit the man whose arms were cutting off his air. Unable to land a blow, he sank to his knees, then fell on his face, unconscious. I looked up at the man who had defended me, praying his intentions were not sinister. My kerchief had come off in the struggle, and the wind blew my hair over my face, obscuring my view. I pushed it out of my face, wanting to know if I needed to flee.

I swallowed—not out of fear, but out of a different sort of panic. It was Gavin. What little air remained in my lungs was forced out by the weight that settled solidly onto my chest. He stood larger than he had been—much more solid. Any boyishness was entirely gone, and it was intimidating. He took a step forward, reaching out his hand, then stopped himself, closed his fist and stepped back again. I opened my mouth to try and say something, but a guard from the wall above cried out and my attention was diverted. I heard the incoherence of shouted orders. My scream had alerted the guard and they were coming to investigate.

I heard the rumble of orders being given and men running about, but then Gavin turned to me. And as I looked up at Gavin, whose chest heaved and whose eyes bore into mine, a strange deafening silence filled my ears. I slowly stood, never letting my eyes leave his, the wind blowing my mass of curls into a tangled mess behind me. My shawl had fallen and blown away, as had my kerchief. I didn't care. I stood straight, my breath rolling through my body as I allowed myself to savor his presence. Somehow, his gaze sustained me, giving me strength. It had been so long since I had felt this way, I didn't want to miss even the smallest moment. My lower lip trembled as a solitary tear slipped down my cheek, but still I just stood there, allowing that feeling to wash over me, to fill me up until

———

Voices. They came into my consciousness slowly, as though my mind were hesitant to let them in. Only a few guards rounded the corner tower to investigate. I turned toward them and the man in the lead

143

stopped dead. "It's the princess!" he shouted and ran headlong at me.

I turned back to Gavin, but my eyes were drawn beyond him. The man who had attacked me had regained consciousness and was starting to rise. When Gavin heard my startled yelp, he spun to see the man rising and protectively pushed me aside just as the soldiers reached us. The commotion tripled as a dozen unseen guards descended upon us. They surrounded me in a flurry of motion, dragging me away. I tried to keep my eyes on Gavin, but only managed a glimpse or two.

As the guards escorted me—rather roughly—toward the palace, they shouted panicked questions at me, trying to ascertain my well-being. I answered as well as my scattered thoughts would allow. I arrived in the great hall still disoriented, surrounded by guards, but came to an abrupt halt when Jeshua captured me, wrapping me in his arms. I stiffened and heard him ask, "My darling, are you all right?"

His voice made me cringe, most especially because he called me 'darling.' I didn't respond, just stood there with my arms hanging at my sides, staring ahead as he babbled on, asking me about my clothing. I shook from the panic or from the cold—I didn't know which. I wanted to be held, to be wrapped in someone's arms—but not his.

My father's entrance was a welcome distraction.

He pulled me into a fleeting, stiff hug. "Ariella." His voice was cold, barely restrained.

"Father." My voice was a monotone and shook only slightly as he pushed me away to look me over.

"Are you hurt?" His question seemed unnecessary. I knew the captain had already given him a full report. At the same time, he looked slightly vulnerable, and I wondered if perhaps I had frightened him.

"No," I answered.

"Follow me." He turned and strode swiftly and stiffly toward the passage leading to his office. I followed in silence, trying to keep pace with his long stride but feeling as though I were moving through molasses. When we reached his office, I barely made it through the door before he slammed it shut.

"Sit," he barked without looking at me. I obeyed as he circled his desk. I expected him to sit in the chair there, but instead he stared at the books lining the back wall with his hands on his hips, shifting his weight in an agitated manner.

In truth he was more than agitated. He was trying not to lash out physically. Not that he would strike me, but I feared for the books, and even more for the statuettes sitting on the shelves. I didn't know how to act. My father had never disciplined me in person. He left that to my mother, or my tutors, or a note sent by a page.

After a silent minute, he finally turned. "Is this about the gardener?" he demanded.

My stomach tightened and I involuntarily sucked in a quick breath. I had been ready to defend myself, to fight back, regardless of the fact that this man was both my father and the king. But the mention of Gavin kept me silent. I stared at the floor, afraid the moisture in my eyes would show.

He raised his voice. "Ariella, is this about the gardener?"

Yes, I answered in my mind, *this is about Gavin, how could it not be?*

"It is, isn't it? Did you go and meet him tonight?"

"Meet him?" I asked incredulously. *Meet him? For what purpose? So he could show off his intended bride and break my heart even more thoroughly?*

"Yes, meet him. Did you meet him? Did you two have a plan to meet and—"

"No." I stopped him before he could accuse me of the one thing I wanted.

"Ariella, you will tell me the truth." His voice was barely controlled.

"I have." My voice sounded calm, much calmer than I felt. "I did not meet him. I did not plan to meet him. I…"

"Well then what could you possibly have been thinking going out on your own, without telling anyone?" I caught a hint of concern before his anger took over. "Where did you go? Why would—"

"I went into the village."

His nostrils flared as he tried to breath steadily. "Why?"

"Because I'm suffocating." If I had been thinking about my responses, I would certainly have said something else, but this conversation was causing me to be very honest. Because I *was* suffocating —very slowly, very painfully suffocating.

My father rocked back. "What are you talking about?"

"Father, I don't—" I broke off, hesitant. "I don't feel as though I have a purpose—or maybe that isn't the best way to put it. I don't know what is expected of me. Am I honestly supposed to do nothing but look the part? I feel as though my days are filled with nothing, just mindless tasks and diversions with no point to them. Is that all that is expected of me?"

My father said nothing. This worried me; I had never seen my father speechless and I didn't know what it meant. Was he angry? Did he think me impertinent? Was he surprised, shocked? I couldn't tell.

I don't think he knew either, because he chose to ignore what I had said and changed the subject entirely. "Your engagement celebration will be held next week." He started rifling through the papers on his desk as though this news should have no more affect on me than news of the weather.

Now I was speechless. An engagement celebration? Had I allowed things to get this far out of control? Did my father honestly believe I would marry Jeshua? There were no coherent thoughts that I could voice, so I turned to leave.

Then I stopped myself. I may have let it get this far, but it would go no further. My mother had assured me that my father would never give me to anyone. I was about to test her theory.

Turning back, I remembered something Gavin had once told me. *You say no.*

"No."

The king's hands froze and he slowly looked up at me. "Excuse me?"

"I am not engaged, Father." My voice was quiet, but firm.

"But you will be by next week." He went back to sorting things as though this settled the matter. Funny that though I was his daughter, he still treated this as though it were a business transaction.

"No, I won't." I spoke as calmly as ever, willing myself to keep standing straight.

"Jeshua will be proposing in the next week and—"

"I have no interest in marrying Jeshua."

His hands stilled and his eyes came up slowly. "What are you talking about?"

"Jeshua may propose as many times as he wishes, but you may want to warn him that he will certainly not be accepted."

The papers dropped from his hands. "If that gardener has jumbled your head so much that you—"

"That gardener has a name. And my refusal has nothing to do with Gavin."

I could see my father fighting to keep his composure, so I tried to explain. "I really don't know how I could have given the impression that I was interested in Jeshua in any way. My sisters may find something in him to be admired, but to me he has been nothing but repulsive. He cares for no one but himself, least of all me." Shock crossed his features at my declaration, but he also appeared much more calm, so I continued. "I'm sorry I didn't say anything before now, but I hoped my actions would be taken into account and that perhaps...it would all go away. I don't know." I looked at the floor. I was uncomfortable making such a speech to the king, and my words failed me.

"You have no affection for Jeshua?" Obviously this was not something he had anticipated.

"No, Father." I spoke clearly but kept my eyes down.

"Did you ever, in years past, have a regard for him?"

The conversation I had overheard years before by my waterfall came clearly to my mind. "Never, sir." I raised my head, and seeing that he was not going to immediately speak again, decided to clarify. "When I was young he frightened me, but as the years went by, I realized he was

147

selfish and domineering. I don't like him, Father. I don't respect him. I can hardly stand him." I did not mean to be overly critical; after all, Jeshua was a Prince of Tride. But I also wanted to leave no question about my feelings.

He looked at me for a moment, as though seeing something in me for the first time, and was on the verge of speaking when a knock sounded at his door.

A messenger was allowed to enter and handed the king a roll of parchment, which he read as the messenger exited and then summarized for me. "Your attackers have been dealt with." *Attackers?* "They have both been arrested." *Both?*

"Father, only one man attacked me."

He glanced up briefly, then back down, unconcerned. "There were two men at the scene when the guards found you. You probably only saw one, but there was another."

"No, I'm very sure there was only one—"

Dread filled me so quickly that my knees nearly collapsed. *There were two men found.* Of course there were. One was the man who had indeed attacked me, but the other man saved me. The other was Gavin. "Oh, no..."

I didn't ask permission to leave. My feet carried me from my father's office and I was running before I had the conscious thought to do so. Running through the great hall, I was vaguely aware of Jeshua. He reached out to me but I refused to be hindered. I must have looked ridiculous. Not only was I running flat out through the corridors and halls of a palace, but I still wore the dress of a commoner. I didn't care. I would not let Gavin suffer, not for me.

As I raced outside and down the palace steps, I came upon Marilee. I begged her cloak away from her, and she handed it over, clearly appalled by my appearance, but perfectly willing to help. I continued to run, flinging the cloak around myself and pulling up the hood.

For the first time in many years, the authority I had been born into would be put to use. I would find whoever was holding Gavin and they would do as I asked.

Chapter Fifteen

I HAD NEVER been anywhere near the prison before. Thus my forcing my way past guard upon guard to get through the entrance caused many blank stares, many questions of what to do with me, and much confusion when I ordered them to tell me where they were keeping their most recent prisoners.

"The men who attacked you, Highness?" asked a confused young guard. "They are being interrogated, of course."

"Only one man attacked me. The other is entirely innocent. In fact, he saved me from the man who did attack me."

"Your Highness, both men have implicated the other. We must do a full—"

"I know what happened and I demand you release him."

"But Highness—"

"Where is he?"

"Who?"

"The prisoner. Not the massive, drunk man who did attack me, but the other man, where is he?"

He bumbled for a moment.

"Who is interrogating him?" I demanded.

"The captain, Your Highness."

"Go get him this instant and tell him he must talk to me before this interrogation goes any further."

He stuttered, then gave a hasty bow and hurried down the corridor to my right, disappearing through a door halfway down. The captain of the guard emerged moments later. "Princess Ariella." He bowed low, then looked up, puzzled. "I understand there is some problem?"

"I was attacked by one man. One. The other man, who you are now interrogating, delivered me from the other."

The captain blanched, a look a horror crossing his face. "You are certain, Your Highness?" He sounded as though he hoped I was not. Uneasiness stole over me.

I brushed past him, intent on the door I had seen him come out of. "Of course I am sure."

The captain overtook me and blocked me from opening the door. "Princess, I beg you to allow me to take care of this."

My unease increased. "Stand aside, or open the door for me." He remained where he was for the space of a heartbeat then closed his eyes and opened the door.

I had imagined Gavin sitting in a chair, answering questions. That was not the case. His bound hands had been looped with a rope that connected to the ceiling. He had been hoisted by his wrists so much that his toes barely touched the floor. His breathing sounded shallow and labored, his eyes pinched in pain.

I gave an unintelligible yell of horror and rushed to him. "Get him down!" I screamed. My command was unnecessary. The captain was already there, lowering him to the ground. Gavin tried to steady himself but his legs wouldn't hold him. I tried to catch him, but my strength was insufficient, so I only succeeded in breaking his fall as his weight brought me to my knees.

Gavin grunted as we hit the floor, then started pulling in great deep breaths. His eyes stayed closed as he slowly tried to make his muscles work again after being locked in the same position. I tried to calculate how long he might have been here. A quarter of an hour? More? Had he been strung up the entire time? I turned to the soldier I had spoken to and ordered him to get water. The captain untied Gavin's hands and I just stared at him, his head cradled in my hands, trying to think what I should do.

The water arrived just as his hands were freed. I snatched it from the guard. "Now, both of you, get out!" They hesitated, so I turned to glare at them. "Go!" They left.

I watched the door slam and couldn't make myself look back at Gavin. What had he suffered because of me? I shut my eyes as tears of shame and aching sympathy forced their way down my face. "I'm sorry," I sobbed out, letting my forehead drop to his shoulder as I continued to mumble, "I'm sorry...I'm so sorry..."

I heard him breathe in and hold it for a moment as if afraid to let it out for fear of pain. "I'm fine," he breathed out.

This falsehood made my heart hurt ten times over. "You're not fine." I remembered the water and instantly pulled my head up. "You must drink this." My hand shook as I lifted his head and tried to put the cup to his lips with the other. Much of it spilled down his chin and I felt useless and ridiculous as I fussed over him, wanting to help and not knowing how. "I'm sorry. I'm sorry," I said again.

He covered my hand where it held the cup and helped me to guide it more steadily to his mouth. After several swallows he laid his head back on the floor. "I told you, I'm fine."

I stifled a sob. "No, you're not. What did they do to you?" My voice sounded hysterical.

"Nothing of consequence. It hadn't progressed very far yet. And in a moment I will stand on my own and prove to you that I really am fine."

"They weren't interrogating you, they were torturing you."

He lifted a shoulder in what could only be described as a shrug. "That's the way it goes."

I stared at him. "How can you say that? It's not right, you didn't do anything wrong!"

"I was suspected in connection with an attack on a royal—a princess, no less. Of course they would use drastic measures to interrogate me."

"But—"

"They know I've taken you away from the palace before. I'm not supposed to be anywhere near you, Princess. But when I saw you alone in the village—" his lips tightened and his nostrils flared. "You cannot be out alone." It sounded like a reprimand—it probably was. "I could not let you return alone."

"You were following me to protect me?" He stayed silent. "Are you out of your mind? You cannot protect me at your own expense. You cannot."

"What would have happened to you if I hadn't been there?"

"Why didn't you leave when you heard the guards coming?" I demanded. "You knew they wouldn't harm me, but look at you." My point was made for me as he sat up with a groan. "Don't protect me, Gavin."

He cast his eyes skyward for moment, lips pressed together, head shaking. Then he looked me full in the face. "I'm sorry, Princess, but protecting you is ingrained in me. I cannot *not* protect you."

From the moment I had walked into this room my dominant emotion had been agonizing sympathy and pain at seeing how he had been treated. But suddenly I felt as though I needed to be on my guard. I moved away from him, creating distance between us, remembering that he had broken my heart. "You don't have the right to protect me." He could not be engaged and continue to care about me; it would break my heart all over again.

"That's a bit hypocritical," he said, forcing himself to his feet and walking stiffly over to a chair standing in one corner of the room. "You protect me. You walked in and saved my hide just now. Why do you have the right and I don't?" He sounded...sad, with only a hint of anger.

"I am not the one," I began, not able to meet his eyes and trying to be tactful, "whose responsibilities lie elsewhere."

"We both have responsibilities," he said in a tired voice, "and as a subject of this kingdom, one of my responsibilities is to protect you."

I decided to be more blunt. "I'm not engaged."

He turned to face me. "What about Prince Jeshua?" He spat the name, a lot like I did.

"Please don't speak to me of Jeshua; he's the reason you're in this place." I thought back to my reasons for running to the dance and had to swallow the disgust as I remembered Jeshua's advances. "He's the reason I snuck out without thinking. He—" I looked over at him in time to see his brow furrow in anger and his nostrils flare. I couldn't blame him for being angry with me. His being here was my fault.

"What did he do?" I scarcely heard his question, his voice was so low, filled with menace. His anger was not directed at me, but at Jeshua. How ridiculously ironic: Gavin—engaged Gavin—coming to my defense.

I dropped my gaze, unable to watch his emotions as they roamed freely across his face. "I don't want to talk about—"

"Did he hurt you?" The fear in his voice made me look up. His eyes studied me, trying to surmise if I was hurt, but enfolded in Marilee's cloak, he could see only my face and my hands. So he stopped taking inventory and waited for me to answer.

"No," I assured him. "No, he just—" I paused, not wanting to say it aloud. "—kissed me, is all." I closed my eyes and shook my head, trying to rid myself of the memory. Why did I feel the need to tell Gavin anyway? I couldn't keep myself from reassuring him and I hated it. His anger remained, and I sensed that now it *was* directed at me.

"Well, I suppose that leads back to my original question. Are you going to marry him?" He tried to sound cold, uninterested, but it didn't quite work.

Anger seeped in through my sympathy. How dare he care? How dare he act like he had a right to care? He was the one who was engaged and yet he was getting angry with me when he only suspected that I was engaged. "I don't know why you care. Why should it matter to you if I marry a man whom you *know* I loathe?"

Disbelief was written clearly on his face. "If you hate him so much, then how is it he kissed you, Ella?"

He questioned my actions and it was humiliating to defend myself to him; it was heartbreaking and wrong. It was none of his concern what I did or didn't do. And yet I had to make him understand. And calling me Ella? I was so taken aback by his accusations that I'm sure the hurt and betrayal showed clearly on my face. "Because he had a mind to and he's stronger than I am." I could hear the vulnerability in my voice but hoped he didn't.

He thought that over for a moment and I saw his anger shift back to Jeshua. "He had no right—"

"Stop," I commanded in desperation. "Quit acting as though you have the right to accuse *or* defend me. You have neither." My voice had started out strong, but broke on the last two words. I stared right at him and he couldn't hold my gaze.

"You're right. I'm sorry. I'm sorry for..." He shook his head, trying to clear it and I wondered why exactly he felt sorry. For leaving? For coming back? For saving me? For what? "So, your father's promise of betrothal has not come to pass?"

"No." I spoke with conviction. On this subject, I was certain. "And it never will." His reaction to this news looked like surprise, relief, and quite a bit of disbelief. He didn't entirely trust my conviction, but I tried not to care. I pulled my feet beneath me and got up clumsily. I had to get away. "Goodbye, Gavin. You may leave whenever you are ready."

"The captain may not be done with me yet."

"The captain will answer to me," I snapped. If he insisted on snubbing me for my rank, then I might as well use it to my advantage.

I walked away, slammed the door behind me, and stalked to the main entry where the captain stood with several others. As I approached him without slowing my pace, he snapped to attention. I stopped only a foot from him, and though he towered over me, there was no question as to who was in control. He stood straight and unmoving, looking me in the eye, waiting for my order.

I wanted to say something, feeling justified in transferring my furious anger into power. It was then I felt something for the first time: an instinctual need to exert force over another person. And while I reveled in it, I also recoiled, disgusted with myself.

I had no right. My position should not have offered me this power. I knew that this man standing before me, who had earned his place and the respect of those under him, should not have been cowed by me. But I did have that power—it had been given to me long ago; I had just never had a reason to use it. And now I wondered if I could go back. It felt so good to feel in control. Having control over others was a heady experience, but to feel as though I were directing my own path left me intoxicated.

I consciously reeled myself in. I could have given any order, doled out any punishment. But I couldn't—I wouldn't. I did not want this absolute power, because it would ruin me. And so with a deliberate effort of will, I took a step back. "I was attacked by one man; he was intoxicated and belligerent. This other man saved me. You must allow him to leave when he is ready." My voice was thick with emotion and didn't sound powerful at all.

The captain appeared stunned. "As you wish, Your Highness."

I wanted to scream at him for what he had done, but more than that, I wanted to use my power as little as possible. "I will trust in your discretion in this matter."

"Of course, Highness. Though the king will, of course, be apprised of the situation," he reminded me, still looking like he didn't know quite what to think of me.

I nodded, lost for words, hoping that my father would trust the captain, and turned directly to the door. I made my way up to the palace with resolute step, refusing to cry, viciously holding on to my anger.

I moved silently through the deserted corridors and into my room. It was very late and exhaustion consumed me. I sat down in a chair by my bed and felt my anger flatten into numbness as I waited for the motivation to get undressed. But I never found it. I sat there, thinking of the events of what seemed like an endless day.

This morning, I had seen Gavin's fiancée for the first time. Just this afternoon, Jeshua had shown up unannounced, taken me for a walk, kissed me. I had fled to the village dance and seen Gavin dancing with his bride-to-be—the nameless girl I couldn't seem to hate even though it seemed like I should. I had spoken with Eli, fled from Gavin, had my life threatened. I had declared my independence from my father and from Jeshua, then used my influence as a royal to have Gavin released and exonerated. And I had had one more heart breaking conversation with Gavin. This day had lasted a year, yet it was all so fast.

Sleep claimed me eventually, and I woke up a few hours later, fully clothed and slouched in my chair. I convinced myself to unfasten the cloak and let it slide to the ground as I climbed onto my bed and fell immediately back to sleep.

The next morning I woke late, though I would have welcomed more sleep. I still felt exhausted, but I was wide awake and decided to go riding.

Weston saw me approaching the stables and had Fancy saddled and ready to go by the time I arrived. Though I usually took a moment to speak with Weston, today I simply mounted and nudged Fancy out of the stables and into a gallop, wanting to be alone with my thoughts. I rode into the forest and urged Fancy to follow along the stream that ran down the mountain until I found myself sitting on top of my waterfall.

I had never viewed it from this direction before and it gave me the feeling of sitting on the precipice of my world. So much of my time with Gavin had been spent right here—so many good memories. Then there was the memory of my father and Jeshua. I had been devastated by that conversation, had the breath knocked from me completely. But last night, I had said no. After more than a year and a half, I had finally been given the chance to say no. Suddenly I could breathe again, and while I reveled in that feeling, I also felt the loss of Gavin even more keenly. Now that the inevitability of a forced marriage no longer stood in my way, I realized just how dim my prospects were.

There had to be more. There had to be something I could do to make somebody's life better. I couldn't be with Gavin, but I could do something for someone. And if he would just stay away from me, perhaps I could even forget him a little.

Chapter Sixteen

I REQUESTED AN audience with my father for the first time. I hadn't wanted to speak with him since Gavin left. And before that, requesting an audience wouldn't have been necessary; I could have just talked to him. I hated having to do it this way, but despite my anger over his treatment of me, his permission was necessary. So I stood in his study, my back straight, awaiting his presence.

When he entered, he didn't look past me, as had been his habit lately. Instead he stopped just inside the door, regarding me carefully. I tried to keep my face passive but polite. He issued a weary sigh, then closed the door and sat at his desk.

"You requested an audience." It was a prompt for me to speak, but it also sounded like a question.

"I have a request to make."

His eyebrows rose. "You're not going to give an explanation of your actions—?"

"I didn't know you wanted one." He had never asked.

He leaned his elbow on his armrest and thoughtfully pushed his fingers along his jaw. "I think I deserve one."

I didn't know exactly what he wanted an explanation for, so I decided to cover everything, trying to rush through it. "The evening Jeshua and I went for a walk, I could tell that his interest in me was increasing and I didn't know how to deal with that. My anxiety caused me to act irrationally. I went into the village for only a few minutes and as I was returning—" I swallowed and blinked, trying to maintain my composure. "I should not have been out alone." I forced myself to take a deep breath. "As for Jeshua, I should have made my feelings clear long ago, but I didn't know how."

We stared at one another in silence. He didn't appear particularly angry. He looked more like he was trying desperately to figure something out.

"The gardener was the one who delivered you from your attacker?"

My chest tightened. "Yes." He just looked at me, as though requiring further explanation. "The reason I only stayed in the village a few minutes is because I saw him. Apparently he saw me as well. He saw I was alone, and he was rightly concerned."

The silence unnerved me, but at least he was listening to my words.

"This behavior cannot continue, Ariella." The anger I had been waiting for finally came out. I stared at my hands, forcing myself not to argue. I still needed to make my request. He blew out a breath, his anger deflated by my lack of response. "Your request, then?" His voice was tight, but most of the anger was gone.

"I want to make regular visits to the village." His eyebrows shot up and he opened his mouth. "Please let me finish," I rushed on. "With your permission and with whatever escort you choose, I would like to make regular trips into the village. I want to get to know the people. I want them to know me. I want to show them that we care for them, not just as a whole, but also as individuals. I know you can't take on that responsibility, but I want to." He sat silent, but I thought I glimpsed approval in his eyes.

I guess that he was resistant to my proposal, in part because of his protective nature, but mostly because he didn't want to give me what I wanted when I had so recently defied him—again. I believe what won him over in the end was that the idea was a good one. He had told me once that caring for individuals would make his job nearly impossible.

That didn't mean he didn't want someone else to care for them.

✳✳✳

It had been two months since Gavin had come back. I still spent some time each day with my tutors and I continued to draw, but the best parts of each day were my visits to the village.

The first couple of weeks had been strange; the people didn't know how to react to me. But eventually they came to accept my presence, and then trust me. Each day found me, trailed by two guards, walking through the village streets. I could see that the people would have been content to just see me among them, but that would not have satisfied *me*. I wanted to *do* for them, not just be seen by them. It turned out to be a more difficult endeavor than I expected. Adults were far too wary to accept my help at first because they did not wish to disrespect me.

Children, however, were much easier to convince. For though they recognized me as the princess and were in awe of that fact, they still weren't inclined to turn down help with chores. So I spent my first weeks helping children carry water from the well to their homes, or assisting them in weeding a little patch of garden. I found myself drawn to the poorer neighborhood. They were the most in need of help and the most likely to take it.

Of course, people stared and talked quietly behind their hands. But eventually some of the mothers allowed me to hold their fussing babies while they went about the market, or pull up a few vegetables after I came back with their children from the well to find them harvesting their garden. By the end of the month, they were inviting me into their kitchens, where I learned to knead bread dough and chop vegetables to put in a stew.

By the middle of the second month, they were smiling as I approached and some of the children would run to me, calling, "Princess Ari!" and wrap their arms around my middle, inviting me to play hide and seek. The women would call out a greeting and the men would nod their heads and smile.

I found myself more content and wondered many times why I had never done this before. I was still a princess to these people, but in a different way. I wasn't Princess Ariella; I was Princess Ari. And with that title, given to me by children, being a princess didn't bother me so much. Though hide and seek was difficult, since the children only had to look for my guards to find me. I didn't mind, and sometimes even took pleasure in making them climb into small places. They tried to appear surly, but sometimes caught them on the verge of smiling. I also understood why I had protection, and I thanked my father for his extreme lenience. Our agreement was simple—he allowed me to go into the village so long as I went as myself. Once in a while I imagined he might even be proud of me for the work I did. But he never said and I never asked.

My mother, however, did say something. I was in my sitting room, writing down the names of the people I had promised to visit the next day, when the door opened. Assuming Gretchen had come in, I finished writing and started to unfasten my cloak while looking over my list to be sure I hadn't forgotten anyone.

"Well, I must say." I was startled to see my mother standing in my doorway. "You've come back to life."

I looked down, struck by how sad her statement sounded, but also how true. "I know." I draped my cloak over a chair, then sat down, quite exhausted. "I wasn't much use after he left, was I?"

"You tried, just…not very hard." She smiled in a knowing way and walked farther into the room. "But now—now you've taken charge of your life." I nodded, considering her words. I was surprised though, as she voiced her next thoughts. "I hesitated in letting him return. I was afraid having him here would make it worse, make you not want to try at all."

"You knew he was coming back?" My parents did not usually deal with the hiring of workers around the palace.

She nodded as she sat down across from me. "The head groundskeeper, Joseph, came to your father. He thought that since Gavin had grown up and changed in many ways, he should at least approach us with the idea of allowing him to return. The maze hasn't been the same in his absence. He's a skilled laborer."

"Why didn't you tell me?" I wasn't upset, just curious. A little warning would have been nice.

She thought for a moment. "I'm not sure. Perhaps I thought his presence would go unnoticed." I gave her an incredulous look and she smiled. "Or maybe I just thought you would deal with it better on your own. And I think I was right about that."

"Well," I said, not sure I had dealt with it well at all, "I dealt with it."

"You've done beautifully, Ariella. You'll make an extraordinary queen one day."

I gazed at her for a moment. "You know I'm not going to be queen, Mother."

She smiled. "No matter where your life takes you, Ariella, you will be a queen, with or without the title."

She rose from her chair, kissed my forehead, and left me wondering what she meant.

✳✳✳

A few days later, I found a group of children playing by the river and informed them that we were going to have a treasure hunt. I had hidden my treat-filled satchel somewhere in the village and sent them on a wild goose chase to find it. I gave them clues, sending them running to different locations, and when we all arrived there, I would make them do something silly in order to earn the next clue.

At the moment we were at the well, all of us hopping around it on one foot. These children were inexhaustible. I had to do each assignment right along with them, no matter that I usually carried one of them while we ran to each location. My once carefully secured curls were now hanging down my back and I had left my cloak somewhere along the way. Hopefully one of my trusty guards had picked it up for me. They hadn't joined us yet. They had given up running with us and tended to amble to each location, arriving just before we took off to the next.

I hopped around the well only once before I gave up and collapsed on the cobblestones, pulling my hair away from my damp neck. I wondered at that moment what my sisters would think if they saw me. Then I laughed, shaking my head at the absurdity of my situation—an absurdity I loved. Among my family I felt like a misfit, but somehow I fit in here. These children didn't care that I sat cross-legged on the cobblestone while they bounced around me with their endless supply of energy. They didn't mind that my hair had come down or that I often looked unladylike as we stormed through the streets in search of the next clue. I was one of them.

As the children started dropping one by one, their legs exhausted, I let my hair down and looked around the square in preparation for the next clue. My guards needed to catch up before I sent the kids off again. But it wasn't my guards that I spotted watching over me.

Gavin was here. In the shadows of one of the lanes, he stood with his arms folded, watching me. I didn't allow my eyes to linger on him. What brought him here? Was he following me? I had never seen him in the village during the day. That was one of the benefits of coming to the village—distance from Gavin. And yet here he stood.

My guards came into sight and I decided it was time to continue. I needed to get away from Gavin. I got up on my knees, sat back on my heels and waited for the children's attention to return to me.

"Our next stop is to the pastry maker, the keeper of cookies. Let's go see the—"

"Baker!" The children shouted in unison, bursting to their feet and scrambling toward the lane leading to the bakery.

I rose as well and called toward my guards, "Did you happen to find my cloak?"

"No, Princess."

"No matter," I called back as Sasha and Henry dragged on my hands. "I'll find it later." Turning to follow the children, I nearly tripped over Jordyn, who crouched, investigating his shoe. I picked him up. "Come, young squire, we must off to the baker!" I said as I ran along the street with Sasha and Henry still keeping hold of the sides of my skirt. "This way!" I shouted when some of them headed off toward the wrong bakery.

Thank goodness my mother had seen my need for plain dresses. After a couple weeks of going into the village, she realized my usual attire just wouldn't work. My seamstress had been asked to make me several casual dresses, with practical fabric. No frills, no trains and no overabundance of skirts. I loved these dresses. They allowed me to move, and breathe, and run.

I arrived in front of the bakery amidst bouncing children begging for their assignment. The couple that owned the bakery came outside to see what all the fuss was about, so I explained our endeavor and asked them to give us a task.

We were instructed to spin around until we fell down. I laughed to myself, then took a deep breath and started my turns. The four and five-year-olds around me dropped quickly, but the older, more experienced spinners were still going strong as I realized that I was about to fall down. I had intended to "fall down" before I got too dizzy, but spinning on the cobbled street with my arms spread wide and my hair fanning out around me gave me such a feeling of carefree abandon that I kept going without thinking. I attempted to sink to the ground gracefully, but someone caught me beneath my arms and lowered me carefully into a sitting position. He crouched behind me, using one hand to support my back as the other rested on my arm.

Did my guards think I couldn't handle a simple children's game? I laughed as my head continued to drift. "You needn't have done that. I'm perfectly fine." I glanced up just in time to catch Marin as she stumbled, giggling, into my lap. She sprawled across my legs and I watched as her eyes tried to focus on the guard behind me.

My head had almost stopped spinning when Marin grinned up at the man behind me and asked, "Mr. Gavin, did you see me twirling?" The smile slipped from my face. It was Gavin who perched behind me with a hand on my back.

I wanted to jump up and put as much distance between myself and *Mr.* Gavin as possible, but I was still slightly dizzy. Fine. I would crawl away if that were what it took. But Marin was still happily draped across me, giggling as she watched the upside-down view of the other children afforded her as her head lolled back over one of my arms.

I arched my back forward, hoping he would drop his hand away. He didn't. Instead I saw his hand, clutching my cloak, as he laid it beside me. "You left this," he murmured, and I flinched away. His voice sounded much too close. I closed my eyes, waiting for him to leave while cringing away from the warmth spreading through me. There was nothing to say. I just wanted him away from me. It was too hard and I loved him too much. Marin sat up in my arms at the same time I felt Gavin stand up, his hand brushing through my hair as he rose.

Marin put her hands on my cheeks, "What's wrong, Princess Ari?" I opened my eyes and struggled to smile into her sweet face as Gavin moved away.

"Nothing," I lied, trying to ignore the feel of his hand that still lingered on my skin. I distracted myself by watching people as they tried to weave their way through the maze of sprawling children. For a moment I wondered if we were causing trouble, but then I noted the smiles on each of their faces as they stepped over limbs and torsos. They didn't mind. I finally pulled myself together enough to gather the children around me for one last clue.

Chapter Seventeen

AFTER SPENDING SO much time in the village, palace life seemed even worse. My life lacked a sense of purpose inside the palace. The only occasions of note were the many parties requiring my presence. I attended mechanically. I sipped my drink and joined in conversations and tried to use the time to observe people, to try and make sense of the life I lived. I took my turn spinning around the grand hall. Dancing had been so ingrained into my person that it took no thought. My dancing was flawless regardless of where my thoughts were.

Tonight's party was for Jensa and Prince Goran. He had proposed and she had accepted—not because she loved him, but because she could think of no practical reason to say no. He was an amiable person, a good prince; that was all she required. I should have been happy that she seemed happy, or at least content. But I couldn't help thinking of my own betrothal, and what would have happened if I had gone along with my father's plan. I knew, absolutely, I would have been miserable. But I also knew that Jensa and I had very different temperaments, and so I hoped, I *hoped* she would find happiness, that she would grow to love her fiancé.

This celebration had been hastily pulled together. Goran had proposed after the ball held for Lorraina's sixteenth birthday. Our guests were more than happy to stay a few extra days when my parents decided to throw the event together. No one objected to prolonging the revelries.

Unfortunately, the short notice didn't allow much time for new gowns to be made. Thus I found myself stepping into a dress I had been avoiding ever since it had been presented to me. It was red, and oh, it was ghastly. Instead of a deep red, or even a rich red, it was just bright red and it practically hurt my eyes.

After Gretchen had laced me into it, we both stood before the mirror, frowning at my reflection. "Well," Gretchen began, trying to sound enthusiastic, "It's...very..."

"It's awful."

"Absolutely horrifying, Miss."

I couldn't help laughing. Though there was nothing about my appearance that I wanted to laugh about, it was so wonderful to have Gretchen be brutally honest with me that I laughed nonetheless. "I can't believe the seamstresses think this dress is flattering on me." I turned to see the back of the dress. "They must be utterly mad."

Gretchen stood back to examine me for a moment. "You know... it might not be so terrible if it weren't entirely red."

"Well, there isn't much I can do about that now."

"Actually..." Gretchen murmured as she walked toward my wardrobe. She rifled around until she found a wide black sash belonging to one of my other dresses. "Let's try this," she suggested, and proceeded to wrap it around me in several different ways until she was satisfied. It ended up wrapping from just under my bust on my right side, down to the left side of my waist, where it crossed over, and then around to my right hip. There we tied it and let the ends hang down to mingle with the folds of my skirt.

"I still hate the red," Gretchen proclaimed as she stepped back, "but it's much better."

I agreed. The shade of red still made me wince, but the black made the dress dramatic instead of gaudy. "Are people allowed to wear black to an engagement celebration?" I wondered aloud.

Her brow scrunched together. "You do look a little like you're mourning something."

I smiled at that, but then found myself frowning as I thought of the different losses I could be mourning. I decided not to dwell on it and so said lightly, "I'm mourning the enjoyment I could have had at this affair if it weren't for Jeshua."

Gretchen wrinkled her nose in distaste, then went about setting my hair.

Jeshua hadn't gone away as I had hoped. My refusal of his affections had been conveyed to him in no uncertain terms. Unfortunately he seemed determined to become my shadow. He had come, in all his pomp, to Lorraina's birthday. He had flirted as usual with my sisters, all the while keeping his eyes riveted on me. I tried my best to ignore him, but he kept popping up at my side to engage me in conversation or ask me to dance. This evening's festivities just gave him one more opportunity to make uncomfortable advances toward me.

When I was ready, I proceeded to the top of the stairs and took a deep, fortifying breath. I made my regal entrance and took a turn around the ballroom, greeting guests and trying to be sociable. Then I found an out of the way spot at the edge of the ballroom and tried to relax.

My reprieve was short lived as Jeshua sauntered toward me. I squared my shoulders, ready for battle.

"My dear Ariella," he said loudly, approaching me with that unmistakable air of confidence. "You do look ravishing tonight." He plucked my hand from my side and forced a kiss on it.

"Prince Jeshua," I responded, giving only the slightest nod.

He kept my hand, though I pulled on it with some effort. "You have not been dancing much this evening. I think I must save you from being a wall flower."

"Chivalrous of you, but I assure you, I am content to simply watch."

"An amiable response, to be sure," he said as he yanked on my hand, forcing me onto the dance floor. "But I don't believe it for a moment." He pulled me abruptly into dance position and I had to will myself not to stamp directly on his foot. Instead I held my frame rigid, turning my face away.

"Oh, Prince Jeshua, how little you know me." I kept my voice pleasant, but allowed an undercurrent of malice to flow through my words.

He pulled me a little closer, breathing on my neck. "On the contrary, Ariella, I know you better than you know yourself." He finally moved us into the flow of dancers and I managed to create a little more distance between us. I wondered if he were trying to irritate me, or if he thought this domineering behavior would somehow endear him to me.

I remained stiff throughout the entire dance, refusing either to smile or to look at him. I had grown tired of these games; I was tired of him trying to undermine my ability to choose for myself. He seemed to believe my affections could be forced from me.

As the last notes of the song were played, he stepped back, holding only my right hand and bowed while I sank into a curtsy. As I rose, he leered at me. "Another dance, perhaps?" He tried to pull me back toward him, but I jerked my hand away.

"No, thank you," I said flatly. "I need some air."

He gave a regal bow and smirked as I brushed past him. He infuriated me.

As I glided at a ridiculously quick pace toward an exit, I found myself flanked by Lorraina and Marilee.

"In a hurry, Ariella?" Lorraina asked in a tone that hinted at being snide.

"I just need some air."

Marilee latched onto my arm, trying to slow me to her pace. "Why didn't you stay to dance with Jeshua? Or at least talk with him?" she asked in her usual conspiratorial tone.

"The dance was finished and we had nothing to discuss."

Lorraina grabbed my upper arm and made me stop. "You are being rude, Ariella. Father would disapprove. Jeshua is a great friend to our family and for some reason he's chosen to pay you special attention. I think you need to apologize," she declared, her nose in the air.

Typical Lorraina, trying to dictate the behavior of others. "If you're so concerned about Jeshua, why don't you go speak with him? I'm sure you'll be more than polite."

Her lips pursed and her nostrils flared. "All right then, I will." And she turned to seek out Jeshua, while I breathed a sigh of relief.

"Honestly, Ariella, I don't understand you sometimes." I turned to Marilee, who had curious bewilderment written on her face. I had to smile; Marilee could always be depended on to lighten the mood.

I just shrugged. "What is there to understand?"

"Sometimes you act as though you don't even like Jeshua." She took my arm again and we made our way toward the exit while I puzzled over her response.

"Marilee," I finally said. "I don't like him." Was that not obvious?

Her eyes widened and she leaned in to whisper in my ear. "You mean you aren't just making him chase you?"

"No, I'm really not," I assured her. It would have been amusing, if I weren't so tired of everyone's mistaken assumptions.

"Well," she huffed, and then seemed to have an idea. "Do you mind if I try for him?"

This time I couldn't help being amused and a smile broke across my face. "Be my guest."

"And let's not tell any of the others. I don't want any of them getting the same idea." She gave me a warning look, as if this were the most serious of subjects. To her, it probably was, and I couldn't help but wrap my arms around her.

"Oh, Marilee," I let out a laughing sigh. "You always make me smile." I pulled back to look at her bewildered face, but didn't bother explaining. I just linked my arm, once again, with hers and we finally made it out into the fresh air.

After wandering outside with Marilee for a few minutes I returned in a better mood, ready, once again, to face whatever or whomever came my way. Or so I thought.

I was speaking with Jensa for the first time that evening. She appeared genuinely excited about her upcoming marriage and we were having a good talk until Goran joined us—with Jeshua at his side. It surprised me when they approached together. I had never had the sense they liked each other. We were only together for a moment before Goran escorted Jensa away, with a gentle hand on the small of her back.

Jeshua's hand closed around my upper arm and he immediately started pulling me with him as he murmured, "A moment, if you please, Princess."

He had caught me off guard and succeeded in pulling me into an adjacent chamber before I could get my bearings.

"Let go!" I finally managed as he pushed the door shut. He unhanded me with a patronizing smile and positioned himself directly in front of the door. My chest tightened. "What is it, Jeshua?"

He stood with his feet apart, hands clasped behind his back. "I thought it was time you and I worked through this misunderstanding we seem to be having."

"What misunderstanding?"

"Your father seems to be under the misapprehension that you've refused my offer of marriage."

My nostrils flared. "It's not a misapprehension, Jeshua. I *have* refused your offer."

He smiled. "Now, dear, you know that's not how these things work."

"But it is how *this* is going to work. I'm not marrying you."

He gave a patient sigh and advanced toward me. "Ariella. Forgive me, but I have put a great deal of effort into our relationship, and I'm not going to allow you to destroy it because of a childish tantrum."

He continued to advance and I backed up—I couldn't help it—for though he spoke in niceties, as though placating a small child, a threatening undertone ran through his words. I tried to speak calmly. "We don't have a relationship, Jeshua. And this isn't a tantrum. This is my decision."

He reached toward me. "I think you need to reconsider."

I pulled my arm from his clutching fingers and dodged around him, heading for the door. "There's nothing to consider."

I hurried away, reaching for the door, but he got to me first. He spun me around and then took hold of both my upper arms, pinning me against the door. I stared at him, frantic, as he smiled congenially. "I think it's only fair you give me a chance to change your mind."

"Fine." My voice quivered as I spoke in desperation. "Say your piece and let's be done with it."

One eyebrow twitched upward. "I wasn't planning on talking." His hands relinquished their vice grip on my arms and went instead to the sides of my neck as he pulled my face to meet his. He smashed his mouth into mine, kissing me with a ferocity I did not wish to understand, his lips trying to open mine. I used both my hands to push up on his chin, heaving his face away from me. When his grip broke, I slapped him soundly. His head snapped to the side, but he did not bring a hand to his cheek or even turn his head to look at me. He just smiled—actually smiled—and said, "My apologies, Princess," before stepping back and gesturing for me to leave.

I fled the room, trying to get a handle on what had just happened. He had assaulted me while speaking as if we were having afternoon tea.

I tried to wipe my lips free of the disgusting feel of his mouth on mine as I made my way up the grand staircase. When I reached the top, my breath was stuttering and shallow—and it had nothing to do with climbing the stairs. I sank down on the top step, leaned against the stone pillar and sat, feeling vulnerable and exposed. One oddity kept coming to mind: he had released my arms when he kissed me. If he had truly wanted to force himself on me, then why let me go? The way he had held me almost gently was reminiscent of a lover's embrace. It was as though he truly endeavored to change my mind, honestly trying to make me want him. It was demented and I was so tired of it.

Why me? Why, when he could take his pick of any of my sisters, did he choose to fixate on me, the one who did not want him?

I studied my hands, which sat trembling in my lap, and noticed the hideous red of my dress, contrasted with the black sash. I ran the silk through my fingers, musing that black seemed eerily appropriate at this moment.

"What are you doing wallowing on the floor, Ariella?" I looked up to see Lorraina and Lylin coming up the stairs.

I considered telling them nothing was amiss, then felt the tears in my eyes. I blinked them away and tried to say matter-of-factly, "Jeshua and I argued."

"A lovers' spat," Lorraina sneered.

"No, it wasn't a lovers spat! I don't like him."

"Then pray tell why a quarrel with him would make you so upset." She sat down a step below me, off to my right, and seemed truly interested. Lylin, who had yet to say anything, sank into a sitting position as well.

I didn't want to talk about it. Or at least I didn't want to need to talk about it. But with two sisters awaiting my answer, the words tumbled from my mouth. "He tried to force me to kiss him."

"He did what?" Lylin exclaimed, alarmed. I was about to reassure her when Lorraina spoke up in her usual tone.

"Oh please," she scoffed. "Do you really believe you are so irresistible that every man is trying to seduce you? You are extraordinarily vain." She rose and swept down the staircase, leaving me with a stark reminder of why I didn't confide in my sisters. It was a wonder she had bothered to ask in the first place.

I stared at my lap, until Lylin moved to sit right beside me. I had almost forgotten she was there. "Did he really do that?" she asked quietly.

I put an arm around her shoulders and rested my cheek on top of her head. "He was just trying to make a point."

We sat in silence until Lylin spoke again. "You want to know a secret?"

I pulled away to look at her. "Of course."

"I hate these parties," she said, sounding disgusted.

I laughed out loud. That bit of honesty, with which I wholeheartedly agreed, was just what I needed. I stood and offered her my hand. "Come along. Let's endure the rest of the evening together."

Chapter Eighteen

THE NEXT MORNING, I went into the village earlier than usual, anxious to make up for lost time. Because of the impromptu nature of the party, I had been forced to postpone previous commitments.

As I approached Jordyn's home, he was playing in the yard with a stick in his hand as his mother watched from the porch.

"Princess Ari!" four-year-old Jordyn hollered. He threw down the stick, yelling over his shoulder, "Mama, the princess is here!" apparently entirely oblivious to the fact that she too could see me. He ran to me in his usual manner, ducking under my cloak and circling behind my back before coming around the other side with his arms reaching up around my waist.

"Katrin," I greeted his mother, "I'm so sorry I wasn't able to come yesterday."

She waved my apology away. "Don't you worry about it, Princess. I hear there was a quite a to-do up at the palace."

"Yes, there was." I paused to help Jordyn retrieve a treat from my satchel. "But I was still amazed it took the entire day to prepare for it."

"We also hear they were celebrating an engagement," Katrin had a knowing look on her face. "Have you been keepin' secrets from us, Princess?" She raised her eyebrows in anticipation, but I just laughed.

"I may have a few secrets, Katrin, but none of them involve being married any time soon."

"Is that so?" She looked disappointed. "Well then, I suppose that fellow who works the grounds around the palace doesn't know as much as he thought he did."

"I'm sorry?" Surely she didn't mean…

"The chatter among the children was that Mr. Gavin, who works the grounds, had told them they were celebrating your engagement to Prince Jeshua up at the castle last evening."

The accusation shocked me, lodging in my throat. "No," I managed to respond, gathering my thoughts. "It's Princess Jensa who is marrying Prince Goran." I was taken aback, not only by the idea that Gavin assumed the engagement would be mine, but also that he would share his suspicions with the townspeople. For the moment, though, I tried to let it go so I could have a coherent conversation. "Katrin, would you like me to invite Jordyn to come along with me today so you can rest?"

She put her hands to her swollen midsection and sighed, relieved. "As long as you don't think he'll be a bother."

"Oh, he's never a bother," I assured her, then raised my voice so that Jordyn, who was fighting some shrubs with his stick, could hear me. "Jordyn, would you like to come along with me today?"

He stopped mid-swing and looked at me, wide-eyed. "Oh, could I, Princess? Mama, could I? Princess Ari wants me to go with her! Can I go?"

"Yes, Jordyn," Katrin agreed as she rose to her feet with some difficulty, "but you must be on your best behavior and do just as the princess says."

"Oh, I will, Mama, I'll be so good!" And with that he grabbed my hand, said, "Let's go!" and started pulling me toward the gate.

"Rest well, Katrin," I hollered back to her. She just smiled and went inside.

As we continued down the lane, Jordyn put his hand in mine, swinging it back and forth as we walked. "Well, Jordyn, what shall we do today?"

He tipped his head back, crinkling his nose as he thought. "Umm…can we go to the bakery?"

I laughed. Jordyn was always thinking about food. "Not now, but perhaps we'll stop by later. Would you like to visit Marin with me?"

"All right," he agreed with a shrug.

Marin only lived two streets away, but on the way over I received more than ten congratulatory greetings from various women, children and even a few men. Each time, I stopped to explain that it was not I, but my sister who would marry not Jeshua, but Prince Goran.

"Well, I'll be," was the reply from Marin's mother, Maggie. "Marin made it sound as though it were absolutely certain."

"Yes, well," I said, exhausted from the repeated explanations on my way over, "he was very much mistaken."

"Well then, I'm certainly glad to know we'll be keepin' you for a while longer."

"That makes two of us," I admitted with a smile.

She smiled sweetly and hooked her arm through mine as we walked toward the river together, where Marin was playing with some other children. As we went, I received more well wishes from more townspeople, but instead of having to explain myself, Maggie took over.

"Oh, don't be congratulating this one quite yet. Turns out it's Princess Jensa that's to be married. Princess Ari will be free for a while yet."

"Well then," one man said, "give Princess Jensa our best regards."

"I will," I replied. And so it went until we arrived by the river, where several children were playing on the banks. I realized as Jordyn went to join in the fun that I knew each one of them by name. They were among the poorest and tended to band together.

As Jordyn approached Tanner, a boy several years his senior, I heard him say, "Hey Jordyn, I thought your Mama said you were too young to come out by yourself."

"I'm not by myself; Princess Ari brought me."

At the mention of my name, all seven children turned toward me, then made a mad dash in my direction. "Princess Ari! Princess Ari!" I quickly moved my satchel behind me so they wouldn't crush its contents as they swarmed around me. I received all their hugs gratefully and kissed each child on the cheek, making the older boys turn red.

"Gracious sakes," I said, after their unusually enthusiastic greeting. "You'd think you all hadn't seen me in years with a greeting like that."

"Is it true?" Lessia asked.

"You gettin' married, Princess?" Marin inquired, crinkling her nose.

"To a *boy*?" Sophie's wide eyes declared her astonishment.

I saw Maggie about to come to my defense, but I wanted to answer these little ones myself. "Now, where did you hear such a thing as that? I'm not getting married at all."

"You're not?" Tanner asked.

"I'm not."

"But Mr. Gavin told us you were gonna marry some Prince from over yonder." This came from Tanner's brother Henry.

"Well, don't you think if I were going to get married I'd tell you all myself?" The looks on their faces told me this was, indeed, how they expected things to be done.

"Besides," Jordyn spoke up with the authority of one who had heard the explanation many times. "It's a whole other Prince that's marryin' Princess Ari's sister."

"Ohhh," the children said in unison, as if this were all the explanation they needed. They then proceeded to rifle around in my satchel in search of the goodies I always brought. I noticed that a small crowd had gathered and that the news of my not being engaged was quickly circulating. Hopefully by the time I finished entertaining the children, I would be able to walk back to the palace without receiving any more congratulations.

The children and I ended up playing run-around games in the knee high grasses growing along the river. At one point I feared I had lost Lessia and Sophie, but then heard them giggling and discovered their hiding place in the grass. The games relaxed me, but once I had delivered the children back to their homes, I found ample time to get worked up again.

My guards left me as we entered the palace grounds and I made my way into the gardens. Coming here was unusual for me, but I was in the mood for a fight and knew exactly with whom I meant to have it.

It didn't take me long to find Gavin. He worked on a garden path alongside another groundskeeper. As I approached at my irritated pace, he looked up, startled by my appearance. I gave him a meaningful glance without slowing down and kept walking toward the maze.

I went straight to our favorite garden room, knowing he would follow. I was in the process of discarding my cloak when he came tentatively through the hedges, rubbing dirt from his hands. I dropped my cloak on a stone bench and threw my satchel down with it, not looking at him, as he stood at the entrance, uncertain.

"Princess?" he ventured when I continued to stare at my things, hands on my hips.

I turned to glare at him. "So, I am engaged, am I?"

His brows shot up. "Aren't you?"

"No!" I exclaimed, wondering how he could truly believe me capable of such a thing.

"But," he floundered. "Jeshua is here, he has been courting you for years, your father promised you to him—I heard it myself, remember?" Of course I remembered. "There was an engagement celebration. If you aren't—"

"I have six sisters, Gavin." I cut him off. "And Jeshua was, by no means, the only nobleman visiting for Lorraina's sixteenth. My Father managed to work his magic on Goran and Jensa."

"You're not engaged?" He still sounded stunned.

"Of course I'm not. I said no." My voice was harsh. "I'm glad to know you have so much faith in me." I glared at him, insulted that he would think me so weak. "Didn't I tell you? Didn't I say it would never happen?"

He looked down, penitent. "Ella, I'm—Princess, I'm sorry, I should have known…" He drifted off and I could see that while he felt sorry for hurting me, his dominant emotion was relief. It hurt to see him so relieved by this news. It made me think he still cared about me—the same way I cared about him.

"Yes, you should have known. And you certainly shouldn't have told the entire village."

"I didn't tell the entire village," he said in a quiet monotone.

I narrowed my eyes. "You mentioned it to a group of children; surely you didn't think they would keep it to themselves?"

He seemed about to retort, then thought better of it. I realized how odd this must seem to him. I had avoided him at all costs and now he would think I had sought him out to reprimand him. My intent had been to take to task a former friend of mine, but it must have looked to him as if I were scolding him in my official capacity as a royal. My suspicions were confirmed when he spoke.

"My apologies, Princess. It was not my intent to spread rumors. I believed I was speaking the truth and sharing the good news." He kept his voice carefully controlled and entirely flat. That irritated me even more. I had wanted an argument.

"Oh yes, the loveliest of news. The princess is going to marry a leech whom she hates because she has no spine and no independent thought. I'm sure you thought I was simply thrilled at the prospects, since just a few months ago I told you just how loath I was to—" I stopped myself. I didn't know how to handle this. I had thought that yelling at him would make me feel better, but as the minutes went by, I just became more aware of him standing there, looking at me with dirt on his knees and hair falling into his eyes.

This had clearly been a very bad idea. I picked up my things. "Never mind, it doesn't matter. I shouldn't have yelled at you no matter how much you deserve it."

He still stood in the middle of the only path leading out of this garden room and did not move as I approached. "Excuse me," I said, but he just stood there.

"Ella—"

I met his eyes. "Oh, so it's Ella again, is it? No more of this titled nonsense—"

"Princess—"

"Don't call me that!" I said in frustration. I wanted him to move his rather large form out of my way so I could escape. It had been impulsive and stupid to try to talk to him. I'd thought my anger would sustain me.

"What shall I call you then?" He took the tiniest step toward me as he said it.

"Nothing. Don't call me anything. I just need to go now." I used my satchel as a barrier as I pushed past him, determined to get away, though I felt something very real pulling me in his direction. I made it only a few steps before his hand wrapped around my arm, pulling me to a stop as he moved to block my path once more. His eyes searched mine, making me swallow.

"Do you hate me for not fighting for you?"

His question shocked me, not because he asked, but because of what he was admitting. My shoulders fell and I met his eyes, answering with as much honesty as he had shown by asking. "Sometimes, I really wish I could."

"Ella—" His voice caressed my name.

"No." I stopped him from saying anything more as I pulled my arm from his grasp. "You come back here, engaged, and have the audacity to accuse me of accepting Jeshua?" My lip quivered as I stepped back. "How dare you! I am not the one who left you; *you* left *me*."

His face was stricken. He opened his mouth to respond but I ran him over. "Just go away," I begged. "Please, Gavin, just go."

"Ella…" His tone was pleading.

"What do you want me to say?" I snapped. "What exactly would you like to hear from me, Gavin?"

He opened his mouth, but ended up shrugging slightly, unable to come up with anything.

"Go away," I begged him, then rushed on, hoping to quicken his departure before I lost the last shreds of my composure. "I don't want to be having this conversation. I don't want to stand here, knowing what I know and feeling how I feel with you here to watch." My chin quivered as I watched his emotions play out on his face. "Please," I whispered. "Go. Away."

He still looked at me in that horribly familiar way. I hoped he would just leave, and yet I couldn't help wanting him to stay. I wanted to argue with him more. I wanted him to hurt. I wanted him to know just how much he had hurt me.

"It wasn't my choice to leave, Ella. You know that. You know I wouldn't have left, but they made me leave." I heard in his voice the anguish I had wished upon him and it tore at my heart.

"I wasn't talking about then!" He winced, knowing exactly what I meant. "You're here now, and you don't want me."

"I do want you, Ella." He said it quietly, as though it were a simple fact. "I do, but——"

"Don't say that." My anger was quiet, but he heard me clearly.

"It's true."

"It's not!" I held on to my anger, hoping it would give me strength. "If it were true you wouldn't be marrying someone else."

"You are a princess." He raised his voice as though this fact should have made me understand.

"I was a princess when you kissed me a year and a half ago. You chose to ignore my title; we *both* made that choice." There was a ringing silence as I felt an irrational calm settle over me. "You were the one choice I made for myself. And that one choice was taken away from me, because the night I realized I was in love with you was the same night you left."

He reached out as if to touch me. "I hated leaving you——"

"And then you came back." My voice was suddenly strong, accusing. "And you came—and you found me—and you stood there—

and told me of your engagement—so calmly." I was incredulous, wondering. "And you didn't care that I was still in love with you." I stared at him, letting my words hang in the air between us, letting him feel the grief emanating from me. "You should have just stayed away."

He stepped forward, reaching for me, but I recoiled and he stopped himself. I could not let him touch me now, because if he did, I wouldn't be able to let go.

Chapter Nineteen

I STARED AT him, wary. He hadn't lowered his arms, hadn't retreated. I saw his determination just before he moved toward me again, and in one swift movement he had his arms around my waist and his mouth pressed to mine. He enveloped me with his entire being. He kissed me. Oh, how he kissed me. I was stunned, shocked by the feelings coursing through me. My body reacted before my mind even knew what was happening. I dropped my satchel and wrapped my arms around his neck, just wanting to be close to him again. This was nothing like the way we had kissed before. Then we had both been tentative, our feelings more child-like, sweet and delicate. But this? This was entirely different. Suddenly his assertion that he wanted me was more than just words. And so I responded with all the desperation, all of the missing him and wanting him and hurting for him that I had been doing for the past year and a half. I poured all of the angst and anger and love I had for him into his lips as I kissed him back.

I felt myself spinning, spiraling down into something blissful. I wanted so desperately to sink into it and just be…happy.

But he wasn't mine, and so I sought for the strength of will to stop myself when I only wanted to hold on to him, to feel his arms surrounding me. I wanted to keep him for myself. But I knew he would not let me keep him, and in that I found my resolve.

I made myself unwind my arms from around him, and managed to cram them into the nonexistent space between us. I shoved him away. It took all of my physical strength to release myself from his hold, pushing away his face and his chest and his arms and his hands as they reached for me when I stepped back. But I did it, letting out a cry as I turned my back on him. If I looked at him, I would be undone, and it had taken every rational particle of my being to make myself let go of him. I could feel myself being almost physically dragged back in his direction as my breathing filled my ears just above the sound of my pulse. I focused on the feel of the breeze on my wet cheeks and the rhythm of my breathing.

"Ella?" he asked breathlessly from behind me.

"You are engaged." It was all I could say—the only thing that could make me stay away from him. *You are not mine. You are not mine. You are not mine.* But, oh, how I wanted him. It hurt to be away from him.

There was a moment of silence before he asked quietly, "And what if I weren't?"

The question caught me so off guard that I turned to him. "What if you weren't what? Engaged?"

"Yes. If I weren't engaged—what then? What would we do?"

It was the question I had avoided asking myself for the past year. What then? Could we even consider the possibility of marriage? And though I had never let myself consciously think about it, I knew there was only one way I could answer.

"I don't know." I pulled in a stuttering breath, feeling as though I were falling apart at the seams.

Never had I felt more alone than I did at that moment—standing in front of Gavin, trying desperately not to cry. He stood only feet from me, and yet the loneliness in that moment surpassed anything before or after. I wanted to reach out to him; I needed to be able to reach out to him. But reaching out to him was wrong. So I stood there, suffocating in loneliness.

But even worse—he did reach out to me. He approached slowly and wrapped me in his arms. I suppose he was waiting for me to cry or pull away, waiting for me to react in some way. And if I had been smart, if I had been thinking clearly, I would have pulled away the moment he approached me. I would have fled his presence as quickly as possible.

Instead I let him hold me, let myself breathe in his presence. But I had to let him go and so I started to pull away. It was the moment of impending separation that nearly did me in: to go away from him, knowing I could never go back, knowing that there would never be anyone else who would give me this feeling. If I was going away, I wanted to be selfish—just once. I wanted to make him feel what I felt. My head was tucked against his shoulder, so if I lifted my face toward him, I could kiss him one last time.

But I didn't do it. I lifted my head, I met his eyes, I moved toward him. Then he moved toward me and I came to my senses. He would have kissed me back—he would not save me from myself. So I dragged my face away from his, my eyes closed, reprimanding myself. I had more strength than this. I had more discipline. For a moment I listened to the sound of Gavin's breathing, still so close to me before I took one step back, and then another. He stood there, defeated and sad, but he said nothing. I bent to pick up my bag but as I walked past him—ready to leave him behind—he caught my wrist. "Ella—"

"Gavin," I whispered, cutting him off before he could ask anything of me. He turned to study my stoic face as I held his gaze.

"Yes?" he asked, his voice husky.

"Let me go," I pleaded in a whisper. And I saw in his eyes that he understood.

His face crumpled slightly as he groaned, "I can't."

My teeth clenched and my eyes narrowed. "You cannot hold us both."

He abruptly released me as if my words had physically struck him. I walked away, refusing to let myself cry.

The pain continued, but my anger had taken over. He wanted me. He had come out and said it. And by the anguish I saw in his face, which so closely mirrored mine, I could guess that it wasn't just want; it was need, and love.

Why was he marrying her? Why would he do that to me? To himself? To her? He must have had his reasons, though I couldn't fathom what they might be. Then his question came back to me. *"If I weren't engaged, what then? What would we do?"* I had always thought that if he ever came within my reach again, that if we were ever given a second chance, that we would know what to do—that somehow we would figure it out. But life didn't work that way. I knew that; I had known it for a long time. Perhaps we always think we are the exception, that somehow matters of the heart will magically resolve themselves and come forth triumphant of their own accord.

Amazing how, at the age of seventeen, there were still childish dreams and ideas to give up. Love did not always conquer all.

And so I was left to find a way to conquer love. Heaven help me.

***

✳✳✳

I didn't see Gavin during the next week, for which I was grateful. And yet I had the inexcusable desire to see him, though I couldn't stand the thought of another encounter, knowing it would all come to nothing— nothing but a quickening of my pulse and a dead weight in my stomach when it was all over.

It had been ten days since our heart-wrenching encounter, and each day I awoke with the memory of his kiss so fresh in my mind that it nearly suffocated me. I awoke to the knowledge that even though it was Gavin, I had still kissed a man bound to another. And so each day I went into the village and did all I could to not think about him.

I stood in the courtyard, waiting for my guards to join me, when next I saw him. A movement at the corner of my eye caught my attention and I turned to see Gavin. He had just rounded the corner of the castle when he stopped, having seen me. He stood there, seeming to debate whether to go forward or back, before resolutely turning and walking away. I kept my lips tight and my eyes wide as I tried not to let my emotions overtake me.

"Your Highness?" I turned to see Wyatt looking at me with

concern and realized I had pushed a hand into my chest, trying to dull the ache piercing through my heart.

"I just need a moment," I said, trying to shake away my tears.

"You are not well, Princess." There was obvious stress in his voice.

"I am well enough."

"Princess?"

I tried holding my breath, to keep the pain inside, to control it somehow. But it would not be controlled. It flowed freely throughout my being, tearing me to shreds.

"I'm sorry, Wyatt, but I need to postpone my visit. Will you go ahead and tell Taya that I will come this afternoon instead?"

"Of course, Highness." I turned to go inside and saw Rowan coming toward us. Before he could ask anything, I waved him off and Wyatt stepped in to explain. I felt their eyes on me as I walked through the towering front doors, back into the castle.

An idea struck me and I turned toward the library, determined to focus my emotion on a task. I locked the door behind me and made my way past my usual chair, past all my beloved books of fiction and adventure. I went to the back wall lined with volumes of legal books. Laws, both past and present. Books filled with royal decrees.

I wanted to know for myself what was wrong with my having a relationship with Gavin, what boundary I had crossed that gave my father the right to keep him from me. Gavin seemed sure that the wall between us was impenetrable, but I wanted to *know*.

My morning slipped by and I returned the books to their shelves without having found an answer. I ate my mid-day meal quickly and met Wyatt and Rowan in the entry hall for my postponed visit to the village.

As we walked once more through the gate and down the path to Taya's house, I contemplated what I had learned that morning.

The answer to my original question had eluded me, but it hadn't been a waste of time either. I had learned a lot about the laws governing our land and the reasons for them. But it wasn't enough. And so I returned to the library as soon as the evening meal finished. I shut myself in and continued to pour over any book or document I thought might hold the answers I sought.

And then I found it. Late into the night, after my eyes had started to water from exhaustion, I found it.

And the answer was this: nothing. There was nothing wrong with my having a relationship with any citizen in the land. I could marry him. If he wanted me, I could marry him. I would not be able to take my mother's title. When Mia and Jensa had decided to marry, there had been serious discussion about whether they would be the one to take the throne. Mia and her husband did not feel that the role of king and queen was right for them. Jensa would marry Prince Goran, who was already slated to take his father's throne. My parents did not want to force any of us onto the throne, so it had become the unspoken expectation that each of us would consider it when our marriage became imminent. If I wanted to be queen, I would have to marry nobility. But being queen had never been my aspiration. I only wanted to live a life of my choosing.

Knowing this gave me a great sense of relief. It left me feeling empowered.

But it didn't change anything. It didn't matter that the law of the land allowed me to choose Gavin. He had chosen someone else. Not only that, but even if he broke his engagement, what of my father? I couldn't imagine that the king would ever be inclined to allow his daughter to marry the gardener whom he had already banned from his presence once.

That was my reality. The law was not an obstacle. Our situation was not utterly impossible, just mostly impossible. I was free to do what I would; society's opinion hadn't meant much to me in a long time, anyway. However, my father was still king and could stand in my way. And Gavin had already made his choice. He would marry his bride; he would live his life and leave me in his past.

I would go on. I would live my life and do my best to leave him in my past. It was time—time to stop crying, time to stop allowing my heart to break repeatedly. It was time to find a way to be happy without him.

And I would find a way to be happy; I would find a way to make myself better because of him. Because despite the way it had turned out, he was still the one who had led me to myself and given me the courage to take my own path—the path no one else had seen or even bothered to look for.

I took in a long breath, closed my eyes, and tried to release Gavin along with the air leaving my lungs. It was time.

Chapter Twenty

SIX WEEKS LATER, I walked up the deserted, rain sodden path that led to the palace gate. The path was quickly turning to mud, and my guards fought to guide me over the slippery ground while sheltering me from the rain. We should have come back earlier, but I had been determined to make sure each of my small friends returned to their homes before I returned to mine. Plus, I was trying to stay away from the castle as much as possible because Jeshua has shown up last night—unannounced.

At the edge of the village, I noticed a cloaked figure huddled against a wall. I was about to look away when he lifted his face. Gavin. My foot slipped, forcing Rowan to keep me from falling. I thanked him and regained my footing before peering back to see Gavin still looking at me. He gave me a nod of acknowledgement and I wondered at his determined stance. I would have thought that he would be less inclined to look out for me after our argument, yet there he stood.

My thoughts distracted me and we had only walked about halfway from the edge of the village to the gate when three men, dressed in the cloaks of commoners, made their way toward us, carrying bundles of wood on their backs. Their faces were down, their hoods drawn up to protect them from the rain. As we approached, two went to walk around us to my left and the third went around to my right. When the man to my right slipped in the mud, dropping his bundle, Wyatt bent to assist him as Rowan and I paused to make sure all was well.

It happened then. I saw the fallen man rise up and simultaneously felt Rowan's hand ripped from my arm. In that moment I realized we were under attack, and in the next moment I saw that our assailants had won. It was quick and entirely silent. The three men had rendered both my guards unconscious. At least I hoped they were only unconscious. The horrifying thought crossed my mind that they could be dead. I turned away, hoping to flee, but felt arms wrap around me from behind. My assailant hauled me off my feet, dragging me away just as Gavin came into my line of vision.

"No!" I cried out, but a hand quickly silenced me and I watched in mute horror as Gavin grappled with one brute for only a moment before crumpling to the ground. Gavin was left lying in the mud as the two men turned toward me where I struggled in the third man's arms. Despite my thrashing, one of them forced a length of cloth between my teeth as the other caught my hands and bound them tightly with another length of cloth. The one who held me ignored my flailing and flung me over his shoulder, carrying me away. I raised my head and had a shaky view of Wyatt straining to gain his feet and falling back to the ground. My captors slipped swiftly into the trees and I was left to wonder what the fate of my guards and Gavin would be.

I felt my heart in my throat, where my voice should have been. I needed to scream. I should have screamed when my guards first fell, but everything had happened before I realized it was happening. And even though I knew any sound I made now would be muffled not only by the gag but by the rain as well, I pulled in a deep lung full of air and let it out in the longest, loudest, most piercing scream I could muster. A hand immediately covered my mouth, so I started flailing instead. Even if they didn't lose their grip, I would at least slow them down. The struggle ended abruptly as he flung me to the ground. I landed on my back, the air knocked out of me, as one man pinned my bound arms above my head and pushed one knee into my ribs, stopping any further struggle. He held a knife up in the space between us to discourage any more screams.

Not a word was spoken. I knew there were three, but I could only see the man kneeling on top of me. He held the knife against his lips in a silencing gesture. Staring at his face, he looked... stern. Not hateful or malicious or even threatening; just stern. His features in any other situation would have been disarming. He was clean with a neatly trimmed beard—the exact opposite of what I would have expected. Even his handling of me had not been violent, only powerful and controlling. He was not trying to hurt me.

And yet this was so much worse than my encounter with the drunk on the road. These men had planned; their actions were calculated. They were efficient and worked well together. They had an agenda, which meant that however this ended, it would not end soon and it would not end well.

My panic took over as I tried to look anywhere but at his calm, controlling face. My harried breathing finally reached my ears. I was wheezing, almost squealing as my lungs worked to pull in enough air against the restraint of a gag, my fear, and the large man pushing his knee into my ribs. When I planted my feet into the ground to try to push myself out from underneath him, he simply applied more steady pressure with his knee and shook his head, admonishing me.

I had to calm down. I could barely breathe through my panic, and now the cloth gag wedged between my teeth was becoming soaked along with the rest of me as the rain continued to fall. I tried to blink the rain out of my eyes and slow my breathing. It seemed clear that I would not be let up until I had no air to breathe, if necessary. I despised the idea that I might have to stop fighting, but I felt myself slipping toward a faint, and that would be even worse.

When I stilled, the man shifted positions and I tensed, wondering if he was finally going to hurt me. But he just leaned over me so the rain stopped pounding my face. Confusion almost overrode my terror. It made no sense—no sense for him to shelter me from the rain, no sense for him to stay perched on top of me, so close to where my guards had fallen. We hadn't made it far into the trees before I had screamed. Why was he content to keep me here?

In a flurry of motion, the man sheathed the knife and stood up, pulling me with him. I twisted away furiously, but he kept a steady iron grip on my arm. I lashed out with my feet, and his grip tightened so much that my eyes watered and a cry escaped my throat. I stopped my struggle and heard horse hooves. I turned, hoping to see castle guards. Instead, three horses emerged from the forest. Two carried the dark cloaked figures who had helped bind me, and the third held no rider. They stopped the riderless horse in front of us and hoisted me unceremoniously into the saddle, where I immediately sought to throw myself off again. Horses meant distance. But my captor quickly mounted behind me and used a rope to tie my bound hands to the saddle horn as I thrashed and pushed back against him. I started screaming again, but I was so out of breath I could barely make any noise. Then the galloping started beneath me, and my screams were choked off by the ragged sobs forcing their way out of my gagged mouth.

And still they said nothing. Not a threat, not an order, not a curse, and most certainly not a reason for why I was being carried away by three men who didn't look as though they fit into this nightmare.

As we rode, I started shivering uncontrollably, not only because of my emotional upheaval, but also because I was freezing. We were riding swiftly, and the wind and rain had no trouble finding their way beneath my cloak.

It surprised me when, after only a few minutes, we slowed. I had expected them to ride hard for hours, as far away from my home as they could get. I was also surprised when the man seated behind me took the opportunity to wrap my cloak more securely around me. I didn't understand.

My captors meandered for a couple of minutes, looking for something. I hoped it would take them a very long time to find it, because the less we moved, the closer I stayed to my home. I wondered if these men were fools or geniuses. Their actions were swift and intentional; they seemed to know exactly what they were doing and how to do it. And yet, as far as I could tell, we hadn't gone far at all. We were probably close to the northern roads leading to Tride. Were they madmen or masterminds?

We stopped. Perhaps they really were fools. We had come to a large and conspicuous tree. It was knotted with age and three times as wide as a man.

A rope hung from one of the high branches.

I thrashed wildly, trying to throw myself from the horse. I didn't care about hurting myself. My injuries certainly wouldn't matter once they had hanged me. But those inescapable arms restrained me once more, and when I started throwing the heels of my sturdy shoes back into his shins, he quickly used his own legs to pin mine to the side of the horse and threw his weight into my back, flattening me against the horse's neck. I groaned in pain and frustration as I felt his hands working with the rope that bound my hands to the saddle. I twisted my hands underneath me to make it harder for him. Between being tied to a horse and hanging from a tree, I wanted the horse.

But the reality was that I was entirely at this man's mercy. The rope loosened and he sat up, his arms like steel bands around my torso. He slid us from the horse and dragged me over to where his two comrades waited by the rope, all the while putting up with the barrage of kicks I inflicted on his lower legs. When we reached the tree, he unceremoniously released me and let me drop to the ground. If I tried to get up and run I would have no success. So instead I curled into a ball and locked my bound hands behind my neck, praying this would somehow deter them in their efforts to put a rope around it. Almost immediately, I felt a tugging on my hands and tensed. But the tugging never intensified, and after a moment it stopped. What was going on? Did they have to make a noose? Something touched the back of my neck and I tried to jerk away, but once again—beyond all reason—the movement wasn't violent. The gag loosened. I stayed still, waiting for their next move. The silence was making me crazy. They never spoke— not to me, not to each other. Only their footsteps reached my ears.

Keeping my arms locked around my head, I turned my face so I could see beneath my arm. They were back at the horses, about fifteen paces away. Two were mounted, and the one who seemed to be the leader—the one who had been physically restraining me the whole time—was standing by his mount, holding the reins and looking back at me. I uncurled and raised my head, prepared to duck back into my protective ball if need be, but they didn't move.

It made no sense. What were they doing? I had been their captive for all of ten minutes and now they were leaving?

I pushed the gag out of my mouth with my tongue and tried to swallow. They just stayed where they were, two on horses looking anxious to leave, the other on foot just staring at me. I pushed myself to a kneeling position and still they didn't move. I struggled to my feet, never allowing my eyes to leave them as I stumbled back several paces. They were still and silent. I turned my back on them so I could run, but after three steps my hands caught on something and I was jerked to a stop.

I had been so intent on keeping an eye on my captors that I hadn't noticed that the rope dangling from the tree was now tied to the cloth binding my wrists.

It made no *sense*! I turned back to my captors and saw the leader mounting his horse.

"Why am I here?" The question escaped my lips before I had made the decision to ask, but they just looked back at me with that maddening calm and started to turn their horses away. "What are you doing? Why am I here?" I yelled after them, but they just urged their horses forward. "Say something!" I screamed. My nerves were frayed, nearly gone. I felt my sanity slipping as I strained against the rope tethering me to an immovable tree.

The rain had let up, but the tree continued to shed moisture from its leaves. I blinked water out of my eyes, my mind spinning so fast that I had difficulty forming any coherent thoughts. They hadn't hurt me. They hadn't delivered me to somebody else. They hadn't asked me anything. They hadn't even left me gagged! I was just stuck to this tree until someone or something found me.

"Hello?" I yelled. I didn't know how deep into the forest they had taken me, but I really didn't think I was very far from the northern roads. "Hello? Is anyone out there?" I listened, but of course no response came. It was futile, but I kept yelling anyway. "I need help! Please, somebody! Hello?"

I thought I heard a movement somewhere off in the trees and screamed once more, as loud as I could. "HELP!"

Ringing silence met my ears, and then hoof beats. I strained to look toward the sound and saw a lone rider galloping toward me. My heart lifted for a moment until I recognized the cloaked rider. One of my captors had returned. I backed to the other side of the tree until the rope pulled against my wrists. He reined his mount to a halt, dismounted, and walked toward me, pulling out another length of cloth.

So they didn't want me yelling. "Help! Help! Someone help me, plea—" He tried to shove the gag back in my mouth but I clamped it shut and tried to knock his hands away with my bound fists. He used his body to pin me against the tree with my hands locked between us. I jerked my head back and forth and tried to cry out again, but his overwhelming strength won out and he jammed the cloth between my teeth as I endeavored to stamp on his feet. I heard him grunt in pain as I found his foot and ground my heel into it. He did not retaliate, only forced my head into his shoulder so he could make a knot behind my head. When finished, he released me, backing away from my flailing limbs. "Coward!" I tried to scream through my gag.

I considered trying to go after him, but knew that he could easily get out of range before I did any damage. Besides, I didn't know if at some point something I did would break the cool calm and cause him to lash out at me. So I slumped down against the tree and watched him mount his horse and ride away.

I tried to pull the gag from my mouth, but it was too tight. I reached my hands over my head, trying to reach the knot, but could only touch it with my thumbs. I turned my head and reached over my shoulder, picking at the knot with my fingers. The knots were firm, and my bound hands were inadequate for the job. I gave up. I had no need to speak at the moment anyway. I tried to pick at my knotted wrists with my teeth, but the gag wouldn't let me bite down to get a grip.

After several minutes I went to stand directly beneath where the rope was tied so that I had as much slack as possible. The rope seemed long enough to allow me to lie down with a couple of inches to spare. Again, this sent my head reeling. It seemed they wanted to keep me in one place, but they also wanted me to be comfortable. Or at least as comfortable as I could be under the circumstances.

I stepped back until the rope was taut and pulled as hard as I could, throwing my weight into it. I screamed through my gag as my bindings cut into my wrists, but I kept pulling until I could no longer stand it. Nothing even budged.

I pulled my cloak around myself and put the hood up, then hunkered down by the trunk of the tree, hoping to retain my body heat as much as possible. It wasn't as cold as it felt, but with my mind battling to make sense of the situation, I couldn't stop shaking. There must be something else coming. There had to be more to the plan than just leaving me tied to a tree like an animal. For that's what I felt like: an animal on a leash. Was the point of this charade merely humiliation? There were easier ways, and without anyone here to witness it, mere humiliation didn't seem likely. There had to be something else, some*one* else. The men who took me were like soldiers, following orders. So who was giving the orders? Not only did I not know the motive; I didn't even know who may have *had* the motive.

Maybe they wanted a ransom. Maybe they didn't want to hurt me but my father. They moved me out of the way so they could threaten my father with my life and demand money or information or land. Maybe, maybe, maybe.

I soon tired of thinking about the why. There had to be something I could do. I stood up and examined the tree above me, trying to think my way through climbing it. The branches were sturdy and close together, but with my wrists tied, it would be very difficult to get up onto the first branch jutting out just over my head.

I wrapped my hands around a small branch and tried to push my feet against the trunk, but my hands soon gave out. Trying to slowly work my feet up the trunk of the tree wouldn't work. The strength in my hands wouldn't last long supporting my weight, especially with the added pain of my wrists. I took a moment to rest, then grabbed the branch again and jumped, pulling my feet up until I was able to wrap my legs around a thick limb. I pulled my upper body onto it and from there, I could only pull with my elbows and shimmy myself up on the branch. It felt as though my arms were torn to shreds, but I finally lay on my stomach over the branch.

Once I had my feet under me, I made my way up the tree with great difficulty. I had to plan each step and each handhold. When I wasn't careful enough—when I forgot to take into account the rope dangling from my wrists or my dress constantly underfoot—I would slip and be forced to catch myself any way I could. My wrists were raw. My forearms were bleeding. I couldn't see my knees to know the extent of damage, but I knew they hurt. It didn't matter though; I could not give up on the one chance I might have of getting away from here, of ending this nightmare before it reached its climax.

Halfway up the tree, I stopped to rest and assess my position. My heart sank as I craned my neck to look up into the tree and I realized why they had chosen the branch from which the rope hung. It was large and sturdy and could support plenty of weight; there was no chance of it breaking. Unfortunately, I realized that there were no other branches close enough for me to reach it. Someone taller—someone the size of the men who had taken me—could easily reach it, but I would be too short. I could try to get to where the rope was knotted, but in all likelihood I would fail at best and fall at worst. I didn't bother climbing any higher, and for the moment, I didn't have the energy to climb down.

My knees stung and my forearms were dripping blood mingled with rain. I had several nasty cuts and scrapes where I had fought against the bark. My wrists were burning from straining against their binding. For the moment, I just sat on a sturdy branch and lay the side of my head against the trunk with my eyes closed, rethinking, planning and listening. I tried to focus on the sound of the leaves moving with the wind, to slow my pounding heart.

An unnatural rustling reached my ears and my eyes snapped open. I sat far enough up in the foliage that I could see for quite a ways in most directions, but unless someone were specifically looking for me, they wouldn't see me. I waited, listening and watching.

It seemed to be a lone man, on foot. This buoyed my spirits; I didn't think any of my mastermind captors would be on foot. Of course, neither would a search party from the palace. I caught a glimpse of a cloak several times, but it seemed to be made of rough fabric—a commoner? He was moving very slowly, pausing every couple of steps. When he made his way close enough, it was clear in the way he carried himself that he was indeed a commoner. His hood was up, so I had no view of his features, but he seemed to be examining the imprints left by the horses. Had he tracked the horses? He came right up to where my captor had dismounted to gag me the second time, and then continued to the base of the tree where my captor and I had struggled. He stared at the trunk, lay his hand on it and gazed in every direction.

And then he looked straight up into the tree and his hood fell back. Tears of relief sprang to my eyes. "Gavin!" I choked out through my gag.

Chapter Twenty-One

"ELLA!" HE UNCLASPED his cloak, letting it fall to the ground, then jumped up, catching hold of the lowest branch and swinging himself up in one swift motion. As he climbed I tried to tell him what had happened, how they had taken me and bound me and brought me here. How I had thought they were going to hang me, but they just left without saying a word, without hurting me. And of course, it all came out in a garbled mess because of the gag and my tears. I watched him, his entire body working to pull himself from branch to branch. I kept talking—needing to do something, but afraid that my body, weak with relief, wouldn't hold me if I tried to move.

He pulled himself onto my branch, straddling it, and I reached out to him, grabbing the front of his shirt with my bound hands to assure myself of his presence. He put one hand over mine and used the other to push my hair out of my eyes, then pulled my head onto his shoulder. I kept mumbling incoherently and he made soft shushing noises in my ear as he worked on the knots at the back of my head. He pulled the gag out and I pushed myself back so I could see him while I talked and he worked on my hands. "And I don't know when they're coming back, or if they're coming back or who it will be or what they want or where I am—and how did you find me? Are you all right? I saw you fall. I don't even know where I am, but they didn't take me all that far and that doesn't even make sense, none of this makes sense, Gavin."

He gazed at my face as his hands continued to fumble with the knots. His eyes were so deep, his brow creased with worry, but he said nothing.

"Say something!" I begged. "They wouldn't talk to me, they never said a word to me or even to each other. Say something!"

He abandoned the rope for a moment and put his hands on the sides of my neck, his thumbs caressing my tear stained cheeks. He searched my eyes before wrapping his arms around me. "Ella...you're all right. We'll get you out of here. Are you hurt?" He pulled back and examined my bleeding forearms that had been scraped and re-scraped, answering his own question.

I shook my head as he went back to picking at the knots at my wrists. "Those were my fault, from climbing the tree." Blood trailed down to the tip of my elbow. "What about you? You were unconscious, just lying there in the mud." I pulled my hands from his so that I could take a hold of his chin. Turning his head from side to side, I found a lump above his left ear.

He pulled my hands away from the injury and kept trying to untie me. "I'm fine. Did they hurt you?"

"No, that's what I was trying to tell you. They were so well-planned and exact in what they did, but they were very careful not to hurt me if they could avoid it. It didn't make any sense. It wasn't just that they didn't hurt me on purpose; sometimes it seemed like they were even protecting me and trying to make me more comfortable. Ahh!" The bindings on my wrist had finally come loose, and I could feel the pain of my raw flesh much better now that they were free. "Ouch." I whimpered, trying to blink away the tears. Gavin's hands hovered helplessly over the welts, and he furrowed his brow, clearly frustrated that he could do nothing to fix it.

"You climbed the tree on your own? With your hands tied?" He sounded both amazed and horrified.

"I had to do something. I wasn't just going to wait around for someone to come back and decide to hurt me or to...to—" All the nightmare scenarios ran through my head once more, but I shoved them aside as Gavin wrapped me in his arms. I was fine now. I had Gavin here.

He pulled back, once more pushing my hair from my face. "Take off your cloak."

"What?"

"It will be easier for you to climb down without your cloak. We are going to go down, aren't we?"

"Yes," I answered, unfastening my cloak. I enjoyed being part of a "we" again. He helped me pull the cloak from around and under me and then held it out and dropped it to the ground.

"Well, climbing down a tree in a dress will still be difficult, but I'm relatively certain it won't compare with climbing a tree in a dress, a cloak, and a gag, while your hands are tied." His expression still held a mixture of sadness and amazement.

We made our way down, and Gavin stayed behind me the entire time, often stepping with me from one limb to another. He moved agilely, holding on with one hand and steadying me with the other or holding my skirt out of the way so I could see where to put my foot. We went mostly in silence, not needing to communicate verbally. Working with Gavin didn't require words; it never had. Twice I slipped, but he was there, wrapping an arm around my waist, holding me anchored against him as I regained my footing.

By the time we reached the lowest branch, I was pretty well spent and wondered if I could manage to land on my feet when I jumped down. But Gavin jumped first and was able to help me to the ground without much effort on my part. I immediately sat down.

"We really should move away from here, Ella."

I looked up at him, exhausted, and took a deep breath. "All right."

He helped me to my feet and kept a hand on my lower back as we put some distance between ourselves and the tree.

When I tripped over the hem of my dress, he decided we should take a rest. He got no argument from me. I sat with my back against a tree and closed my eyes until Gavin spoke.

"Can you tell me what happened? All of it?"

I nodded, took a deep breath, and told him everything—everything I remembered and everything I suspected all interlaced with my frustration at not understanding why or who.

While I talked, I ripped off the tattered hem that I had tripped over and examined the scrapes on my arms. I wanted to check the scrapes I could feel on my knees and shins. A couple years ago I might have done it, even with Gavin sitting right there, but things were different now, and I couldn't do much for my knees anyway.

When my explanation was finished, I watched him, more than a little stunned and overwhelmingly grateful to have him sitting across from me. "How is it that you were able to find me?"

It took him a moment to decide whether or not to answer. He picked up one of the strips of fabric I had ripped from the bottom of my dress and started winding and unwinding it around his hand before answering. "Ever since the incident three months ago—" he looked up to make sure I knew what he referred to. I nodded. Of course I remembered the last time he had saved me. "When you started visiting the village regularly, it made me nervous. So, whenever I can get away, I've tried to be around when you come to and from the village."

He paused, expecting some sort of response. I had none. I just stared at him, my eyes stinging and my lip quivering as I realized why he had been standing there by the road. He was waiting for me.

"I was following you when the ruckus started. I ran up the road to see what had happened and was practically on top of the situation before I realized how bad it was. One of them knocked me pretty good and when I came to I heard you scream." His voice caught on the last word, and I wondered what his experience would have been, seeing it from the outside. "I ran in the direction your scream had come from, but they were already putting you on the horse." He took a steadying breath. "I ran after them, but all I could do was follow the horses' prints. I was lucky it was raining. The soft ground made the prints a lot easier to follow. I honestly didn't expect to find you. I certainly didn't think I would catch up to you so quickly. I planned to follow the trail as far as I could and when it ran out I'd at least be able to give the guard some idea as to where you had been taken, which direction, something. But then I heard horses coming. Three riders passed by, none of them small enough to be you. I felt pretty sure they were the ones who had taken you, but you weren't with them, so I just kept following the trail." He reached across the space between us and took my hands. I didn't know if he was aware of the action or not. "I'm still baffled that I actually found you."

"I'm not." Somehow it made perfect sense that he would find me.

He gave me a real smile. "Thanks for your confidence in me—however undeserved." He looked me over. "Are you all right to keep going?"

I nodded and allowed him to pull me to my feet. The strip of my hem he had been playing with had ended up tied around one wrist, and I wondered if he realized it was there.

We made our way through the woods, walking mostly in silence, but it didn't feel awkward. Gavin led the way, glancing back often to make sure I could keep pace with him. He helped me over any obstacles we encountered and though the undercurrent of attraction was there, both of us were content—if not eager—to let our friendship take over.

Still, there was something that needed to be said. I had an answer to his question now, and I couldn't let him marry someone else if our difference in station were really the only thing keeping him from me.

"Gavin."

"Yes?"

"Tell me about your fiancée."

He stumbled, as if knocked off balance by my request.

"She is—" He furrowed his brow, fighting for the words. "Her name is Brinna."

When he did not continue, I prompted him. "Have you known her long?"

"Most of my life." He continued to walk, staring at the ground.

206

"Our families have been acquainted for years. We have always been friendly."

"So, she is a friend? You get along well?"

"Yes. She's very easy to be with. We're comfortable with one another. We know what to expect from each other because we have so much in common."

I swallowed and tried to make my voice bright as I said, "She'll make a good wife, then."

"I've no doubt of that."

We lapsed into silence. I had heard enough.

We had been walking about half an hour when the sound of voices reached us. Gavin silently took my arm and hurried us over to a fallen log amid a denser group of trees. When the voices didn't move nearer or farther away, we crept closer for a better look. It could be someone who could help us, someone searching for me.

Or it could be them.

Chapter Twenty-Two

My three captors sat quite a ways from the beaten path we had been following. As soon as they were in view I pulled Gavin down. He looked at me, confused. I think he had planned to approach them. They appeared perfectly harmless. But I shook my head, and he saw by the slight panic in my eyes what was going on. He looked back at the men and then once more at me. "Them?" he mouthed. I nodded and his brow furrowed in confusion. I knew the feeling.

We couldn't move or we'd risk being seen, so we sat down carefully on the damp earth and waited. There would be no continuing on until they left.

"How much longer?" one of them finally asked.

The leader didn't even look up, just kept carving on a stick with the same knife he had used to threaten me. "Not long. He's probably already found her and is just taking his time receiving her thanks." His voice was bland, sounding mildly disgusted.

A half-formed suspicion started at the back of my mind but I had to keep listening. I wanted to know who 'he' was.

"You think it will work? From what I can tell, she made it pretty clear she doesn't want him." The suspicion was more than half-formed now.

"That may be so, but a damsel likes to be rescued now and then. It's not difficult to get a maid to fall in love with you once you've saved her life." The disgust in his voice was obvious now.

"Still, I don't know why we have to wait around."

"Doesn't matter why; we have our orders. Now quit complaining and start listening. There may be a search party out, and if so we're going to have to convince them that we're out looking on the prince's orders."

The other two grumbled, indicating they knew the plan. But I had heard enough. I was seeing red. The only prince I had ever had the opportunity of rejecting was Jeshua. What kind of a spineless, pathetic person has their friends kidnap a girl just so he can pretend to rescue her? I wanted to scream and hit something, but I kept my mouth tightly clenched, trying to think my way through the white-hot fury. I labored to keep my breathing under control and my fingers dug into the earth beneath me. My mind felt so consumed with my internal battle that I didn't notice the rider approaching. He was just there, pulling his horse to a halt and shouting at his comrades.

"Where is she?" he demanded. The hood obscured his face, but I didn't need to see him to know who hid beneath the cloak.

The leader looked stunned. "At the tree, sir."

"Don't fool with me, William; she's not at the tree! What have you done?"

"We left her there, sir. Are you sure you went to the right one?"

"The rope was there as were some of her bindings, but she wasn't there." Panic was starting to taint his anger. "What did you do?" His horse pranced beneath him, upset by his master's anxiety.

"She was there, sir, I…" he trailed off.

For a moment they all just stared at one another, silent, not knowing what to make of it. "What have I done?" Jeshua murmured, then kicked his horse into a mad gallop toward the castle.

I stared into the air in front of me, only vaguely aware of Gavin sitting stalk-still, his clenched fist pressed tightly against his mouth.

The three men finally roused themselves and jumped onto their horses, immediately heading away from my home and back toward

Tride.

When the sound of their horses had disappeared, I finally let my voice loose. "Who would do such a thing? What kind of a person *does* something like that?" I pulled up a fern from nearby and beat it against a tree until there was nothing left of it, wishing the tree was Jeshua. "I could have killed myself climbing that stupid tree, all so that he could fake being a hero! How *could* he?" I went to pull another switch from the ground, but Gavin's arms came around me from behind and gently made me drop it. I almost let myself lean back against him, but instead I pushed away, stumbled, and fell to my knees, letting out a scream of frustration through my clenched teeth.

After a moment of kneeling there in quiet fury, Gavin spoke from behind me. "That was Jeshua, wasn't it?"

I nodded my head.

"I can't believe he would do that." He let out a breath as though he were forcing the tension out of himself. "What a miserable—human being." He had been about to say something else, but caught himself in time. I heard clearly the revulsion in his voice. "No wonder you always despised him."

My bitter laugh sounded harsh. "'Despise' doesn't begin to cover what I'm feeling right now."

"Come on." He put his arms under mine and lifted me to my feet. "Let's get you home." He took my hand and we continued picking our way through the forest. I let Gavin pull me along, too consumed in my own thoughts to pay attention to where we were going. I wondered how to tell my parents what I had seen when they thought they knew who Jeshua was. Explaining Gavin's involvement would be difficult as well. And I came to the conclusion that I could do neither. No one, absolutely no one would believe that Jeshua would do something so depraved, especially when I hadn't seen his face. And as for Gavin's involvement, trying to explain that would just make a mess and would likely end up getting him in trouble.

We crested the top of a hill and looked down to see the road winding away to our left and the palace wall a short distance beyond the foot of the hill. If we followed the wall left, we would come to the gate, which was just beyond our sight. I turned to Gavin. "All right, tie my hands together."

He stared. "What?"

"Gavin, I have to go back on my own. No one can know you were anywhere near me when this happened."

"But—"

"Last time you saved me, you ended up under interrogation." I looked him in the eye, trying to make him understand. "The best thanks I can give you is to make sure no one has even a chance to suspect you. You've been in trouble because of me too many times before."

He looked toward the sky and sighed, then clenched his jaw. He knew I was right. "All right, I agree I should let you go back on your own. But why in the world would you want me to tie you up?"

"I'm not exactly a tough girl, Gavin."

He huffed. "That's debatable."

I smiled weakly. "I shouldn't have been able to get away on my own, and if I had, I wouldn't have taken the time to try to free my hands; I would have just run. I can tell them the scrapes on my arms and knees are from falling. But I need to have my hands tied, and I should probably have the gag around my neck to make it look like I was able to pull it out of my mouth but not untie it."

"Ella—" he started to object.

I held out the cloth for him. "Just…tie my hands please."

He glared at the binding. "I do *not* want to tie you up."

My smile was sad. "I appreciate that, but I really need you to. I won't be tied for long. As soon as the guards spot me, they'll cut it off."

He still made no move to take it from me, so I shoved it into his hand. While he continued to debate with himself, I took the gag and tied it loosely around my neck.

I heard him sigh again and turned to see him shaking his head. "It needs to be over your hair."

"What?"

"They tied it over your hair, not under it." I could tell he gave me this advice reluctantly, so I shoved my hair inside the loop of cloth and then held my hands out to Gavin so he could tie them.

He glowered at my wrists. "They've barely stopped bleeding; this will make them worse."

"Gavin, please? The sooner you tie them, the sooner I can get back home and have my nurse bandage them."

He finally stepped forward and gently wound the cloth around my wrists. It only made the stinging a little bit worse.

I took a deep breath, then went up on tiptoes and kissed his cheek. "Thank you for everything. I hope you're happy with Brinna." He didn't say anything, just swallowed and nodded while looking at the ground. I started to turn away, then instinctively told him the truth. "I miss you." He still wouldn't look at me, but I saw him mouth the words *miss you* before I turned to stumble my way toward the castle and home.

I planned on getting quite close to the wall before drawing attention to myself in an attempt to ensure Gavin would not be found. But as I started down the hill, I saw a swarm of soldiers patrolling the ground outside. I guessed either they were expecting a full scale attack on the castle, or they were preparing to come out and find me en masse. I rushed down the hill, wanting them to find me as far from Gavin as possible.

My stumbling approach resulted in many weapons pointed my way for the few seconds it took them to recognize me. Then they froze, no doubt shocked as they watched me approach—dress ragged and torn, arms bloodied, wrists bound, hair wild—walking awkwardly in an attempt to keep my balance while my hands were restrained in front of me. I heard a deep voice resonate, "Princess!" then they broke into an uproar, each running toward me on foot or on horse. The first horseman to reach me barely slowed his momentum as he swept me up in front of him and then rounded toward the gate. The soldiers completely surrounded me. We reached the gate before I knew it and were met by even more guards. They all shouted questions back and forth, but the captain was the first to speak to me.

"Princess Ariella, are you well?"

"Well enough," I managed to answer as the horse pranced in agitation beneath us.

He looked me over, seeming to take in every detail. "Are you seriously injured?"

"No, but—" I held my hands forward and he quickly drew a knife from his forearm and cut my bonds. I sucked in a breath; my wrists stung.

"Are you being pursued, Your Highness?"

"No." I replied, but he signaled his men to continue their search anyway.

"Take the princess home," was the captain's next order.

The horse took off toward the castle, past all the curious onlookers and vigilant guards.

News of my return reached the palace before we did. My parents and all of their attendants were making their way toward me. I slid from the horse just before they reached me. My mother was there first, crying, stroking my hair and kissing my forehead, asking over and over if I was all right and murmuring, "You're home, you're home."

My father didn't say anything to me, just held me tightly against his chest for a moment, then began drilling the guards. It was more affection than I would have expected from him and I appreciated it. Though he and I were still at odds much of the time, that didn't matter at this moment.

I passed into the entrance hall, leaning against my mother while my father kept a supportive hand on my back. I vaguely heard my father ask that my mother, the captain, and my nurse join us in a chamber off the main hallway, but instead of allowing myself to be propelled along, I stopped.

Jeshua stood outside the fray of people, anxious and guilty. My vision went red. His audacity had me acting before I could think. I asked my parents to give me a moment, but still had to pry myself from their embrace.

I barreled toward Jeshua but had enough sense to pass him by and duck into an alcove that was mostly concealed by tapestries. He followed me.

"Ariella—"

I spun, and in response to him daring to use my name at this moment, I slapped him across the face with so much force that the sting of my hand registered through my fury, my adrenaline, and all my other pains.

"Don't," I whispered fiercely. "Don't you dare say a word to me, you horrid bit of filth."

His mouth hung open in shock. "But—"

"I know it was you."

He went a bit pale. "I—I'm afraid I don't understand."

I could not speak through my fury and only pinned him with what must have been a withering glare because he took a step back.

"I only wanted—"

"Don't speak to me. Don't touch me, don't you dare to ever come near me again." He took a step back, away from my fury. "I know that no one will believe it was you, but I want you to be aware that I know what you are, you *wretch!*" He actually had the nerve to appear indignant at the insult. "Now, *get away from me!*" I shrieked through clenched teeth. He took two more steps backward, then turned and strode quickly out through the hall. I stood there, attempting to gain some sort of control over my emotions. I seethed, so angry I could barely make my eyes focus as I tried to breathe evenly before leaving the alcove. My parents waited a short way away and their expressions made it clear that my last demand of *get away from me* had been heard. They may have even heard me slap him. Good; now they knew how I felt about Jeshua even if they didn't know why.

My mother's arm came around my shoulders and I feared she would want to talk about Jeshua, but she said simply, "Come along, dear," and led me to a room off the main hall where I was situated in a chair as my nurse tended to my arms. I would wait for the captain to leave before telling her about my damaged knees. My parents stood just behind my chair, my nurse knelt beside me, and the captain sat down across from me, asking his questions.

I tried to keep myself aloof and numb as I answered as honestly as possible while leaving Gavin out of the telling. I let them believe that I was able to free myself from the tree on my own. I told them about overhearing the conspirators, about the fourth conspirator who had wanted to rescue me. I even mentioned that his sounded familiar, almost like Jeshua's voice...but they brushed that notion aside and moved on to other details.

I was so exhausted by the time I was bandaged and delivered back to my room that it took me a moment to realize I had been handed over to Gretchen's care. It was her sniffling that finally broke through my foggy mind. I focused on her and saw a stream of tears running down her face, though she continued to work steadily at helping me prepare for bed.

My brow furrowed, wondering what had upset her. Then she met my eyes and I realized her distress was for me. Her hands stilled and then she wrapped her arms around me. "Are you all right, Highness?" she whispered through her tears.

I returned her embrace and opened my mouth, intending to say, "I'm fine." Instead I heard myself say simply, "No."

That one word was my undoing. I had been able to remain stoic and numb while my mother and nurse had worked over me, while the captain questioned me about the events of the day. But Gretchen's question and the utter truth of my answer brought the reality crashing in.

My mother came in to check on me a few minutes later and found me crying in Gretchen's arms. I was transferred to my mother's solid embrace and fell asleep with my head in her lap.

Chapter Twenty-Three

My WRISTS STUNG as Nurse Mary replaced the bandages. I ignored the pain, staring out the window as she fastened the velvet cuffs over the bindings. I hated seeing the evidence of my wounds hour after hour, so I insisted on something to cover them. It had been three days.

My mother thanked Mary as she left then settled in the chair opposite me, taking my hands in hers. I looked at her face and gave a weak smile. Next she would ask if there was anything else I could remember and I would tell her the same thing I had told her each day. I described the three men in detail, and told her once again that the man in charge had sounded very much like Jeshua. She gave me the same indulgent smile, kissed my head and left.

She always left me glad that I hadn't mentioned Gavin. She obviously thought me too muddled and emotional to be trustworthy. Only Gretchen heard the entire story. She was the only one who would ever know what Gavin had done for me.

My family members' reactions to what had happened varied greatly. My mother hovered whenever she had the time. Most of my sisters were silently curious, never asking about it, but looking at me as though I might break at the slightest provocation. Marilee treated it as a grand adventure and Lorraina acted as though nothing had happened. My father became wildly protective, but also standoffish, and we ended up having a rousing fight about my being allowed to return to the village.

"That is out of the question," he declared when I told him I felt well enough to go back.

"What?" I asked in desperation.

"Do you suppose for one minute that I would allow you to continue these frivolous visits after what happened to you?"

I wanted to scream and throw things, and I was on the verge of doing just that when I saw the undiluted fear cross his face. It so shocked me that I lost my vehemence and found myself begging in a whisper, "Please, Father. Please don't take this one thing away from me."

He would have continued to say no. I only won the argument because of my mother. The number of times my mother had gone against my father could be counted on one hand, but when she did, she won. The truth was that my father would give my mother anything she asked.

Even so, I almost lost that freedom only a few days after I resumed my visits to the village.

I had been kneading dough with Josephine, while little Logan sat on the kitchen table, "helping." I went outside to wash off my hands after the loaves were finished. As I shook the water from my fingers, I glanced up and down the lane, noticing two children playing in a puddle while their mothers stood by in earnest conversation.

A wagon had just passed and stopped at the cottage two doors down. A chair was sitting in the back, tied down with several ropes. The driver jumped down as the lady of the house came out the front door and rushed out to the wagon, eager with anticipation.

When the driver turned to greet her, my heart jumped. It was Gavin. He took the woman's hand in his own to greet her and she turned back to admire the chair. I wondered at her enthusiasm. I couldn't see anything special about it, but then I knew my perspective was skewed. I focused my attention back on Gavin as he took off his hat to wipe his forehead, grinning unabashedly.

I heard a throat clearing behind me and turned to see Rowan gazing at me with eyebrows raised. He had stationed himself on the porch when we first arrived and had obviously seen me staring at Gavin. I went immediately back into the house, just in time to pull Logan's fist from the middle of a doughy loaf.

Josephine turned back as I laughingly extricated him. She sighed. "I swear, Princess Ari, every time I turn my back for even a moment..."

"He is a quick one, isn't he?"

She just shook her head as I carried him out to the rain barrel for his own hand washing. As I rinsed him off, I glanced over to see Gavin hauling the chair up the pathway to the house. He didn't appear to have noticed me.

By the time I had finished at Josephine's house, the wagon was gone.

The next day, I rounded up all the children I could find and let them choose the activity.

"Hide and seek!" was the consensus.

I couldn't help laughing. My guards had been especially vigilant since the kidnapping. The children would certainly win this one.

"All right, who wants to seek first?" Three of them raised their hands, and I designated all of them as seekers. It always worked best if several of them worked together. They quickly took their place beside the well, with their heads buried in their arms, and started counting.

The rest scattered every which way, and I set out to find a niche of my own—hopefully one big enough to hide both of my guards with me.

I ran down a lane leading to the edge of the dwellings, where the blacksmith resided. "Jeffrey," I called as we approached the smithy. "Quickly, we need a place to hide."

"Is there something wrong?" he asked in alarm. Jeffrey was a grandfatherly figure and had a protective nature.

"Of course not, we are just playing hide and seek," I explained while crawling over and under equipment in order to get into the heart of the shop. "Stop rolling your eyes, Wyatt."

Jeffrey laughed as Wyatt cleared his throat in embarrassment.

"How did you know I was rolling my eyes, Princess?" Wyatt asked as he followed behind me.

"You always roll your eyes when you think I take games too seriously." I settled myself among some feed sacks that appeared relatively clean as Jeffrey resumed his hammering.

My guards settled beside me, Wyatt looking as though he may have been blushing. "My apologies, Highness, I did not know you had noticed."

"I am much more observant than you give me credit for, I assure you." I said this lightly as I tried to reorganize my skirts, which were twisted beneath me.

"Is that so?" Wyatt's tone of voice caught my attention and I glanced at him, but his gaze was directed elsewhere. Both of my guards were looking at something or someone out in front of the smithy. My skin prickled and I turned my head reluctantly to see what they saw.

I shouldn't have been surprised, but I was. Gavin—again. My face felt heavy and expressionless as I watched him approach Jeffrey and converse quietly. I studied him, letting my eyes take in the state of his dress, the stiffness of his back, the way his hands kept clenching and unclenching, the strip of fabric wrapped round his wrist, peeking out from beneath his sleeve. He kept his eyes only on the blacksmith until his business was concluded. It was only as he turned to leave that his eyes barely skimmed my face.

I sat absolutely still as he walked away, moving nothing but my eyes. I refused to let my feelings show on my face.

"Your Highness?" I turned my head only a fraction in order to see Rowan as he spoke to me, concern lighting his eyes. "That is the third time in the last two days that we have seen that man." I didn't move or speak, just waited for him to continue. "Your father made it very clear that if he did not maintain a suitable distance from you, something would have to be done."

I sat silent for a long moment, wanting to defend him, wanting to tell them he was only trying to protect me. I had been kidnapped; he worried. But I didn't have any idea how much Gavin would have known if he hadn't been there. I couldn't risk it, so I spoke defensively. "And what do you expect me to do about it?" The question came out sharper than I had intended. "I cannot predict nor control where he goes. If it is a problem, then fix it."

I got to my feet, making my way toward the front of the shop. My guards got up to follow me, but we heard Jeffrey whisper, "Stay low, I see some young ones coming." I crouched down just behind Jeffrey's work station while my guards remained on the other side of a long work table.

The sound of children's voices reached my ears and came closer, but it was Jeffrey himself, standing above me, who spoke. "Princess." I cast my eyes up at him, and he continued to speak so only I could hear. "He was only asking after your welfare, wanted a glimpse of you. He is a good lad, and loyal to you."

As if I didn't already know that. No one knew better than I of Gavin's goodness and loyalty. I dropped my eyes as the disinterested mask fell from my face. The strip of fabric wound around his wrist—it came from the torn hem of my dress, the one I had destroyed while climbing the tree.

I didn't have time to dwell on what it meant, for our hiding place was discovered and I was dragged into the open by five enthusiastic children. I forced myself to smile and continue in the game, but my focus was lost and I ended up returning to the palace earlier than usual. Unfortunately, just as I was saying my goodbyes and leaving the square, Gavin wandered into my path. I felt my guards stiffen and Wyatt went so far as to take my arm and steer me around him. He only stood against the wall, staring at the ground with his hat pulled low.

When we entered the palace grounds, I made to hasten away from my guards, but Rowan caught my arm. I spun to glare at him, looking pointedly at his hand. He dropped it. "My apologies, Princess, but I want you to know that we will have to report Gavin's whereabouts to your father."

I fought for a dismissive tone as I answered, "It matters not to me what you report to my father. You will excuse me."

But it did matter, for I received a summons to counsel with my father a short while later. He wasted no time on pleasantries, only launched into his accusations. "He is seeking you out in the village?" His anger was apparent, and I found my patience very thin.

"No," I replied.

"Your guards report he was seen three times today."

"I have no reason to dispute that claim."

"Ariella, I cannot allow any fraternization—"

I cut him off. "He lives in the village, Father. I am surprised I did not run into him sooner. It was unavoidable, and it was not my fault."

"If it is unavoidable, then perhaps your excursions to the village should be put off for the time being."

"Of course, Father. Punish me more; why not?" My patience was gone.

"Don't be insolent," he said with a quiet fierceness.

"Haven't I been punished enough? Do you not think that almost two years of your blatant disapproval has made its point? And if not, shouldn't the terror of being abducted count for something?"

He was taken aback. "You have seemed to be doing well, I had hoped you had put it behind you, forgotten it a little."

I pushed the velvet cuffs from my wrists and thrust my arms forward, putting my scars on display. "How can I forget when the evidence still marks my skin?" The pain crossing his face was obvious and something I rarely saw. I dropped my arms to my sides, embarrassed at having been overly dramatic. "I am the first to admit that what happened to me could have been so much worse. I'm fine—I am. But I cannot forget what happened, nor how I felt while it was happening."

"You haven't wanted to talk about it."

"How would you know? You never asked," I snapped. I saw the guilt and also the defensiveness rise in him, but I'd reached my limit. "I would beg your leave, *Sire*."

He dropped his eyes, saddened—whether because I was leaving or because I had called him 'Sire,' I didn't know, and I refused to let myself care. He nodded his permission and I left. I was tired of being in the wrong when I felt very clearly in the right.

✳✳✳

Oddly enough, the situation with my father got better, in a manner of speaking. Though our conversations remained aloof and stilted, the way he looked at me changed. He started seeing me again. And he seemed glad to see me. Instead of constant disapproval, I sometimes saw simple sadness, but he no longer tried to see past me. It was a pleasant surprise, having something positive come from my kidnapping.

Unfortunately, there was a very unpleasant surprise as well. I had expected never to set eyes on Jeshua again, but three weeks after the incident, as I walked along the upstairs balcony overlooking the entrance hall, I saw several of my sisters rushing down the staircase. I went to the railing to see what had drawn their attention just as the doors were pushed open by two guards, and in walked my father with Jeshua at his side. They spoke for only a brief moment before my father went his own way, leaving Jeshua to walk over and greet Kalina, Marilee, and Lorraina. Only he didn't greet all of them. He walked right up to Kalina and took both of her hands in his, not even glancing at the other two.

And I just stood there, shocked into stillness, watching from above as Jeshua slid back into my life.

That evening he dined with us, sitting at the opposite end of the table from me and never looking my way. He seemed to have decided that since my most fervent wish was his death, he should pretend that I had never been the object of his affection. It became apparent throughout the meal that he had dedicated himself entirely to winning Kalina over. She seemed thrilled and completely willing to ignore the fact that he had never given her a second glance until now. Truly, his arrogance astounded me. It crossed my mind that it was a good thing there were no knives within my reach. The temptation may have been too much.

I started to regret having told him that I would not share my suspicions with anyone. At the time I had thought only of getting him out of my life; I had never considered the possibility of him pursuing one of my sisters, not after what he had done to me. I was tempted to tell my parents the truth about his involvement, but seeing my father's reaction to him convinced me that it would do no good. They would wonder why I hadn't spoken up sooner. They would laugh off my suspicions just as they had when I mentioned that my captor's voice sounded like Jeshua. They would ask if I had seen his face, and the truth was that I hadn't, and Gavin was the only one who could confirm my story. And if I mentioned Gavin? Not only would my father go back to despising me for the relationship Gavin and I had shared, but I also feared what he would do to Gavin. The memory of him being strung up, ready for torture, still made me ill.

Besides, I had never been in any real danger, and Kalina was happy. So I bit my tongue and made the best of it.

He stayed the night and took the opportunity to be charming during breakfast. I tried my best to ignore the entire affair. Only after he departed for a hunting excursion did I start paying attention to the conversation again.

"He seems to fancy you, Kalina," Marilee said in a conspiratorial voice. We were all standing just inside the doors of the entryway as Prince Jeshua rode off with the hunting party.

Kalina turned to Marilee, her eyes bright. "He does, doesn't he?" She grabbed a hold of Marilee's hand, trying to channel her excitement. "It's so unexpected, we all thought—" she cut herself off, glancing over at me.

I held up my hands. "Don't look at me, I don't want any part of him." I wished I could tell them just how much I despised him, but I had the feeling I would come across as jealous and insincere. We turned to make our way up to our day room to meet with our tutors.

Kalina stared at me, incredulous. "How could you not? He's Jeshua! I've wanted a part of him for as long as I can remember!" My younger sisters burst into giggles. "We were all certain he would ask you, but now…"

"I suppose he finally came to his senses and realized who the true prize would be." I was being much more generous than usual, but for some reason I felt the need to bond with my sisters in that moment. I had been such a solitary creature for so long, it was nice to be a part of this sisterly prattle and affection.

"Either that or he didn't want to play second fiddle to that gardener of yours."

The giggles stopped. The camaraderie dissipated and I turned to stare, thunderstruck, at Lorraina. Her face told me this had not been a slip of the tongue.

"Raina!" Kalina admonished.

Marilee and Lylin stood silent. They had all stopped mentioning Gavin long ago. Though my sisters did not often understand me, they could see how his memory hurt me. Lorraina just gazed right at me, her eyebrows raised, daring me to react.

"Gavin doesn't play the fiddle," I stated. "He sings." I turned away from Lorraina's confused and disappointed face and made my way upstairs.

Jeshua stayed for several days. He took his meals with us, but spent the majority of his days on hunting expeditions or other gentlemanly endeavors. His evenings were spent strolling with Kalina.

I prayed that he wasn't the wretched human being I supposed him to be and tried to keep myself from glaring whenever I found myself in his company. Not because I would mind him seeing the loathing on my face, but because I knew that anyone else who saw me would assume I was jealous of my sister, that I was being petty to spite them both.

Jealous I was not.

In fact, I felt lighter since my ordeal. Not because of the ordeal itself but because of the place it had taken me in my relationship with Gavin. I felt calm where Gavin was concerned. I missed him terribly, of course, but something had passed between us that day—something that made me feel more whole. Perhaps he had given back one of the portions of myself that he had taken when he left. Whatever the reason, I was conflicted, being wound up and edgy about Jeshua's pursuit of Kalina, while at the same time feeling more calm in my soul than I had felt in a long time.

✳✳✳

A week after Jeshua's departure, I decided to go into the maze. Ever since my kidnapping I had wondered if I should try to talk with Gavin. Perhaps if we had a conversation devoid of fighting or threats against my life, I could bring our relationship back into perspective. Perhaps we could be friends again now that I knew where he stood. He may have wanted me, but he had chosen Brinna.

I had only been into the maze once since he returned. I had entered angry and hurt and our conversation had turned into a fight, ending with a kiss. That couldn't happen again. So I entered calmly, trying to avoid any expectations. I had brought my art kit and decided to sit in one of the large open areas of the maze and draw, relatively certain he would happen upon me eventually. I ended up in the room where I had helped him trim the branches of a tree. I sat down facing the tree and pulled out my pencils.

I had done several sketches before he walked in, beating his gloves against his thigh, and I tried not to notice how his arms strained against his rolled up sleeves. He looked up, slowing to a stop, and I wondered if he had the same sense of déjà vu as I did. This situation felt so familiar: me, sitting cross-legged on the ground, sketching; him, working with a satchel of tools slung across his body.

"You haven't been here much," he finally said.

I gave him a smile. "You know I couldn't."

He nodded, seeming happy to see me. "I do know. But I'm sorry you've been driven from a place you love."

"It's all right," I assured him.

His eyes went to the gloves in his hands. "So, why can you now, when you couldn't before?"

I shrugged. "Just…time, I guess."

He walked a little closer, still maintaining a sizable distance.

"You still draw."

I focused on the paper in my lap. "Not as much, but yes." I didn't tell him most of my sketches during his absence had been of the castle's harsh lines and dark interior. I brought my eyes up, admiring the maze. "And you still work wonders with this place."

He peered around, scrutinizing. "It's still not what it was, but I'm working to remedy that."

"Do you know why they didn't keep it up better?" I remembered my mother admitting it was partially the maze's disrepair that brought Gavin back.

"I'd been tending this maze for so many years…everyone knew how I felt about it. I think they left it alone out of a sort of respect, I suppose." His gaze fell to the ground. "It sounds ridiculous."

"It doesn't, actually."

He seemed embarrassed, mumbling, "Thank you," before clearing his throat and looking at me. "How are your wrists?"

I swallowed, surprised by how this question affected me. My wrists had been bandaged for two weeks after it happened. The velvet cuffs I had worn to cover them remained after the bandages came off, hiding the scars. I fidgeted with them before answering, "They're fine."

"And the rest of you?" His jaw twitched.

I swallowed again and tried to be honest. "I've recovered well enough."

"I hope so," he said quietly, then shook off his emotion and grinned. "You've created quite a stir in the village."

I laughed. "That's one way to put it."

"And how would you put it, Princess Ari?" He was trying to keep a straight face, but smiling underneath it.

"I would say I've finally found a purpose."

"I'm very glad about that." Silence settled between us and his eyes darted about. "I should be getting on with it."

"Gavin." He turned back to me. "I…I need you to not let my guards see you when I'm in the village."

Confusion swept over his face before understanding set in. "I've caused problems for you?"

"No," I assured him, "but it might cause problems for both of us if they keep seeing you."

He nodded. "Understood, Princess." He gave me one of my favorite smiles, so I took no offense at the title. I suppose it was good to remind ourselves of where we stood. "It's good to see you back here."

"I'm very happy to be back. Good luck with your work, Gavin."

He inclined his head. "Princess."

He left and I went back to sketching, relieved it had gone so well.

Chapter Twenty-Four

I HATED MY dress. I was accustomed to inconvenient formalwear, but the design Kalina had chosen was extreme. In addition to the bodice being tighter than any dress I'd ever owned, it was also fitted down to my hips, instead of just my waist, making it not only difficult to breath, but also impossible to sit down.

Tonight we celebrated an engagement. Jeshua had done it. Only seven weeks after his desperate last effort to secure my hand, he had managed to secure that of my sister. It horrified me that this conniving little pretender would soon take my sister to wife, but I could do nothing. Besides, he may have been a sniveling little whelp, but he wasn't really dangerous. At least, that's what I hoped.

Throughout the evening I contented myself with being quietly disgusted and hoping I wouldn't be forced to dance. Having never fainted in my life, I was left to wonder if this dress would finally get the best of me. I kept a keen eye out for any gentleman who might be coming my way in the vain hope of getting me onto the dance floor.

In all fairness, Jeshua and Kalina seemed to make a good couple. Kalina wasn't as giggly and ridiculous as some of my sisters, and Jeshua was seen as charming by most everyone. In fact, he seemed even more charming than usual. I suppose having Kalina reciprocate his affection had made him redouble his efforts. They were quite a sight to see; their children would be gorgeous. I just hoped Kalina would be the one instructing them in matters of ethics.

The main part of the gardens had been transformed for the party. I was relieved to be outside, for I could only imagine how much more uncomfortable I would be if this many guests had been forced into the great hall.

"Your Highness?" I spun in the direction of the voice. I had been distracted by Kalina and Jeshua and had not seen the young lord coming. I fought for composure as I dipped my head and extended my hand as custom dictated. He took it in both of his and bowed over them. "You look stunning tonight, Highness."

I tried to smile in a flattered sort of way as I said, "Thank you, Lord Wilden," then pulled my hand away with a little more force than necessary. "And how are you enjoying your evening?" I would have just excused myself, but I was on thin ice with my father and it would not do for him to hear that I had snubbed nobility.

"Very well, indeed. This is an exquisite celebration." He looked around in appreciation and sucked in a large breath as if preparing himself. It was now or never.

"It is that," I responded. "And if you'll excuse me, there is something I must see to." I stepped away before he could say anything else. I didn't want to be rude, but I also didn't have the energy to appear interested. Fighting my way through the throng of people, I slipped into the maze. I didn't go far, for I didn't want to be missed, but I needed the reprieve.

I leaned back against a pillar not too far from the edge of the maze. I didn't want to be at this party. Not only because I couldn't stand the thought of Jeshua being my brother-in-law, but also because I would rather have been at a different dance. I couldn't go to the village dances as Ella anymore, since I would surely be recognized, but I could have gone just as myself. That is, if my father allowed it, if I ever got up the nerve to ask.

Even worse, my trip into the village had been cancelled today. My morning had been spent in last-minute dress fittings and then having my hair pulled and twisted and fluffed just the right way. Kalina had made Gretchen do my hair four different ways, and then declared she liked the first one best. I nearly strangled her before remembering that her engagement to Jeshua was largely my fault. I forced myself to hold my tongue.

"The children missed you today." I opened my eyes, instantly recognizing Gavin's voice, but I didn't move, his presence catching me off guard.

I turned slowly to see him sitting on a stone bench several paces farther into the maze. It was the spot I would have rested if I dared sit down in this dress. His feet were planted wide, his elbows resting on his knees and his eyes fixed on the ground. I wondered how long he had been there and why. When I didn't say anything, he finally looked at me. "They were quite disappointed you couldn't be there."

"What are you doing here?" Gavin never stayed so late.

He shook his head, shrugging as he rose to his feet. "Just…enjoying the frivolity." His voice sounded accusing as he stepped toward me. "I hear it is an engagement celebration. Jeshua of Tride is to marry one of our dear princesses."

My brow furrowed. "And?" I prompted him, wondering why I felt as though I should be ashamed of myself.

He shrugged in a would-be casual gesture. "I'm just surprised is all." He slapped his gloves against his thigh, causing puffs of dirt to fall to the ground. "I would have thought a man of his *caliber* wouldn't warrant anything kinder than a knife in his gut, much less your sister's hand in marriage."

I was taken aback by his harsh tone. "And what do you propose I do?"

"Why haven't you told them?" He still maintained that disappointed expression and it set me on edge.

"Told who what?" I asked defensively.

"About the kidnapping, about Jeshua. Why haven't you told your family it was Jeshua?"

I tried to remain calm, tried to remember the camaraderie he and I had shared. "They wouldn't believe me."

"Since when do they not trust you? Are you secretly some great liar?" His words were gentle, but I could hear the underlying disapproval.

"They wouldn't understand."

"What wouldn't they understand? Jeshua had you abducted; how can that be misunderstood?"

I stared at him, trying to convey my fears, to make him understand. "I never saw his face! It's only my suspicions, and if I tell them anything more, I'll have to tell them everything. Everything, Gavin, including you."

"So tell them everything!" he blurted impatiently. "I didn't do anything wrong. As I recall, I was the only one who did anything right!"

"Do you really think they'll see it that way?"

"Why would they not?"

"Because you're you! Because in my father's mind, you are the villain. My father hasn't trusted a word I've said since you happened." He was surprised by this, having been unaware of the disintegration of my relationship with my father. "Do you think I want this? Do you think I want Jeshua skulking around, courting my sister? They'll think I'm jealous, or they'll think I'm trying to get you back. I want, so much, to be able to scream out loud that you were the one who found me, but they won't believe me. They'll think I went off to meet you, that there was no kidnapping. They'll find a way to blame it on you. If there were anyone else who knew the truth, that would be different. But for you and I to try to convince my father that our meeting was a coincidence—he won't believe me."

"So, you'll let your sister marry him?" It was a reprimand and it made me angry.

"I'm not letting her do anything. She makes her own choices, just like everyone else."

He remained calm, missing the accusation and spoke gently. "She, at least, should know. She's going to spend the rest of her life with this man. What if he's not just an arrogant fool? What if he's worse?"

I pinched my eyes shut, trying to block out that possibility. "He's always been above reproach—"

"How do you know?" he interrupted, his voice impatient.

I kept my eyes closed, trying to keep a hold on my rationale. "He's royalty. Everyone knows everything about him. Someone would know, someone would say something."

"Like you?" I looked up at him. "You know something and you say nothing."

"I can't."

"Why?"

"I won't let them blame you for anything else, Gavin. I won't!" I looked away, not wanting him to see how desperately I was trying to protect him and what that meant.

He chose his next words with care. "I am honored," he began with emotion burning through his voice. "And grateful that you are trying to protect me." He took a deep breath and spoke deliberately, making me listen to each word. "But you can't trade your sister's happiness to save me."

"She wants this! She wants him; she's always wanted him."

"She doesn't know who he is. You do." I focused my eyes elsewhere, not wanting to have my mind changed. "You have to tell her, Ella."

"I'm doing what is right." I was saving Gavin from humiliation and possible punishment. Surely, that was the right thing. Kalina knew what she was doing. She wanted to marry Jeshua; why should I get in the way?

"You're doing what you *think* is right."

I bristled, unaccustomed to having my judgment questioned.

"Think about it, and really do the right thing."

I didn't say anything. What *could* I say? I just stared at him, defiant and wanting to be right. He regarded me steadily and then turned away. Our conversation had come to an end.

"By the way," he said over his shoulder, "you look beautiful."

Chapter Twenty-Five

I HAD SUSPECTED this moment might come, and found myself oddly calm when it did. I had arrived in Tride with my family this morning for the festivities accompanying my sister's engagement. The people of Tride were being introduced to their future queen at a grand ball held in her honor. I had been dreading our trip to Tride, but not for the usual reason. I knew Jeshua would pay me no mind, which suited me, but this trip brought Kalina one step closer to marrying a man who didn't deserve to be within fifty paces of my sister, much less marry her. Yet here we were, and I felt physically ill because of it.

In an effort to distract myself, I decided to keep watch in case I came across my captors. It was unlikely, but from the conversation Gavin and I had overheard, we knew they were not hired thugs, but more likely loyal servants or even his friends. I had thought quite a bit about what I would do if I were to encounter one of them. In fact, I had thought about it so much, that I felt very prepared and relaxed when I saw him across the room.

It was the leader, the man Jeshua had called William. He stood against the wall, behind a large pillar in the formal raiment of a knight. He was turned to the side with one shoulder leaning against the wall and his arms crossed over his chest. He was trying not to draw attention to himself, but his eyes were constantly scanning the crowd.

I made my way around the outside of the room, picking up a drink on my way, keeping my eyes on him. I expected him to appear menacing, skulking in the shadows, but he seemed more watchful than anything.

I approached from behind until I stood only a few feet from him. Then I leaned my back against the wall and gazed out at the crowd while I spoke. "Can I ask you a question?"

In my peripheral vision, I saw him turn, recognize me and freeze. I continued to speak without looking at him. "Did you think I wouldn't recognize you, William, or did you just not care?" I kept my voice friendly and took a sip of the drink in my hand before turning my gaze on him.

I looked at him with open, innocent eyes and waited for him to find his voice. He cleared his throat and tried to look at me. "I follow orders, Your Highness." His anxiety was obvious, but controlled. "There are few things I do and few places I go that are of my own choosing." He stared into my eyes, searched for understanding. "I follow orders." He said this heavily, no doubt trying to convey that his actions had not been his choice.

It struck me that this man might be willing to tell me about Jeshua and his intentions. He obviously took no pride in what he had done. I peered down into my drink, still leaning against the wall, and couldn't help asking. "And you were ordered to scare me senseless but not hurt me?"

The silence stretched until I glanced up at him, surprised that he hadn't confirmed my suspicion. "I was ordered to bring you to the tree; he gave me no specific instructions as to your physical well-being."

I stared at him and digested this for a moment. My opinion of Jeshua was already so low that his wretchedness didn't concern me. However, my opinion of this man was still negotiable and suddenly very blurry. His gaze held no animosity. The way his eyes kept examining my own felt as though he were asking forgiveness, though he couldn't say the words out loud. And I started to wonder if I *could* forgive this man—this man who seemed so trapped by the position he held serving Jeshua—

serving a royal.

And oddly, I did feel some understanding—only a small portion, but it was understanding nonetheless.

I blinked and looked down, unable to hold his gaze. I didn't want to understand him. I didn't want to feel this compulsion to forgive a man who had held me captive. This entire situation felt ludicrous. Here I stood, chatting with the perpetrator of my own kidnapping, and I couldn't muster the loathing I should feel.

"What would he have done?" I focused on my drink, trying to keep my head clear.

"When?"

"If I had stayed tied to the tree, and he had found me. What would he have done?"

"Rescued you."

"You mean, *pretended* to rescue me?" He dropped his gaze. "He would have saved me from the wicked clutches of his own stupidity? And then what?"

He considered me for a moment before turning his gaze back to the dance floor, trying for a casual appearance once more. "I believe he thought his actions would endear him to you, and perhaps you would consider marrying him."

I turned to admire the dancers as well. "And if that had happened? If I had married him and come to live here, what exactly would he have done with you? Did he expect me not to recognize you or the others?" I could feel his eyes on me, though I still looked out at the festivities. "Or are you just an expendable resource?"

Instead of bristling at this suggestion as I expected, he remained calm. "I may be the closest thing Jeshua has to a friend, but I've always known I was expendable."

I studied his face, and felt my sympathy returning, trying to get under my skin. He seemed wise in that moment—as though he could see his entire life laid before him, holding nothing but orders to be followed.

My eyes were pulled from his as Marilee came giggling and

tripping her way in my direction, towing Lylin behind her. I acted on impulse.

"Ask me to dance," I ordered, setting my drink on the nearest table.

Williams eyebrows shot up. "I beg your pardon, Your Highness?"

"Just ask me to dance, quickly."

He straightened to his full height, looking awkward, and then sucked up his courage and bowed, extending his hand to me. I placed my hand in his and he led me onto the dance floor.

Marilee and Lylin came to an abrupt halt and started a whispered conversation, staring at me in astonishment.

William pulled me into a formal dance position and we stepped together into the flow of dancers. I held myself with all the grace that had been ingrained in me, and kept my eyes locked with his. I could have looked over his shoulder, but I felt the need to prove my mettle to this man, and thus refused to back down.

I allowed myself to be distracted by the motion, allowed the rise and fall of our movements and the swishing of skirts to clear out my muddled thoughts. I let myself examine the difference of feeling William's hand in mine as opposed to the feel of dancing with Gavin. I was aware of William—aware of his eyes traveling over me with an intense curiosity. But it differed greatly from my awareness of Gavin. When Gavin and I were together, there was a pulse between us, a very distinct pull that often trumped my own better judgment. With William, the awareness was interesting, but not overwhelming.

"How did you do it?" William interrupted my musing.

I focused on him, wondering to what he referred.

"The tree," he clarified, "the ropes. How did you get away?"

I hadn't anticipated this question. In fact, I hadn't anticipated him asking me any questions.

I wondered why he asked—if it was to satiate his own curiosity or to report back to Jeshua. My instincts told me this man held no true loyalty to Jeshua, but even so, I couldn't tell him the truth. I couldn't tell anyone the truth. Gavin was the truth, and I would not let his name be caught up with mine.

So I just smiled at him, using the smile that turned me into a mystery and reminded men of my position. I had never used this smile on Gavin.

"I'm afraid that is something you will continue to wonder over."

He tried to dissect my composure with his piercing eyes, but I was much better at this game than I should have been. He finally gave up, his eyes going from searching to intent and determined.

"I suppose I'll never get this opportunity again, so I'm going to take it." He took a deep breath and I noted the utter sincerity swimming over his face. "I want to apologize for what happened to you—most especially for my own involvement in it. But I also want you to know that in some ways, I'm glad Jeshua asked me to carry it out." My eyes widened in anger and he hurried on, "Because I really do believe anyone else would have been far less…"

He trailed off and I knew what he was thinking. He was thinking of all the words he could apply to his actions toward me, but discarded each one. They would have been far less what? Kind? Gentle? Merciful? Protective? They were the same words running through my own mind. And I knew he had as much difficulty as I did using those words to describe what he had done to me.

He tried again. "I believe it could have been far worse for you."

"I know that," I told him, but kept my face carefully aloof, unwilling to give him too much.

He nodded, appearing slightly relieved, but I didn't want to let him off the hook too easily. "But that didn't make it any easier at the time."

He nodded once, accepting my refusal to forgive and we lapsed into silence. He started to focus on the dance and I noticed that when he tried, he was a superior dancer. I found myself trying to match my skill to his, until I noticed our audience.

Chief among those watching us were Jeshua, who had gone a bit pale, and my father, who looked distinctly suspicious.

As a general rule, I avoided dancing, especially when we were away from home. Part of me wanted to tone down my performance to avoid the curiosity of my family, but another part of me enjoyed our little battle.

I was spared the decision as the dance came to an end and William brought us to a stop. I could hear his breathing close to my ear before he released me with seeming reluctance. I think he still hoped for me to give some sign of forgiveness.

He stood stiffly before me for a moment until I looked at him.

"I am sorry," he stated, then bowed lower than was necessary and walked away without noticing that I couldn't bring myself to even nod.

I forced myself to walk off the dance floor and was immediately accosted by my sisters. Lylin surprised me by speaking first. "You danced, Ella! You never dance."

"Was he terribly interesting?" Marilee gushed. "You looked as though you found him very interesting indeed. What was his name?"

Was that what it had looked like? That I found him interesting? I suppose that was as good an explanation as any.

"William." I managed to answer her question.

"William who? And of where?" As always, Marilee must have all the particulars.

"I don't know; I didn't think to ask," I responded, trying to move away from them.

"Didn't think to ask?" Her reproving look suggested I had been remiss in my duties. "Well, when you dance with the next gentleman, you really must be more thorough. Details are important when considering suitors."

I rolled my eyes, but smiled all the same. "Firstly, I am not considering suitors," I began, and they each gasped as if this were a horrifying statement, "and secondly, I don't plan on dancing with any more gentlemen tonight."

"That's going to be difficult," Lylin muttered as she peered past me. I glanced back and saw two gentlemen eyeing me with interest and another striding toward me with purpose.

"I'll catch up with you two later. Enjoy the dancing." I slipped past them easily and looked back in time to see Marilee distracting the gentleman who had been in pursuit. Marilee could always be counted on as a good distraction.

Hurrying to the nearest door leading off the main hall, I passed by Jeshua, who latched onto my arm, pulling me to a halt.

"You desert too early, dear sister," he sneered in his most charming voice. I was surprised at his talking to me. I suppose my dance with his henchman had gotten under his skin.

Taking hold of one of his fingers that wrapped around my arm, I bent it back until he let go with a wince. "Let me make one thing perfectly clear." I stared at him, but he was avidly avoiding my eyes. He tried to appear genial while I continued to bend his finger back. "You have no say—in anything—to do with me." I released his finger and strode away.

Crossing the entrance hall, I threw aside a heavy tapestry, entering what appeared to be an empty and dimly lit corridor. Then I stopped, not knowing where to go next. I hated being here in Tride. I hated the inevitability of Jeshua marrying my sister. I didn't want to stand by and let it happen.

I paced for a moment, wondering where exactly I could go from here. It was so confusing to be a royal when I didn't feel like one.

"Can I help you with anything, Your Highness?" I looked up to see William standing in the shadows farther down the corridor. It seemed we had found the same place to collect ourselves. "You look as though you might be in need of an escape."

"I do not wish to speak to you," I said bluntly and turned away from him, toward the entry hall once more. He confused me. I already felt as though I were a paradox in my world; matters were not helped by this man, who seemed also to be a paradox in his world. And now we two paradoxes had collided and I worried the earth would fall out from under me.

"My apologies, Highness."

I spun to glare at him. "Stop doing that," I insisted. "Stop being nice. I don't want you to be nice to me."

He didn't look surprised, only calm, and it reminded me of that maddening calm he had possessed when shoving a gag in my mouth. "Might I ask why?" he inquired.

"Because I want to hate you," I spouted, fueled by the distinct memory of his actions toward me. "I have the right to hate you, I *should* hate you and yet somehow I can't manage it."

"Might I speak freely, Your Highness?"

My eyes narrowed. "Trying to uphold the rules of polite society seems a bit silly, don't you think?" He stared at the wall and said nothing. "So, speak on. Speak as freely as you wish; at least you'll be talking, which is more than I can say for the last time we met."

His head snapped up. "You're angry I didn't strike up a conversation? Do you really think anything I would have said could have made a difference?" He had the audacity to sound angry.

"Yes." My voice was rising but I didn't bother checking it. I had been checking myself for too long.

"What could I have said?" he demanded in a whisper.

"The truth!"

"I was following orders."

"But you could have said something. You hold no real loyalty to Jeshua. You didn't want to carry out those orders. You're not a lowly servant; you're a knight! You could have done something, even a small something. I understand that all royal commands must be followed. Believe me—I understand that." He didn't retort because I was right. "A few words. 'Someone is coming; you'll be fine.' 'No one is going to hurt you.' 'The rat of a Prince will be along to collect you shortly.' 'We're not going to torture and murder you!' Something!" My calm was breaking. I had convinced myself that because I had never been in any real danger, I could control my emotional response. But it was slipping out now, as I was reminded what it had felt like in those moments. "Anything would have been better than the silence!"

And silence is what followed. William regarded me with his honest eyes and I tried desperately to hold on to my anger.

He walked slowly toward me, looking tired, resigned somehow. I tried to appear strong and angry. His hands came toward me and I refused to flinch away. I was strong. I was not intimidated, and he would not succeed in making whatever point he was trying to make. His hands came to rest on either side of my neck and I reflexively tried to push him away; but he just made me look at him and said earnestly, "*I'm sorry.*"

I stilled, shocked by the pain and vulnerability written on his crumpled face. My calm broke, my breath catching in my chest.

"I'm so desperately sorry for what I did to you. I know I have no excuse and I'm so sorry."

I started heaving sobs and he pulled me to him, wrapping his arms around me.

"I'm sorry," he repeated as I tried to push at him, tried to remember my anger, to remember all the reasons why this man had less right than anyone to touch me. But he just held on, binding me gently but inescapably against his chest, until I gave in to my need. I *needed* to be held. And so I rested my forehead on his shoulder, held my arms to my chest, and just let him hold me as I forced my sobs to quiet.

Standing there, clutched in the embrace of this stranger of all strangers, I remembered being attacked by the drunk in the road and afterwards coming into the entry hall and being held by Jeshua. I had hated it, wishing it had been anyone but him—because I had needed that comfort, but not from Jeshua.

As I steadied my breathing, my mind went back further, searching for the time when this sort of comfort had gone missing in my life. And I realized that ever since my Father had sent Gavin away, ever since he had started ignoring me as punishment for my defection, I had been missing this. Because my father had deprived me not only of Gavin, but of himself when he had sought to punish me. And I hadn't realized the toll it had taken until now.

I gave up completely and let my arms go around him, fisting my hands into the fabric at the back of his coat. I breathed in the calm he offered, taking it in methodically, because I knew this was something I was not likely to receive again for a long time. I leaned into him, relaxing, pouring my stresses into him.

It was one of the strangest experiences of my life—to give myself over to the comfort offered by *this* man. I must have taken leave of my senses—and yet so had he. He should not—absolutely should not—have allowed himself to touch me. Dancing was one thing, but to hold me in a deserted corridor against my will was lunacy on his part. And yet I silently thanked him for it.

That was how Jeshua found us.

Chapter Twenty-Six

I HEARD THE tapestry draw back, but William was quicker to react. He shifted, putting the bulk of his body entirely between me and whoever had come into the corridor. He glanced back over his shoulder, but kept his arms around me. I froze, inexplicably trusting William's instincts.

"Prince Jeshua, I'm afraid I'm a bit busy just now." William chuckled in a conspiratorial way I didn't recognize, having never had an opportunity to observe the brotherly bond these two seemed to share.

"So I can see," I heard Jeshua reply. He sounded amused. "All the same, I'll need to speak with you as soon as you are available." The amusement was still there, but the authority overrode it.

"I'll only be a moment," William promised, and I sensed Jeshua had gone. William released me slowly. I let my arms drop but didn't bother stepping back.

"What was that about?" I asked.

"He thinks I was in the midst of seducing you, but he didn't realize who you were."

I was surprised for a moment, wondering if Jeshua and his friends could often be found seducing maidens in deserted corridors. And then I remembered Jeshua's several attempts at seducing me and felt my nose wrinkle in disgust.

William misread my expression. "An unpleasant prospect for you, I'm sure."

"No, I was actually thinking of—" I stopped myself and leaned against the wall, realizing how tired I felt.

"Of?" he prompted.

I looked up at him. "You seem to have muddled my brain a bit."

"How so?"

I put a hand to my forehead, trying to keep my rationality intact. "I have this absurd inclination to confide in you, but I know I cannot."

His hand moved toward me but he stopped himself. "Why can't you?"

I stared at him, not bothering to answer. He probably hadn't expected an answer anyway.

"Very well," he said. "Then I shall confide in you." I smiled as he folded his arms across his chest with determination. It was admirable what he was doing, trying to distract me.

"But you have to answer to Jeshua," I reminded him.

He sighed, resigned. "Right," he muttered to himself. "So, what shall I tell him?"

"What do you mean?" I had no idea what Jeshua would want.

"He'll want to know why we danced, what we talked about, and if you recognized me as…"

"My captor?" I supplied blandly.

"Yes." His arms fell to his sides and his eyes dropped.

I thought for a moment about Jeshua, about why I was here in Tride—to celebrate the fact that my sister would marry him. The situation was suddenly unacceptable. I don't know if it was William's taking on my burden, or just a sudden epiphany, but whatever the case, I couldn't sit through it. "I can't let her marry him," I said to myself. "He's such a wretched human being; she deserves better."

I should have told my family the truth. That was obvious now. But the situation seemed so unbelievable and my instinct to protect Gavin was so overpowering that I had lost my sense. By protecting Gavin, I had thrown Kalina into the jaws of a snake.

Gavin had been right. She deserved to know what I knew. It was wrong for me to keep this from her for the sake of protecting anyone.

"Are you going to tell your father what happened?"

I studied him, realizing what a ridiculous web had been woven. This would affect not only me, but Kalina, Jeshua, Gavin, and now William. But I nodded my head anyway. "He probably won't believe me, but there is nothing I can do about that. No matter what happens, Kalina needs to know the truth. Perhaps I can leave you out of it." Even as I said it, though, I knew it wasn't true. If I was going to tell this story, it had to be the whole story.

"Your father won't believe you?" He sounded a bit incredulous.

A bitter smile flitted over my mouth. "He has his reasons."

"You lie often?" he asked sarcastically.

I offered a small smile and answered with a partial truth. "He doesn't approve of some of my associations. He doesn't trust my judgment."

"You shouldn't leave me out of it." He continued to shock me. I wondered if he realized what he was volunteering for.

"I know, but the consequences..." He just shrugged his shoulders, resigned. "Unless, of course, he doesn't believe me, in which case he may not even let me tell him about you. Perhaps that's what you should wish for."

He frowned, puzzled by my continued assertion that my father would not believe me. "What if you weren't the one to tell the story?"

I panicked at the thought of Gavin being involved in the telling of it. "Who else would tell it? I'm the only one who knows the whole story."

"Neither of us knows the whole story, but together we could paint a clear picture."

Once again—shock. He would accuse Jeshua of planning my kidnapping? He would admit to carrying it out? "Do you have any idea what my father would do to you?"

"He couldn't do anything to me. If he wanted me punished, he would have to turn me over to Tride authorities. A criminal must be punished in his own kingdom, except in cases of murder. If I had killed a

Dalthian subject, then he could do with me whatever he liked, but other than that, he must seek retribution through my own monarchs."

"And is that any better? You are talking about accusations against your own prince."

"I'm hoping that once your father hears the whole story, he won't be inclined to turn me over—that he will instead seek retribution against Jeshua. I was, after all, following a royal command, and your father knows what that means. Perhaps we will be able to make him see the situation clearly." He didn't appear optimistic, but he did look determined. "Either way, I've done Jeshua's bidding long enough."

The enormity of what we were considering overwhelmed me. "But my family is only here for two days. If we do this, then it has to be…"

"Now," he stated.

I sucked in a deep breath, trying to keep my composure. I tried to think through our options—whom we should tell, and how. I had to tell my father, but should we tell only him? No, Kalina needed to know, and it would be easier to get it out all at once and not have to repeat ourselves. I also decided I wanted my mother there. She would help my father keep a level head.

"All right," I said, after I had worked through the details in my head. "I will get my father and mother and Kalina. We need a place to meet where we won't be disturbed or overheard."

"All the guests are on the main floor, so we can go up to the library. Do you know where it is?"

"Yes." I had hidden there quite a bit during our visits here over the years.

"Gather your family as quietly as possible and meet me there. I'll go up directly so I can avoid Jeshua. How will you get your sister away from him?"

This was easy enough to answer. "Marilee."

It was easier than I had expected. My parents and Kalina were all tired enough that they welcomed the idea of getting away from the commotion for a while. It wasn't until I was leading them up the stairs that their curiosity piqued.

My father stopped. "Ariella, what is going on?"

"There is someone I would like you to speak with."

"And it couldn't wait until after the festivities?" He sounded alarmed and I couldn't blame him; this was entirely out of character.

"I believe the information he has needs to be heard as soon as possible."

"Ariella," Kalina interjected, "if this has to do with matters so important that Father needs to be involved, then surely I don't need to be here."

I looked at her, guilt crashing through me. "I'm afraid this concerns you more than anyone." This caught her attention and she started moving forward again. My parents moved on reluctantly, but my father's questions continued.

"What is this about, Ariella?" he asked as we reached the second floor.

"My abduction."

My father grabbed my arm, pulling me to a halt. "You have said very little about the situation since it happened, and now suddenly you need to discuss it?" He seemed a bit angry, but also worried.

"There is a man waiting for us in the library who has information concerning it."

My father started breathing angrily through his nose. Then he strode quickly to the library door, towing me along with him. My mother and Kalina caught up with us and slipped through the doors, not knowing what to expect. The king closed and locked the door, then turned to the seemingly empty room.

Then I saw him. William stood very still beside a chair with his feet apart, his hands clasped behind his back and his head down.

"Father, Mother, Kalina. This is Sir William."

He raised his head, brought his feet smartly together and bowed to each in turn. "King Forrester, Queen Lorilai, Princess."

Kalina curtsied, my mother stared, and my father glowered.

I walked over to stand a little ways from William, so that I could face my family. "Before William tells you what happened, I need you to know I trust him and he is giving us this information at great personal risk to himself." I felt as though I should have said more, but I couldn't think what or how to say it. I looked at William and he began.

"I've had a close association with Prince Jeshua for many years. His parents were good friends with mine and we grew up together. First we were playmates, then friends. After my parents died, I ended up relying on the grace of the royal family. The king helped me in my ambitions for knighthood, but it came at a price. Jeshua leveraged the debt I felt toward them and started asking favors. I am no longer so much a friend to him as I am a convenient way for him to get what he wants, to accomplish his designs without having to do much himself. We still act as though we are on friendly terms, but his purpose for keeping me around is to do his dirty work.

"When Jeshua was informed that Princess Ariella had no intention of accepting his planned proposal, he became quite put out. He started to obsess over it; I don't believe he had ever before been denied something he wanted." He paused and swallowed, knowing we were coming to the pivotal point. "In an attempt to win the princess's affections, he commanded me to take her captive and deposit her at a predetermined location, where he planned to find and rescue her."

Kalina paled, her eyes moving rapidly, but seeing nothing as she tried to sort through this information and what it meant. My mother stood unmoving and stared at me, a hand on my father's arm, disbelief frozen on her face.

I saw my father silently building his fury, not quite knowing where to direct it. "And you carried out these orders?" he asked in a voice of stone.

"Yes, Sire. It was a royal command." William's voice shook just slightly under the terrifying gaze of an angry father.

My father then turned to study me. His face looked somewhat bewildered, and also horrified and disgusted. "This man took you?" It sounded more like an accusation than a question.

"Yes, Father."

"And yet you stand beside him? You—" His eyebrows shot up as he remembered. "You danced with him earlier. Did you know then…" He paused for a moment, trying to get a grip on his next words. "What do you expect me to say to this?" he asked me, then turned his fury on William. "You held her captive?" he demanded.

"Yes."

"Tied her up, forced her onto a horse, and took her away?"

William swallowed. "Yes, Sire."

"And yet she stands beside you?" I couldn't tell if his anger or his incredulity won out. "Of her own free will? Or do you hold her captive again, forcing her to say these niceties about you? Have you threatened her?" He thundered and advanced, but I stepped in front of him.

"I am not being forced, Father. I know this is all very backward, but if you would just consider for a moment." He could have easily brushed me aside and pummeled William, but he stayed himself long enough for me to speak. "Jeshua gave the order, Father. Jeshua."

He finally tore his glowering eyes from William and focused on me. He seemed as though he were in pain. Suffering the pain of betrayal. "Jeshua? He did this, he… you told us you had heard his voice."

The guilt that leapt to his eyes left me unable to say any more than, "Yes."

"Why would he do that? How could he stoop…" He trailed off at the incomprehensibility of it. "Jeshua had my daughter abducted?"

"Yes, Sire."

"Why?"

I saw that William was reluctant to engage in conversation with my father, so I explained. "It seems he thought if he had a chance to appear as though he were a hero—if he had the opportunity of being my rescuer —he thought I would accept his proposal out of gratitude or hero worship."

"But that didn't happen?" he asked and I shook my head. "What went wrong?"

I took a breath. "I need to start at the beginning."

I told him everything. I told him all the details I could remember—how the men didn't look like criminals, how William had never hurt me, how he had protected me as much as possible. I told them about the horses, the tree, the rope, the fear, the climbing, the pain... and then I got to Gavin. And I told them all of that too: how he had seen me and followed the tracks, how he had planned to report back to the guard which way I had been taken, but then ended up finding me. I told them of his helping me out of the tree and then coming upon the conspirators. I told them all the conversation I could remember, about my suspicions that they were carrying out Jeshua's orders, and then of Jeshua himself appearing.

"You knew?" Kalina's voice surprised me. "You knew it was Jeshua and yet you told no one."

My eyes were brimming with tears of guilt, realizing how close I had come to letting Kalina marry a man capable of such deceit. "I didn't think anyone would believe me. And I never...I never thought he would court you. I told him. I told him when I spoke to him after I came back. I told him I knew it was him. I thought he would go away; I thought he would never show his face in our home again, but..."

"But he did, and you still didn't tell us."

"I had never seen his face and everyone thought it ridiculous when I said his voice sounded like Jeshua's. Then I convinced myself that it wasn't so horrible a thing as I had thought. I told myself since I hadn't been physically hurt—since his only objective had been to win me over—that he was only a fool, and perhaps not dangerous." I saw sympathy in her eyes as a tear streaked down my face. "I thought I would be accused of slandering his name for jealousy's sake. There was no one to confirm my story. I—" I stopped speaking, not wanting to defend myself. That was not the point. I had come here to tell them the truth, not to justify my mistake.

"There *was* someone to confirm your story, Ariella." My father pointed out after a moment of silence.

"Yes, but I had no idea William would be willing until tonight when—"

"Ariella," he interrupted. "The young man who did rescue you could have supported your story. Why didn't he come forward?" This wasn't an accusation, and it wasn't a slight against Gavin's character. It was an honest question.

I laughed. I was so tired and emotionally wrung out that his suggestion seemed funny to me. My amusement was short lived—cut off by the tears clouding my vision at the thought of Gavin being able to approach my father in any capacity. I took a deep breath to center myself before answering. "He wanted to. He suggested we come to you and tell you what happened, but I told him no." My parents appeared confused. "Would you have put any credence in what Gavin had to say?" I could see my father thinking it over. "Just imagine what it would have looked like if Gavin and I had shown up together, accusing Jeshua of such an outrageous crime." My father remained silent, probably unable to reassure me of what might have happened. "But I should have come to you myself. I know that, and I *am* sorry. I just didn't want to cause more problems for him." I swallowed, forcing myself to add, "And I didn't think you would believe me."

No one spoke. There was so much to consider—so many more questions to ask.

"So what now?" Kalina was the first to break the silence. "What do I do now? Because, clearly, I'm not getting married." I looked at her and saw the betrayal she felt. "I am engaged, Ariella. I would have married him and you would have let me?" I ran to her then and wrapped my arms around her. I couldn't express my sorrow or my relief, so I just hugged her and she squeezed me with a fierceness I had never witnessed in her before.

We finally broke apart when my mother took control. "We will leave. That is all we can do. Prince Jeshua is royalty and cannot be punished; thus we will have to be content with his never being allowed within our borders ever again. We shall go as soon as the ball is concluded."

"Jeshua will need to be told," I pointed out.

"I'll take care of it," my father said, but I saw his jaw twitching in fury as he thought of a confrontation with Jeshua. Out of all of us, I believe my father had been the most deceived.

"I'll do it," Kalina volunteered. We all turned to gape at her. "I want to face him. I want to be the one to break it off. I don't want to be the hapless victim."

"Kalina…" my father started in a doubtful voice.

"I can do this, Father. I *want* to do this." My father was about to shake his head. "I *need* to do this."

My father closed his eyes and nodded, acquiescing. Kalina turned to me and held out her hand. "You need to do this, too."

I took a breath and held it for a moment, fortifying myself before I let it out, and grasped Kalina's hand with my own.

"And you all expect me to say nothing to him?" My father asked, quiet fury seeping into his voice. "You expect me to be satisfied when he has suffered no consequences?"

"Forrester…" my mother placated.

"It was my daughters he hurt!" His fury was growing; we could all feel it. "And I cannot stand by and do nothing. I would be justified in bringing an army against him."

"But you won't." I was surprised to hear Kalina say this, but unsurprised by my father's response.

He jabbed a finger at me. "He had her kidnapped. That is a crime against my kingdom, against my *family*." His breathing was labored. "I cannot stand by."

"Yes, you will." Again, Kalina's response was measured and confident. "Because you know, father. You know what the result would be, what the price would be."

His jaw shook in anger.

"And you are wise enough to know that though it might be

justified, that would not make it right."

He let out a harsh breath, and with it came some of his fury. Kalina's words had made him pull back. I was stunned by not only her insight, but her courage as well.

"And what of this man?" My mother's rancor was obvious. I turned to see her scrutinizing William, confusion and indecision written all over her face.

My father took a deep breath and fixed William with a piercing stare. I had seen him do this many times before. He had a sort of gift for judging the character of his subordinates. He took several long moments to make up his mind.

Then he turned to me. "I leave this man's fate in Ariella's hands. She is the only one qualified to make this decision."

I blinked in stunned surprise. The idea of my father turning such a decision over to me had never entered my mind. However, I didn't take long thinking it over. I knew what my decision would be.

Chapter Twenty-Seven

FIVE MINUTES LATER found Kalina and me in Jeshua's private study, still hand in hand, standing across from Jeshua himself, who tried to cover his nervousness with curiosity and amusement. He was unsuccessful.

"Well, darling, what's this about?"

"I am not your darling," Kalina replied bluntly, and Jeshua's smile faltered. "I've just been informed by two very reliable sources of your role in Ariella's abduction."

Jeshua's eyes widened and he unconsciously shifted into a defensive stance.

"You are a liar." Kalina's voice was calm. "You are a fraud. And I will not be connected with you any longer."

Jeshua took a moment to draw himself up, then demanded, "Might I ask who these two very *reliable* sources are?"

"I am one," I stated. "And William is the other—William, who will be taking up residence in Dalthia, where you will no longer be welcome or even permitted."

"And what in the world should stop me from running him through this very hour?" he asked, with a menacing glare.

"This is your kingdom, Jeshua," Kalina replied, perfectly calm. "Or at least it will be. We are not going to interfere with your rule. We are not going to make accusations; we are not going to slander your name with the truth of your actions—so long as you never cross within our borders ever again."

"I am a crown prince; I can do whatever I please," he spat.

"And I am a princess and will do what *I* please. And it does not please me to marry you." Kalina's temper flared and it was gratifying to see the effect of it on Jeshua. "However, it would very much please me to go downstairs right in the middle of this lovely celebration and publicly humiliate you by leaving in the middle of it." She paused, letting the threat of public humiliation prick at his pride. "Instead, we will wait until the ball ends, and then leave quietly. You may tell your people we parted amicably."

Jeshua stood there, seething, his nails digging into the palms of his hands. "You will regret the day you tried to dictate *anything* to me."

"I very much doubt that." Kalina spoke my thoughts aloud, and then we both turned and left the study. Our father and mother were waiting for us just outside, along with William, who didn't seem to know where he fit. We all walked to the great hall, my parents' arms linked, and my arm linked with Kalina's. William walked silently, and I allowed him the space to sort through what was happening. Before we reentered the dance, William excused himself to gather his things, since he would be leaving with us.

We didn't see Jeshua again. I guessed he remained in his study, angry and brooding. That was fine with me. We finished out the dancing. I joined my father for the last dance, while Kalina danced with William —though she did so in a daze. Lylin, Marilee and Lorraina remained blissfully unaware of what was going on until the event had ended.

We all gathered in the suite of rooms we had been given for accommodations and Kalina was the one to explain the situation. My sisters cast curious and astonished glances at both me and at William as the truth was told. Then we all arranged to have our things packed away and made our way out to the waiting carriages. Since Lorraina, Marilee and Lylin were not sure if they trusted William, they rode with my parents in the larger carriage, while Kalina and I were thankful for the opportunity to ride in silent contemplation with William. None of us said a word throughout the entire ride, which took all night, though none of us slept. There was too much to consider. William had a new life ahead of him. Kalina was back to being single and had to deal with the reality that the man she thought she loved did not exist.

And I? I had entered a new life as well. One where my father respected my opinion, one where he trusted me—trusted me enough to allow a stranger who had admitted to being my captor to ride in a carriage unescorted with two of his daughters. I had a new respect for my sisters; they were not as silly as I thought. It would be a new life where my parents knew my recent encounters with Gavin, and accepted them.

I had no idea what it all meant—only that it was good.

We arrived home as the sky was pulling itself from the blackness of night into the grey of dawn. Kalina jumped out as soon as the carriage stopped. The other carriage had arrived before ours, and Lylin reached out to Kalina as she passed, but Kalina slipped from her grasp and ran, headlong, into the palace. I sat in the silence, grieving for my sister, realizing I might have prevented this if I had not been so selfish.

"Your Highness?" William finally spoke into the silence.

"Did I do the right thing?" I asked, still staring at the place where Kalina had disappeared.

"For whom?" he asked softly.

"For everyone," I murmured. "For you, for Kalina?"

"Yes."

I turned to him. "But—"

"Yes," he insisted. "Your sister is hurting, but it will come nowhere near the hurt she would have experienced being married to Jeshua. You need to believe me about that." I already knew this, but it was good to hear it from someone else. "And as for me," his voice quavered, "you will probably never realize the gift you have given me." He slipped his hands into mine, and gazed at me as though there were more he needed to say, but couldn't find the words.

Finally he leaned toward me and kissed my cheek. "So, thank you," he said, and kissed my other cheek. I closed my eyes, welcoming the affectionate gesture without thought. Then I had the sensation of his mouth hovering close to mine, and my eyes opened.

He abruptly pulled back when he realized what he'd done—what he'd been about to do. He leaned back into his seat, stunned by his own actions. I sat frozen, staring at him—not because I was angry, but because I wasn't.

He scooted even farther from me. "I seem to have momentarily taken leave of my senses. My sincerest apologies; I forgot for a moment who you were, Princess." I found myself smiling, glad I had made yet another person forget my title, if only for a moment.

That was why I wasn't angry. That and the fact that his actions had not been intimate, only friendly and affectionate.

I wondered for a moment if, in other circumstances, I might have fallen for William. If our relationship hadn't started with lies, if I hadn't been completely in love with Gavin—

"I need sleep," I concluded aloud. He immediately opened the carriage door and stepped out, holding a hand out to assist me.

"Good night then, Princess."

"Good night, William," I replied, then forced one foot in front of the other until I reached my room. I pulled myself mechanically out of my clothing, determined to sleep for a long time. Then I fell into bed and drifted into blissful unconsciousness.

✳ ✳ ✳

When I woke, I found Gretchen sitting by my bed, mending a piece of clothing. "You're lurking," I said to get her attention.

Her hands stilled and she looked at me. "You did it." She sounded surprised.

"Did what?"

"Got rid of Jeshua."

I smiled as I pushed myself into a sitting position. "I did."

"How did that happen? You aren't even supposed to be here. You're supposed to be in Tride for four days."

I winced. "And you were supposed to have the next few days to yourself," I realized. "Oh, Gretchen, I'm sorry."

"Oh, pish." She waved my apology away. "I don't mind at all. I'm just relieved to be rid of him. Perhaps it will be some time before we see him again."

"We won't ever see him again."

Her eyebrows raised impossibly high. She put her mending on the ground and crawled onto my bed. "All right, start at the beginning."

The explanation took some time. When I finally made it down to breakfast, it had been cleared away. A steward asked me what I would like, but I told him I would prefer to just eat in the kitchen. This is something I had done several times before. It always caused a bit of a stir, but the kitchen staff actually seemed to enjoy it now.

When I entered the kitchen, everyone glanced up, smiled, dipped into a bow or curtsy, and then moved on with their work.

Marta approached me. "Mornin', Princess Ari. Miss breakfast again?"

"I'm afraid so. Do you mind if I just eat in here? I hate sitting at that giant table alone."

"Course not, Princess. Come on back." I followed her silver bun back to the alcove where a table and chairs were kept for anyone needing to eat in the kitchen. It was set back far enough to be almost completely private. It was one of the reasons I enjoyed eating here. No one but the kitchen staff ever knew I ate there, and they weren't likely to disturb me.

But the table wasn't empty as usual.

"William?"

He stumbled to his feet and bowed deeply, still clutching his napkin with both hands. "Princess," he mumbled. The mumbling seemed odd.

"Oh, then you know our guest, do you?" Marta asked and I nodded. "Well then, I'll let you sit to it. What can I bring you, Princess?"

"A plate from this morning would be wonderful." No need for them to make something new.

I settled in a chair across from William and found him studying me.

"What?" I asked. He seemed ill at ease, not his usual demeanor at all.

"Nothing." He glanced away, then looked back only a second later and answered, "I'm waiting for you to change your mind."

"About what?"

"About my being here."

"Why would I change my mind?"

"I can think of a number of reasons."

He was right, of course. Perhaps I was a bit crazy to have invited him into our home, but I felt he was a genuinely good person. Somehow, we understood each other.

"I'm not going to change my mind."

He sighed. Not a sigh of relief so much as a sigh of acceptance. "Well then, what shall I do?" I furrowed my brow, not sure what he meant. "I must have an occupation of some sort," he explained. "There has to be some way I can make myself useful to you, to your family." I considered this for a moment. William was a knight, used to following orders and completing tasks. Of course he should be given work of some sort—he would go crazy otherwise.

"I'm sure there is something." Our plates were set before us. "Thank you, Marta." She curtsied and excused herself. "I will speak with my father about it," I told him, and then bit into my breakfast.

"Thank you." He did not touch his food.

"Are you not hungry?"

"Uh..." he went to pick up his spoon but was uncomfortable doing so. "I'm not used to eating at the same table as royalty, much less beautiful royalty." He said this almost to himself.

I smiled, finding it adorable that he would be nervous about eating with me, and couldn't help poking fun at him. "Says the man who once sat on top of me." He stared at me, shocked and horrified, then picked up his spoon and defiantly shoveled a bite into his mouth. I quirked an eyebrow, then went back to eating my food. His statement had made me curious, though. "You never sat to eat with Jeshua?"

"No." He sounded as though the idea were slightly absurd. "I stood and watched him eat many times during our discussions, but I never ate *with* him." This made sense of course, but I had always thought of them as friends, ever since seeing them in the woods together. William had made it clear last night that there was no bond between them, but it took some effort to realign my thoughts. I was chewing my food thoughtfully when he addressed me. "I should apologize."

His phrasing made me smile. "You *should* apologize or you *are* apologizing?"

"I would like to apologize."

"For?" I asked, because there were a great many things to which he may have been referring.

He shifted in his seat. "I realize the list is rather extensive. But at this moment I'd like to apologize for the familiarity I treated you with last night in the carriage. I had no right to—"

"Don't," I cut him off, shaking my head. "Please don't."

"Princess, I—"

"No, really. I don't want you to apologize for that. Apologize for something else."

His eyes studied my face, trying to figure out what I meant, then he nodded his head. "All right," he said slowly, "then I apologize for sitting on you."

I smiled and we ate the rest of our meal in silence. He finished before I did, but continued to sit. "You don't have to wait for me."

He shrugged. "I have nowhere else to be."

That afternoon, I managed to waylay my father in between appointments. I suggested he might find some use for William, and that little nudge was all it took. They spent more than an hour that afternoon locked in my father's study, discussing I don't know what.

I stayed close to my father's study as much as possible, hoping I might speak with William and see if they had reached a suitable agreement. I was curled up on a cushioned seat down the hall, reading, when the door opened. They shook hands in parting before my father left alongside his personal aide, who had been waiting right outside the door.

William turned my way and walked slowly down the corridor, two fingers running along his jaw in deep contemplation. He didn't notice me until I spoke. "How did it go?"

He looked up, startled, and opened his mouth to answer, but it took him a moment to get a coherent thought past his throat. "Your father is an interesting man."

I raised my brow, waiting for him to explain this very broad statement about my father.

"He reminds me of my own king—former king, I suppose—before his illness."

"Is he much different now?"

"He's much too weak to rule now, and even before he was weak, he was confused. Jeshua has been ruling for over a year now, though people don't realize it. Most of the kingdom believes the king is simply too tired in his old age to make public appearances, but it's much more than that."

"I didn't realize." His smile said clearly that he knew I didn't realize that, which was exactly the point. "He was a good king?"

I was still sitting casually and he took the seat next to mine, leaning his forearms on his thighs. "He was. He served his people to the best of his ability. I was proud to be a part of his household." His remembrances had lent a softer quality to his eyes, but they went steely once again. "Now there is very little in that household to be proud of."

"Because of Jeshua?" He nodded but didn't say any more, lost in contemplation. "Did you come to a suitable arrangement with Father?" I asked, trying to draw him back into the conversation.

He turned to me. "Not...yet." His slightly cryptic answer intrigued me. "I think he wants to get a better handle on who I am before he gives me any responsibility. I respect that; I understand it. I'm just glad he's giving me the benefit of the doubt after everything that happened."

I had my elbow up on the armrest, my chin resting on the back of my fingers. He stopped talking and ran the back of his hand over my forearm, where my scars were still visible from scraping my arms on the bark of the tree. "What happened?"

I glanced down and pulled my arm away. The velvet cuffs covered the dark, angry scars on my wrists, but my arms I had left visible. I felt bad answering, but I couldn't lie. My hand rubbed over my scars as I answered, "I...climbed a tree." I brought my eyes to his before clarifying, "With my hands tied." I raised my eyebrows and shrugged my shoulders apologetically.

His face was stricken, his mouth open to speak, but unable. His eyes shot away and then back. The regret and self-loathing obscured his features until that was all I saw. His eyes darted from my face, to my arms, to the wall and back again until he was so agitated that he pushed himself to his feet. He paced for a moment then turned to me suddenly.

"Every apology running through my head is so pathetically inadequate." There was a fury in his voice. A revulsion for himself, I guessed, and probably a good deal for Jeshua as well.

I wanted to say something to make him feel better, but I didn't think I could. I sensed any forgiveness I gave him at this moment would make him feel worse, not better. So I sat silent and let him work it out himself.

"Tell me what to do." He sounded desperate. "Give me something to do for you. Anything. I know it won't be anywhere near sufficient, but please let me do *something* for you."

I opened my mouth, knowing there was nothing he could do for me. He couldn't give me what I wanted. No one could. But before my refusal could pass my lips, I thought of something else. I closed my mouth, thinking over this request before laying it at his all too willing feet. "Help Kalina." Confusion replaced the mask of self-loathing for a moment. "I don't know how to help her through this. I think I'm the wrong person to help with Jeshua's betrayal. But I think you could."

"I couldn't—" he started, but seeing my expression he rerouted his thoughts. "I will find a way. If that is what you ask of me, then I will do everything in my power to help your sister."

"I think she mostly just needs a friend. And a distraction," I offered, finding myself very pleased with the potential of this endeavor.

He gave a nod of acceptance, then glanced once more as my arms. "Dare I ask why you cover your wrists?"

"I'm fine," I assured him. "Now, go find Kalina."

Excitement filled me as I walked away. It had been years since I had been excited about anything, and now I was—not only about William and Kalina, but about so many things that had happened over the past couple days. Jeshua was gone. As that realization sunk in, I was nearly overcome with relief. I had been living in dread, terrified that I had doomed my sister to a miserable marriage; terrified that any other choice would ruin Gavin's life. Now that weight had been lifted, and I could see just how crushing it had been. Jeshua was gone, my relationship with my father was inexplicably better, and I had discovered a friendship in the most unlikely way. William was a godsend.

Caught up in my thoughts, I found myself outside before I realized where I was headed. I stopped for a moment, making sure my actions were wise before continuing toward the maze. Gavin deserved to know what I'd done—that I hadn't sacrificed my sister. I wanted to tell him my family knew he had saved me, and that he would receive the credit he so rightly deserved.

It took only a few minutes of wandering to find him. He was hard at work, and I watched as he spread dark, rich soil over a patch of ground, crumbling the larger pieces in his hands. His arms up to his elbows were dark with soil, as was his forehead where he had swiped his hand across it. I shook myself from my observations, determined to keep my thoughts in their appropriate place. "Good day, Gavin," I said to get his attention.

He turned to look at me. "Princess," he said in surprise as he rolled off of his knees into a sitting position. "I had heard your family returned early." It sounded like a question.

I just smiled, happy to have such good news to tell him.

"Is there going to be a marriage?" he asked.

"No," I said, smiling even more broadly.

He blew out a breath and chuckled. "I'm glad to hear that."

"I'm very glad to tell it."

"Well done, Ella." His sincerity touched me.

"It shouldn't have taken me so long." I dropped my eyes, appreciating his praise, but knowing I should have done the right thing long ago.

"Did you tell them about the kidnapping?"

"I told them everything, including you and your—heroics."

He didn't respond, rendered speechless by this revelation. It took him a moment to recover. "I, uh—" He blinked back his emotion. "I very much appreciate that, Princess." I didn't know how to respond to his obvious emotion, so we were silent until he spoke again. "Your father believed you, then?"

I nodded. "I don't even know how it happened, but things with my father have greatly improved."

"So he's not going to have me hanged for being too close to you?" He was fighting a smile.

"I don't know; he might. He is rather unpredictable."

"Very comforting, Highness." He allowed himself a lopsided grin.

It was good to see him smile—to smile with him—but I didn't want to slip into the flirtatious teasing that had been our habit years ago.

"I just thought you should know." I clasped my hands in front of me, preparing to leave. "After all, I don't know if I would have been able to do it without your—" I searched for the right words. "Without you telling me to." I laughed a bit and a look of chagrin crossed his face, but he still smiled. "So, thank you again. I'll let you alone now." I turned to go.

"Thank you, Princess." I turned back. "For coming to tell me. I'm very glad to hear about it."

"You're welcome. Good day, Gavin."

"A wonderful day, Princess."

I left him, glad I had been able to speak with him, but still missing him. I would always miss him.

✻ ✻ ✻

Over the next few days, I tried to be around whenever William and Kalina might have the opportunity to cross paths. She kept to her room much of the time, so I followed her after lessons, hoping it would give me some chance of seeing their meeting.

I didn't have to wait long. Only four days after his arrival, I left the study and noticed William standing inconspicuously down the hall a ways. Kalina passed without noticing him; she appeared to be in a daze, which was not uncommon. I stayed just outside the door, waiting to see what William would do. When she had gone ten paces beyond him he pushed away from the wall and walked after her. I, in turn, followed him. I'm sure it would have been an odd sight, if anyone had been paying attention—a somber parade progressing down the corridor without any apparent destination.

Just as I was wondering how William would approach her, she gave him the perfect opportunity. In her apathy and distraction, her shawl dropped to the floor without her noticing its departure. She kept walking. William paused, took a deep breath and then hurried his pace.

"Your Highness," he called as he scooped up her shawl.

She did not turn—too wrapped up in her own thoughts.

"Princess Kalina!" he called again, this time raising his voice.

Her head came up and she turned slowly, as if she were surprised to hear someone calling for her. She took a moment to focus on him before saying, "Yes?"

He held out the cloth. "You dropped your wrap, Highness."

Her eyes went down to the offering in his hands and her brow furrowed in surprise and confusion. "Oh." She took it from him slowly, as though her mind was still not focused on the situation at hand. She stood there, staring down at the fabric running through her hands.

William opened his mouth as though to speak, but didn't manage to get any words out until his third try. "Might I walk with you a ways?"

Kalina's eyes darted up, startled by the question. "Of course," she replied without any real conviction, then turned and started walking.

William fell into step beside her, his hands clutched behind his back. The murmur of their voices started just before they turned the corner. It was a start.

In fact, it turned out to be a very good start. William seemed easily able to persuade Kalina to spend time with him. Within a few days, she appeared less distracted and more cognizant of her surroundings. Her eyes lit up each time she saw him, and over the next several weeks I was able to watch as William coaxed my sister out of her melancholy over Jeshua's betrayal and into a fragile romance. Watching their relationship develop was wonderful and difficult at the same time. Kalina was being introduced to genuine love, as opposed to feigned love. The stark contrast between Jeshua's arrogant pursuit and William's sincere interest gave her a startling perspective on the relationship she would have had with Jeshua. I saw her become much more of herself and less of what everyone expected.

As I watched them greet each other one morning, William spotted me and waved me over.

"I was just telling your sister: your father has decided to give me a try."

I raised an eyebrow. "And what exactly does that mean?"

"I'm joining the guard. I'll be working directly under the captain, helping to assess defenses and make improvements. If I prove myself useful, they'll keep me around."

I offered my sincere congratulations to him, and then silently congratulated myself for a match well made.

Chapter Twenty-Eight

SOMETHING ABOUT MY sketch was off. Trying to draw the village square from memory was proving to be more difficult than I had hoped. As I contemplated the idea of just giving up for the day, the door opened and my father walked in.

My muscles tensed, but he only sat in the chair across from mine and offered a small smile. My grip on my pencil relaxed and I was able to return his smile, after which we spent the next half hour in comfortable silence.

I resumed lessons with my father after that day, and though our time together still felt a bit strained, I was relieved to feel his approval.

My life settled into a comfortable rhythm once Jeshua's presence no longer plagued me. I was able to enjoy my work in the village as well as time with my family without that oppressive sense of dread invading my thoughts.

I saw Gavin working many times, and I was able to acknowledge him and continue on my way without the extreme emotional upheaval that had ruled my reaction to him previously. He would smile and continue with his work, at least at first. After a few weeks, I noticed his smile was slower in coming and there was sometimes a distinct sadness in his eyes.

I had never seen Gavin so grave, so out of sorts. I wished I could talk to him, find out what was wrong, but that was no longer my place. I missed his smile.

✳✳✳

I pushed the ivy aside and heaved the door open. This was likely to be the last time I went to the waterfall. It was unwise for me to go on my own, but my purpose today required the serenity and solitude offered by the waterfall. The change I had seen in Gavin over the past several weeks was weakening my resolve. Every time he gazed at me with his sad eyes, every time he failed to greet me in his casual friendly manner, I found myself becoming weaker. Wasn't he happy? I needed him to be happy. Because if he wasn't, then what was the point? I truly wanted his happiness, and if Brinna could give that to him, then I would be content.

So I walked through the trees and changed out of my dress before slipping under the waterfall, into my sanctuary. I was determined to let him live his life in the way he had chosen. That life did not include me, so I would let him go. But first I would sit here, completely alone, and I would let myself think of him one more time. I would remember every beautiful moment of our friendship, every joyous moment of having someone who truly loved me, someone I had loved in return. And when I finished, I would leave him here in this place. I would not let his happiness or unhappiness shake my resolve.

I sat in the water, my knees pulled up and my head resting against the stone behind me, and I allowed myself to feel just how much I had loved that boy—how much I still loved the man. I let the memory of him —his crooked smile, his fascination with my hair, his walking backwards when he teased me—I let them all fill my mind as his voice drifted through my head.

"Princess," his voice said. I frowned, not wanting to remember him calling me by my title. I tried to imagine the many times he had called me by my name, the many times he had called me—

"Ella," he whispered in my mind, and it was exactly how I wanted him to say it. With all the tenderness and love I had hoped would be suffused in it. Then I felt something touch my cheek and my eyes flew open. I gasped, sucking in some of the water running over my face, and

269

started to sputter as I scrambled away from the man crouching in front of me. I had only retreated a couple of feet when I realized it was Gavin crouching in the water, a startled expression on his face.

"Gavin!" I gasped, as I tried to wipe some of the water from my face. "What are you doing here?"

"I—" he began, but seemed distracted as his eyes studied me.

I looked down at myself and shut my eyes in embarrassment. As usual, my dress and cloak lay on the shore, safe and dry, and I was only left in my under things. And though they were, in actuality, entirely modest (even wet, the layers of fabric were thick enough to not become see-through), it still felt very revealing and entirely inappropriate for him to see me in such a manner.

I decided I needed to talk, so perhaps he might stop staring at me. "What are you doing here? How did you find me?"

He still didn't answer, but he did look away, or at least tried to. He kept glancing back at me every couple seconds. "I…I have suspected for some time that you come here."

I stood in water up to my knees, and as he continued to steal glances at me, I was suddenly conscious of the fact that I was drenched from head to foot, with my hair hanging unkempt about me. I must have looked like a drowned kitten. "But why did *you* come here?" I demanded as I pushed the hair away from my face and tried to smooth it. But as I did so, my hand brushed a tender spot and I winced. I realized that my head hurt—a lot. My eyes pinched shut and my hand pressed gently against the swelling at the crown of my head.

I heard Gavin moving through the water, then he spoke very close to me. "Are you well, Princess?"

His hand rested on top of mine and I pushed it away. "I'm fine."

"Did you hurt your head?" he asked in alarm.

I pinched my eyes tighter. "Yes, I think I must have bumped it when you startled me."

"I'm sorry. Will you let me have a look at it?" My eyes popped open. I did not want him to touch me; or more accurately, I knew I should not let him touch me. But he was only being kind, so after an agonizing moment of staring into his eyes, wondering if my apprehension was written as clearly on my face as I felt it, I nodded my head.

He took my elbow and had me sit where the water was shallow. I instinctively curled into a ball, wrapping my arms around my legs.

I felt his hands in my hair and realized I had overestimated my control, or underestimated the way he would make me feel. As he tried to move my hair aside in order to see if my head was bleeding, I clasped my hands even more tightly to prevent them from trembling.

"You have a bump, but it isn't bleeding," he concluded, while his fingers continued to weave their way through my hair.

"Are you cold?" he asked after a moment.

"No, of course not." I responded automatically.

"You're shaking."

Oh. I hadn't realized my trembling had moved beyond my hands, or I would have told him I was cold. As it was, I didn't know how to explain my body's reaction to him. I shut my eyes again in a vain attempt to block out my feelings.

"I'm fine." But I wasn't fine, because his hands still ran through my hair, no longer concerned with the bump on my head. He just played with my hair, running his fingers haltingly through the wet strands, pulling it back over my shoulders until it all lay in one solid sheet down my back. The sensation of his fingers grazing my neck felt so wonderful, and so wrong. What was he doing?

"Gavin," I whispered in desperation. "Please stop."

He slowly moved his hands away and settled beside me. "You're still shaking." He pointed out the obvious.

"I know." I kept my eyes shut, not wanting to see the way he would be staring at me.

"Tell me why you're shaking, Ella."

I shook my head. This wasn't fair. He had surprised me, intruded on my sanctuary. I had let myself remember everything I felt for him. I wasn't prepared to have him so close to me, especially when he was being so… so *Gavin*. "Please don't ask me that."

"I am asking," he said, covering my hands where they were clenched around my knees.

I opened my eyes and made the mistake of catching his. He was leaning toward me and looking at me in the way only he could. It was the expression that made me want to crawl into his arms and never leave. Instead, I uncoiled my body and moved deliberately away without taking my eyes off of him. I curled back into a ball, pinning my hands between my chest and my legs so he couldn't reach them and they could not reach for him, then took a fortifying breath. "Tell me what you're doing here."

He looked hurt, or disappointed, as though my moving away from him had somehow been a slight to him. Then he took a breath and said, in an almost defeated voice, "There was something I wanted to discuss with you."

"And what would that be?" I asked, still only able to manage a whisper, for fear my voice would break with the strain.

"I have heard some news, and since there have been times in the past when I've made mistaken assumptions," –I almost smiled at that reference—"I decided to come directly to you and ask you to verify what I've heard."

I appreciated that he was finished making unfounded assumptions, but I wondered why he had sought me out here. "What have you heard?"

"A new knight has joined the guard."

"Yes. William," I confirmed.

"And he has won the favor of your father and plans to declare his intentions toward one of the princesses."

"He does?" I was delighted, having wondered if William's insecurities and guilt would cause him to pass up even someone as tempting as Kalina.

As Gavin registered the delight on my face, his eyes closed, as though he were in pain. "You didn't know?" he asked with a catch in his voice. Perhaps he disapproved of William being accepted among us after what he'd done.

"No, I didn't know. It's rather fast and I thought perhaps he would not have the courage to ask for her hand."

His eyes caught mine suddenly, clearly surprised. "Then it's not you?" he asked.

I felt a bit put off by the utter relief he expressed at my not being attached to someone when he was very securely attached. "No, indeed. That would be very strange." I said this more to myself than to him. My relationship with William was, indeed, strange.

"Why would it be strange?" he asked.

"Because..." I suddenly realized he would not know. "Because this William is the same William that you and I encountered after you found me at the tree." A look of horror crossed his face. "He is the one who carried out Jeshua's orders—"

I stopped speaking when Gavin shot to his feet, hit his head on the low cave wall, and cursed. He clutched his head and flailed for a moment in wordless pain and anger. I couldn't help but go to him.

He was doubled over, holding his head, and if he hadn't been so angry, I might have found the situation funny. As it was, I just put my hands over his. "Hold still," I insisted when he started to shake his head. I tried to examine his head, but he grabbed my wrists and lifted his face.

"Are you all mad?" he asked. "You aren't playing some horrible joke? The man who abducted you is now responsible for your protection?"

"Gavin, calm down. It's not as simple as all that." I tried to sooth his anger, though I knew it would take a lot of explaining.

"It doesn't sound simple at all. It sounds dangerous and completely insane."

I slowly pulled my wrists from his hands. "William was acting under Jeshua's orders. He tried to protect me as much as possible during the whole ordeal, and it was he who came forward and told my father what had happened. He's the reason Kalina didn't marry Jeshua. He's the reason I was able to tell the truth about you. Yes, it is a rather insane situation, but William is an honorable man and only did what he did to me because he was ordered to."

Gavin winced as he put pressure on his head. "That doesn't mean you should invite him to join the guard."

I shrugged, hoping to convey that since I wasn't worried about it, he shouldn't be either. "My father made the decision. But I do agree with it. He has quite a brilliant strategic mind." I went to him again. "Now, let me look at your head." I pushed down on his shoulders so he would sit down and I would be able to see the top of his head. Instead, he rested his forehead on my shoulder and put his hands at my waist.

I froze for a moment, then forced myself to move, to push my fingers into his hair as he had done to me only minutes before. He winced and I forced myself to speak in the hopes of dispelling the tension saturating the air around us. "We're quite the pair, you and I." I tried to chuckle, but it came out as more of a whimper. "But I'm sure we'll both be fine." I put my hands on his shoulders and tried to push him away from me. But instead of moving away, he moved into me, wrapped his arms entirely around my waist and buried his face in the curve of my neck.

I stood there stiff, my hands frozen in the air, not willing to embrace him back, but not able to push him away.

"Gavin." I cleared my throat in the hopes of lending my voice strength when I told him, "Please let go."

"There was something else I wanted to discuss with you," he murmured against my neck as he pulled me closer, and I forgot for a moment to breathe. Tears stung my eyes, and I wondered once again if he had any awareness of what he did to me.

I pushed on his shoulders, trying to heave him away from me. "Let go, Gavin," I demanded, my voice sounding desperate.

He lifted his head to catch my eyes, but his arms remained around me. "Just listen for a moment."

"Let go," I insisted, trying to pry his arms from around me.

He finally released me, only to grab hold of my wrists and anchor them against his chest. This was less torturous, but torture all the same. "Not until you listen."

I closed my eyes, wondering how he could be so calm at this moment, and pulled in vain against his hold. "Please, Gavin." The strength of my voice was gone. "Please. I'm listening, but just please let me go. I can't think when you touch me."

"That doesn't sound like such a bad thing." He had the audacity to sound amused, and I jerked my hands away, glaring at him. I don't know if he could differentiate between my tears and the water dripping from the ceiling onto my face, but I could. My tears were hot and angry. I backed away from him slowly, then turned and swam beneath the waterfall. I dragged myself to shore and clawed my way onto dry ground.

"Ella."

"Don't!" I spun to face him and he stopped, knee deep in water. I stood on shore, once again shaking.

"Why are you angry at me?" he asked.

I blanched. Was he in earnest? Was he honestly asking me that question? "Because you are toying with me, Gavin! You cannot be unaware of it. And I cannot fathom what I could have done to deserve such cruelty."

"I am not toying with you."

"How can you say that? How can you look me in the eye and say that?" He took a step forward in the water, but I stepped back and he halted, his eyes running the length of me. "Everything you have done in the past five minutes has hinted at intimacy and flirtation. In what world would that not be considered toying with me?"

His face was intensely serious for a moment before asking, "You don't know?"

"Know what?" I shouted to keep from wailing.

He stared for a moment more, then said quietly, "My... engagement"—I winced at the word—"was broken off several weeks ago."

I stopped breathing. My face went numb and my vision blurred. I could not speak; I could barely convince myself to start breathing again, and when I did it was quick and shallow.

He very slowly started to move toward shore while he explained, "She and I both realized that while our marriage would have been practical, we both wanted more. She was not what I wanted, and she knew I was unable to give her what she wanted." I blinked the tears from my eyes, wanting to see him clearly. He had stopped at the edge of the water, penitent. "I thought you would have heard. The news circulated all through the village only days after it happened. I thought for certain you would have heard of it. So when your indifference toward me continued, I thought perhaps you had found someone else. Then when I heard of William—" He stopped speaking when his words finally registered in my head. The barrier fell down; the conscious effort to stay away from him that I had been making for what seemed like forever was gone. I felt my body being pulled to him and found my arms wrapped around his neck. In the same instant, he wrapped his arms around me, fisting his hands into my hair.

He lost his balance and we fell into the water. Gavin used one hand to push us up so our heads were above water, and though I gasped for breath after having my head submerged, I wouldn't let go of him. It had been too long. I had been without him for much too long.

He pushed us into a sitting position and then pulled back enough to see my face, pushing my hair out of the way. His eyes fixed on my mouth but he hesitated. I was not in the mood for hesitation. I put my hands to the back of his neck and brought his lips to mine. I had meant to kiss him firmly, but then his lips brushed mine and all of those tiny, lovely sensations flitted through me. I slowed my advance and savored the sensation for just a moment before letting my exuberance take over. I kissed him in earnest, saying haltingly between kisses, "I—missed you—so much."

He met each kiss with the same passion and longing as I. Once I had exhausted myself with kissing him, I wrapped my arms around his neck, burying my face in his shoulder as I reveled in his closeness. While

I continued to cling to him, he picked me up out of the water and walked us onto dry land.

He dropped my feet beside where my clothes lay, then picked up my cloak and draped it around me.

"I'm not cold," I told him.

He fastened it securely around my neck before admitting, "This is for my sake, not yours."

I put my fingers to my lips to suppress a smile. It all felt so very new and yet so very familiar. He moved my hand away. "Don't cover your mouth."

He moved to kiss me, but I needed the answer to a question first. "Gavin." He stopped himself, only inches from my face and looked at my eyes. "I told you months ago that I was in love with you, but you've never said—"

"I love you, Ella. I'm in love with you. You're the only thing I've ever wanted." I smiled at his thorough answer, and kissed him just as thoroughly, but then he pulled away, an expression of quiet sadness plaguing his face. "But in addition to not deserving you, you're also the one thing I know I can't have."

"Gavin, there is nothing you don't deserve." He smiled as though I were being overly kind. "And there is nothing you can't have."

"Ella…" he said, trying to prevent me from giving him false hope.

"I did some research. After our last…fight, and after you asked me what we would do if you weren't engaged. I researched the laws on royalty and marriage." His eyes were curious, but without hope. "Marriage of royalty to nobility is a tradition—a long-standing, well respected tradition, a tradition no one has broken in generations. … But it isn't law."

He looked utterly shocked. "What?"

"I'm not bound by law to marry someone with a title." I didn't want to push him, to make him think I wanted a promise from him right then, just after we had come to understand each other, but I wanted him to know our situation wasn't as impossible as we had thought.

"So, you can marry…"

"Anyone I want."

"Me?" His eyes delved into mine and my breath caught. Was he really asking? "I don't know how the details would work out, and I'm sure your father would want to kill me, but I could have you? If you chose me, I could have you?" he asked quickly, wanting the answer as soon as possible.

"Yes." I answered his hypothetical question, and he kissed me fiercely then, without the sense of reservation that I now realized had been a part of our kisses moments before. I felt nearly smothered, and it felt wonderful to be smothered by Gavin. I finally had to stop him so I could get my breath back.

"Marry me?" My eyes snapped to his as I heard him ask. The intensity of his gaze mesmerized me. "Ella, will you marry me?"

He didn't wait for an answer though, just kissed me over and over, murmuring, "Marry me, marry me, marry me," until I finally got out a "yes."

Chapter Twenty-Nine

WE SAT TOGETHER—his back against a tree and me curled up under one arm—watching the sun dip in the sky over the waterfall, his hands running constantly through my hair. "So what happened?" I asked.

He took a deep breath and let it out in a relaxed sigh. "I finally took my own advice."

I looked up at him, my brow furrowed.

"I said no," he clarified, making me smile. "I dreaded breaking things off with Brinna, but when I went to talk to her, she started sobbing with relief. She'd been struggling just as much as I had with our decision. We cared for each other, but we both became more and more uncomfortable as the time for our wedding drew closer."

"I am glad she was not hurt. Were your parents upset?"

He shook his head. "Did you know my parents never knew about you and I?"

"Never?"

"No, it was too dangerous."

"Not even after you left?"

He shook his head. "They didn't know what to do for me. They watched me struggle through that year and then talked me into the arranged marriage. I had no reason to say no, at least none that I could tell them. I was convinced I would come back here and you would barely remember me."

"As if that would be possible," I said, burrowing into his shoulder.

"I am rather unforgettable."

I snickered. "The boy who told me the only thing worse than nobility was royalty."

"I'm not entirely sure I wasn't right about that," he quipped, running his fingers through my hair.

I closed my eyes, smiling sadly. "I know you were. I'm a terrible person."

"And what terrible things have you done lately?"

"I almost let Kalina marry Jeshua."

He tightened his arm around me. "But you didn't."

"But I came so close," I whispered. "If not for William, I honestly don't know if I would have been able to tell them."

"Ah, William," he mumbled into my hair.

I stifled a giggle. "You would like him."

"Oh, would I?" he questioned as he pulled the cuff from my wrist, his fingers caressing my scars.

I smiled up at him. "I know it's utterly bizarre, but William is one of the most honorable persons I know."

He sent me a mock glare. "But you still love me more, right?"

"Yes, but only just," I said on a laugh.

He silenced me with a kiss. "Only just, indeed," he muttered against my mouth.

When he pulled back I stared into his eyes without guilt or regret and couldn't stop my smile. "We're getting married, you know," I said in a conspiratorial whisper.

"I do know, yes." He gave me his crooked smile. "And how do you propose we go about telling your father?"

I sighed, thinking through our options. "We could try to tell him together."

"If we showed up together, do you think he would allow me to live long enough to tell him the good news?"

I laughed, only because I knew my father's attitude toward Gavin had improved significantly since he found out Gavin had been the one to rescue me. Otherwise I would have taken his question seriously.

"Perhaps that's not the best idea," I admitted. "I could tell them on my own," I volunteered grudgingly.

"I don't want you to have to do that." He looked so serious, so concerned, and I loved him for it. "Do you think your father would grant me an audience if I requested it?"

I grimaced. "I really don't know."

He brushed a curl back from my forehead. "I think I should try anyway."

✳✳✳

Gavin was not granted an audience. So it was left to me. I told them. My mother sat silent, her face unreadable. My father sat there, silent, obviously fuming.

"I know you're disappointed. I know you're probably much more than disappointed. But you have to know it doesn't change anything. I've made my choice, and it is *my* choice. I'm marrying Gavin. I know I can't control how you will react, but I hope you will remember that I'm not foolish or flighty. This wasn't a rash decision made on a whim. I know what I want. I've agonized over it and this is my decision."

"I thought we had reached an understanding with one another." My father was holding on to his composure, but only just. "And here you are, defying us once again."

"That's where you're wrong, Father. This has nothing to do with defiance. I'm not petty or vindictive. You know that! This is simply what I choose, what I want."

"You choose to toss our traditions aside. You choose to shirk your responsibilities."

"What responsibilities?" I shouted, unable to help myself. I was so tired of the implication that there was some great work I was expected to perform. In my way of thinking, the only worthwhile work I had done was in the village, and that I had done in spite of the king's wishes.

My father's anger brought him to his feet. "You were supposed to

281

be queen!"

His voice reverberated off the walls, shocking me into silence. The weight of this declaration settled painfully on my shoulders, forcing me to rock back. The silence stretched out until I found my voice.

"Don't you think it's a little bit late in my life to be putting that expectation on my shoulders?"

"You can't possibly be surprised."

"I am very much surprised," I argued. "You have six other daughters; I am certain at least one of them would love that responsibility. They would each be better suited for it than I."

"You don't really believe that, do you?" His question was sincere.

Perhaps not all of them would be better suited, but if I knew anything, I knew this: "I don't want it."

"Exactly," he said simply.

"Exactly what?"

"Do you think the best person to rule is the person who *wants* to rule?"

Of course not. I knew very well that anyone who wanted power was just as likely to corrupt that power once it was obtained. However, I had never considered that not wanting power would make *me* a likely candidate.

"What do you think all of our lessons in the library were about, Ariella?"

His words stung me, and my voice had lost all its force when I answered, "Forgive me for believing you were spending time with me because you wanted to. If they were so vital, then why did they stop for two years?"

He closed his eyes and sighed heavily, but before he could respond, I went on. "I'm sorry you wasted all that time grooming me to become something I'm not. If I had known, then perhaps the path of my life would have taken me to a place where I could accept that responsibility. But it hasn't. I've lived my life, I've become who I am, and *I am* going to marry Gavin. You will be ruling for many years to come; you have no need for a successor right now. And I can't let go of my entire life on the off chance you'll need me some time in the future. I have to live my life now, and I truly believe one of my sisters will be up to the task if you put your faith in them."

My father's face was like stone, and just as silent for several long moments. Then a sadness crept over his face.

"We were relying on you, Ariella." His words soft, like I'd hurt his feelings.

My calm broke. "You almost married me off to Jeshua!" My voice rang through the hall. All of the anger and hurt over the way my father had treated me in those years came spewing from my mouth in that one accusation. His hypocrisy hurt me deeply, especially since I had thought our relationship had made such strides. "For almost two years, you planned on my marrying Jeshua while not breathing a word of it to me." The accusation surprised him, perhaps even more than my initial outburst. "How exactly did that fit into your plans of my being queen?"

He didn't answer me, only closed his eyes, looking pained.

"I'm sorry you are incapable of understanding me. I truly wish it could be otherwise." My hurt melted into tears. "I am going to marry Gavin." I turned and walked away, the echo of my footsteps ringing through my head as I crossed the grand expanse of the great hall. I passed through the doors, intent on leaving the castle, but the words of my sisters stopped me.

"Ella, you cannot be serious." I whirled around to see Lorraina, Lylin and Marilee all standing just outside the doors of the great hall. Lorraina had spoken, her tone condescending and disgusted. I was about to snap out a reply to her, but Lylin spoke first.

"Are you leaving, Ella?" She sounded worried and sad.

I swallowed my anger, choosing to respond to Lylin instead of Lorraina. "Not right away." I glanced back at the great hall where my parents sat. "At least I don't think so."

"You're marrying a common man?" Marilee sounded more bewildered than judgmental.

"Yes."

"Why?" Her brow furrowed; she was honestly curious.

"Because," I began, trying to think of how to say it, "he's the other half of my heart." I shrugged a little, knowing it sounded fanciful and romanticized. "I can't be myself without him."

A moment of stunned silence was followed by Marilee asking, "Are you in love, Ella?" Again the tone of mystified curiosity.

"Of course."

All three were silent, and I took a moment to study their reactions. Marilee appeared baffled, but pleasantly so. Lylin's eyes were bright and hopeful. Lorraina's expression was almost angry, but mostly hurt. I wondered what about my situation pained her.

Lylin was the only one to move. She hugged me and whispered only, "I'm glad," before letting me go. I squeezed her hand and touched Marilee's arm as I passed her, headed for the entrance hall.

I found Gavin. I told him everything that had been said, then asked him when we should go speak with the clergyman.

He had been silent throughout the telling, a look of deep concern on his face, until he finally asked, "What if he is right?"

My stomach dropped. "About what?"

"What if you are the best choice to lead when the time comes?" he asked in all sincerity.

"I'm not."

We were sitting facing each other, our knees almost touching. He took hold of my hands where they wrung in my lap, then looked into my eyes. "But what if you are?"

I didn't answer right away. He had asked an honest question and I wanted to give him an honest answer. I stared at our hands for several moments, squeezing his fingers as I thought through my answer.

I let out a breath before focusing on him once more. "If they have need of me, if it comes down to it and I am the one who needs to take the crown, then my father will simply have to change the laws."

Disbelief crossed Gavin's face.

"He could do it. He is the king, and if he saw fit to alter the laws of succession, then he could. He could make it so that I would be allowed to rule with you at my side." Panic replaced his disbelief. "So, now I suppose the question is, if it came to that, would you be willing?"

I saw a myriad of emotions cross Gavin's face in rapid succession. I hated laying this possible responsibility at his feet, but our situation required that we both know what we were asking of the other. At length, he took a deep breath and let out a quavering, "Yes."

I smiled, leaned in to kiss him briefly then said, "Then let's just hope it never comes to that," before I kissed him once more and felt him smile in the midst of it.

Chapter Thirty

We were married a month later. There was no reason to wait longer; we had been waiting forever. My mother helped me with the planning, and my father grudgingly complied with all her requests, including our wedding gift. My parents gifted us a villa near the capital. I was overwhelmed by such a gift, but it was the only thing that really made sense. We could not realistically live in either the palace (Gavin would not be comfortable) or in a common house (I would not be safe). And so we ended up with our own home, our own small piece of land, and we were both anxious to start our own life away from the scrutiny surrounding the palace.

Our wedding day arrived with sunshine and fresh spring air. The ceremony took place in the small village church, and the only royalty in attendance was my family. I knew my father was still reluctant about the situation, and I suspected he came for appearance's sake more than anything. But when he saw the way the village people crowded the church to overflowing—people standing outside, children perched on windowsills—I think it made a difference. I think he saw the love that his subjects so freely gave to his daughter, to Gavin, and especially to the two of us together. I think he found it difficult to fault something that created the kind of unity evident at our wedding. I took a moment to observe him, in the moments before the ceremony started. He stood beside me, waiting for our cue to enter. The joy and ease of the people surrounding him had made him drop his guard, and he seemed content. I was overwhelmed with gratitude when he turned to me with a smile on his face—a sad smile, for he could not fully approve of my choices—but a smile nonetheless. He wrapped me in his arms and I had to blink away the moisture in my eyes.

"I do wish you the very best, my Ariella."

I smiled to myself. "I'm still me."

He pulled back to look at me. "I know," he said, and I knew he meant it. "Now, go marry that man of yours." He ran the back of his finger over my cheek before giving me one of his rare smiles.

When the ceremony began, Gavin and I entered separately, as was tradition. The doors on each side of the chapel were thrown open at once. Gavin came in from one side, my father escorted me from the other, and we walked toward each other until we met in front of the clergyman. I'd never before wished for a moment to hurry up, yet at the same time want it to last forever. Walking toward Gavin felt so entirely right, I could barely remember to breathe. When we met in the middle, my father could have simply stepped back after placing my hand in Gavin's. Instead, he looked Gavin in the eye and grasped his hand in acceptance before stepping away.

We said our vows—simple, but more meaningful than any other words I'd spoken. The atmosphere was hushed, as though every person in the room breathed in unison with the two of us. Then as he leaned in to kiss me, the crowd erupted, all shouting and most jumping to their feet. We left the church through the throng of people, making our way into the wide-open marketplace. It had been emptied of its usual stalls and decorated for a celebration befitting a royally common wedding. A group of musicians, the same that played during the common dances, sat at one end.

We reached the middle of the marketplace and Gavin spun me once before bringing me close and whispering in my ear, "I have something for you."

I pulled back to look at him, intrigued. He reached behind his back and from out of nowhere pulled a beautiful scarf into view. I was so stunned and so elated that I had to fight down tears. I grabbed it, winding it around my wrists and unable to hold back a delighted laugh. I had wanted a scarf like this for so long that it felt almost surreal holding it in my hands. I never wanted to let it go.

I quickly looped it around the back of Gavin's neck, took the ends in each of my hands and held them behind my back, binding us together. "I've wanted one of these for a very long time."

"I know," he said, lightly kissing my lips.

"How did you know?"

He shrugged one shoulder and gave me a crooked smile. "I know you."

I rose up on my toes, smiling. "Yes, you do." I kissed him once more, and he spun me into a dance.

The End

About The Author

I was born in Utah, but I migrated to Arizona, Missouri, and Virginia before settling in Idaho.

Though I dabbled in writing throughout school, being an author seemed like an unattainable dream. It took me seven years to write *Just Ella*. During that time, I taught myself how to write a novel. Not the most time effective method, but it gave me an education I wouldn't have received from a class or a how-to book. Something about the struggle of writing without a formula or rules worked for me.

I write clean romance because I love it. Jane Eyre is the hero of my youth and taught me that clinging to your convictions will be hard, but it will bring you more genuine happiness than giving in ever can.

I love chocolate, *Into the Woods*, ocean waves, my husband, and my five littles. And I love books that leave me with a sigh of contentment.

To My Readers

Thank you so much for choosing to read *Just Ella*. If you enjoyed it, I invite you to read the stories of Ella's sister, Lylin, in *Missing Lily*. As a self-published author, I rely greatly on reviews and word of mouth, so if you could take a minute to review *Just Ella* on Amazon and/or Goodreads, I would really appreciate it!

You can also visit my blog (www.annetteklarsen.com) and leave me a comment, follow me on Twitter (@AnnetteKLarsen), Instagram (@AnnetteKLarsen), or Facebook https://www.facebook.com/authoraklarsen.

Happy reading!

Annette K. Larsen

Indoors

(A Scene from Gavin's Point of View)

I walked to the servants' entrance of the kitchen and stepped inside. I had been here only a few times before, preferring to walk home for a good meal rather than eat in the clamoring kitchens of the palace.

I caught the eye of one of the cooks and raised the flowers I was holding. "I'm supposed to give these to the house mistress."

The cook pointed with the knife she was holding, indicating a door across the room. "Through there."

I crossed the room, dodging servants carrying steaming pots and silver trays laden with dishes before pushing the door open with my shoulder.

The house mistress looked up from where she seemed to be scolding a lad. "Mr. Gavin. Very good. Bring them here."

I handed over the bundle when she reached for them. She set them in a vase, already filled with water, and fussed with their position.

"Will that be all, Missus?"

She made another adjustment before answering. "Now you can just take them up," she said, thrusting the vase into my hands.

"You wish me to go above stairs?"

"Of course. Joseph always does, you know. Likes to deliver them himself."

But I wasn't Joseph. "I've never been above stairs, Madame."

"Oh. Well, follow me." She brushed past and I had to rush after her. She led me up the steps and through the palace as I cast my eyes about, trying to keep track of where I was going, while at the same time trying to keep my eyes down out of respect.

She stopped at the bottom of another staircase. "Her room is just up there, third door on the right." She turned around and I realized she meant to leave me to my own devices.

"Should I really be interrupting—"

"The princesses are busy with their studies, young man. You needn't worry about that. Now, off you go. I trust you can find a suitable place for them, and be quick about it."

"Yes, Madame," I mumbled as she headed back to the kitchen. I forced my feet to move up the stairs, baffled that she had left me alone to find the bedchamber of one of the princesses.

I found the door and breathed a breath of courage as I pushed it open, hoping she had been right in assuming all the royal misses were busy with their studies. No one was inside and breathed a sigh of relief. Looking around, I noted the mantle over the fireplace, as well as a writing table, both good spots for the vase I carried. Though perhaps a less obvious spot would be better, maybe the little table beside the bed or the low one in front of the fireplace. How many tables did one princess need? I was turning slowly, taking in the entire room when the door burst open. Ella's hair flew out around her as she spun to close the door, then leaned against it, as if she were relieved to have arrived.

I was not relieved. She wasn't supposed to be here. The house mistress had said she wouldn't be here. This was bad, very bad. I couldn't be here with her. It was inappropriate and wrong, and her hair was down. Why was her hair down?

She pushed away from the door and walked toward her dressing table without seeing me. The clink of hair pins scattering across the table's surface reached my ears as she thrust both hands into her hair and shook it. I swallowed, unable to speak as the image of her wheat-colored hair held me transfixed. After she was finished brandishing her hair at me, she tossed it over her shoulder and then looked up into the mirror before her. That's when she saw me.

She gave a startled yelp and spun around, one hand pressed to her heart while the other clung to the table. I was stuck in the same position I had been in when she entered the room, my body stiff as I tried to contain the feeling of panic caused by the realization that this creature whom I had spent day after day with out in the wilds of the garden had never looked more like a nymph than she did now, her eyes bright, her hair tumbling around her. I pulled my focus back to her eyes and realized she was waiting for me to speak, to offer some sort of reasonable explanation for my standing in her room.

"I—" was all I managed before my nerves choked me and I had to start over, the words spilling out, tumbling over one another in my rush to explain. "I was told that one of the princesses wanted an arrangement of flowers, so I took the liberty of arranging one and when I brought it to the house mistress, she showed me to this room and told me that all the highnesses were doing their studies and I should just place them where I thought best, so I...."

Her hair fell into her eyes and my thoughts scattered. If she would just put it up where it belonged, I was sure I would be able to maintain my train of thought. She pushed the curls out of her eyes, a mystified "Oh," being her only response.

I needed to give a better explanation. "I would have been gone before now, but I couldn't decide where they looked best and I had no idea of anyone returning any time soon." Otherwise I never would have entered in the first place. "I certainly didn't know it had been you who requested them, though I suppose I should have guessed." Why hadn't I guessed? The girl was obsessed with every plant she encountered.

She didn't respond, just looked at me, her eyes still wide, tempting me to kiss her surprised mouth.

It was time to leave. I was a servant, she was royalty, and I had no right thinking about kissing her just because she had befriended me. What *had* she been thinking? "I should go," I tried to say it in an offhand way, and headed toward the door. I needed to get out, back into the real world, the world where I belonged.

"Gavin."

Did she have to say my name like that? I stopped, turning to face her. I tried to look at her eyes, but her blasted hair kept distracting me. I looked away.

"The vase," she said and I looked down to realize I still held her flowers. "On the table would be fine."

I hurried to the table, my toe catching on the rug as I went. I set the vase down, not paying attention to where on the table would have been best, and fled toward the door once more, avoiding looking at her and barely remembering to give a bungled bow as I yanked the door open and made my escape. A delicate "Thank you" followed me from the room.

I walked, practically ran, down the corridor and was grateful to find my way back to the kitchens and out into the fresh air. I scrubbed my hand over my face, inhaling. The wind and the smell of dirt were right and normal. Not like the barely perfumed scent of the room I had just escaped, the room where Ella slept, no doubt with her curls splayed out on her pillow.

So much for friendship. It felt like I was falling off a cliff.

I was terrified.

The End

Books of Dalthia, Volume 2

Chapter One

I pulled my horse to an abrupt halt. A sound—or a lack of sound —made my limbs freeze up. My guard said nothing, but stopped and listened as well. What was it? My horse, Willow, pranced in agitation as I strove to keep my wits about me.

The road curved just ahead, and beyond that, we would come out of the trees and cross the river before entering the village. I tugged my hood up over my head, seeking the anonymity it provided, and continued to listen while my eyes cast about for anything unusual. The dimming light was turning everything to shadow.

A branch snapped.

"Hear that?" Nathaniel whispered.

"Yes," I breathed.

He gestured for me to follow, and we moved our horses into the trees. There, Nathaniel dismounted with care. "Stay here, Milady. Keep the horses quiet."

"Don't leave me," I whispered frantically.

He hesitated before gesturing for me to follow. I slid from the saddle in an awkward attempt to keep silent, and stayed behind him as we walked. We hugged the side of the road and crept forward until the trees opened. We crouched there and watched.

I saw nothing out of the ordinary, but we remained still, sensing something beyond our vision. The unnatural stillness continued to pulse beneath my feet. Nathaniel gestured for me to stay, then started to rise. I latched onto his arm, but before I could plead with him to stay with me, I heard a rustle in the trees and movement caught my eye. Two hulking figures stepped into the road in front of us, a mere twenty paces away. My breath hissed as I sucked in and we watched both men unsheathe their large swords.

"Princess Lylin," Nathaniel said quietly as he drew his own sword with precision. "Get on your horse and ride."

"Nathaniel—"

He thrust me away as a third man charged from his right. "GO!" he screamed and lunged forward, his sword raised.

I stumbled, barely able to maintain my balance, then turned and ran flat out, driven by unconstrained fear. Willow sidled as I skidded to a halt and crammed my foot into the stirrup.

Through the clash of swords, I heard someone yell, "Go after her!"

I pulled myself into the saddle and fumbled for the reins. I yanked on them to pull Willow around before digging my heels into her sides. "Go! Go!" I sobbed, urging her into a trot. Only when she was at a full gallop did I glance back. The clash of swords rang through the night, but beyond that there was only blackness, so I looked ahead and rode. I had to get back to Ella's house; there was nowhere else to go.

Riding across the open countryside, I glanced behind me and my heart lodged in my throat. A rider followed a good distance behind.

I pulled my horse in a different direction, refusing to lead danger to my sister's doorstep. I urged Willow to go faster, my harried flight across the uneven ground made nearly unseating me. Moving past Ella's estate, I looked back to see the rider closer than before. Willow could not keep this pace for long, and he was already closing in on me.

Rain spattered my face. My early departure from Ella's house had been useless. If I had just stayed put, I would not have been forced to hatch the reckless plan that entered my mind. The path I followed entered a grove of trees ahead. My pursuer would lose sight of me for at least a few moments once I was among the trees. It was my only chance, so I pushed Willow toward it.

Just Ella

The sheeting rain blurred my vision as I entered the copse of trees, but I was determined. I pulled my right foot from the stirrup and swung my leg over. Just before the path opened to another field, I slapped Willow's hindquarters and threw myself to the ground. My left side slammed onto the ground, scraping across the rough terrain before I skidded to a stop. Gasping for breath, I dragged myself on hands and knees away from the trail. I flattened myself to the ground and watched Willow continue to gallop. She disappeared into the rain without slowing. A second later, my pursuer galloped past at full tilt, his black cloak whipping behind him.

There was no time to waste. I had to move before the rider discovered my deception and turned back to look for me.

I rose to my feet, wincing in pain, and leaned against a tree, preparing myself for movement. Pain pulsed through my body with every step I took. My left shoulder was bruised and bleeding from hitting the ground, and pain radiated from my hip where I had slammed into a jagged rock. But I stood and found my ankles to be blessedly stable. I staggered off into the drenched night, putting as much distance between myself and my pursuer as possible. Every step hurt, but I clenched my teeth and kept up a lurching run until the stitch in my side forced me to stop. My wheezing breath sounded in my ears as I struggled for air. I tried slowing to a walk, but had to stop altogether to cure the stitch in my side. The wind tried to pull my cloak from shoulders. My face stung with every raindrop that pelted my face. Once able to take in a full breath, I continued on. I tried to run but didn't have the energy, so I put my head down and trudged forward, watching as the water dipped from my hair. I could hear nothing but the roaring storm.

I walked without direction, my legs aching as I slogged through the relentless downpour and the muddy ground for what must have been hours. I had never been so alone, so entirely dependent on myself, and everything inside of me seized with anxiety at the thought.

As I continued placing one foot in front of the other, Lorraina's words of warning rang through my head.

"It's not safe, Lylin." She stood in my doorway, her posture rigid as always and her arms crossed in certainty. At twenty-one, Lorraina was three years my senior, and obsessed with appearances.

I sighed, tired of the same argument. *"I can't stay here in the castle every hour of every day. It's healthy for me to leave."* I returned to searching for a trinket to bring Ella's two-year-old, Guinevere.

"What's so wrong with being at home?" Her tone indicated that I had offended her, but I refused to rise to the bait.

"Nothing is wrong with it. I like being at home."

"Then why are you always running off to Ella's house?"

"Because I miss my sisters. I'm so grateful that you're still here, but we had five sisters leave in barely more than five years. I love visiting Ella and she's close enough that I can." I crossed the room to add the little bracelet to the trunk that Missy had already packed for me.

Lorraina shook her head. *"I don't understand the appeal."*

"I know you don't, which I assume is why you don't accept her invitations. And that's fine, but it doesn't mean that my going is wrong."

"I didn't say it was wrong."

"But that's what you meant." I closed the lid.

"I said it isn't safe. You have one guard, and you insist on riding, which means you don't even have a carriage to protect you."

I stood up and turned to face her. *"Nothing is completely safe. That doesn't mean it's not worth it."*

At the moment, it certainly didn't feel worth it, but all I could do was continue forward and try to trust in my own capabilities. I trudged on, determined to arrive somewhere, and my persistence paid off. The rain was so heavy, that when I saw a light, I was practically on top of the manor house already. My heart pounded, ecstatic about the prospect of shelter, but terrified of the unknown. The house was surrounded by a wall, only as tall as my waist. I circled carefully until I found the stables, then pulled myself over the rough stones. I cracked the door open just enough to creep inside, overwhelmed by relief as I stepped out of the storm.

The stables were dark, but held the familiar sounds and smells of horses. I walked down the aisle, jumping when a horse stuck its head over a wall, its curious eyes reflecting the small bit of moonlight seeping through the doors. Moving past, I reached the other end and tried to sit down, but the pain in my left side forced me to stretch out on my right. I pulled my sopping cloak around me, trying to bring some warmth back into my body and failing. Shaking with cold and fear, I thought through my options. Approaching the house would leave me vulnerable to whoever resided here, and I couldn't trust anyone at this moment. I had never been so alone and found myself incapable of making a decision, so instead I just lay there, shaking.

Just as I started to relax, the sound of voices made my eyes pop open, and I sat up, forcing my breathing to quiet. The doors at the other end of the stables slid open and someone entered, carrying a lamp and shaking water from their clothes.

"I'm not seein' things, Lord Fallon. Someone is in here," a voice whispered. I sat still, unable to move. The lamp shifted, casting two men in ominous shadow.

"I believe you, Giles. That's why we're here." His Lordship sounded not at all concerned, as though he were merely humoring his hired man. He sounded more tired than anything.

"The lamp, Giles." The light transferred to His Lordship's hands, illuminating his face and leaving me astonished by his youth. He looked to be in his twenties, and I wondered how such a young gentleman held the title of Lord. "You're sure it wasn't an animal of some sort?" he asked as he took his first steps down the long line of stalls. He would find me soon enough, and yet this prospect didn't terrify me as it had moments ago. Lord Fallon looked not at all frightening. He wore trousers, a loose fitting shirt that hung untucked, and a full-length coat that fell in languid folds from his shoulders. Water dripped from his rumpled hair, sliding down his face and into his well-trimmed facial hair.

"T'weren't no animal, sir."

"The horses aren't agitated. They would be if someone

threatening were about."

When the light fell on me, Lord Fallon's eyes widened. I tried to push myself to my feet, but he drew a sword that I had not realized was hanging at his side and pointed it at my throat. I fell back against the wall, crouching, my chest aching from the heavy beating of my heart.

"I don't take kindly to vagrants on my property." His fatigue had vanished. Now he looked menacing—terrifying.

My voice was barely audible as I forced a reply. "I'm not a vagrant, sir."

His eyes narrowed in question. "Remove your hood."

I raised my hand slowly and pushed the fabric back. His eyebrows raised, even more surprised by my appearance than by my voice. The sword lowered. "Giles, take her inside and put her in front of a fire. She's freezing." And with that, he walked away and I slumped back to the ground, numb with relief.

"Come along then, miss," Giles said as he helped me to my feet. "What in the world is a pretty thing like you doing wandering about in the middle of the night?" He seemed to be mumbling to himself, so I didn't answer.

Giles' face was lined and his shoulders were stooped, but his smile was kind. He pulled my hood up for me and put a gentle arm about my waist as we left the stables. My body shook and I was glad for the help as we braved the storm once more. We entered the house and he helped me into a room with a rough wooden table and chairs. We must have been below-stairs, since I was certain the Lord's living quarters would be much finer than this room. From my perch on a stool, I watched as Giles crouched before the banked fire and coaxed it back to life. I pushed my hands toward the flames, grateful to feel the warmth on my fingers.

Once the fire was well stoked, Giles turned to me, rubbing his hands together. "If you'll hand me your cloak, we need to wrap you in something dry."

It took a moment for my hands to reach for the clasp at my

throat. I was drowsy with relief and fumbled to unfasten my cloak and give it to Giles. He pulled a blanket from somewhere behind me and draped it around my shoulders.

"Very good, miss," he said with a little bow and then left the room.

I stared into the fire for quite a while before it struck me as odd that they had left me alone. I was a complete stranger to these people. They had no reason to trust me. Likewise, I had no reason to trust them.

I moved each of my limbs in turn, taking note of the pain. My left shoulder, arm and hip seemed to have taken the brunt of my fall. During my flight through the storm, I had tried to ignore my injuries, but now I felt each and every one.

Hearing footsteps approach, I turned toward the door, expecting someone to walk through it. But the footsteps ceased, replaced by voices.

"And how is our little vagabond?"

The corner of my mouth twitched upward. Lord Fallon was making no attempt to keep his voice down.

"That's no vagabond, sir. Feel this." I furrowed my brow as Lord Fallon made a noise of interest. "Look for yourself, sir," Giles prodded.

Lord Fallon came through the door, his eyes falling to me. We each studied the other. He no longer appeared as though he'd been roused from his bed. Though water still glistened in his dark hair, he was impeccably dressed and I wondered at his reasons when he had assumed I was a beggar. Giles had entered behind him, holding my cloak.

"I see what you mean." His Lordship sighed, relaxing his posture somewhat before grabbing a chair and placing it next to me.

I turned toward the fire and pulled the blanket tighter around me, unable to meet his gaze as I felt him staring at my profile for several moments.

"You are injured, miss."

My eyes darted to him in surprise. I had expected him to demand my name. "Sir?"

"Giles," he said while still looking at me. "Go wake your wife.

Our guest needs someone to tend to her injuries, and some dry clothing as well."

"She'll be right pleased to have someone to fuss over," Giles murmured as he left.

In Giles's absence, I realized I was alone in a dimly lit room with a handsome man. I turned my attention back to the fire, ignoring my discomfort.

He scooted closer and I stiffened as he reached for my straight, dark hair, pushing it away from my cheek. "How were you injured?" I glanced over and realized he was inspecting a wound on my forehead.

"I fell from a horse." My voice was barely above a whisper.

"Why would you be riding so late at night?" He moved closer, getting a better look. "And in the middle of a storm?"

It took me a moment to find my voice with him leaning so close. "I wasn't. I was riding this evening, trying to make it home before the storm. I've been walking since I fell."

His eyebrows shot up. "You were riding alone?"

My heavy eyes blinked as I stared at the fire. "I was returning home with an escort. We found our way blocked by bandits—miscreants —I don't know who they were." I shook my head in frustration. "My escort told me to ride away and I did. But I was pursued and they were gaining on me. The only thing I could think to do was to jump off the horse and hope they followed her long enough for me to get away."

"And then you walked?" His voice was hushed.

I glanced at him but couldn't hold his gaze. "Then I walked…or ran when I could."

Out of the corner of my eye, I saw him nodding to himself as he looked at the floor. "Forgive me, miss." His eyes returned to me. "I do not recall ever having made your acquaintance, but you look very familiar."

I studied his face, surprised that I did not know him since I knew most of the nobility. "I have never seen you at court, sir."

He let out a bitter laugh. "This estate is falling to ruin. I do not have the time to play at being a socialite."

"And your name, sir?" I knew that he was Lord Fallon, but thought it polite to ask.

"Rhys Fallon." The dropping of his title surprised me.

"A pleasure, sir."

He smiled at my hollow formality. "And who might you be?"

I looked away, not wanting to lie, but unwilling to confess my true identity. I was royalty, this man's superior, but I couldn't make myself admit it, determined to protect myself. "Lily," was the lie I came up with. "Lily Josten."

"And how—" he began but was interrupted by the abrupt entrance of an older woman. Unlike her master, she had not taken time to fully dress. She was in the midst of fastening her dressing gown as she walked toward me.

"My gracious, what have we here?" she crouched before me, taking my face in hand. She was a lovely woman, all gray hair and compassion. She set about fussing over me—removing the blanket so that she could search for injuries and quietly inquire about others. I was shocked when she gave orders, not only to her husband, but to Lord Fallon as well. "Giles, put some water on to boil. Rhys, go pull some bandages from that cupboard over there."

I looked up to see how he would respond to being ordered about by someone who worked for him, but he simply rose and went to the cupboard. She focused mostly on my arm. My sleeve had been torn, revealing a long, ugly looking scrape from shoulder to elbow.

Once she had acquired everything she needed, she waved the men away, "Now get out, the both of you. I must tend to her injuries."

"It is only her arm, Rosamond," Rhys protested.

Rosamond shot him a steely glance. "There are others," she stated, and I ducked my head in embarrassment. Rhys just cleared his throat and walked out the door. Giles followed.

As Rosamond helped me to peel off layer upon layer of sopping fabric, she found bruises running from the back of my left shoulder down to my thigh. There was a fist-sized wound at my hip. It had turned my underskirt pink with blood and still bled feebly. She cleaned up the scrapes on my head, arm and hip as quickly as possible and put some sort of salve on my bruises before helping me into a dry chemise and bundling me once more in a blanket.

By the time she had finished patching me up, my exhaustion made it difficult to stand. After trying to help me walk a few steps, Rosamond called out, "Your Lordship!" He appeared immediately at the door. "She's in no state to be walking up those stairs, sir."

With only that prompting, Rhys picked me up gently, blankets and all, and carried me from the room. Though he was as careful as possible, I still had to bite back a groan of pain as his arms pressed on my injuries. Rosamond bustled ahead of us and entered a room at the top of the stairs. "Just set her down. I'll take it from here."

Rhys set me on my feet, made sure I had my balance, then gave me a nod and a small smile. I gazed after him, barely recalling my manners before he stepped out of sight. "Thank you, sir," I managed to blurt. He just nodded once and closed the door.

"You've certainly got the master in a bunch," Rosamond commented.

"I'm sorry?" I asked.

"His Lordship isn't usually so quiet, is all." I didn't know what she meant, so I gave no response. She worked in silence, removing the few pins that remained among my hair, then pulling back the covers on the bed. "I know you won't be comfortable with all the pains ailing you, but I hope you can rest."

"Thank you." I was already half asleep when I heard the door close behind her, but I didn't slip off right away. My mind was too full of my ordeal, the memory of fleeing across the countryside racing through my head. The hours spent wandering in the dark and the rain had left a shadow of fear in my heart.

My eyes remained wide open for a good portion of the night, the questions finally forcing their way into my mind now that I found myself in relative safety. A sick feeling settled in my stomach as I thought about my parents and what they must be thinking at this moment. What conclusion had they drawn when I did not return? What had happened to Nathaniel? Had he been able to return to the castle and tell the tale of our attackers? I had no way of knowing.

Missing Lily is available on Amazon.

CPSIA information can be obtained
at www.ICGtesting.com
Printed in the USA
LVHW080829271119
638451LV00026B/873/P

9 781492 175391